**From the Land of Shadows**
**the Old Ones have returned.**
**The curse of Gokaleh has**
**not been forgotten.**

Jim Feathers's mind reeled. For a time he couldn't move, frozen there while he stared down at the floor of the cave. And the shape he found there.

The body of a man, decomposing in dry heat, lay at the rear of the cave, his features distorted by feeding ants and swarming flies. But it was his belly that bore the signature of Gokaleh and the Old Ones, where it lay open with entrails scattered like twisted ropes over the rocks.

Jim was shaking from head to toe as he backed slowly out of the cave, and his coppery face felt cold when he rubbed his eyes.

*It is a dream. The spirits are telling me it is time to die. My eyes play tricks on me. Look again and the body will be gone.*

His breathing was shallow. He edged closer to the entrance and peered inside, feeling his stomach boil. He blinked, and brushed a fly away from his nose. *It is not possible. The Old Ones are no more. But who else would do this?* The body was scalped, he noticed now, leaving no doubt. The Old Ones had come back from the Land of Shadows to have their vengeance.

*Bantam Books by Frederic Bean*

EDEN
MURDER AT THE SPIRIT CAVE

Rivers West:
The Pecos River
The Red River

# MURDER
## at the
# SPIRIT CAVE

◆

# Frederic Bean

**BANTAM BOOKS**
New York   Toronto   London
Sydney   Auckland

*12096756*

## MURDER AT THE SPIRIT CAVE

A Bantam Crime Line Book/December 1999

CRIME LINE and the portrayal of a boxed "cl" are trademarks
of Bantam Books, a division of Random House, Inc.

ISBN 0-553-58017-5

*Published simultaneously in the United States and Canada*

Bantam Books are published by Bantam Books, a division of Random
House, Inc. Its trademark, consisting of the words "Bantam Books"
and the portrayal of a rooster, is Registered in U.S. Patent and
Trademark Office and in other countries. Marca Registrada. Bantam
Books, 1540 Broadway, New York, New York 10036.

PRINTED IN THE UNITED STATES OF AMERICA

OPM   10 9 8 7 6 5 4 3 2 1

# MURDER
## at the
# SPIRIT CAVE

# PROLOGUE

ABOVE A WINDING limestone escarpment he saw buzzards circling in the air, a certain announcement of death. He waited for rheumy eyes to adjust to the distance the way they must when someone has been too long on the face of Earth Mother. He watched the vultures from a patch of mottled shade below brittle bushes smelling of creosote, long accustomed to the acrid scent, noting how the birds swooped lower with every pass. *They are careful, making sure,* he thought. This was the way of all creatures from the desert, making certain no danger lurked beneath an agave plant or cactus bed. *They do this in order to survive. It is the Way.*

He gazed across miles of low hills to the Rio Grande, and beyond, to towering Coahuilan mountains purpling with distance. Then his eyes returned to the vultures, measuring how far they were from his creosote shade. *Half a mile. No more.* Sand flies darted to his face and he ignored their stinging bite, wondering what could be attracting buzzards so late in the year. It was fall, and no cattle grazed here during the dry season, unless some maverick had escaped the fall roundup. *It could be anything. A deer or a wild pig killed by a rattlesnake bite.* In his youth, before his legs got too old to carry him without complaining, he would have investigated the vultures' meal. But now, with the spirits of his ancestors beckoning to him from the Spirit World every night before he went to sleep, he no longer cared as much when death occurred. Very soon it would be his own death bringing buzzards to the sky. *I have lived too long anyway. I feel as old as the rocks.*

An inner voice whispered to him, like gentle wind moving among the occotillo, lechuguilla, sotol stalks and cholla spines growing on the desert floor. *See what brings the sky scavengers. Something is out there.*

He was disturbed by the voice. Lately, he'd been dreaming strange dreams, waking up in a cold sweat when visions of the Old Ones came to him. He told himself it was because he was about to die that he dreamed of his ancestors. Old men had nothing else to dream about.

He got up slowly, squinting in the sun's fierce glare. Why should he care what lured the vultures to this place? It was not his land by right of deed. Only in his heart was the land his. Only in his mind.

"I will look," he said, his voice lost on a breath of hot wind blowing out of Mexico. He said it aloud, hoping to satisfy whatever spirits had come to haunt him and goad himself into looking when he didn't care to look. He walked away from the creosote bushes with soundless steps.

The sun was gauzy over his right shoulder, dimmed by dust risen from the desert during fall when no rains came, and with each gust of wind more particles of Earth Mother's skin became part of the sky, carried by the winds to some other place. This, too, was the way of things here, the ways of change in an empty land too harsh for all but the most determined creatures. No one had ever tamed this place and in his heart he was sure no one ever could. It was once the land of his ancestors and they had understood it, living in timeless harmony with its sharp thorns, scant wa-ter and brutal elements, stinging ants and scorpions, poisonous snakes and gila lizards, javelina and cougar. Now it belonged to men of another race who cared nothing for the land itself and because of this, it was dying. Dying slowly, eroded by overgrazing, turning to fine dust borne away by endless winds, a sad thing to behold over a lifetime for a man who loved its raw beauty, its vastness. No longer was it a safe refuge for herds of deer and antelope, home to the People. Now it was only a dying desert full of memories for those who knew it before.

He came to an arroyo that twisted through layers of jagged limestone. Brush choked the floor of a dry streambed. A vulture perched on the lip of rock and peered cautiously into the mouth of a small cave entrance almost hidden by bitterweed. He saw the bird and laughed softly. "Are you afraid? Does a serpent guard the passageway?" Rattlers sought shade this time of day, making the cave a perfect place for a venomous ambush.

As he climbed up the side of the arroyo the buzzard took off clumsily, flapping its heavy wings, warning the other vultures of his intrusion with an angry squawk as it climbed slowly into the sky. *They will not go far. They smell death and they will be patient.*

At the mouth of the cave he tossed a tiny pebble inside to awaken dozing rattlers. When nothing sounded, he leaned closer. It was a very small cave—more of a pocket in the rock. He could see the back wall in slanted sunlight. Bending down, he crept inside until he saw something near his feet. Two big feathers, probably from the tail of a hawk, lay close to the entrance. He had picked them up to examine their strange brownish color when he noticed they were joined together by a strand of rawhide. He noticed a soft buzzing sound, not a rattler's warning—the swarming noise made by hungry blowflies deeper inside.

Now his attention was drawn to a shape at the back of the cave, and a smell he knew well—the scent of death. His eyes narrowed. He took a deep breath and went closer, feeling tiny hairs prickle on the back of his neck. He held the pair of feathers until his hands started to tremble, then he let them fall.

For a time he couldn't move, frozen there while he stared down at the floor of the cave. And the shape he found there. The voice whispered to him again. *From the Land of Shadows the Old Ones have returned. The curse of Gokaleh has not been forgotten. Earth Mother has no more tears to shed. Gokaleh comes again to spill their blood for what they have done.*

The body of a man, decomposing in dry heat, lay at the rear of the cave, his features distorted by feeding ants and swarming flies. But it was his belly that bore the signature of Gokaleh and the Old Ones, where it lay open with entrails scattered like twisted ropes over the rocks. His shriveled genitals had been pushed into his mouth, testicles the color of dried plums protruding grotesquely between his lips. Maggots squirmed in the hole where the penis and scrotum had been severed from his abdomen.

He was shaking from head to toe as he backed slowly out of the cave, and his coppery face felt cold when he rubbed his eyes.

*It is a dream. The Old Ones are no more. My eyes play tricks on me. The spirits are telling me it is time to die. Look again and the body will be gone.*

His breathing was shallow and he felt his stomach boil. He blinked, brushing a fly away from his nose. *It is not possible. But who else would do this?* The body was scalped, he noticed now, leaving no doubt. The Old Ones had come back from the Land of Shadows to exact their vengeance.

He looked up at the sky before he took off in a lumbering trot down the arroyo. His legs did not complain now of old age when he asked them to run. He ran as hard as he could until his lungs ached, forcing him to rest in the meager shade under an ocotillo.

When he looked back he noticed the vultures were gone. *It was a dream, a vision. I am old and my mind is wandering. There was no body. Only an empty cave and a crazy old*

*Indian. I will say nothing to anyone or they will lock me away in a place for crazy people and leave me there to die.*

With his mind made up he walked away from the ocotillo into a setting sun. It would be dark before he got home, since he had to cross a sixty-thousand-acre pasture on foot to reach his battered pickup truck parked at the abandoned line shack. No one at the ranch said anything to him when he wandered around the place. They felt sorry for him, he supposed, an old man with nothing else to do. Perhaps they all thought he was slowly losing his mind, walking the desert for no apparent reason, no reason they would understand.

His hands had stopped shaking. He had only imagined seeing the body, he told himself. Spirits of the dead did not come back to kill people in ancient ways, mutilating corpses the way his ancestors did more than a hundred years ago. He had dreamed the whole thing, the vultures, the cave, the body. Perhaps it was the heat. . . .

# PART 1

# ONE

TEXAS RANGER CAPTAIN Claude Groves glanced at the initial report from Terrell County Sheriff Walter Casey, idly wondering how long it had been since a Texas Ranger investigated a scalping. A hundred years? This was 1992, at least a century past an era when Indians scalped white settlers across the west Texas frontier and yet here was a written request for the DPS Crime Lab in Austin to perform an autopsy and attempt identification of a body found in a shallow cave outside of Sanderson with its scalp neatly excised, not merely eaten away by scavengers. And there was more—the penis and testicles had been severed, placed in the victim's mouth as some sort of gruesome signature, along with an opening in the body cavity made by a sharp instrument. Four photographs taken at a Sanderson funeral parlor proved Sheriff Casey was not given to exaggeration. A bloated corpse that looked like something out of a horror movie lay on a mortician's table, only vaguely human in appearance, extremities and some facial features partially missing where feeding ants or scavengers had made a meal of decaying flesh. The dead man's scalp had been removed with almost surgical precision, but it was the sight of his genitals dangling from his lips that gave Claude an eerie feeling, that made him think what had been captured in these photographs was the work of a madman. A killer whose mind would defy all conventional methods to track him.

He looked across his desk at a pretty blond woman. She had been watching him expectantly while he examined the report and he knew she wanted an explanation for his lengthy silence. "This'll be one for the record books," he said, closing the folder as he considered the wisdom of showing her the pictures, deciding against it until they'd had more time to talk. It wasn't as if he didn't know her, or know about her qualifications to examine a case file. She was three days away from certification as a Texas Ranger, the first woman appointed to the state's most reknowned police force. The furor her commission created still hadn't fully died down in the press. To complicate matters for Claude, she was the daughter of his mentor and first training officer with the Texas Rangers, Captain Alfred Jenkins. He'd known Carla Jenkins almost from the day she was born, although he hadn't seen her for a number of years, not since her graduation from high school and a stint with the El Paso Police Department. Carla hadn't been told she was being assigned to Claude as her field training officer. Claude and Alfred had arranged it in secret with Major Tom Elliot weeks ago.

"A tough case?" she asked, a slight frown wrinkling her forehead.

"A little on the gory side, but you see all sorts of blood and guts with this job." He recalled a few odd details from her personnel folder . . . thirty years old, divorced, no children, seven years as a traffic cop in El Paso. He hadn't expected her to be quite so pretty, remembering her as a tomboy who liked to climb trees and ride horses. Her file photo—the one hidden in his desk drawer—did not flatter her. If she wasn't Alfred's daughter he might have . . .

When he made no move to show her the case file she leaned back in the chair with one foot resting on her knee, a foot that twitched unconsciously, showing how nervous she was. Perhaps it was because this was their first meeting after more than a dozen years, or perhaps it was the circumstances, with her appointment as a Texas Ranger. "I've seen plenty of blood, Captain," she said. "I don't think anything can shock me."

It could have been her way of asking to see the case file, but again he opted against it. When she was told of her assignment to Headquarters Company with Claude as her training officer, he'd show it to her. He wondered if she would smell a rat, realize that her assignment had been arranged. And he wondered if this would be the right kind of case to break in a rookie, after looking at the photographs.

"If I'm in town I'll come to your graduation," he said, to turn their discussion in another direction. "Your dad won't be driving to Austin because of his eyes, I suspect."

"I asked him not to come," she said quietly, averting her gaze to an office window. She offered no further explanation and Claude didn't press her. All the public pressure, attention from the newspapers, and several notable resignations by distinguished Rangers with long, outstanding service records had been hard on her.

"I'll be there if I can," he said again.

She looked at him briefly. "There's no need, Captain. I'd just as soon go through it alone. Thanks anyway."

"I guess the boys have made it a little rough on you. It'll pass."

Her face darkened. "I can handle it," she said, coming to her feet abruptly. She offered her hand. "Thanks for seeing me, Captain Groves. They haven't given me a company assignment yet so I don't know where I'll be going. I promised Dad I'd drop by before I left Austin. For old time's sake."

Claude hoped his blush didn't show when he stood up to take her handshake, or that the truth—that he knew where, and to whom, she was being assigned—wouldn't show in his eyes. "Good to see you again, Carla. The next time I talk to Alfred I'll tell him you came to see me. If I can ever do anything to help, let me know."

Her emerald eyes betrayed a moment of suspicion before she turned for the door, then she smiled and it was a pretty smile, full of sparkling white teeth in an oval, suntanned face with high cheekbones. Her badge was pinned to a white short-sleeve shirt that did little to hide a generous bosom, but Claude was quick to avoid more than a passing glance at her body. She was, after all, Alfred's daughter.

She closed the door behind her, leaving him with several impressions. Some problem existed between Carla and her father, one she didn't care to talk about. Nor had Alfred ever mentioned it, other than to vent his disappointment when she entered the police academy in El Paso, married a man he disliked and moved so far away from Brownwood that he seldom saw her. All her life she had been the apple of Alfred's eye and Claude guessed it must have wounded Alfred when she moved away.

He picked up the case file on the Terrell County investigation again, but not before he gave one last thought to how much Carla Jenkins had changed. If only things had been a little different, he might have made an attempt at a slow seduction: a dinner date, perhaps a night of dancing to slow country tunes. He opened the file and dismissed the notion entirely. What kind of man would try to seduce his best friend's daughter? Maybe if he were a little younger. . . .

He shook his head and turned back to the photographs, examining them one at a time. It was abundantly clear the killer meant for his victim to suffer, unless—the man was already dead when the mutilation occurred?

The victim's identity would hold the key to everything. If Claude ferreted out the details of the dead man's activities prior to the killing, who he knew, where he lived, the places he frequented, someone would give him a scrap of information that would lead to the murderer. It worked every time, if you looked closely enough.

Terrell County was a virtual wasteland. Sanderson, the county seat, was a tiny place with only a few thousand residents in a section of Texas bordering both the Rio Grande and Mexico. It seemed an unlikely place for something like this to happen, and a hard place for a killer to hide.

One notation in Sheriff Casey's report surprised him. No one had been reported missing anywhere in Terrell County or in any of the surrounding counties Casey notified. That the victim might be a stranger seemed odd, making a motive harder to figure.

Claude stared at the corpse's face for several minutes, oblivious to the traffic sounds outside his office windows. It almost looked like a Hollywood movie creation, a monster made of wax or gray latex, formed to look like a creature risen from the grave.

The report from DPS Crime Lab would clear up several things, whether the victim was alive or dead when he was mutilated, and how long he'd been dead. Fingerprints and dental records would then put Claude and Carla on the killer's trail, mostly routine investigative work, little real danger for Carla until the killer had a name. Then Claude could devise some excuse for making the actual arrest himself.

Now all that remained was to drive out to Brownwood tomorrow to tell Alfred about his meeting with Carla, and about the first case they'd be working on. It was the sort of thing Claude could have done over the phone, he supposed, but it would be good to see his old friend again—a lonely man after a bullet wound forced his early retirement, and his divorce from Alice. In truth, Claude still missed those years he and Alfred had spent together as

Rangers, and he was certain Alfred missed them every bit as much as he did.

Later, in a bathroom down the hall, he glanced at his reflection while washing his hands, thinking about Carla. He was twenty years her senior, showing his age more and more lately, a thick mane of black hair turning gray around the temples, deeper lines around his eyes and mouth. It was foolish to think that she might find him physically attractive. Too much difference in age even though he was still reasonably fit: muscular, six feet two in his socks—a little flabby in places, perhaps. But he stayed in good shape because of the demands placed on him by the nature of his job.

"She's Alfred's daughter," he said to the mirror. But even spoken aloud, the words didn't dismiss the attraction he felt for her.

# TWO

Wallace Baker, director of the Department of Public Safety Crime Labs, stood a safe distance away from a stainless-steel autopsy table, breathing through his mouth to avoid the overpowering smell as much as possible. A giant black man wearing rubber gloves and a rubber apron placed a dull gray corpse on the table as though it weighed nothing, stretching it out, placing a body block underneath the remains so the chest was elevated. Baker swallowed, wondering how Dr. Grossman's pathology assistant could perform his duties without any show of emotion, especially in a case like this where the corpse, or what was left of it, hardly seemed human.

"Jesus," Baker whispered as Grossman's assistant turned on a small spigot, sending a stream of water down the metal gutters around the edge of the table to wash away blood and fluids. Baker was thankful he hadn't eaten any breakfast this morning. He closed his eyes, preparing himself for what was to come.

Dr. Saul Grossman, chief pathologist and medical examiner for Travis County, entered the lab wearing scrubs and two pairs of latex gloves, a surgical mask covering his nose and mouth. He nodded to Baker, pointing to a cart near the morgue doors. "Put on gloves and a mask, Wally. Rub some of that mentholatum on your upper lip. It helps kill the smell—fatigues the odor receptors in your nose. You don't need to be brilliant to know this piece of rotten meat is gonna stink."

"Spare me your slaughterhouse slang, Saul," Baker said as he put the menthol cream on his lip. He was in no mood to watch an autopsy, especially one where the body was so badly disfigured. He put on a mask and latex gloves before he approached the table, standing back a few feet while Grossman examined a tag affixed to the corpse's right toe. Then the medical examiner took a clipboard from his assistant and glanced at the page on top.

Grossman addressed a microphone dangling from a cable above the table. "This is Dr. Saul Grossman, medical examiner for Travis County, beginning postmortem examination of John Doe, case number 128-674-8-21-92. Present during this examination are Wallace Baker, DPS Crime Lab director, and Sammy Jones, Morgue Diener and my pathology assistant." He spoke in a dull monotone, as though he'd repeated these same lines too many times.

Grossman read from the clipboard. "The subject appears to be a well-developed Anglo male, standing five feet nine inches tall, weighing one hundred sixty-four pounds. He was found in a cave near Sanderson, Texas, at approximately three-forty-five P.M. on the twenty-first of August, 1992. No core body temperature was taken at the scene and it was moved prior to a coroner's examination. The time of death is very difficult to estimate initially, until we get tissue samples under a microscope. Partial mummification of tissues is noted, perhaps due to a dry climate. There are numerous insect and scavenger bites over the entire body, and a number of eggs of the blowfly are present, indicating they had not yet become larvae. Thus I estimate the victim has been dead five or six days." He glanced at the report again. "The subject was found naked. No clothing or identification. Due to advanced decomposition and tissue gases, I can only estimate he was between twenty-five and thirty-five years of age."

He put down the clipboard and spoke into the microphone while leaning over the corpse. "His scalp has been excised at the top of the neck to the hairline, leaving the entire calvarium bare. The scalp was not found with the body. The subject's penis and testicles have been severed and placed in his mouth. Bruising at the edges of the penis shaft and at the top of the skull indicate both events occurred premortem, while the subject was still alive."

Baker swallowed once more, the menthol on his lip making his eyes water.

Grossman glanced over his shoulder at Baker. "I've never seen anything like this before, Wally."

"Neither have I," Baker replied thickly, wishing he hadn't seen it. He had been director of the crime lab for nine years, but he rarely watched actual autopsies, since his staff's main function was to evaluate autopsy data when a cause of death was less obvious. He wouldn't have been here now, witnessing the examination of this poor disfigured creature, had not an official request come from Texas Ranger headquarters asking for his personal attention to this case. Someone in a high place wanted quick and accurate results. Puzzling, unless the bizarre circumstances of the crime made a high-ranking officer believe this was the beginning of a string of serial murders.

Grossman turned his attention back to the table. "Subject has a vertical incision in the midline of the abdomen, extending from the xiphoid process down to the pubic bone." He fingered coils of purple intestine aside. "Extending through the skin and subcutaneous fatty layer, rectus muscle, and peritoneum into the abdomen. This wound also occurred premortem, and it suggests some anatomical knowledge on the part of the killer since it precisely bisects the median raphe of the rectus muscle. This area is almost entirely avascular, with no major blood ves-

sels, meaning it took the subject considerable time to ex-
sanguinate—bleed to death," he added, looking up. "The
pain must have been unbearable, lasting as long as several
hours."

Baker didn't need any more details from Grossman to
understand what had transpired. "I don't see the need to go
any farther, Saul. The cause of death is painfully obvious.
See if you can get me some fingerprints and dental X-rays.
What I need more than anything now is to know who he
was, and your best estimate as to time of death after you
look at the tissue slides."

Grossman picked up the subject's hands one at a time.
"No way to get prints, Wally. Some partials, maybe, but
probably not enough to help. By the way, there are ligature
marks on both of his wrists, so his hands were tied." Then,
as Baker was about to leave the room, he saw Grossman
remove the penis and testicles from the dead man's mouth,
poking a gloved finger into the corpse's mouth. "No apparent dental work at all. Not a single filling. He bit the tip
of his tongue off, but that's easy enough to understand,
undergoing so much pain."

Baker closed his eyes again, briefly, as stomach bile
rose higher in his throat. When he opened them he saw
Grossman using a scalpel inside the corpse's chest.

"We'll remove all the organs at once, the Rokitansky
method, unless you have another preference."

Baker's only preference now was to get the hell out of
this room before he threw up. "Do whatever you feel is
best," he said. "I don't think it matters."

"Here's something," Grossman said, lifting a mass of
green-white membrane from the subject's stomach. "Unless I miss my guess, this is partially digested peyote pulp.
When I was a pathology resident in Phoenix we found it in
the stomachs of a few Indians who inhaled too many spray
paint fumes. You'll also note the liver has fatty infiltration,
meaning our subject was a heavy drinker, just this side of
cirrhosis. Add that to the fact that his penis was uncircum-

cised and you may have an Indian here, or a part-blood. At least it's something to go on." He dropped the greenish membrane to look closely at the dead man's face. "If he had eyelids I could look for traces of a Mongolian fold common to some Indian tribes, but the ants got there ahead of us. A cephalic index might help, since most Indians have quite large skulls. His nose has been eaten off so we can't get a nasal index measurement or look for any distinctive aquiline features. Odd, but it looks like his left earlobe was cut off. I'll test the pulp to see if it's peyote, and we can try for at least one good fingerprint, although it looks like there's too much skin damage. Care for some lunch?"

"I may never eat again," Baker replied, pushing through the swinging doors dreaming of fresh air and sunshine. He decided he needed to lose a few pounds anyway.

# THREE

As Claude drove up to Alfred Jenkins's house he saw a black-and-white Border collie streak across the road in front of his Ford truck.

"He's throwing pecans at his dog," Claude muttered, braking and pulling up to the curb. Since Alfred's retirement from the Texas Rangers, he'd get so surly at times he was hardly fit company for man or beast, unless you knew him the way Claude did. On the drive out from Austin he'd been thinking about the years they'd spent as Rangers. Alfred had taken him under his wing and treated him like a son when they first became partners. He owed Alfred a debt he could never repay.

Now Claude switched off the motor and heard the telltale hiss of a leaking radiator. "Damn." He gazed across the hood of his blue pickup, watching steam rise like a ghost come to haunt him. He spoke to the truck. "Time I took you to the mechanic's shop, Blue. Seems like your bladder dribbles just like mine does first thing in the morning."

He got out and slammed the door, not out of disgust or animosity but because the door latch needed fixing. He took measured steps toward Alfred's front porch until his arthritic knee stopped hurting so much—his right knee, the result of a calamity with a rodeo bull more than thirty years ago that never healed properly.

"Mornin' Alfred," he said. "I see you're mad at your dog again. What sort of terrible crime did ol' Spot commit?"

Alfred watched Claude through thick lenses while Claude climbed the steps. Alfred's vision had gotten so bad he could scarcely drive anymore. His Chevrolet had dents in the fender and a crumpled rear bumper from backing over his neighbor's mailbox. Claude saw it as his duty to remind Alfred he wasn't aging well. It was the way they'd gotten along for years.

"The son of a bitch killed another one of Miz' Wilkerson's hens. Makes the second one. I hate that dog, Claudie. If it wasn't for the fact he's Alice's dog I swear I'd shoot him dead before sundown. There's nothing on earth more useless than a chicken-killin' dog, unless it's a goddamn communist."

Claude eased his weight down in a metal lawn chair next to Alfred's. They looked out at the front yard, shaded by pecan trees. "If you shoot him your neighbors might complain. It's against the law for a man to shoot an animal inside the city limits. Move out to the country like I did. That way, you can kill all the defenseless animals you want."

Alfred glared across the road to where Spot sat beside a trash can, just out of range of hurled pecans. "That animal needs to be killed. He's earned it. He's a proven chicken killer an' he should be destroyed."

"You know you love that dog, Alfred. Besides, if you feed him maybe he won't feel like he has to hunt down your neighbor's chickens for his supper."

"I feed the rotten little bastard," Alfred growled. "I buy him the best dog food money can buy. Maybe he'll choke to death on a chicken bone the next time. If it wasn't for him belongin' to Alice . . ."

"Alice isn't coming back and you know it. She filed for divorce five years ago."

Alfred made it plain he didn't want to talk about it. "Is that a leaky radiator I hear hissing out front? Damn near every part on that Ford has quit on you one time or another. I've been tellin' you all along to buy a Chevrolet. Do you know what the letters in Ford stand for, Claude? Found on the Road Dead. Fix or Repair Daily. A Chevrolet keeps runnin' no matter what."

Claude took two pecans from a basket near his feet, cracking one shell against the other. "That Chevrolet of yours keeps on running, all right. Running over mailboxes, running into that parking meter in front of Bob's hardware store last winter. There's times when it's a benefit for an automobile to stop running."

"It was the brakes," Alfred said quietly.

Claude knew it was Alfred's eyes and he said so, since Alfred was already in a foul mood. "You're going blind. Those new glasses the doctor prescribed look like Coke bottle bottoms. Another reason not to shoot that dog. They can train some breeds to lead blind folks around."

"I can see like an eagle with these glasses. I could shoot a fly off a buzzard's beak at three hundred yards, if I wanted."

Claude let it drop. Lately Alfred had become more sensitive about his vision. "I ran across that pretty gal again. She was riding a good Steeldust gray stud this time. She stopped along the fence and invited me over to have supper with her sometime real soon."

Alfred shook his head. "You've never given up lookin' for a trashy woman, have you? At your age, you'd think you'd recognize a few of your failings. You've never known a decent woman in your life, if you don't count the time you were married. And it could be argued you never really got to know Martha. I've had head colds that lasted longer than your marriage."

Claude broke open a pecan and popped the pieces into his mouth. "There's no such thing as a decent woman, Alfred. It's a myth, like flying horses and unicorns. Women were put on this planet to make men miserable. Remember, it was Eve who talked poor ol' Adam into eating the apple. She told him she wouldn't give up any more of her goodies unless he took a bite. What else could the poor bastard do?"

"It doesn't say any of that in the Bible, Claude. Tinkering around with Scripture can get a man sentenced to damnation for all eternity. If this was a cloudy day I wouldn't be caught sittin' on the same porch with you, fearing a bolt of lightning could strike any minute."

"Have you ever had an intelligent conversation with a woman?"

"You've never kept company with a woman who could count all the way to ten, not including Martha."

"Martha couldn't count. Why are you always bringing her up?"

"Because she was the only decent, God-fearing woman you've ever known and you ruined things with her when you wouldn't stop drinking."

"I drank because of her, Alfred. She was a bitch. She's still a bitch. . . ."

"You drove her to it. I found her quite pleasant, really."

"You never saw her dark side. Let's talk about something else, like the pretty redhead who's my new neighbor. She's got tits the size of Rio Grande Valley grapefruit and a smile that'll melt your heart. I may be falling in love with her."

"You don't even know her name, Claudie. All you've ever worried about is finding another cheap woman, one more sleazy tramp who'll make your life miserable again.

You go from one ruined affair to the next, wondering why you're unhappy."

"I'm not unhappy. Every now and then, when I think about it, I hate myself for needing a woman. I'll be glad when it's over, when my pecker won't get hard again. I'd always been told that a man's pecker was the first thing to go, but in your case, it was your eyes. 'Course, I can still see without glasses and my pecker still gets stiff. Maybe not as often as it used to . . ."

Claude chewed thoughtfully on more pecan pieces, wishing Alfred would get in a better humor. Their visits usually began like this, one gripe after another. It was Alfred's way of telling him he was lonely and restless. They'd been friends almost twenty-five years and Claude understood his black moods. Those who didn't know them well never understood the way they got along, arguing back and forth like they couldn't stand the sight of each other. Arguing with him was just a role Claude was expected to play, letting Alfred blow off steam. "By the way, her name is Rita."

"Rita sounds trashy, a name like that. First thing you know you'll be trying to get her drunk so you can get her pants off in a hurry, without making any sort of honorable commitment."

"You woke up in a bad mood, Alfred. When you get like this I can't hardly stand to be around you. I think I'll head down to the coffee shop. Maybe find a mechanic to fix Blue's radiator, and some friendly folks to talk to."

"You'll always be fixin' something if you drive a Ford."

Claude tossed his pecan shells into a flower bed and dusted off his pants. "I'll run you a race anytime you feel like it, only we'd better do it someplace where you're not liable to run over some unsuspecting pedestrian. A Ford can outrun a Chevrolet any day." He stood up like he was ready to leave. "I drove out to talk to you about Carla, only you're in such a rotten mood I think I'll skip it."

"Care for some coffee?" Alfred said suddenly. "I made it before you got here."

He watched the dog inch closer to the curb, wagging its tail hopefully. "Only if you'll promise not to talk about my taste in women anymore. I know what I'm looking for."

Alfred got up. When sunlight brought out the colors in his hair, it was easy to see where the dye failed to cover streaks of gray. He was still in good physical shape for a man in his late fifties, enough muscle tone to pass for a younger man until you saw his thick glasses and realized he could no longer be a Marksman. He had retired early at a captain's rank after a bullet lodged so close to his spine that it couldn't be removed safely. Alfred Jenkins was a dead shot with a pistol even after his eyes started to go bad, a fact learned too late by four armed drug dealers in Eagle Pass three years ago. Alfred got all four of them before a bullet took him down. He still didn't walk as straight as he used to, not the way Claude remembered.

"I'll bring the coffee. Keep an eye on that goddamn dog so he don't get back in this yard."

"I'll strangle him with a chicken bone, if you've got one."

"Miz' Wilkerson's got plenty of chicken bones scattered all around her henhouse, she says. I 'spect she'd be more'n happy to lend me a few if I told her what we aimed to do with 'em."

Alfred opened his screen door and disappeared into the house. As if it were a signal, Spot crept across the street with his tail between his legs, hiding behind the hedges.

Leaning back in his chair, Claude thought about the real reason he had come. Major Elliot had readily agreed to assign Carla to Claude's supervision for her first case in the field. The commanding officer wanted to make certain Carla did nothing to embarrass the Rangers. Alfred knew why he had driven out to Brownwood and he was avoiding the subject.

When Alfred came back with the coffee Claude's nose told him something was different about it.

"Coffee don't smell the same." He took a cracked china cup Alfred gave him and tasted it. "What the hell did you do to this stuff, piss in it?"

Alfred took his chair, spilling a small amount of coffee on the front of his khaki pants when he sat down. "I boiled it on the stove like I always do. Coffee made any other way tastes terrible."

"It tastes like shit. What's wrong with fixing it in a real coffeepot?"

"It's delicious, and it's easier to boil it on top of the stove. Gives it more flavor."

"I can't drink this shit."

"You're too set in your ways. That's the reason you can't find a good woman. No wonder Martha left you. You've got no taste in coffee or women. You keep tellin' me my eyes are goin' bad, when I've seen you with some of the ugliest women God ever created."

"I've never gone to bed with an ugly woman, but I've sure as hell woke up with a few. In the dark they all look beautiful." He put down his cup. "You haven't taken well to retirement. Maybe you oughtta go fishing."

Alfred finally looked him in the eye. "I thought you said you drove out here to tell me about my daughter."

"I wrangled it with Tom Elliot so she's been assigned to me, just like you wanted. She came by my office yesterday and we talked. She doesn't know I have it fixed so I'll be her training officer."

"If she ever finds out she'll throw a fit. She'll think I was trying to protect her from something she couldn't handle."

"The major said he'd let me handpick the case. Something without too much risk."

"He wants her out of the public eye. He's had enough of all the ruckus over it, the headlines. She'll make a good Ranger, Claude. She'll pull her own weight. Wait an' see.

You won't have to handle her with kid gloves, I'll promise you that. I raised her to be tough, to make her own decisions. She won't disappoint you or Tom or anybody else."

"You know I'll watch out for her. It's hard to believe she's grown up. Hell, Alfred, she's a downright beautiful woman now."

"She's almost thirty-one. That rotten marriage was hard on her. She's still bitter about her divorce, but she's got good cop instincts. She can read people like a book."

"She inherited it. You always could tell when somebody was hiding something. You have a good nose for shit, Alfred, until it comes to making coffee."

"I make real coffee. A city slicker like you can't tell the difference. Air conditioning ruined your sinuses and junk food ruined your taste buds."

"I'm leaving." Claude got out of his chair. "I drove all the way out here to tell you about Carla's first assignment and you offer me coffee that tastes like horse piss and all you want to talk about is what's wrong with me. If this is the kind of welcome I'm gonna get I'm driving back to Austin."

Alfred looked down at his cup. "Sorry," he muttered, a word he seldom used with anyone. "Tell me about the case. I haven't really been myself lately . . . I get so goddamn bored sittin' around this house all the time."

Again, Claude didn't offer any sympathy. "I'm guessing it'll be fairly routine. The Terrell County sheriff sent a body to the crime lab for identification. Nobody's missing around Sanderson, so it's probably some drifter. The strange part is *how* he was killed. Somebody scalped the poor bastard and cut his pecker and balls off, stuffed them in his mouth, and ripped his belly open too. Whoever cut him up like that has to be a psycho, a real fruitcake. The sheriff is wondering if it's a ritual slaying, something like voodoo. Thinks he may have some sort of cult activity in Terrell County, a bunch of crazies hiding out in the mountains over in Mexico, maybe."

Alfred scratched behind his right ear, frowning a little. "Terrell County used to be part of my territory when I commanded Company E. Nothin' ever happened there, not that I remember. One time we arrested this Mexican cow thief who kept comin' over from Coahuila stealin' cattle, drivin' 'em back across the river at night. That's sure as hell empty country. The sheriff could be right about it bein' some screwball militia group or one of those offbeat religious cults, only the scalpin' part don't make a hell of a lot of sense, or what they did to the guy's nuts an' pecker. Comanches used to do stuff like that. I read about it in some history book about the old-time Rangers." He sighed. "It does sound like an interestin' case, only I sure hope Carla will be okay."

"I'll make sure she's okay," Claude said. "I won't let her get in any tight spots."

Alfred stood up and offered his hand. "Thanks, Claudie. I think you know how grateful I am. She's all I've got an' I want her to get the best field trainin' she can. You're the only man I'd ever trust with that. Call me as soon as you know more about the case." He seemed embarrassed when he added, "An' tell Carla I love her, if you think of it."

They shook hands, then Alfred scowled. "Now, where the hell's that goddamn dog? . . ."

# FOUR

BILLY COULDN'T SLEEP. He'd tossed and turned so much that he'd awakened his wife several times. But he could never explain to Carmen what it was that kept him awake. Visions of what he had seen drifted through his mind every time he closed his eyes. There was no escape, no way to erase it from his thoughts even if he lived a thousand years. Worse, he knew he could never tell *anyone* in Sanderson about it; he would have to keep it locked inside his memory forever, his lips sealed until the day he died.

The strain was telling. He couldn't rope a steer the way he used to, and his usual ranch chores had become a series of meaningless events riddled with mistakes . . . pasture gates he'd forgotten to close, water valves at several windmills he left open, the wrong mix of fly spray used on cattle so that it blistered their hides, made far too strong because he simply forgot to add enough water to the spray rig tank. And he had no appetite, leaving the suppers Carmen fixed untouched, tossing his lunches out in a ravine or behind a cattle shed after only a few bites, nothing but coffee for breakfast, sometimes a tortilla or two merely because he *had* to eat something to keep his strength up.

Today he'd almost driven his pickup through a five-strand barbed-wire fence. His mind wandered continuously. All his life he'd thought of himself as a cowboy, rough and tough, able to handle most anything that came along, a hard-pitching bronc or an enraged Brahma bull, a fistfight at the Broken Spoke against damn near anybody on Saturday night. But what he'd seen on a clear night over a week ago topped the worst nightmare he'd ever had, even as a child when fire-breathing dragons or blood-sucking vampires from some movie kept him up all night looking under his bed or in his closet, trembling from head to toe. And what had happened was real—as real as the blood he stepped in the next day when he went back to the cave to get a better look, as real as the screams he heard the night before, echoing across a dark, empty pasture on the Hunter ranch, screams lasting for hours until they grew weaker, turning into plaintive sobs that still resounded in Billy's memory.

He had crept up to the cave carefully after the killer left to see if there might be some way he could help the screaming man end his pain by taking him to the hospital over in Fort Stockton, or to old Doc Grimes's house, Sanderson's veterinarian. But what he found at the back of the cave only proved he'd acted too late. The poor man was dead by then and it was easy to understand why.

Billy knew for certain there was nothing he could have done to save him, and now Billy had a secret he must take with him to his own grave. He had a family to raise, two sons and a daughter, and if he wanted to remain in Sanderson, the only place he'd ever lived since the day he was born, he had to remain silent. The whole county was already divided over this dump thing, friends taking sides against friends, neighbor against neighbor. All Billy had to do now was figure out a way to forget about it so he could get some sleep.

Besides, he sure as hell didn't want to go to jail. Sheriff Casey might see to it that Billy was blamed for the killing. He would almost *have* to if Billy told him who he thought did it. And Casey wouldn't believe him anyway. Hardly anybody in Terrell County would, because what happened didn't make any sense. The guy who got killed wasn't doing anything wrong that day, only what Billy figured he was being paid to do.

"It's pure hell, havin' a secret like this," he whispered into a dry night wind, sitting on his front porch in Sanderson, smoking yet another cigarette, wishing now he'd minded his own business.

# FIVE

CLAUDE WATCHED CARLA very closely while she read the autopsy report, paying particular attention to her expression when she went through the four photographs of the corpse. Her skin color remained the same and she didn't show any signs of revulsion or queasiness, appearing to study each picture carefully before she turned to the next.

So far, so good, he thought. When she came in the office a few minutes ago her green eyes were flashing, and he was sure he knew why she was upset, since she'd learned this morning about Claude being assigned as her field training officer. Carla smelled shit, a fix to put her under the supervision of her father's friend. He wondered idly if she had already called Alfred. Claude headed off her tirade by handing her the case file before she sat down.

"Pretty gruesome stuff," he remarked when Carla came to the last photograph. "I've seen my share of executions, but this one takes the cake. Whoever killed him cut him up with a plan of some kind. The killer wasn't just angry at whoever that poor slob was. Maybe he's one of those weirdos who shaves his head and wears a white bathrobe, or he has shit tattooed on his forehead like Charles

Manson. What doesn't figure yet is why something like this would show up in a place like Sanderson. California maybe, or New York, but not in the middle of a west Texas cow pasture."

"Indians scalped their victims," she said, flipping through pages of typewritten report. "And it says here they think they found peyote in his stomach contents. I'll call someone at the Anthropology Department at the University of Texas. Maybe they know if these other wounds could be part of some primitive Indian practices."

Claude smiled. "We've been at peace with every Indian tribe I know of for more than a hundred years. I think you'll be barking up an empty tree looking for descendants of Geronimo in Terrell County. They're all gone now, moved away, living on reservations, getting food stamps. It's gonna be more complicated than that. And I don't recall ever hearing that an Indian cared all that much about what happened to his enemies' genitals."

"Peyote is still being used by some Indian tribes as a part of religious ceremonies," Carla said. "It doesn't fall under the Controlled Substances Act if it's in the possession of an American Indian, so a peace officer can't arrest them for having it. I remember a memo we got at El Paso PD about peyote, when some of those Tiguas on the reservation there were using it. I can't recall if they ate it or smoked it. It's a bulb, sort of like an onion. It gives them one hell of a high. Loss of motor control and hallucinations. It was hard putting cuffs on someone high on peyote. My partner and I had to spray this Tigua boy with Mace one night at a local bar just to get him in the car. He acted like he didn't hear us or know we were there. And all we could charge him with was public intoxication."

Claude shook his head. "Well, there are no Indians in Terrell County that I know of. When we get to Sanderson we can ask, but I'd be willing to bet there aren't any. We'll leave tomorrow morning. Pack enough clothes for several days. At this point, we don't even know if our John Doe was killed where they found him. Somebody could have chopped him up in Tulsa and dumped him out later. And I'm sure Sheriff Casey is no rocket scientist when it comes to sifting for evidence. Most rural county sheriffs are good ol' boys who get elected in what amounts to a popularity contest without a minute of police training. Some of 'em can't hardly shoot straight."

"We're also missing a motive, Captain. Finding out why our victim was killed and who he was will probably explain everything else."

"We may never know who he was," Claude said. "No fingerprints and no dental work. Not much to start with. Be here at nine and we'll take off for Sanderson."

Carla placed the file on his desk and stood up. "One more thing, Captain," she said, staring him in the face. "Did my dad have anything to do with me being assigned to this company, and to you for my field training?"

"I doubt if he even knows about it yet," Claude lied, with his fingers crossed behind his back so the lie wouldn't count.

Muscles in her cheeks tightened, then relaxed. "At the risk of being insubordinate, Captain, I don't believe you." She turned on her heel and walked out of the office before he could protest his innocence.

He took a deep breath when he heard the outer door close. "She knows, Alfred," he muttered, as if Alfred were there to hear him. "Caught red-handed." He reached for the phone to call Brownwood. "I'd better tell him she's onto us. He won't be happy to hear it."

Dialing the number from memory, he thought about his second impression of the grown-up Carla. She was thorough, unruffled by the grisly pictures, all good signs. And she was still pretty even when she was angry. Beautiful, in fact. He told himself he had to stop thinking about her in that way. "Alfred may be going blind, but he'd shoot me right between the eyes if I ever laid a hand on his daughter," he said into the telephone while it was ringing, preparing himself to deliver the news. Carla knew what he and Alfred had done and she was not taking pains to hide her resentment.

# SIX

POST OAK JIM FEATHERS sat on the back porch of his shack in a daze, watching a brilliant sunset, remembering stories he heard from his grandfather. A Lipan Apache learned about his ancestry from oral tradition and it had been thus since the Great Spirit gave them breath, for they had no written language in the time of the Old Ones. Jim had gone to school as his father had, learning English, living among white men because the People were no more. Jim's grandfather was one of the last of the Old Ones who remembered the Way, the life of a Lipan before the white man came. He instructed Jim in the Way and even now, as Jim approached the time when he would begin his walk to the Spirit World, those memories lingered in his thoughts. During his lifetime he lived outwardly as a white man, but in his heart he had always been Lipan.

As a young man he felt anger and resentment toward all white people for the way they treated him, looking down on him because he was an Indian, the butt of their jokes, never fully accepted in a world where he didn't seem to belong. When he was small his grandfather, Four Feathers, told him he must accept the white man's ways because

Powva, the Great Spirit, had turned His back on the People and there was no choice. Death would be his only escape from oppression and ridicule. In the Spirit World a Lipan would be with his forefathers as a free man. Until then, there was only the white man's way . . . and memories handed down to him in the form of stories about what it was like to roam free upon the face of the Earth Mother, to be in harmony with all living things, to know the quiet rhythms no white man could ever experience because they only listened with ears, not with their hearts and minds.

Jim had lived seventy *taums* as both a white man and a Lipan. One was only an outer skin, the other his true self, the inner man he had always been because of his grandfather's lessons. And now he was dying. He was certain of it. Finding the corpse was a sign from the Spirit World that death was near. He knew this in his heart. The spirits were calling to him in a way only a Lipan would understand. Gokaleh, shaman from the Land of Shadows, had returned to dismember the white man Jim found in the cave. It had not been his imagination. Almost everyone in town had seen the body before Sheriff Casey sent it away to find out who he was.

Already, so soon after the body was discovered, there was talk in Sanderson that only an Indian would kill someone in this ceremonial way. It was just a matter of time before the only Indian living in Sanderson was blamed. They would take him off to prison, or to the place where crazy people were kept, to live out his final days. No one would believe him if he told them Gokaleh, the Spirit Warrior, was responsible. Gokaleh had been dead more than a hundred years. People would say Post Oak Jim Feathers was as crazy as his father.

Too many white men would remember his father, how he drank too much whiskey and caused trouble in town, how he beat Jim's mother until she died of head injuries. Big Jim Feathers succumbed to the white man's disease called alcoholism, dying young, only thirty-three *taums* when the illness made him turn black and bleed internally. Everyone believed Post Oak Jim was sure to become like Big Jim, a drunk, a crazy man because he was a Lipan. An Indian. Jim never drank whiskey or beer, not even once, in an effort to prove them wrong. And he had succeeded in convincing them he was neither a drunk nor crazy. Until now. If he told them who he truly believed killed the man in the cave, he would be taken off to an asylum.

He watched the sunset as though the sun were setting on his life. Very soon, Sheriff Casey might be coming to take him to jail and that would be the end of it. He could never tell Sheriff Casey it was Gokaleh who performed the ceremonial killing. Everyone would laugh at him. White men did not believe in spirits.

Fading sunlight turned the skies above the horizon pink. Shadows lengthened beneath the desert's plants as the sun lowered with the coming of night. Once, before Danny Weaver, one of Mr. Hunter's ranch hands, found the body, Jim considered telling Mr. Hunter about Gokaleh. But Mr. Hunter would have ridiculed him for believing in spirits and their friendship would be over. Mr. Hunter had been the only white man to offer Jim a job after his father and mother died, even though he paid him only half what the white cowboys were paid for the same work. Still, Mr. Hunter was kind and generous and it would be foolish to tell him what he thought happened to the body Danny found. Jim decided it was better to go to prison in silence than to lose a friend over something no white man could understand.

With a deepening sense of sorrow Jim continued to watch the sun go down. Life had been good, for the most part, although he would have enjoyed it more if he had found a wife, like the girl who came to visit him recently. None of the girls at school had wanted to spend time with him because he was an Indian, the son of crazy Big Jim Feathers. It was even difficult to find friends among the boys in school. Everyone treated him as if he were different. As he grew older he earned some respect from other cowboys because he knew horses and cattle so well. As the years passed he grew accustomed to being alone. The Hunter ranch became more than a place to live, it was home. And it was his ancestral home too, perhaps explaining why he felt this way about a piece of land. Out on the ranch he was at peace; he was where his spirit belonged.

A stirring near his feet drew his attention from the horizon. He spoke to the dog curled beside his chair. "I know you are hungry, Sata. Be patient. I am thinking." He'd named the blue heeler the day he got it as a pup, a gift from Mr. Hunter's best litter that year, calling it Sata, the Lipan word for dog. Sata bore countless scars over his blue roan hide after years of battling wild cattle, rattlesnakes, and cactus thorns as he helped Jim drive cows to the corrals. A good cow dog was far better than a mounted cowboy at rounding up strays, able to give chase through thorny brush while tirelessly nipping a cow's heels until it went through a gate. Sata had been bitten by rattlers half a dozen times and survived. Now at the age of fourteen he was too old to chase cattle, providing companionship for his owner and not much else. "You are always hungry," Jim added as he looked to the sunset again. "You are too fat anyway. Lie still and be quiet while I think. There is much to think about. My spirit ancestors are calling to me. . . ." He wondered what would happen to Sata if he went to jail, or if he died in his sleep. No one would take care of an old crippled dog, especially not a dog belonging to Post Oak Jim, a crazy old Indian accused of murder. "They will blame me, Sata, for scalping and torturing that man. No one will listen when I deny it. I will go off to prison and you will be alone. You are too old to catch rabbits for your supper." He could ask Mr. Hunter to care for the dog, although it was unlikely he would agree to waste food on a dog who couldn't earn his own keep penning cattle.

Sata cocked his head, listening to his master's voice

with his ears raised, ears ragged from years of running among the thorns of ocotillo, cholla, and cactus. Sata's left ear had a notch missing near its tip, torn away by a barbed-wire fence. He wagged his tail, whimpering softly.

"Do not beg," Jim scolded, unwilling to take his eyes off the last rays of sunshine beaming above purple mountains. "All we have left is our pride, foolish dog. Begging for things is the way of a white man. I have never begged for anything from them and you will not beg me for supper. I would rather see you starve. If they take me to jail for something I did not do I will not beg them to set me free. The Great Spirit Powva knows it was Gokaleh who killed. I will say nothing."

When dusk turned to darkness he arose from his patchwork bullhide chair, the legs of it held together with bailing wire, to stretch aching muscles. Sata stood up painfully, keeping weight off a paw which had lost two toes after a rattler's bite, wagging his tail in anticipation of supper. Carl Bass at the meat processing plant gave Jim frozen entrails for his dog from time to time, since they could not be used for anything else. But as Jim turned to go inside, he noticed again how Sata kept sniffing the air with his nose turned toward Jim's old Dodge pickup, which was parked beside the shack.

"Why do you question the truck with your nose?" Jim asked. For a week or more Sata had shown unusual interest in the truck, often limping around it with his nostrils flared as if he scented something unusual in the bed. There was nothing in the truck bed but old kerosene rags and a gas can. So why was Sata behaving so strangely?

The old dog whimpered, hair rising on his back, ears pricked forward toward the truck.

"Old age has robbed us both of our senses," Jim said. "Come and I will show you there is nothing but cloth and a rusty can." He went down sagging wood steps and walked to the pickup bed with Sata close at his heels.

"You see?" he asked, holding up a handful of oily

rags, the vapors of kerosene still pungent on cloths he used to fill a hole in the neck of his gasoline can when he went to buy fuel for his ancient lanterns. He saved precious money on electricity while at the same time preferring the softer glow of lantern light at night, a reminder of better days before he had electric service, when he was a younger man. "Nothing but rags. Your nose plays tricks on you, foolish beast."

Sata gave a low growl, hair still rigid along his spine.

Jim peered into the bed of the truck again, and saw a piece of burlap sacking he didn't remember putting there. He picked it up and felt something wrapped inside.

Opening the rough cloth, he stood there, staring at what he saw while Sata's growling grew louder. Then Jim's hand started to tremble as an inner voice spoke to him in a whisper. His heart was beating so fast he could hear it thumping inside his chest.

A white Ford with an emblem on its doors stopped in front of his shack, as Jim had known it would. He sat on his porch steps in the dark with tears in his eyes. Sata lay beside him, growling, when a man Jim recognized got out of the car.

"Be still," Jim whispered to the dog. "My time has come and barking will change nothing. We have spoken our last good-byes. Do not let anyone see our fear. I will ask that someone take care of you. It is all I can do for you now. They will take me away and we will die alone, apart. Be brave, my old and dear friend. We will meet again in the Land of Shadows, for it is the Way."

Sheriff Casey stopped a few yards from the porch. "I gotta ask you a few questions, Jim," he said. "Hell, I've known you so long I'd nearly forgotten you was an Indian. It's about that cut-up body Danny Weaver found." He held a flashlight in his hand, shining it in Jim's eyes.

"I know," Jim answered hoarsely, softly. "I knew you would be coming soon."

"The guy was scalped, an' several of the cowboys out at the Hunter place saw your truck at the ranch that day."

"I was there," he replied. "I go there almost every day."

"Funny," Casey said, "that I didn't remember you was a full-blood Indian. Seems like you've lived here so long folks don't hardly notice you anymore, but it's a fact you're an Indian an' so was your daddy an' mamma. I remember Big Jim from way back, all the hell he raised 'round here when I was a kid. Some folks used to call him Tonto."

"I remember," Jim said, remaining motionless. He didn't want to remember the cruel names or the jokes.

"Let's get right to the bottom of it, Jim. Did you scalp that poor bastard Danny found out at Hunter's? For the life of me, I can't figure why you would. You're about the most harmless feller in Sanderson, if you ask me. But the Texas Rangers said they found some peyote in his stomach an' everybody knows he was scalped. I told Harlan you was too damn old an' crippled up to kill anybody. You gotta be gettin' close to seventy, ain't you?"

"I have lived for seventy years."

"I forget what kind of Indian you're supposed to be."

"I am a Lipan Apache. All are gone now."

Casey shook his head. "You never did answer me. Did you kill him?"

Jim reached down to stroke Sata's neck gently. "What will it matter if I say I did not? You will take me to jail no matter what I say."

Casey frowned. "Then you ain't denyin' it?"

Jim struggled to his feet, standing as straight as his old arthritic bones would allow, stiffening his spine to show pride, that he was not afraid of the white man's laws. "Look in the back of my truck," he said, pointing to the Dodge, doing his best to hide a slight quiver in his voice.

"The Spirit Warrior of the Old Ones, Gokaleh, placed something there. It was meant that you should find it. I will say nothing more, for it is the Way and my time has come. I cannot speak against my ancestors. This is the law of the Lipan."

"You ain't makin' any sense," Casey remarked as he walked over to the Dodge and shone his flashlight into the bed. For a time he stood still, wearing a puzzled expression, then he touched the object wrapped in burlap with his fingertips. "I'll be damned," Casey said. "It's that poor bastard's scalp." Now he aimed his light at Jim. "Turns out you're just as crazy as your old man. Sorry, Jim, but I'm gonna have to take you to jail. . . ."

Jim refused to look at Sata when the dog whimpered. "I am ready to go," he said quietly, forcing his feet to move toward the sheriff's car.

Once, he looked over his shoulder across the darkened desert to see if Gokaleh was watching from a distance, but there was no horse, no rider he could see. Perhaps it had only been a vision when he saw a mounted Indian riding between the ocotillo stalks. But he'd been sure of what he heard, the hoofbeats, and hadn't Sata growled when he too heard them?

# SEVEN

CARLA JENKINS SAT beside him reading through pages of notes she'd written on a legal pad, while Claude drove west along U.S. 84 toward Brownwood, over Carla's initial objections. Claude told her it wasn't out of the way by much, which was part truth. It puzzled him somewhat, that she wouldn't want to see her father. "He'll try to tell me how I'm supposed to conduct myself," she had said. "The last thing I need right now is somebody else looking over my shoulder. Dad won't understand why I'm a little nervous over making a good impression. He'll preach another one of his long-winded sermons." Until now she'd made no further mention of her suspicion that her assignment to Claude had been prearranged.

Before they left Austin, Claude told her about the call from Sheriff Casey early this morning, how he'd arrested some old Indian named Post Oak Jim Feathers who had what looked like a human scalp hidden in the back of his pickup. Casey was sure it would turn out to be John Doe's scalp, and that the case was virtually solved now. The scalp was on its way to Austin for analysis.

Carla looked up from her notes, staring through the

windshield of Claude's new Ford sedan. The car was the ugliest color he'd ever been assigned by the Rangers' purchasing office, a dark green reminding him of fresh cow shit.

"It's too easy," she said thoughtfully. "Why would the guy who committed the murder leave something as incriminating as the dead man's scalp in his truck?"

"I agree," Claude replied, steering around a curve at eighty miles an hour along an empty stretch of highway surrounded by dry mesquite scrubland. "Something stinks. Maybe this Jim Feathers is being framed. Casey told me the guy was seventy years old, and that don't exactly fit the profile of a violent killer in my book. It took a hell of a lot of strength to cut the victim up like that and the guy would have been half his age. Although I suppose the peyote could have helped subdue the guy. I asked Casey what he knew about Feathers. He said as far as he knew Feathers was just a harmless old Indian who'd retired on Social Security five or six years ago."

"So where's the motive?" Carla asked, dropping her pad in her lap.

She looks pretty, Claude thought, making sure to avoid any glances at her bosom, continuing to remind himself she was Alfred's daughter, not fair game for gawking. "We won't know till we get there. I also got a call from a guy by the name of Bill Thompson with the Nuclear Regulatory Commission. He's got some sort of title, like acquisitions specialist or something. He's staying in Sanderson for some hearings, giving expert testimony as to the potential for environmental damage from some sort of low-level nuclear dump site planned for Terrell County. We'll talk to him as soon as we can, after we see what Casey has. Thompson insists it's all connected, the corpse and the nuclear thing. He told me the dump is a red-hot issue there. Dozens of lawyers are involved. One faction wants it because of the jobs. The others, mostly big landowners, are worried it'll lower the value of ranches all over the county.

They want an injunction to stop it. Big money is involved, Thompson said. Some landowners claim they'll fight it all the way to the Supreme Court if they have to."

"Why would a seventy-year-old man living on Social Security have a stake in this," Carla wondered aloud, "unless somebody hired him to kill our victim? And who is our John Doe? None of this computes."

"I've been thinking the same thing," he said as the skyline of Brownwood appeared over a group of wooded hills, "only I would have said things don't add up. I'll never understand computers. I'm too old to learn anyhow."

"It's easy, Captain. I brought my laptop. I'll show you how."

He grinned and wagged his head. "Not me. You'll be wasting your time. We won't stay but a few minutes at Alfred's." He was changing the subject, and he knew it. "I owe it to him and he'll be happy to see you. You know he loves you more'n anything in his whole life. He won't tell you how to work cases . . . and even if he does, it's because he wants to help."

"I know," she said, something new in her voice and her expression. "Sometimes I think he loves me too much. I've tried to make him understand I have to do this on my own."

"He knows," Claude said quietly, slowing down for the outskirts of town, reminding himself that Carla couldn't find out about his visit to her father earlier in the week, or any of their recent phone calls.

◇ ◇ ◇

He parked in the shade of a pecan tree on Vine Street, a quiet neighborhood in an older part of a small railroad town fallen on hard times. As he switched off the engine, Claude noticed Alfred's Border collie chained to a corner of his front porch. "Appears Spot's been killin' chickens again," he said, before he caught himself. "The last time I talked to your dad . . . must've been a few weeks ago, he told me Spot killed some of his neighbor's chickens.''

He got out with his lie ringing in his ears and slammed the car door, out of habit from driving his old blue pickup with a malfunctioning door latch. Alfred's favorite lawn chair was empty. Carla came around the car appearing edgy, blinking more than she usually did, smoothing the front of her white shirt.

"He's here," she said, glancing at Alfred's Chevrolet. "He hasn't got a straight fender anywhere on that pickup. I wish he wouldn't drive, but that would be like telling him to stop breathing. I asked him not to drive to Austin for my graduation. . . . I was afraid he'd kill himself. He's going blind as a bat and won't admit it."

"Don't tell him that," Claude warned, starting up the cracked sidewalk toward the house. "He's been real touchy lately about his eyes. I used to be able to tease him about his glasses, but not anymore."

Spot's tail wagged furiously when he saw Claude and Carla. He made a soft whimpering sound, stretching his chain as far as he could.

"Hello the house!" Claude yelled when he saw only the screen door was closed. It was an old-time way of announcing a visitor he and Alfred had used with each other for years.

Carla went over to Spot and squatted down, smiling, rubbing the dog's neck and ears. "Hey, boy," she said as Spot's tail whipped back and forth. "Long time no see."

Alfred came to the door wearing his usual khakis and short-sleeve shirt. He pushed the screen open, offering Claude his hand. "Hello, Claudie." They shook and he quickly looked past his old partner to Carla. "Hello, my little darlin',"' he said, grinning from ear to ear. "Come give your poor ol' lonely daddy a hug an' a kiss."

Carla came up on the porch to embrace her father, her complexion a fiery red. She kissed his cheek. Claude took a stroll to the end of the porch where Spot was chained, to avoid being too close to their reunion.

"I've missed you, Dad," she said, hugging his neck while Alfred wrapped his arms around her waist.

"I've missed you too, honey. Sit down an' tell me about your graduation. I'm so very proud of you."

"I've been through hell, Dad. You know what the academy is like, so let's skip it for now. Tell me how you've been. You look well."

Claude found himself thinking how formal Carla's greeting sounded. Stiff. Why was she so nervous about seeing her father today?

Alfred and Carla took the lawn chairs while Claude reached down to pat Spot's head, accepting wet licks from a long pink tongue in return. "You been killin' any more chickens?" he whispered.

"I know they put you through hell, honey," Alfred said as he held her hand, "but there isn't a woman on earth who's better at takin' all the hell anybody can dish out. You'll make one of the best Rangers they ever had. Don't let them get your goat."

"I won't," she said, squeezing his palm gently, smiling in a way that seemed forced to Claude when he took a sideways glance.

When their silence lasted too long, Claude said, "Why have you got your faithful dog chained up like a prisoner, Alfred? Has he bitten the mailman or something?"

"He's a crazed chicken killer," Alfred replied, scowling, glaring at Spot through thick lenses. "Miz' Wilkerson across the street threatened to have him gassed at the dog pound unless I chained him up or fenced my yard. It'd cost three thousand dollars to put up a chain-link fence. I've thought about shootin' him. I decided I'd make him do hard time instead. He's wearin' that chain till he dies of old age."

"No parole?" Claude asked. "Seems to me the punishment far outweighs the crime. What about the winter? He'll freeze to death out here."

"Serves him right," Alfred snapped. "When it turns cold he can think about all those chicken dinners he ate. I don't give a damn if he freezes solid. I'll bury him in the spring . . . after he thaws out."

"Poor Spot," Carla said, sounding a bit more relaxed when she wasn't the topic of discussion. "I agree with Captain Groves. You're being too harsh."

Alfred looked at Carla. "You used to call him your Uncle Claude. Remember?"

Claude hadn't remembered, until now.

"Things are different, Dad. I'm not a little girl anymore and Captain Groves is my superior officer, my field training officer, which I'm sure you knew a long time before I did. You never will stop treating me like a child."

"That isn't true, honey," Alfred protested, wearing innocence all over his face. "Claude didn't tell me until a couple of days ago that he'd asked for you as a trainee. Am I right, Claudie?"

"As right as rain," Claude answered, turning away, caught in an outright falsehood. "I told Alfred about it after I'd already done it, so he couldn't object to the idea."

"You're both lousy liars," Carla said. "I wanted to do this on my own, Dad. I'd hoped you wouldn't interfere."

"I wouldn't dream of it," Alfred insisted, making his weak performance worse. With no attempt at subtlety, he changed the subject. "Tell me about your first case, Carla. Claude did mention somethin' about the two of you bein' headed back to my old stompin' ground in west Texas. Sanderson, I think he said."

Claude wouldn't look at Carla, since Alfred had just gotten them caught in another lie, mentioning the case they'd only known about for a few days when he'd said it had been weeks since he last spoke with Alfred. He could almost feel Carla's eyes boring holes through his back.

"I'm sure you already know all about it, Dad, so let's

stop playing games. We're going to Sanderson and you know why."

Alfred sat quietly for a moment. "Listen, honey," he said in a much softer tone, "I love you more than anything in the whole world. Have since the day you were born. The Almighty blessed me when He gave you to me an' I only want the best for you. If it seems like I'm bein' too protective or somethin' like that, it's because you're the only thing that matters to me. You're all I've got. Don't get mad at me for lovin' you. . . ."

Claude swung off the porch when he heard the plea in Alfred's voice. A proud man like Alfred wouldn't want anyone else to hear what he was saying now, what amounted to an admission that he had arranged things for his daughter, hoping to make the beginning of her career as a Ranger a little easier. Claude walked over to the shade beneath a pecan tree while Alfred and Carla talked in private.

"He'll turn you loose in a few days," Claude promised when Spot followed him pulling on his chain. "He talks tough, but we both know he's an old softy deep inside when it comes to things he loves . . . even a chicken-killin' dog."

Spot licked his wrist as though he understood. Claude risked a glance toward the porch. Carla was standing up as if she were ready to leave.

"Women," Claude whispered. "All she had to do was talk to him about the case for a while, make him feel like he was a part of something again. Can't she tell how lonely he is? He's so damn restless he can't stand it."

Carla hugged Alfred, saying something Claude couldn't hear. She kissed him and started down the steps.

Claude gave Spot a final scratch before he straightened up, feeling a sharp pain in his damaged knee when he took the first step toward Alfred to shake hands before they left.

"You're damn near a useless cripple, Claudie," Alfred

said when he noticed Claude's limp. "You oughtta think about takin' an early retirement, like I did. Can't hardly stand all the excitement. We could go fishin' together."

He took Alfred's palm, ignoring his friend's bitter sarcasm. "I may call you in a few days if this case gets complicated. You know that region better'n I do. Be seeing you, Alfred. Maybe if you tried giving Spot some chicken necks from the grocery store he'll get tired of the taste of chicken after a spell."

Alfred was looking at Carla, not listening to a word Claude said. Perhaps it was the way sunlight beamed through his thick glasses, making it appear as though he had a tear in his eye.

Carla stopped halfway to the car and turned around. There was no mistaking the tears glistening on her cheeks. "I'm sorry, Dad," she said, strain elevating her voice, "but if I stay any longer you'll start lecturing me, telling me how to do my job. I can't let you do that. I have to make my own mistakes. I can't be perfect like you want me to be."

"No, honey," Alfred said very softly, shaking his head side to side, spreading his arms in a helpless gesture, "I never planned to lecture you, I swear. I know you'll make mistakes. It's impossible to do this job without makin' mistakes. Hell, I made 'em all the time." He lowered his hands. "I made so many the last ten years of my career they sent me to Company E out in Midland. It's the same as bein' sent to outer Mongolia. How could you believe I'd expect perfection from you when I couldn't stay out of trouble myself? I screwed up reports, an' lost crucial evidence. One time I forgot to read some bastard his Miranda an' the case I'd worked on for months was dismissed by the DA. You're always gonna make mistakes, an' I know it damn near better'n anybody. In the beginnin' I was a damn fool, because I wanted to be tough an' fearless, like ol' Frank Hamer. I'm lucky I didn't get my head blown off. I was scared as hell an' couldn't admit it. I know exactly how you're feelin' right now."

Claude realized he was overhearing things too personal for an outsider, admissions Alfred would never make to him even as close as they'd been all these years. He walked past Carla to the car and opened the trunk, pretending to be occupied checking their shotguns and boxes of shells, the kit containing plaster for taking tire and footprint molds, another kit with fingerprint dust and tape for removing fingerprints or fibers and skin cells from victims' fingernails.

Carla remained in the middle of the sidewalk. It appeared she was drying her eyes with the back of her hand. "I don't want sympathy either, Dad, just a chance to prove I can be a good Ranger."

"I know," Alfred replied, coming down off the porch. "You can do it, an' it's not just because you're my daughter. I've got faith in you, honey. You'll do just fine."

Carla started toward him, and this time their embrace was as genuine as any could be. They held each other, saying nothing for a while and now Claude felt much better about his gamble on a side trip to Brownwood, a calculated risk that Alfred would let his real feelings show. It was something Captain Alfred Jenkins wasn't very good at.

# EIGHT

MILES OF SHIMMERING asphalt highway stretched across Tom Green and Crockett counties southwest of San Angelo, heat waves dancing from dark pavement under a blistering summer sun. Carla had not uttered more than a few words for a pair of hours after her tearful good-bye at Alfred's. Claude thought it best not to mention it. Carla had her laptop computer open, making entries from time to time while Claude simply enjoyed the land they drove through, as rugged as any in west Texas, arid plains and flat-topped mesas, twisting limestone canyons, dry creek beds so late in summer. There were desert plants as far as the eye could see, the ocotillo's spiny stalks like fire-blackened skeletal hands reaching toward pale blue sky; cholla spines and sotol growing in clusters, broad-leafed agave in every hue ranging from bright green to purple or brown. Yet by far the most omnipresent feature in this region was rock—higher country full of jagged shapes where solid slabs ended to form overhangs and ledges, or smoother surfaces sculpted by wind and water with hollows and larger basins, a few meager patches of yellowed grass where thin topsoil and scant shade allowed it to survive months without rainfall when temperatures soared above a hundred degrees from late May until September. Across canyon bottoms and streambeds a chalky yellow caliche soil and sand permitted more growth even during the dry season. Cottonwood trees marked underground springs. Mesquites sent roots half a dozen feet in all directions to draw precious moisture, yielding beans in brittle green pods that would keep cattle, sheep, goats, and deer alive. A cow with a calf required over a hundred acres of this type of land to survive, and only then if the cattle were dry-country breeds like Brahma, crosses with hardy longhorns, or other mixed bloods. A ranch in this part of Texas needed thousands of acres of land to support enough livestock to make ranching worthwhile, and it had been Claude's experience that the men and women who made a living in west Texas were just as tough as their animals. Oil and gas wells had been the salvation of many a ranch during particularly lengthy droughts. An older rancher Claude knew south of Midland described his cattle herds as a hobby, that his real "herd bulls" were the giant steel pumpjacks above his oil reserves.

"You seem mighty busy with that electronic toy," Claude said, ending a lengthy silence between them as they topped a ridge south of Sheffield, still hours away from Sanderson.

"It isn't a toy, Captain. I'm pulling up information about Terrell County and Sanderson that I downloaded from our main computer banks. Sanderson has a population of about two thousand and it's the County Seat. Terrell County is mostly white, unusual for a county bordering Mexico, with only six hundred ninety-one Hispanics, no blacks, and one Native American recorded in the 1990 census. It's a ranching economy with oil and gas production in limited locations. It's among the leading counties in Texas in sheep and goat production. It gets less than twelve inches of annual rainfall. Virtually no crime statistics, other than a few stolen pieces of oil-field equipment. The last murder in Terrell County occurred in 1977, over fifteen years ago, when a Hispanic shot his brother-in-law over a beating the man gave his sister."

"I'm impressed," Claude said, "only you didn't tell me much of anything I didn't already know except the killing in '77 and the Indian. Hardly anything ever goes on in Terrell County because nobody lives there. That's one reason why the NRC decided to bid for a nuclear dump near Sanderson, or so Thompson said. Maybe there'll be fewer folks who glow in the dark if that stuff makes people sick."

Carla pushed another series of buttons, frowning at her computer screen. "The dump site comes under the authority of the Texas Low-Level Radioactive Waste Disposal Commission, established by the seventy-second legislature in May of '91. The Sanderson site was selected because water tables are very deep, over eight hundred feet below the proposed site area, while annual rainfall is less than a foot and it is deemed marginal range land for livestock. There are no industrial facilities and no significant cultural resources, thus no adverse effects are predicted for any existing businesses or population. The commission estimates that one hundred thirty-two construction workers will be employed at the site initially, and the project will provide thirty-three full-time jobs upon completion, with an annual payroll of over one million. Low-level waste is defined as contaminated items from nuclear power plants having a Class A or B designation for radioactivity, whatever the hell that means, which must be stored in stabilized containers underground, conforming to requirements established by the NRC in Washington. It goes on to describe packaging safety and all sorts of transportation regulations. I suppose if we need to know any more, Bill Thompson from the NRC can fill us in."

"You've done your homework, Carla, but let's not forget we were asked to solve a murder, and Thompson thinks there's a tie-in with this dump. That little computer is real nice, but it ain't gonna tell us who John Doe is, or who killed him. My gut tells me it isn't the old Indian, although he may know more than he's saying. It'll boil down to old-fashioned detective work, and asking the right questions of the right people."

She gave him a quizzical look. "You sound just like Dad. You don't have much faith in the latest scientific methods, do you?"

"It's not that I mistrust the science, but somebody has to get the facts and the evidence to a lab so a scientist can tell me what it is, and how it fits in the case I'm investigating. A computer and a scientist can't get a confession out of a criminal or haul him off to jail." Claude smiled. "As to the comparison to your father, I'm flattered by it. Probably don't deserve it. He was the best peace officer I've ever known, and he could tell more about people just by looking at 'em than any man who ever wore a star." His smile faded. "It's sad to see him the way he is now, frustrated, lonely, bored out of his skull. He reminds me of that old firehouse dog who barks when he hears a siren. Every time I tell him about a case I'm workin' he asks all sorts of questions, the facts, what some guy looked like and did he seem too calm or too nervous. Alfred's luck ran out when he took that bullet down in Eagle Pass. I expected it to change him, being retired, but I never dreamed it would get him down in the mouth like he is. Too bad that him an' Alice had to break up. I think the loneliness is eating on Alfred as much as anything."

Carla pushed a button and closed her computer, staring out the windshield. "Dad always took such a hard line on everything. He brought his work home with him, in a manner of speaking. He was always talking to Mom about investigations, like there wasn't anything else in the whole world. After a while Mom got tired of it, I suppose. She seems happier now, living in San Antonio. I don't talk about Dad when I see her. He doesn't talk about her either, like there never was a marriage between them."

"Shit happens," Claude said, then he corrected himself when he remembered he was with a woman. "Feces occurs. I had my own dose of marital bliss. Lasted six years. Martha was a bitch, if you'll pardon the expression. She got a court order denying me visitation rights with Bobby, our son, because she convinced this wimpy judge in Waco I was a bad example . . . drinking too much in front of the boy, using foul language, and that I cheated on her with another woman."

"Did you?" Carla asked, watching him now.

He shrugged. "No sense lyin' about it. Living with Martha made me so miserable I did stray from the fold now and then. It got to where I couldn't stand to go home and fight with her. If I opened a beer, it was like I'd unzipped my pants in church. I looked for any reason not to go home until she went to bed, so I could have some peace and quiet."

"Dad told me you used to drink an awful lot."

"I suppose I did. Maybe I still do, by other men's standards. I never drank on the job."

"Dad also tells me you like easy women, that all you want from a woman is to take her to bed."

"I wouldn't put it that way," he replied, feeling embarrassed because it was Alfred's daughter making the accusation. "He's always giving me lectures on the subject of trashy women. I'm a confirmed bachelor, I suppose, so that doesn't leave me much in the way of pickings. I take what's out there. . . ."

Carla chuckled. "It doesn't seem any of us are any good at matrimony. My marriage lasted less than five years. George had trouble dealing with a strong woman. He wanted a mewing kitten waiting for him when he got home. He said he felt threatened by my career, that I cared more about being a cop than I did for him or making our marriage work. We argued all the time, and he didn't like my late hours when I worked the swing shift. Then he started accusing me of having an affair with my patrol partner. That was the last straw."

Claude steered around a slow-moving cattle truck as the sun lowered in the west. "I know all about accusations. Martha used to look in my underwear for—" He couldn't finish, feeling his cheeks turn warm.

"Pecker tracks. Semen. It's okay to say it, Captain. I'm not naive or a prude."

He laughed to help hide his discomfort. "It may take me a while to get used to the difference in our plumbing, if you know what I mean. Don't take it personally. Even though I'm regarded as a despicable creature, a cheat and a drunk, I was brought up to show respect when I'm around a lady."

"But there is a certain class of women whom you set out only to seduce, am I right?"

"Well . . . good grief, Carla. This line of questioning is hard for me, coming from you. You're my best friend's daughter and I hate like hell to admit to some of these things, when it comes to admitting them to you."

She smiled again. "Why is it so difficult, Captain? You're not married. If you seduced a different woman every night, it wouldn't make any difference to me."

"It's a little embarrassing, I guess. Alfred shouldn't have told you all that. It's okay when he and I talk about it, but it doesn't seem proper between you and me."

"Look, Captain, I'm not one of those feminists who wants to be treated like one of the boys. I like having doors opened for me, to be treated like a lady when I'm off duty. But when we're just having conversation I don't want you to tiptoe around me, having to be careful what you say. You shouldn't be uncomfortable about telling me your wife checked your underwear for pecker tracks, or that you try to get laid whenever you can. Please don't treat me any differently than you would any other rookie."

"Okay, Carla Sue," he said, relaxing his grip on the steering wheel. "You've made your point. I'll tell you dirty jokes and use every cuss word in my vocabulary, only you've got to promise me you won't tell Alfred. He'd kill me if he knew I was talking to you about pecker tracks or getting some bar fly drunk enough so I can mount her, if I get lucky."

Carla's laugh was genuine, and for the first time since they left Austin she seemed completely at ease.

"What made you decide to become a cop?" he asked. Back when Carla first chose criminal justice as her major at Howard Payne, Alfred complained endlessly to Claude about it, worrying that she might enter a dangerous profession like police work.

"I thought I wanted to be a lawyer, until I found out most of it was really boring . . . a bunch of paperwork, being inside all the time. I was always an outdoor girl. I guess a part of it is listening to Dad all these years. It sounded exciting. As soon as I graduated I applied with the El Paso Police Department. It was where George grew up. We met in college and he was going back to run the family business. We got married and moved to El Paso. The trouble started as soon as I got out of the police academy and went to work. All the screwy hours weren't good for our marriage, but I liked what I was doing. George never understood me or my work. I shouldn't have married him in the first place."

"Well, I remember all your show steers and your first pony. You weren't afraid of a horse and that's half the secret. Even when you fell off, you got right back on."

She looked at him and smiled. "I *did* call you Uncle Claude back then. You had more patience with me than Dad did. He has always expected me to get things right the first time. I felt that pressure all my life."

Claude nodded, for he understood. "You gotta remember he only wants what's best for you. He loves you, and he's the best friend I ever had. Without his help I'd never have made it through my divorce with Martha or earned my captain's rank. He taught me thousands of things about life I couldn't learn in a classroom. If you can get past the part where you resent him giving you advice, you'll learn a hell of a lot about detective work and it won't include hardly any of that science you believe in."

"I know," Carla said softly, watching the landscape pass by her window, a sunset emblazoning rocky hills and low mountains with a kaleidoscope of color. "I keep hoping one of these days he'll forget I'm his daughter long enough so we can be friends."

He thought it best to let the subject drop when he heard the change in her voice, not wanting to delve too deeply into matters that were none of his affair. "I can't figure any connection between that corpse and a nuclear dump in Terrell County. Since the dead guy, according to Sheriff Casey, isn't a local resident with a stake in the issue one way or the other, there's no way I can put the two together."

Carla took her attention from the land briefly to add her own doubts. "I'm having the same problem finding a motive for a seventy-year-old Indian living on Social Security, unless he owns some of the land in question. But we disagree on one point. I believe the corpse and the nuclear dump are connected somehow. If he was someone with the NRC or the Texas Radioactive Disposal Commission, he'd have been reported missing long before now. I've got a feeling it's more than coincidence when a body turns up in a community at odds over what nuclear material might do to the value of surrounding land, or the potential for a health hazard. This fellow Thompson may be closer to the truth than you think."

Claude thought, but did not say, how much Carla was sounding like her father just now, using her nose to detect a false scent instead of using that damn computer in her lap.

# NINE

⬥

JIM FEATHERS SAT in his Terrell County jail cell staring at the floor. All day he'd watched the square of sunlight from his cell window creep across the cement like a living thing, his mind a blank, refusing the food Deputy Huffman brought him, drinking no water, practicing the meditation his grandfather had taught him when he sought contact with the spirits. And still, no spirit voices came even when he washed his mind of everything. Jim wondered if being in a white man's jail prevented the spirits from speaking to him. Four Feathers said a Lipan should sit on the highest mountain or canyon wall, palms pressed against the Earth Mother with all conscious thoughts banished, watching the sky, reading the shapes of clouds for meaning, listening with his heart for quiet whispers from the Land of Shadows. Perhaps because he could not see the sky or clouds in jail, the spirits were silent. Or was their silence a sign that he would die soon?

He had steadfastly refused to answer any of Sheriff Casey's questions, nor would he ever mention again words that had slipped from his mouth when the sheriff came, words of Gokaleh's return to the land of the living to perform an ancient ceremonial killing and place the scalp in the back of his truck. They would say he was crazy and being locked up in an asylum would be far worse than death in the white man's electric chair when the judge charged him with murder. Sheriff Casey said the laws of Texas required that a lawyer must represent him even though he did not have the money to pay for one. A lawyer would be appointed, the sheriff told him this morning, an old man from Ozona named Bell, since Sanderson had only one lawyer and Jim's case would be tried in Sixth Judicial District Court somewhere else. All he had to do was say nothing to anyone and it would be over soon, sooner than if he tried to explain something no white man could understand.

As sunset came to the window above his metal cot, a key rattled in a lock at one end of the hallway. Deputy Huffman walked in, followed by a man Jim recognized immediately, the only man who had ever trusted him, Jim's lone true friend among the white people of Terrell County.

Cale Hunter ambled up to the bars of his cell, faded blue jeans and denim work shirt clinging to his angular frame, his deeply wrinkled face and mane of snowy hair shadowed from the fluorescent light beaming down on his sweat-stained hat brim.

"You've got company, Post Oak," Huffman said needlessly, a note of disdain in his remark. "Cale said he wanted to talk to you. I'll leave the two of you alone. Sheriff Casey said it was okay."

Hunter thumbed his hat back and leaned close to the bars as Deputy Huffman returned to the front office. Hunter's deep brown eyes riveted Jim—he wrapped work-callused hands around the iron rods between them. "Damn, Jim," he began, a grating sound like he needed to clear his throat. "They told me what Casey found in your pickup. I don't believe a damn word of it. You didn't kill nobody. You're near 'bout the gentlest feller I ever knew an' we knowed each other damn near all our lives. Tell me it ain't so, Jim. Look me in the eye an' tell me you didn't cut up that guy they found in my river pasture."

Jim wanted to tell Mr. Hunter the truth, but it would only prolong his time in jail or even worse, send him to the place for crazy people. "I have nothing to say," he whispered, unable to look Mr. Hunter in the eye when he said it.

"Who the hell are you coverin' for?" Hunter asked. "To my knowledge you ain't got a close friend in this whole goddamn dry-assed county. . . ."

"You have always been my friend, Mr. Hunter. You gave me a job, and you gave me Sata. You helped me get my Social Security money and you gave me my truck. Danny and Chub are friends, and now there is the girl. . . . She was nice when she came to visit me."

"She wanted to meet you because you're an Indian. Sweet Jesus, Jim, they'll send you down to Huntsville an' give you a lethal injection if you don't tell who did it. You know who did it, don't you? Danny an' Chub have worked for me for years an' I know 'em well enough to know they ain't killers. But neither are you, Jim Feathers. Your ol' daddy was mean natured when he was drunk, but you got none of that in you."

Jim looked at the floor, still seated on his cot. "I will say nothing to anyone, Mr. Hunter. There are things about being a Lipan you would not understand."

"I understand you're gonna go to prison if you don't tell Walter Casey what you know 'bout this. You could get a death sentence. Ain't you interested in livin'?"

Jim continued to stare at the floor.

"They have to give you a lawyer, Jim. He's on his way here now. You gotta tell that lawyer the truth. You didn't kill nobody. They'll never get a jury to believe you did. Everybody in town will swear you're the quietest man in Terrell County. You ain't never harmed a fly. I still can't figure how that scalp wound up in your truck, but I know damn well you didn't put it there 'less maybe you found it someplace. What I can't figure out is why you won't tell Casey that. Tell him where you found it, or how it got there, an' he won't have no choice but to let you go."

Jim summoned all his nerve before he looked at Mr. Hunter, to keep the truth from showing in his eyes. "I ask for only one thing, Mr. Hunter. Sata will starve unless someone feeds him. He is too old and lame to catch rabbits now. If you could find him a good home, someone who will feed an old dog who is useless."

"You ain't gonna stay in jail," Hunter said. "Soon as the judge sets your bail bond, I'm gonna make it. You'd be the last person who'd ever run off. I'll make your bond till they take you to trial . . . don't matter how big it is."

"I do not understand these things. What is a bail bond?" Jim remembered hearing Danny talk about it once a long time ago, when he got too many drunk-driving tickets.

"It's money, promisin' you won't leave town until they have your trial. I'll pay a bail bondsman to put it up. I trust you, Jim. Always have, an' that's why I know damn well you didn't kill nobody. But when you talk to that lawyer, you gotta tell him what really happened. You can't just sit there lookin' at the goddamn floor tellin' folks there's somethin' 'bout bein' some kind of Lipan Injun makes you so you can't talk."

He was still thinking of Sata, not himself. "Will you ask if someone will feed the old dog, Mr. Hunter? Mr. Bass gives me frozen intestines for him and Sata does not eat much. . . ."

"I'll take care of the dog," Hunter said, a hint of impatience in the way he said it, "but you gotta promise me you'll tell your lawyer everythin' you know. Is that a deal? I'll put up your bond soon as it's set."

Jim winced inwardly. How could he tell a lawyer why he was not able to explain what happened? And how could he refuse the kindness of Mr. Hunter? The man who had been his employer and friend for so many years? Jim struck a compromise with himself. "I will tell him what my heart tells me to say, if he will hear my words with his heart."

Hunter's puzzled expression lingered a moment. "I ain't all that sure what you mean, but Harlan said your lawyer's supposed to be here later. Tell him everythin', Jim, an' I'll feed the dog an' post your bond. Don't worry. It's gonna turn out all right after you tell that lawyer the truth."

The door to the sheriff's office was open when Jim heard David Bell, a retired attorney from Ozona, speak to Sheriff Casey on his way out at seven that evening.

"The old Indian's crazy. Certifiably insane. He keeps on talkin' about some Apache ghost who came back from the grave to kill whoever it was they found out at Hunter's ranch. He told me this ghost rides a horse close to his house at night sometimes. I can get him off on insanity grounds. They'll prob'ly send him over to Skyview at Rusk for the criminally insane. He still claims he doesn't know whose body it was. He says he found it in a cave when he saw buzzards circlin', an' he swears he don't know how the scalp got in his truck. Schizophrenics sometimes don't remember what they did when it's somethin' bad. I had this case a few years ago where this psychopath chopped off his grandma's head when she wouldn't buy him a new sportscar. . . ."

Deputy Huffman closed the office door and now the lawyer's voice was muffled, indistinct.

Jim promised himself he would never mention Gokaleh or the Spirit Warrior who watched him from the darkness to anyone again. He lay back on his bunk with his hands behind his head, looking at the window. The quiet hum of air conditioning came through a vent in the hallway. He thought of Sata and other material things, since no spirit voice would come to him. He wondered what would happen to his tiny house, or his Dodge, the pictures of his grandfather locked away in an old footlocker beneath his bed, the eagle claw necklace his grandfather gave him from the time of the Old Ones. He supposed all of it would be taken to the city dump east of town, buried like his father and mother and grandfather, forgotten, returning to dust as all things did with the passage of time.

# TEN

BILLY COULDN'T REMEMBER shedding tears since the night his father died over a dozen years ago. Not that there hadn't been plenty of sorrow in his life, his daughter's blindness from birth and Carmen's stillborn baby the first year they were married, all of which he accepted with stoic outward calm because it was expected of him as the head of his family. It was a woman's job to do the crying. But now, as he sat in darkness in the seat of his Toyota pickup in front of Post Oak Jim's house, he drank beer and wept silently, tossing empty cans into the bed of his truck, questioning the existence of God and justice and all the things he'd believed in since he was a boy. The end of this lonely dirt road outside of Sanderson was the only place he could do his crying and drinking unnoticed, so no one would ask him what was wrong.

He'd learned of Post Oak Jim's arrest while he was at Joe's Drive-in a half hour ago, when he stopped off for a six-pack on the way home from work. He'd almost forgotten to pick up his change from a ten-dollar bill when Joe Gomez told him about it, and about the scalp Sheriff Casey found in Post Oak's truck. It was all Billy could do to make it out the door without telling Joe he knew damn good and well Post Oak Jim didn't do it, that he was almost sure he knew who did it because he was *there* that night, only he couldn't be absolutely certain of the killer's identity because it was dark, and besides that nobody would believe him. But of all the people in Sanderson to be arrested for the murder, Post Oak Jim Feathers would have been the most unlikely person he could ever imagine. It made no sense. Why would Sheriff Casey or anyone else believe Post Oak did it? Weren't they smart enough to know the old man was being framed?

He stared at the darkened shack through a veil of tears as he gulped down his fourth beer. Making matters worse, Sata sat beside his pickup door watching him, whimpering, in a dog's way asking why his master was not there to feed him. Now Billy wished he'd remembered to buy dog food for Sata. When he'd learned of Post Oak's arrest he'd been too stunned to think about the old man's dog. Some things, like his father's death in an oil well explosion over in Marfa, were too overpowering to allow a human brain to function properly. Driving out here to Post Oak's wooden shack was something he did automatically, without consciously planning it, as though his truck had a mind of its own.

The scalp. How had it gotten in Post Oak's truck? Had the old man found it somewhere and merely picked it up? How could he not have known what it was? Everyone in Sanderson had been talking about the killing all week, how the dead man was scalped with his dick and balls pushed into his mouth. Post Oak would have known about it. Why would he just leave the scalp in his truck so someone could find it?

Billy sniffled back tears and emptied the beer can, flipping it out the window and into the bed of his Toyota like a basketball hook shot. The aluminum made a hollow rattling noise that made Sata whimper again. "Somebody put it there an' he didn't know it," he said aloud, until

Billy remembered something Joe said, about Post Oak showing Sheriff Casey where the scalp was. Casey's deputy, Harlan Huffman, told Joe all about it after the sheriff arrested Post Oak. That part *really* didn't make any sense—it was like Post Oak *wanted* to be arrested and charged with murder.

"I can't say nothin' to nobody," he said to the night sky he could see through his cracked windshield. "I gotta think about my kids, an' Carmen."

He started the Toyota and made a sharp turn, pulling away from the shack without his headlights on, wondering if he could let an innocent old man take the rap for murder. Post Oak was a friend. He'd known him most all his life.

Billy turned on his headlamps when he reached the Marathon Highway. Sheriff Casey knew where the real power was in Terrell County and he wouldn't buck it, not in a million years. Without a way for Billy to explain what he was doing out on the Hunter ranch late that night, it would be his word against that of one of the richest families in the county. Any fool could figure out which way it would go.

He passed a familiar car coming from town, speeding south down the highway. Its brake lights came on and when he looked a little closer in his rearview mirror, it appeared the car turned down the lane leading to Post Oak's shack. He wondered about it, how anyone in Terrell County could not know Post Oak was in jail. He figured he'd been the last one to find out because he'd been out at the ranch away from everyone, away even from a telephone.

His thoughts quickly returned to his dilemma. No matter how sorry he felt for Post Oak Jim, Billy had no choice but to keep his mouth shut. Nobody ever promised him life was fair. Sometimes you had to turn your head and look the other way. Even when it hurt like hell to do it.

# ELEVEN

◆

CLAUDE ARRANGED FOR adjoining rooms at the Flagship Motel with a connecting door, not with any lascivious intent but rather as a practical way for him and Carla to work closely as partners. He asked for Bill Thompson's room number at the desk, intending to call him in the morning.

"This has to do with that cut-up body, don't it?" the inquisitive clerk had asked while awaiting authorization for a state credit card. "No other reason why Texas Rangers would come down to Sanderson, is there?" He glanced at Claude's badge again.

"We're looking into it," Claude said.

"Everybody's talkin' about it, about who the feller was an' if Post Oak Jim coulda killed him. I've known ol' Jim fer nigh onto thirty-five years. Sheriff Casey's got him locked up in the hoosegow. Seems a damn shame. Ol' Jim ain't never hurt nobody in his life. Harmless as a kitten. Nearly everybody in town is sure somebody framed him. It's on account of that nuclear dump, you know. Rich folks don't want it an' poor folks need it real bad, on account of the jobs. Whole town's divided on it, nearly. I never seen so many lawyers in all my life, comin' from far off as Dallas an' Houston. It's sure been good for the motel business."

Claude couldn't resist asking about the name. "Why did you name this place the Flagship? There's hardly enough water around here to float a bar of soap."

The old man grinned. "It was because of the camels."

"Camels?"

"A camel is called the ship of the desert. Way back in the 1880s the cavalry experimented with camels near here. They was too damn slow, so the army just turned 'em loose when they found out they couldn't sell all of 'em to zoos. They multiplied like rabbits, an' for years there was wild camels all over this part of west Texas. Deer hunters finally killed most of 'em off. A few got shot by ranchers because they ate too much grass that was needed for cows. Me an' Helen, my wife, decided on the name so folks would ask about it."

Claude was sorry he had asked, expecting a simpler and far shorter explanation.

They ate at the City Café, attracting stares from dozens of patrons because of their badges and guns. Carla carried a .38 Colt revolver and she drew most of the looks due to her gender. Not many west Texans had ever seen a policewoman. Towns like Sanderson were among the last refuges for chauvinist attitudes in Texas, where men were taught to swagger and women stayed home to master the finer arts of using rolling pins.

Carla ordered a chicken-fried steak from a pink-cheeked young waitress snapping chewing gum.

"Are you really a police lady?" the girl asked, looking from Carla's badge to her face as she jotted down the order.

"I'm a Texas Ranger," Carla replied, and Claude was certain he sensed pride in her voice even though she said it quietly, with no noticeable emphasis.

"Wow. I didn't know they'd let a woman—"

"I'll have the chicken-fried steak too, ma'am," Claude said, hoping to end any further discussion of women Rangers. "And a beer, a Coors if you have it."

"We don't sell beer," the waitress said. "You have to buy it across the railroad tracks at Joe's Drive-in. It's a city ordinance to keep drunks from comin' to this side of town, my ma said."

Claude couldn't pass up a chance like this. "Next time you talk to your mother, ask her if she thinks everybody who drinks beer is a drunk. I'll bet she's a Baptist. I'll have iced tea."

Frowning slightly, the girl wrote it down and walked toward the kitchen.

"Funny," Claude said, "but that reminded me of somethin' Alfred always said about older towns. You could tell who controlled things by where liquor was sold in relation to railroad tracks. Towns sprung up beside railroads back when a town needed 'em to exist, before good highways came along. He showed me a hundred times how tracks were more than a set of rails. They were dividing lines between rich and poor folks. The poor always came from what everybody called 'the other side of the tracks,' like it meant they were bad. Preachers got hold of this notion and started demanding that vices like booze could only be sold on the other side of the tracks, specially in a town where there were mostly Baptists. A lot of Baptists preach real hard against drinking, but you'll find 'em sneakin' down to the liquor store at night when it's less likely anybody'll see 'em. There's nothing worse than a hypocrite."

"It's because you drink," Carla offered, half smiling. "If you were a good Southern Baptist you'd vote for the city ordinance yourself so nobody could build a saloon next door to *your* house."

"I happen to like the taste of beer."

"Nobody likes the taste of beer. It's the buzz you

want, so you'll have the courage to ask some poor, lonely woman to go to bed with you. That's what Dad told me."

Claude made an exaggerated face. "Alfred thinks he has me figured out. He's dead wrong."

"But you told me yourself he could read a person's mind like a book."

"I said he could read a criminal's mind. It's not a crime to drink beer once in a while, or go to bed with a woman if she gives her consent."

Carla giggled. "Dad used to tell me stories about you, like you were some sort of Don Juan or something. He had a name for you . . . I think it was Romeo of the rodeo set. He said you were quite a rodeo cowboy in your prime."

"You're saying I'm past my prime?"

Carla's emerald eyes sparkled with humor while she tried to suppress another giggle. "I'm only repeating what Dad told me."

He shrugged helplessly and looked away, briefly taking note of the café patrons watching them surreptitiously over the rims of coffee cups or plastic drinking glasses. "Alfred thinks he's an expert on my behavior. He never misses an opportunity to tell me how I oughtta live."

"Maybe now you know why I was nervous about seeing him this morning. If I'd given him half a chance he'd have told me how to conduct every step of this investigation."

Her remark reminded him of something he hadn't done. "I forgot to ask Thompson if anyone else from the government has been down here, someone who wouldn't have been missed right away. Maybe a scientist, whose killin' could have been meant as a warning to the ranchers who plan to sell."

Carla frowned. "The initial sheriff's report said the body was found hidden in a cave. Why hide it if it was meant to be a warning?"

"That's why we're here, Carla Sue. They aren't paying us to take a scenic tour of the countryside or sample the chicken-fried steak."

"I wish you wouldn't call me that . . . Carla Sue. It's what my dad called me when I was little and I'm all grown up now."

His gaze inadvertently fell to her chest, until he caught himself. "I can see you're grown up." He looked away quickly.

She giggled again. "It's okay to look, Captain. I know I've . . . filled out some. I'm used to being stared at. There's no reason to be embarrassed. It doesn't bother me."

"It makes me realize how long it's been since we've seen each other," he said, collecting himself, wondering why he was so uncomfortable. "You have filled out, as you call it. You're a very pretty woman. I remember you as this little tomboy who climbed trees and rode a pony, tagging along behind me and Alfred everywhere we went like a tick on a bloodhound, always asking questions, wanting to learn how to shoot a gun. You never played with dolls or did little girl stuff. . . ." As he spoke he noticed a uniformed officer come into the café, a muscular sheriff's deputy about thirty years of age with what appeared to be a smug expression. "It didn't take long for word to spread that we're in town. Here comes a boy wearing a badge and I'm already sure I'm not gonna like him."

Carla looked over her shoulder as the deputy strolled toward them, nodding to people at nearby tables in a perfunctory way. "I see what you mean," she said quietly. "That's some look on his face, like he's very fond of himself and his high position."

"Good guess," Claude whispered, toying with a paper napkin, wishing he had a beer . . . make that several beers.

"Howdy," the deputy said as he reached their table. "I'm Harlan Huffman, Sheriff Casey's deputy. Miller over at the motel called to say the Texas Rangers was in town."

He needed a moment to examine Carla before he offered Claude his hand. "I read in the newspaper there was a woman Ranger now. Pleased to meet you, ma'am." Instead of extending a handshake to Carla he tipped the brim of his straw Stetson politely.

"Pleased to meet you, Mr. Huffman," Carla said evenly as she held out her hand firmly.

Huffman still seemed reluctant, yet he shook her hand when he felt Claude's stare. "Likewise," he muttered, turning back to Claude. "Sheriff Casey's over in Dryden servin' some civil papers. He told me to let you talk to our prisoner if you got here tonight. The jail's just across the street. He said he told you we got this thing solved. The old Indian had the scalp right there in the bed of his truck. The damned ol' fool wasn't smart enough to bury it someplace. His lawyer came down to talk to him an' he talked crazy, all about Indian ghosts who came back from the grave to kill whoever it was, like he figured we was dumb enough to believe it. The lawyer said he could get him off to a looney bin over in east Texas after he told Judge Thurmond what Post Oak Jim had to say."

"We may drop by for just a minute," Claude said. "To tell the truth we're kinda tired."

"I'd like to get a look at him," Carla remarked, giving Claude a quick glance.

"Sure," Claude agreed, because it didn't matter either way even though his bad knee hurt a little from sitting too long on a car seat in the same position. "We'll walk over after supper." Claude happened to notice where Carla was looking then. Her eyes were on the huge Colt Magnum .44 revolver Huffman carried on his hip.

"See you then," Huffman said, nodding again to Carla as he turned for the front door.

"Talk about overkill," Carla whispered before Huffman went out. "He's carrying a cannon for a side arm. He must be expecting another Mexican revolutionary army like Pancho Villa's to try a raid on Sanderson. Or maybe they've got wild elephants here, too, to go along with their camels."

Claude grinned as Huffman closed the door behind him. "He's fairly typical of rural deputies in a lot of places. Big gun, big hat, big swagger when he walks. Probably dumb as a fence post. Couldn't find his ass with both hands. Alfred used to call his type county Mounties, guys who'd take the job even if it didn't pay a cent because they like having the authority, and wearing a gun."

Carla was watching him as their steaks arrived. "You never stop mentioning what my dad used to say about this or that, do you?"

Platters of chicken-fried steak smothered in cream gravy were placed in front of them, along with side orders of french fries and salad. "He's where I learned damn near everything I know about police work," Claude replied, picking up his knife and fork. "Like I told you before, he could read people. He could almost tell me what some guy was gonna say before he said it. I call it gut instinct. It came natural to him."

Carla looked down at her plate. "If this won't clog up all our arteries, nothing will. As to the part about Dad and his instincts, he may have been good at reading most people but he wasn't worth a damn at knowing what my mother needed, or what I needed. Instead of supporting what I wanted to do, all he ever did was fight me over it. It chapped his butt when I wouldn't let him control me or my choice of careers. I keep hoping he'll give up one of these days."

Claude didn't say it aloud, but he knew Alfred Jenkins was seldom the type to give up on anything.

◇ ◇ ◇

Later, he looked between the bars at an old man with copper skin lying on a cell bunk bed with his eyes closed. "Wake up, Post Oak!" Deputy Huffman shouted.

"The Texas Rangers are here to see you!" He made ready to unlock the cell with a key, until Claude stopped him.

"We don't need to talk to him tonight," Claude said. "My partner just wanted to get a look at him. Maybe Sheriff Casey told me and I've forgotten . . . How old is he?"

"His driver's license says he's seventy years old," Huffman replied. "He'll be seventy-one next April."

Claude shook his head, motioning Carla away from the cell. "We'll drop by sometime tomorrow, Deputy. Thanks for letting us see him."

Huffman seemed bewildered and he simply shrugged, moving out of the way so Claude and Carla could walk back along a dimly lit hallway to the front office.

Outside, as they crossed Main Street in the dark to climb into the car, he heard Carla say, "I know you and I are thinking the same thing, Captain. That old man we just looked at didn't kill anybody with a butcher knife or anything else, not the way that guy was killed."

Claude unlocked the Ford. "You took the words right outta my mouth," he said. "There's a killer still running loose someplace. And maybe he's still in Terrell County."

# TWELVE

"Two Texas Rangers are here," a quiet voice said over the phone. "They ain't buyin' it. They took one look at Post Oak an' walked out of the jail. Never asked him a single question. You said you wanted to know if anything happened. That's the reason I'm callin'. Walter's still over in Dryden servin' a civil judgment. He don't know the Rangers are here yet, but I expect him back shortly. He'll want to know if they said anything. They didn't. Hardly said a goddamn word. Just looked through the bars an' said they'd come back tomorrow."

"Did they ask you any questions?"

"Nope. Get this—one of 'em's a woman. She's wearin' a regular Ranger's badge. Walter told me it's the reason Joaquin Jackson from over at Alpine resigned, because they hired some cunt for a Ranger. She's here."

"I read about it a few months ago. Who's the other Ranger?"

"Cap'n Claude Groves. Mean lookin'. Gives you a hard stare every time he looks at you. I've got him figured for the kind who don't take bullshit from nobody."

"I never heard of him. I wonder why they didn't ask Post Oak any questions?"

"Beats the hell outta me. All they did was look through the bars. That's why I said I don't think they're buyin' it. They acted like they wasn't even interested in ol' Post Oak. They're stayin' at the Flagship."

"That means Thompson will be giving them his ideas. What's important now is to see if the Rangers have identified the body. Let me know if you hear anything. Tell Walter to call me when he gets back. And call me if they've got a name to go with the dead man."

"I'll do it."

"What was that Ranger captain's name again?"

"Claude Groves. A big guy. Walks with a limp. Maybe just shy of fifty but hard twisted, like old rawhide. He don't say much. Walter ain't gonna like him . . . I can tell that already."

"I'll make a few calls. Find out who he is. Keep me posted if anything changes."

# THIRTEEN

BEFORE HE COULD ice down the beer he bought at Joe's Drive-in in the bathroom sink he noticed a blinking message light on his room telephone. Carla was next door in room 105 unpacking her suitcase—their connecting door was still closed. Claude opened a Coors and dialed the front desk.

"Cap'n Groves," a familiar voice said, "you got two calls, one from Alfred Jenkins that was long distance, the other from Mr. Thompson in one-twenty-nine. I saw Mr. Thompson an' told him you was in town."

Claude remembered that the motel owner had also called Deputy Huffman to inform him of their arrival and there was no telling who else had been told by now. Gossip would be a prime commodity in a town like Sanderson, especially gossip over an unsolved murder. "Thanks for letting me know," he said, preparing to hang up.

"Don't you want that long distance number?" Miller asked.

"I know it by heart," he replied, disconnecting so he could call Alfred before Carla knocked on the inner door. He was sure he knew what Thompson wanted, but a call from Alfred puzzled him. He dialed the Brownwood number quickly and gulped down part of his beer.

"Hello." Alfred sounded grumpy.

"It's me. Got your message to call." He stifled a belch.

A moment passed before Alfred said, "I've been thinkin'."

"Thinkin' what?"

"Is Carla sittin' right there so she can hear you?"

"Nope. She's in her room. Why'd you ask?"

"I was thinkin' maybe I could drive down there, maybe help you with things. I know that rough-assed country like the back of my hand. It'd be unofficial, of course, but I was wonderin' what you thought Carla would think about it."

"She'd resent it. She'll figure you're trying to interfere with her first investigation. We talked about it some on the way down. She's real touchy about doing this on her own. If it was up to me I'd appreciate the help. Things are starting to look a lot more complicated. The sheriff arrested this seventy-year-old Indian for the murder because he had what appeared to be the victim's scalp in the back of his truck. Only I don't see it that way at all. Somebody's out to frame the Indian, trying to make it look like this is the 1800s when being scalped by Indians happened all the time."

"What's the Indian got to say for himself?"

"He gave Sheriff Casey and his lawyer some kind of explanation, about this Indian ghost that came back from the dead to kill our John Doe. Carla agrees with me. It's bullshit. The old Indian may be a fruitcake and some asshole decided to pin a murder on him. But unless we can ID that corpse, we're feeling our way in the dark right now looking for a motive."

"And that's all you got?"

"Well, there's another angle to it. Sanderson was picked for a low-level nuclear dump site, which means jobs for folks who live here, but also has the potential for lowering land values. Big landowners are fighting the hell out of it. Carla thinks that it's more than a coincidence." Claude chuckled. "She's more like you than I ever imagined she could be. Stop worrying about her. She's handling things like a seasoned veteran so far."

A lengthy silence passed. "Find out who was close enough to the Indian to know his habits, where he went, who knew him. It's gotta be somebody who knows him fairly well if he's bein' framed. It sure as hell won't be just a coincidence somebody tossed that scalp in his truck. Your murderer is a local."

"According to the motel clerk, everyone in Sanderson knew Jim Feathers, so that still leaves us a couple thousand suspects to consider."

"You know damn well what I meant, Claudie. Somebody who's close to him." Alfred cleared his throat. "If I could help you crack this it'll make Carla look good to the major an' the press. Might take some of the pressure off her."

"I'm sure she'd feel more pressure if you were here, Alfred." He thought of a way to appease his old friend somewhat. "I can keep you posted from time to time, let you know what we've found out. If you've got any hunches I can drop a few hints and maybe she'll think it's her own idea. More than anything else she wants to do this on her own, without having you look over her shoulder."

"She hates me now, doesn't she? It's because of the divorce an' all that shit her mother tells her about me."

"She doesn't hate you. She told me she loves you, and that more'n anything else she wants the two of you to be friends. She believes you still treat her like a child." Claude downed the rest of his beer, wondering if he'd said too much.

"That's bullshit. I never treated her like a baby. I made her stand up for herself damn near since the day she was born."

Claude scowled when he noted the phone cord wouldn't reach the bathroom sink. "Why don't you talk to her sometime, not as her father but as a friend, like you and me used to talk. She's one hell of a smart girl. And she's tough. She won't let 'em intimidate her . . . I've seen that much already."

Alfred's voice broke a little when he said, "I've always been so proud of her. Damn it, Claude, I'd give my right arm to be there. I'm so goddamn miserable, trapped in this little shoe-box house with nobody to talk to, just a dog who can't answer me when I need to hear the sound of somebody's voice so I won't go completely fuckin' nuts. I've tried to make a few friends in this jerkwater town an' all anybody wants to talk about is the goddamn cattle market, or goin' fishin'. I hate the taste of fish, so why go?" He took a deep breath. "There are times when I wish that goddamn bullet had killed me. Livin' like this is worse'n bein' dead, if you ask me. I loved my work. I love the Texas Rangers. I miss the hell outta those times. . . ."

"Take it easy, Alfred," Claude said, wishing for the right words to spare Alfred's damaged pride. "Give me a little time to talk to Carla. I'll call you in a day or two, after we get the lay of things and question some of the principals. You can give me your impressions, your take on what we find out. Meantime, do me a favor and let Spot off that chain. I couldn't hardly stand to see him locked up like that. I wouldn't say this to you if we weren't friends, but you're takin' your frustrations out on your dog, pardner."

"Who gave you the degree in psychology, Claudie? I chained the rotten little bastard up because he's killin' all Miz' Wilkerson's chickens. You're askin' me to go soft on a criminal. I've come to hate that fuckin' dog."

"You don't hate your dog," Claude said gently. "You hate what's happened to you, and so do I. I wish like hell it hadn't happened, but it did. Life goes on, and all that crap. I won't give you a big dose of philosophy tonight, not that you'd listen to me in the first place, but you gotta learn to roll with this punch, compadre. Things'll get easier. Give 'em time."

"If we traded places I wouldn't be feedin' you all that shit you just gave me. You're doin' it outta sympathy an' I don't want your goddamn sympathetic horseshit."

Claude winced inwardly. He'd gone too far. "Sorry. I wish there was something I could do."

"There is. Tell Carla I'm real proud of her, an' that I love her."

The phone clicked dead in his ear before he could say that it might help if Alfred said those things to his daughter himself.

She looked very different out of uniform—the unofficial uniform worn by rangers consisting of boots and colored jeans, white shirt, a straw Stetson in summer and gray felt in winter. Now Carla sat beside a reading lamp punching buttons on her computer, dressed in shorts, a T-shirt, and tennis shoes.

She was in perfect shape, Claude thought, sneaking glances at her bare legs while he thumbed through their case file. He knew he shouldn't be thinking this way, or looking at her the way he did other pretty women. Carla had natural olive skin deepened by a golden suntan. Her legs were slightly muscular, and her shirt outlined a part of her anatomy Claude couldn't help noticing in spite of his best intentions.

"I ran the Indian's name through Motor Vehicle Registration and driver's license computer records," she said. "I had to try it several ways. It's hard to believe, but his legal name is Post Oak Jim Feathers. He was born April third, 1922. No record of any kind. Not even a speeding ticket. His truck is a 1969 Dodge half ton. His address is listed as Rural Route One, Box one-twenty-one. I'll check county records tomorrow to see if he owns the house he lives in."

"I wonder if he has a family," Claude said, returning to the grisly morgue photos for no particular reason beyond a longstanding habit of going over evidence in a tough case again and again, hoping something would click. "We'll want to question any relatives. I've got a hunch our killer is someone who knows him pretty well, so he'd know when and where he could plant the scalp in his truck." He couldn't tell her those were Alfred's words.

Carla looked up from her laptop screen. "A former employer or any close friends might know, but in a town this small, everybody probably knows where he went during the day. It would be hard to hide in Sanderson."

"We need to see the crime scene sometime tomorrow. Alfred taught me that sometimes you get a feeling, an impression, when you see where something took place. And there's a strong possibility we may find something Casey or his deputy overlooked. I've talked to Casey and he's no Einstein. You saw how much thinking Deputy Huffman is capable of. And Casey first reported that a ranch hand found the body. We'll need to talk to him."

Carla was watching him too closely. Something was clearly on her mind, bothering her.

"We can't have a single conversation about this investigation without you mentioning things Dad taught you."

"Is it getting under your skin? Alfred was one of the best investigators I ever met—"

"It isn't that, Captain," she protested, a self-conscious grin forming dimples in her cheeks. "It just sounds like you're saying it for my benefit. I know my dad was a good ranger and he taught you a great deal. You don't need to remind me."

Claude closed the file, tossing down the last of his third beer. "I miss him, Carla. I wish he was here. When I had a difficult case he was always there to help me. I got used to having him for a sounding board, getting his ideas."

Carla's foot began to twitch unconsciously. "I'm glad he's *not* here," she said, turning her attention back to the computer screen. "He'd be pacing back and forth, telling me about some gut feeling he had and that I was doing things all wrong. It wouldn't matter *how* I did it, in his opinion it would be backwards and I should have known better."

Claude dismissed any notion of discussing a visit from Alfred—for now. He wondered why Carla was so adamant about it. Something must have happened that Alfred had never mentioned, some serious disagreement that put distance between them. Maybe it was more than her marriage to George that Alfred hadn't liked, or her decision to become a policewoman. "He can be opinionated as hell, that's for sure," Claude agreed, as he twisted open another Coors.

The hiss of his beer bottle drew a glance from Carla. "You do drink a lot, Captain, if I'm not being too personal. If I'd had that many I'd be lying on the floor."

"I'm off duty," he replied, unruffled. "I'm on my own time, so to speak, even though we're still working on the case. They call it the privilege of rank."

"I didn't mean to imply—"

"It's okay, Carla. I do drink more'n some. I'm carrying a bunch of old scars, and I'm not just talking about my knee, or the one on my chest where this guy stabbed me before I could get handcuffs on him. I'm sure Alfred's told you about my divorce, and my son. I haven't seen him since he was five, but I drank before the divorce so I'm not using that as an excuse. I'd call drinking my hobby, since I don't play golf or go deer hunting or ride bulls anymore. I think I'm being fair when I say I'm a bit lonely, like your dad is now, and I drink to take the edge off loneliness. I go home to an empty house when I'm in Austin, and I guess that's why I understand what Alfred's going through. We both missed out on having a lifelong relationship with a woman, for different reasons. Alfred loved his job too much."

Carla watched him as if she expected more.

"And you missed out because you drank too much and cheated on your wife," she said. "Is that it?"

He shrugged. Her question pointed to the truth. "I guess so. No point in denying what's obvious, is there?"

Then he got up to phone Bill Thompson before he went to bed, a simple courtesy call. Claude was too tired to discuss anything in detail tonight but he didn't care to talk about himself with Carla anymore, digging up old bones he wanted to forget.

# FOURTEEN

BILLY WAS SITTING on the porch drinking beer when his wife came to the screen door.

"The telephone is for you," she said softly, concern in her voice. When he got home she had asked him again what was wrong and he couldn't look her in the eye when he told her it was nothing to worry about.

He stubbed out his cigarette and went in, avoiding Carmen's questioning look. He walked into the bedroom and closed the door, wondering who would call so late. "Hello?"

"Where the hell have you been? I called earlier an' Carmen said you wasn't home yet."

He knew the voice well. "Havin' a few beers. I ain't been feelin' too good lately. It's my stomach. I feel like I'm gonna throw up all the time."

"You hear Sheriff Casey arrested Post Oak Jim? They found that dead guy's scalp in his pickup."

"Yeah, I heard. Everybody knows Post Oak didn't do it."

"You hear the Texas Rangers are in town to investigate it?"

Now Billy's stomach really was hurting, churning. "Nobody told me."

"Two of 'em. One's a woman, an honest-to-goodness Texas Ranger with tits. Harlan says they're probably gonna be questionin' everybody."

Billy needed another beer in a hurry. "No reason why they'd ask me anythin'." His palms had begun to sweat. He fingered a cigarette from his shirt pocket and lit it. "I don't know a damn thing about it."

"I bet we get asked a bunch of questions on account of who we work for."

Billy gritted his teeth and closed his eyes, envisioning what it would be like to be questioned by Texas Rangers, even if one of them was a woman. "They'll be wastin' their time. I can't tell 'em nothin' because I don't *know* nothin'. I gotta go. My belly is killin' me right now. I'll talk to you tomorrow."

A silence. "You been actin' real weird lately. Are you an' Carmen havin' troubles?"

"No troubles. It's just my damn belly. I may have to go to the doctor about it if it don't clear up. See you tomorrow." He hung up and buried his face in his hands. In the living room his younger son was crying above the blaring noise of the television. It was time to make another trip to Joe's Drive-in for a six-pack of beer and more cigarettes, knowing he faced another long night alone on his front porch wondering what to do.

The real trouble was, he couldn't say or do anything about what was happening now. And waiting was the hardest part.

# FIFTEEN

"BILL THOMPSON," a rather high-pitched voice said, creating images in Claude's mind of a small man who probably wore a cheap suit and clip-on neckties, a typical bureaucratic type with very precise speech and mannerisms, a government clone.

"I'm Texas Ranger Captain Claude Groves. The desk said you left a message for me, so I called before I went to bed. I hope we can talk at length tomorrow. My partner and I just drove in from Austin and we're tired."

"I understand, Captain Groves. We have plenty of things to talk about, but I suppose they'll keep. Have you been informed of the arrest?"

"The old Indian? We saw him a while ago. A deputy by the name of Huffman says the sheriff believes this solves the killing. My partner and I have some reservations."

"As well you should," Thompson said. "This runs far deeper than placing blame on some mental-defective geriatric cowboy who happens to be a Native American. Anyone could have placed that piece of hair in his vehicle. Powerful men in this county are at odds with each other over our proposal for a Class A and B dump site. It wouldn't surprise me at all to learn that the bigger land-owners who won't profit from our facility had this done to frighten the others away from selling. A rancher by the name of Cale Hunter has offered us some of the acreage we need, as did his neighbor, Bob McCloud. But several of the biggest landowners have joined in a class action suit to prevent it."

"I'm aware of all that," Claude replied, guzzling beer while Carla fiddled with her computer. "Let's talk in the morning when my partner and I have had some sleep."

"Captain Groves, I believe Mr. Feathers was hand-picked to be blamed. Of course, it's only a personal opinion. I'm not a criminal investigator."

Claude rolled his eyes when Carla gave him a glance. "I'd guess then you've got an idea who would try to blame Feathers," he said in the same lifeless tone he always used when anyone told him he had a particular crime figured out. Texas was chock-full of people who became amateur experts on crime solving while talking to a Ranger in the midst of a case.

"I have a few educated guesses," Thompson said.

Claude wondered how Thompson's guesses could be educated if nuclear dump sites, not criminal investigation, were his specialty. "Tell us about 'em in the morning. We've got to talk to Sheriff Casey first, as a matter of legal protocol, then question Mr. Feathers and drive out to take a look at the crime scene, or at least where the body was found. For all we know the victim may have been killed in Cleveland and then somebody dumped him here. This may all be nothing but coincidence."

"One more quick question, Captain. Have you found out who the dead man was?"

"Got no idea. His body was badly decomposed and that makes it difficult. No dental records because he never had any dental work, and the lab couldn't lift any usable fingerprints." Claude was holding an empty beer bottle and wanted desperately to hang up now.

"I'm certain you'll find this is more than coincidence," Thompson said. "Feelings here are running very high. Please call me when you have time to discuss it. I have a few other things I'd like to tell you."

"G'night, Mr. Thompson," Claude said, hanging up before Thompson could say another word. He looked at Carla. "Another expert on murder investigations," he mumbled, climbing out of his chair to retrieve another Coors from the sink. He spoke to her over his shoulder from the bathroom. "You're about to find out how many folks think they're smarter'n Sherlock Holmes. Every son of a bitch we talk to will have it figured out—who did it, and why, and none of 'em will agree with any of the others. You'll learn to turn a little switch off inside your head every time some local expert starts telling you about his theory. You have to sift through the facts and forget about everything else." When he came out of the bathroom he found her staring at the beer in his hand. "Do I detect a look of reproach?" he asked, heading back to his chair.

Carla smiled. "Not reproach, Captain. Amazement. Not very many men would still be steady after six beers."

"I have a very high tolerance for alcohol. My doctor told me. It's my metabolism. I burn it up real fast. And I do like the taste of Coors."

The smile left her face. She fixed him with an odd stare he couldn't read.

"Are your old scars really that deep?" she asked, pulling her foot up to the chair seat so her chin rested on her knee. "It's none of my business, but some people drink to forget. You don't have to talk about it."

He saw something in her eyes—it could have been caring, or understanding. "No," he replied too quickly, settling into his seat. "Some of them, maybe. I try not to think about 'em, the ones that hurt. Not seeing my son for eleven years. Martha hated my job. She was a very materialistic woman and I didn't see it in the beginning. We fought over money, and that I was gone too much of the time to suit her." He paused to suck thirstily on his beer, uncomfortable. "I suppose that's just an excuse. I started drinking when I was fourteen, because my friends did. It wasn't an escape . . . hell, it was fun. Then I started noticing I wanted a beer all the time. My folks argued damn near every day and it was easier to take after I'd had a few beers. Martha said that's when I became an alcoholic. But I'm not a real alcoholic. I never did drink on the job, not even once. I can control it. I passed all the tests to sign with the highway patrol, and they don't let an alcoholic wear that uniform. I drink at night, on my own time."

"I'm prying, aren't I?"

He shrugged. "I don't mind tellin' you about it. If I had a real problem, I'd get some help. Everybody has little aches and pains, bad memories. You learn to live with 'em. My knee hurts every day. A rodeo bull slammed me into a chute gate. I had all kinds of surgery to repair torn ligaments, but it still hurts. I passed the physical exam to get in the highway patrol. They said I was okay, only I never told that doctor how bad it hurt to do their stupid exercises. I wanted to tell him I couldn't see how doing deep knee bends had anything to do with me being a highway patrolman, like I was gonna squat down every time I wrote a speeding ticket."

"I couldn't help noticing you limp once in a while. You don't appear to be affected by half a dozen beers, although I doubt you could pass a breath test for blood alcohol levels."

He gave what might pass for a grin. "Nobody's gonna give me one. It's sort of an unwritten code—professional courtesy from other police officers so long as I don't act drunk. Which I never do. I just drink. It calms me down."

Carla dropped her foot to the floor and closed her computer. "I think I'll turn in, Captain. I want to go over my notes again so my subconscious can work on it while I'm asleep tonight."

"You believe all that stuff about the subconscious?"

"It works. While I was in college I studied for tests just before bedtime." She smiled as she was getting up. "It's a trick my dad taught me. I know, I was the one who said he came up in almost every conversation we have. This time it was my fault."

"No reason to apologize, Carla. Alfred had a big influence on both of us. Why be so touchy about it? If he was here I'd be asking him all kinds of questions about this case to get his impressions. He was the hardest man to fool I ever met."

She started for the connecting door with her laptop under her arm and now her face was changed, almost sad. "He never let me or my mother forget it, either," she said. "Good night, Captain. See you in the morning. Just tap on my door as soon as you're ready to go. I get up early."

*She's mighty bitter about something,* he thought, listening to the dead bolt lock behind her. *She doesn't want Alfred here. How the hell do I tell him?*

◇ ◇ ◇

Sheriff Casey looked pretty much the way Claude expected, a man in his fifties with a healthy paunch, graying hair, fleshy jowls and a perpetual scowl on a sun-weathered face, thick black eyebrows knitting like hairy inchworms when he talked about anything he wasn't sure of. And this morning he wasn't sure of Carla with a Texas Ranger badge pinned to her shirt. He kept glancing over at her, frowning slightly, unaware of the telltale performance by his eyebrows every time he looked at her.

"Ol' Jim hardly ever talks much to anybody 'cept Cale Hunter or his ranch hands, Danny Weaver an' the Choate boy. Danny is the one who found the body. He saw buzzards circlin' an' he drove over to see what was dead. After I got to thinkin' how the dead feller was scalped like an Indian done it, that's when I remembered Post Oak Jim was an Indian. Hell, he's been around so long I'd plumb forgot. I drove out to talk to him an' he acted like he knew I was comin'. Feathers had that scalp in a piece of burlap in the back of his truck, like he was hidin' it till he could find a better place to ditch it. Damnedest thing I ever saw, a human scalp. It was kinda shriveled up. Stunk worse than a polecat."

"So you took him in?" Claude replied, to get him back to the matter at hand.

"Yep. And Judge Thurmond appointed Feathers a lawyer, ol' man Bell from up at Ozona. Bell's retired, but he takes a court appointed case once in a while. Feathers told him the craziest story you ever heard, 'bout how some Apache ghost killed that feller an' all Jim did was find the body, only he ran off when he got scared an' didn't tell nobody about it. Bell says he can get Jim off on an insanity plea."

"Didn't anyone notice he wasn't playing with a full deck?"

Sheriff Casey's eyebrows moved again. "Lives by himself in an ol' shack just off the Marathon Highway. Got no family, just a three-legged dog. His daddy was the town drunk years ago. Beat his mamma to death one night when he was drinkin'. Crushed her skull with a hammer. That was a long time ago, maybe thirty-five years. I barely remember it. He died in a prison hospital, I think. Feathers has worked as a cowhand out at the Hunter ranch most of his life. Cale knows him better'n anybody, I reckon. I asked Cale if ol' Jim coulda killed anybody an' he said he couldn't imagine it. Cale's gonna make his bond as soon as it's set."

"We'd like to talk to Mr. Feathers first," Carla said, before Claude could untangle these new revelations in his head.

Casey looked at Claude, as if he needed Claude's agreement.

Claude nodded. "Ranger Jenkins wants to get a statement from him, if he'll talk to us. Nothing official, just to hear his side of the story, the part about the ghost. We'll advise him of his right to have his attorney present, if that's what he wants."

Casey's gaze wavered, as though he might be hiding something. "I can call him, Cap'n, but Ozona's over a hundred-mile drive. It'd take Bell a couple of hours to get here if he decides he needs to be present for your questions. All ol' Jim's gonna say is that same goofy stuff, 'bout some ghost. Seems like a helluva waste of a man's time, askin' him to drive so far just to listen to a bunch of babblin' nonsense. Why don't you just go in an' ask him your questions?"

"It's the law," Claude replied. "He's entitled to have his lawyer present if he wants him here."

Now Casey lowered his voice even though no one else was in the office. He winked. "Nobody'd ever have to know. Who the hell is gonna believe a crazy ol' Indian like Jim Feathers if he says his lawyer wasn't there?"

Carla stepped closer to the telephone. "*We* would know," she said. "If you'll give me the number I'll call him myself." She looked Casey in the eye. "You surely wouldn't want your case against Mr. Feathers tossed out on a technicality, would you?" She made no effort to hide the sarcasm in her voice.

The sheriff's cheeks turned beet red. He reached for his telephone index and flipped through a series of cards without giving Carla so much as a glance. He pointed to a name and number scrawled on a card. "Here it is," he muttered. "Why don't you call him, Miss Jenkins."

Carla's mouth flew open to object to the way Casey addressed her, until a wag of Claude's head kept her silent. She dialed the number quickly, muscles working in her jaw angrily. Claude was sure this was only the beginning of what looked to be a very long day.

## SIXTEEN

Post Oak Jim Feathers had all the facial characteristics of
an Indian like the ones Claude had seen in movies and on
television, since he'd hardly ever set eyes on genuine American Indians in the flesh, other than a few Yaqui and Kicka-
poo from Mexico years back when he served along the
border. Feathers sat on his cell bunk staring at the floor, his
broad, time-etched face a total blank. Silver-gray hair fell
below his shoulders. Tiny tufts of gray beard grew here and
there on his cheeks and chin. His nose was oversized, with
a prominent bump midway between his eyes and the tip,
making it appear curved, like an eagle's beak. High cheekbones created the impression of a large head, too large for
his small body. His skin was a mixture of brown and deep
red, with liver spots covering the backs of his hands. He
wore faded denims with holes in both knees, a pair of run-
over cowboy boots, and a blue shirt paled by too many
washings, worn through at the elbows. Claude judged his
weight at less than a hundred and fifty pounds and he
couldn't have been more than five and a half feet tall standing erect. Feathers had badly bowed legs which would
shorten his stature even more, probably the result of riding

horses most of his life. But it was the air of passiveness in his expression that left few doubts in Claude's mind. Jim Feathers was not a killer.

"Why did you refuse to talk to your lawyer over the phone?" Carla asked gently, sitting across from him on an empty bunk bed. "He was appointed by the judge to help you, Mr. Feathers."

Claude saw the Indian's eyelids flutter momentarily.

After a silence, Carla asked, "Why won't you answer me?"

Feathers finally looked at her, but only briefly and then his eyes returned to the floor. "The lawyer told Sheriff Casey I am crazy. He will ask them to send me to a place for crazy people. What more can I say to a lawyer who believes this about me?"

"Perhaps he didn't fully understand what you told him about finding the body," Carla continued, talking to him as if she were coaxing a kitten with a saucer of milk. "As Captain Groves told you, we're Texas Rangers. We intend to find out who killed the man you found, and quite frankly at this point we don't believe you did it. Your lawyer, Mr. Bell, said you could tell us the story about the Apache ghost. All I can promise you is that we won't think you're crazy. It will only be your personal opinion and nothing you say to us now can be used against you in court."

Feathers looked at her again. "I will say no more about it. No one believes me." His voice was low when he spoke, with no trace of accent, and no emphasis on anything he said.

Carla leaned forward, resting her elbows on her knees. "If you cooperate with us maybe we can find out what really happened to the guy. We don't even know who he is. Sheriff Casey told us no one has been reported missing, so we're pretty sure he wasn't from this part of the country. Is it possible you recognized him when you found him in the cave that day? Was he someone you may have seen somewhere before?"

Claude couldn't be sure, yet he thought he noticed a slight narrowing of Feathers's eyes before he lowered his head again to stare at the floor.

"I am finished with talking," he replied. "Send me to this place for crazy people. I do not care. My time has come. I am an old man and I only care about Sata, what will happen to him."

"Who is Sata?" Carla asked, glancing over to Claude when the old man wouldn't look at her.

Claude was certain Sheriff Casey said Feathers had no living relatives and Sata had not been among the names Casey gave as his close friends or acquaintances. For a moment Feathers didn't seem inclined to answer.

"My dog," he said later, without looking up, as though just the mention of his pet made him sad.

"You'll be out on bond very soon," Carla explained. "When I talked to your attorney he told me a man you used to work for, a Mr. Hunter, has promised to post bond for you. A district judge in Del Rio will hear the charges against you today or tomorrow and bond will be set. Then you can make arrangements to have the dog taken care of, in the event you're found guilty. But I don't think you *are* guilty, Mr. Feathers. A case against you now is, at best, only circumstantial. There were no witnesses who saw you do it, nor has the murder weapon been found. A cowboy at the Hunter ranch told Sheriff Casey he saw your truck on the ranch that day. That and the piece of hair Sheriff Casey found in your truck isn't enough for a conviction. A jury has to be convinced beyond any reasonable doubt that you are guilty of the murder."

Feathers seemed unmoved. He sat perfectly still with his eyes turned to the floor of his cell, saying nothing.

Carla looked at Claude again before she stood up. "We can come back later, Mr. Feathers, after you've had time to think about what I said. If you didn't kill the guy you've got nothing to lose by telling us everything you know, even things you may only suspect. If you're trying to protect someone else by remaining silent you have to ask yourself if it's worth it. In the meantime I'll stop at a grocery store and buy some dog food for Sata."

Very slowly Feathers raised his head, looking into Carla's face. "Why would you do this for me?" he asked, just above a whisper.

Carla smiled. "Because I like dogs."

The Hunter ranch lay south of Sanderson below U.S. Highway 90, part of an early Spanish land grant that had belonged to the same family for more than a century, almost two hundred thousand deeded acres of desert and rock hills and mountains reaching to the Rio Grande, according to Sheriff Casey. Danny Weaver, the ranch hand who found the body, would show them the cave and how he removed the corpse. Following directions given by Casey after declining an offer to have him drive them out, Claude and Carla talked about their initial impressions of Jim Feathers.

"He's innocent as a spring lamb," Claude stated flatly. "I did see him flinch once, when you asked him if he knew who the dead man was. That's the line of questioning to pursue when we talk to him again. He knows something he ain't telling us."

"I saw a change in his face too, but not much of one. And he's no half-wit. He's *afraid* to talk. I wanted him to tell us what he told the sheriff and his lawyer, the stuff about an Apache ghost who came back from the dead to commit murder. I think it's symbolism or superstition, not something he actually believes happened. When we get back to the motel I'll tie in with our main computers using my modem. They can switch me over to the Anthropology Department at the University of Texas to see what they found for me on Apache practices. And the fact that the body was found on the Hunter ranch and Hunter is one of the men selling to the NRC is very interesting—I'm sure that's what Mr. Thompson means when he says the dump and the murder are connected, and I'm wondering why Sheriff Casey didn't mention this when he first reported the murder and sent the body to our lab."

"Local politics," Claude suggested. "Hunter is rich and probably very powerful in county affairs. Casey may be thinking about the next elections. But it hardly makes sense that Hunter could be our killer—if he plans to sell to the NRC he wouldn't stir up a big mess right in the middle of his deal by leaving a body on the land he wants to sell. And if Hunter is willing to post Jim Feathers's bond, I can't see him trying to frame the Indian."

"I'll run a computer check on Sheriff Casey and Cale Hunter," Carla said thoughfully, watching the highway. "There probably won't be all that much, if anything, on either one of them, but it's worth a look."

Claude swung into an impressive stone entrance with a sign above it reading Hunter Ranch. An empty gravel road stretched for miles ahead of them, cutting through brush so thick it was all but impenetrable. "That's no way to solve a crime, Carla, with all your electronic gadgets and modems hooked up to some university computer. You get out and talk to people, look for physical evidence, ask questions. Pushing all the buttons in the world won't tell us who hacked that guy to pieces."

"I disagree, Captain. Information may lead us to the right people to question instead of wandering all over Terrell County asking everybody we meet if they committed murder, or if they know who did. A computer can save valuable time."

Claude chuckled. "You do it your way and I'll do it mine. We'll see who gets to the bottom of this first. There'll never be a day when they pin these stars on a computer."

"You sound just like . . ." She didn't finish, turning to her window to avoid looking at him.

"I know. I sound just like Alfred. But we're right to have our doubts. Your gadget can't smell bullshit when somebody's lying to us."

"Have you ever heard of a twelve-lead polygraph?"

"Not reliable. Inadmissible in court. Operator error and a real live human being has to evaluate the result. I've heard a chronic liar can beat a polygraph test anyway."

"I've heard this speech before," she said, still gazing at the thorny brush through her passenger window.

Claude grinned. He wondered if the time were right to mention Alfred coming down to Sanderson, taking a less direct approach. "I wish I could help your dad get over being so lonely, feeling so useless. I've been thinking maybe he oughtta move out West someplace, maybe even around here where he knows the back country. He could get himself a horse and a few cows, something to keep him busy. Next time I talk to him I'm gonna suggest he come out this way to look for some land with a house on it."

Carla drummed her fingers on the armrest and Claude took it as a sign she didn't like the idea at all.

◇ ◇ ◇

"Right yonder's the cave where I found him," Danny Weaver said, aiming a finger at a hollow spot in a wall of limestone. Weaver was whipcord thin, in his twenties, wearing jeans and a greasy cowboy hat with feathers jutting from the crown. He had one distracting feature, a very prominent Adam's apple that went up and down whenever he spoke. They had followed Weaver's truck from a small rock house near the front gate down impossibly rough ranch roads to reach the arroyo. Now Claude gazed across the brushland while Carla opened the trunk.

"There was this set of footprints," Weaver added. "Dry as it is, maybe they's still there. Course, mine's there too from when I pulled the guy out. Had to hold my nose an' wore gloves when I rolled him onto a tarp so's I could drag him. Stunk so bad I damn near chucked. Worst mess I ever saw in my life, the way he was cut up. His guts was strung out all over that cave, his intestines was. It was kinda dark an' I had to make damn sure they wasn't snakes 'fore I touched him."

"There was nothing else in the cave?" Claude asked. "No knife or anything that could have been the murder weapon?"

"No, sir. Just him, naked as the day he was borned, with his guts spilled out, an' no hair." He glanced at Carla. "Had his unmentionable parts stuffed in his mouth, if you know what I mean, sir. Awfulest thing I ever set eyes on."

Carla slammed the trunk as Claude steered the conversation in another direction. "You told Sheriff Casey you saw Post Oak Jim Feathers's truck parked somewhere on the ranch that day."

"Yessir, I did. Only Jim comes nearly every day. Walks all over this pasture in the heat like a feller who's lost his mind. He tol' me one time this was where his ancestors used to live a hundred years ago. Me an' Chub joked about it, how one of these days we'd find ol' Jim dead as a fence post out here, only we had it figured he'd die of thirst. Jim never acted crazy mean, or nothin' like that. He was real gentle with horses."

Claude pointed to a long pocketknife in a leather sheath on Danny's belt. "Did Feathers carry a knife like yours?"

Danny nodded. "Nearly every cowboy who's ever been tangled up in a lariat rope tied to a mossy-horned cow carries a knife so he can cut hisself loose. Jim has one. Leastways he used to. I don't go no place without mine an' neither does Chub Choate."

Carla was walking carefully toward the cave. She stopped and knelt down. "Here's a footprint, Captain. I'll make a cast of it, and if Mr. Weaver will show us the ones he remembers seeing the day he found the body, I'll make plaster casts of them, too."

"Are you wearing the same boots?" Claude asked Weaver as he joined Carla.

"Yessir. Ain't got but two pair, my work boots an' my dress-up boots for when I go dancin' with Sally on Saturday night over in Dryden at the Broken Spoke."

"Can you show us the footprints you saw when you found the body?"

"Right over yonder, runnin' up that draw. Looked to me like whoever made 'em was in a hell of a hurry, 'cause they was real far apart."

Claude surmised the prints would belong to Post Oak Jim and they would prove nothing, only that a frightened old man had run away when he found something he hadn't expected to see.

It occurred to Claude that Feathers might know, or have recognized the murderer, inventing the ghost story to protect someone even though this wouldn't explain the scalp found in his truck. It was time to question Cale Hunter. Alfred always said to follow your nose, and if your nose didn't lead you somewhere, follow the money. Maybe Hunter was trying to buy silence with the old Indian's bail bond, although at the moment Claude had no guess as to what Hunter might be trying to hide. Or why he would hide anything having to do with a murder that could only stand to spoil his chances of selling land to the NRC.

# SEVENTEEN

"THIS IS WALTER. Harlan told me to call you. I got back real late last night an' didn't know Harlan'd talked to you till this mornin'. He said he told you 'bout the two Texas Rangers, an' that one of 'em's that woman everybody got so stirred up about, the reason Joaquin resigned."

"Carla Sue Jenkins. I telephoned a friend in Austin. This is her first case. She just graduated from the DPS Academy last week." Hammond sounded sure of his information.

"She's a bitch. She got right in my face this mornin' when they came to question Feathers. Wanted his lawyer there an' all that crap before they questioned him. She called old man Bell an' he said it was okay for them to talk to Feathers, that he wasn't gonna make any sense anyway, that anything he said was only gonna help with an insanity plea because Feathers keeps on sayin' some Apache ghost did it. Feathers told me the same thing the night I arrested him."

"The other Ranger is Captain Claude Groves from Headquarters Company. My friend said it was unusual that

Company E in Midland wasn't handling this. I was told Groves is like a bulldog, that he'll turn over every rock in the county looking for evidence. He supposedly has one hell of a record with the rangers and he isn't afraid of stepping on toes. According to my information he makes very few mistakes."

"He didn't say much. The bitch did most of the talkin'."

"Be careful what you say around either one of them. I'm sure you know that some influential people want this to help secure an injunction to stop Hunter and McCloud from selling. More folks have signed the petition this past week. People are frightened. No one believes Mr. Feathers did this, which serves as a reminder that a murderer remains free."

"Harlan said the Rangers don't act like they think Feathers is the killer, either, an' after what I saw this mornin', I tend to agree. They hardly spent any time at all talkin' to him, an' he barely said a word to 'em."

"Your deputy said they still haven't identified the body."

"Probably can't. Whoever he was, he was dead too long an' the buzzards an' ants chewed him up too bad. By the time Danny found him there wasn't much left."

A long silence. "The longer this drags on the more it helps our move for a permanent injunction. I'm not telling you what to do, Walter, however there are some people who would be grateful if those rangers stayed for a while, trying to solve this murder. People will continue to be nervous, wondering if it could happen again, and that's good for our cause. Hunter and McCloud are in serious financial trouble because of crude oil prices. Hunter owes several Odessa banks a fortune. He needs money quickly and if we get an injunction and he can't sell to the NRC he'll fold like a house of cards. Whoever killed that man on

Hunter's property did us a favor. It really doesn't matter who he was or what he was doing there. It would be beneficial if things remained just as they are. Your help in that regard would be appreciated."

"I understand. I'll call you if somethin' changes."

# EIGHTEEN

CLAUDE KNELT INSIDE the small cave with a flashlight, moving its beam over the rocky floor slowly, pausing where reddish brown bloodstains darkened pale limestone and caliche dirt. Carla was outside making plaster casts of the footprints.

The medical examiner's report said the guy's hands had been tied either in front of or behind him, he thought, yet there was no rope or cord found with the body. Danny Weaver said the dead man's hands were free when he found him that afternoon. Some sort of binding should be here, unless the killer took it with him, along with the scalp.

Just thinking about it made Claude shiver a little inside. No doubt the dying man's screams filled this tiny cave for several hours until he bled to death. The killer had waited, watching, until the moment when he could push the victim's genitals into his mouth without having him spit them out to continue screaming. As soon as the victim was totally unconscious the killer must have taken off the piece of rope binding his wrists.

"Only a fuckin' lunatic could have done this," he muttered under his breath, satisfied there was nothing in the cave. He turned his flashlight toward the entrance, mindful of rattlers, and crept out cautiously until he could stand fully erect.

He found Carla in an unexpected place, examining the rear tires of Danny's dual wheel pickup, until he suddenly understood what she was doing, and why. While driving the serpentine ranch roads to get to the cave, Claude had told himself the killer must know a great deal about this property in order to find this spot. It was no accident he picked this particular location, and it would have been virtually impossible to get here on foot with a victim in tow. Carla was looking for tire tracks and she was checking the truck Danny drove to distinguish them from any others they might find.

He came to stand next to her as she pressed a soft wax bar into the tread of one tire. "Good thinking," he said. "The problem is we've driven over this road ourselves and so has Sheriff Casey and probably any number of others. You'll have to match casts of what we can find against an awful lot of vehicles, including the truck belonging to Jim Feathers."

Danny was listening, leaning against the tailgate of the truck. "Like I tol' you before, Post Oak don't drive when he comes out here. He walks. Parks his pickup at that old line shack next to the windmill an' walks all over the place. A few times we've seen him just sittin' somewhere, starin' off like he was daydreamin' or somethin'. Me an' Chub used to laugh about it now an' then."

"We'll need to talk to Chub," Claude said, watching Carla peel the wax away with a clear impression of the tire's tread.

"He's probably at the barns puttin' out steer feed right about now," Danny said, "if he ain't ridden off someplace to doctor pinkeye. That's the trouble with a Hereford cross in this country. They git the pinkeye somethin' fierce in the fall when it's this hot."

Claude followed Carla over to the trunk of the Ford

and watched as she put the wax in a container. "We'll need to look around for a few more minutes," he told Danny. "Then you can take us to the house so we can talk to Mr. Hunter and Chub Choate."

Danny nodded and thumbed his hat back, sleeving sweat from his forehead. "Take your time. I ain't got much else to do this time of year."

Claude noticed the plaster casts Carla had made of six boot prints drying in the car trunk. He glanced at her. "Six, and they're all different?" he asked.

"Going both in and out," she replied quietly. "Let's take a look at the top of this ravine. Above the cave. I haven't been up there yet." She lowered her voice even more. "One thing we know for sure now, Captain. Whoever killed the guy had to know this ranch extremely well. No one could have found this cave by accident."

"I was thinking the same thing on the way down here. This is the end of the world unless you've been here several times." They walked down the arroyo to a gentler slope where they could climb to the top. "This means everyone who works here, including Danny Weaver, is a possible suspect, even though right now it don't seem all that likely."

"I agree," Carla told him, edging carefully down a steep incline to the rim, "but it also moves Mr. Feathers back onto our list of suspects. He may not have done it himself, but he knows this land well enough to know about the cave, and you heard Danny say he was out here quite often. He may not be our killer, but we can't completely rule him out as an accomplice, maybe even an unwitting one. And now he's keeping his mouth shut, afraid of the consequences if he talks."

They reached the top before Claude spoke again, giving the brushlands to the south a perfunctory examination. "My gut tells me Feathers had no part in it," he said, turning to the mountains in the distance, across the border in the Mexican state of Coahuila. "We could be overlooking a far simpler explanation, a drug deal from over in Mexico gone sour, a warning from some drug lord that this is what happens to somebody who double-crosses him. We need to talk to the border patrol. They did find peyote in the dead man's stomach."

Carla squinted south into the sun's fierce glare, shading her eyes with her hand since she hadn't worn her straw Stetson. "I suppose it's possible, but then why not dump the body in the Rio Grande? Why leave it here to alert authorities to their drug route, or coincidentally on the same ranch where where a nuclear dump site is being planned?"

"It does seem a bit too coincidental either way," Claude said slowly, studying the ground around them. "And there're no signs of any activity, no trails or roads leading here."

Carla nodded. "And if they were moving drugs across Hunter's ranch, someone would have noticed vehicles driving in and out. Danny Weaver's house is just off the main road."

"Unless Mr. Hunter is in the drug business himself. But then, he wouldn't leave a body on his own land if he killed a guy who double-crossed him. It's all dead ends if you apply any logic to it."

"Which brings us back to the nuclear dump," Carla said. "I can't make anything else compute. Let's hope Thompson can tell us a few things we don't know or haven't already guessed."

Claude frowned. "Don't hold your breath on that one. Let's see if Danny knows anything about the drug trade along here."

Danny watched them descend into the arroyo and walk toward him. In Claude's view he showed no signs of nervousness.

"Find any more tracks?" Danny asked when they stood in front of him.

"Not a one," Claude answered, looking south again.

"Are there any roads or trails leading to the river from here?"

"A few cow trails, only they wander the way a cow will if it's grazin'. Don't none of 'em go straight, if that's what you mean."

"Do you know if the border patrol ever seizes drugs along this stretch of the border?"

Danny shrugged. "Maybe once in a while, every year or two. This country's too rough for 'em, them drug dealers. Some folks claim it crosses down near Langtry, or up close to Boquillas if the river ain't too high. Mostly, what Mexicans we see are them poor ones lookin' for a job. They cross over at night sometimes an' make it to the highway, if they don't git snakebit. In case you didn't know, a rattler feeds at night. It can git mighty dangerous bein' out here on a horse or on foot in the dark on account of the snakes."

Claude leaned nonchalantly against the pickup bed, resting on one elbow while Carla put her plaster mold equipment in the trunk of the car. "Tell me how you think this happened, Danny," he said. "Who was the dead guy, and why the hell was he killed here in this particular spot? Got any ideas?"

Danny grinned. "Me an' Chub talked about it a little, how weird it was to find a dead man in this pasture, an' how bad he was cut up. To me, it don't make a lick of sense. I never set eyes on that dead feller before, an' I know damn near everybody in this county. I was born here. My daddy cowboyed for a livin' here before me. Terrell County don't get many strangers because there ain't nothin' here to see—just this rough-ass dry country an' a few pretty gals like Sally. We git strangers here every Fourth of July for our rodeo. Not many, an' they're gone soon as it's over." He scuffed one boot toe in the dirt. "One thing's for damn sure, since you're askin' my opinion. Post Oak Jim sure as hell didn't kill him or nobody else. He's nearly the gentlest feller I ever knowed in my whole life. Don't drink no whiskey or beer, don't smoke or cuss. Folks are sayin' it's because of the way that feller was cut up that it had to be an Injun who done it. If you'll pardon my way of sayin' it, that's bullshit. I ain't got no idea how that scalp got in the back of ol' Jim's truck, but I'll bet my last dime he didn't kill that feller an' don't hardly nobody else believe it either."

"Sheriff Casey believes it," Claude said offhandedly.

"He don't know Jim the way me an' Chub an' Mr. Hunter do."

"We'd like to talk to Chub today."

Danny grinned again. "Chub, he don't say much. Real quiet most of the time. Soon as you folks are ready to leave I'll show you to the house an' the barns. I figure Chub'll be there. He might git a little nervous when he sees them guns an' badges."

"Why would that make him nervous, Danny?"

"He's been a little edgy ever since this happened. There's a bunch of folks in Sanderson who ain't restin' real easy until the guy who killed that feller gits caught."

"Show us the way to the house," Claude said, pushing away from the truck. "We'll be right behind you."

Carla got into the car and closed her door. "You may be onto something," she said as Claude slid behind the wheel. "Maybe Chub saw something. Or someone."

Claude started the car and turned on the air conditioning. "For that matter he could be our killer. We'll see what he has to say, but it's not unusual for these rural types to get a bit nervous when something like this happens. I did a little cowboyin' when I was a kid. A cowboy sees the same thing day after day, and when something unusual happens it can rattle 'em to a degree—especially a murder." He swung the Ford around to follow Danny's truck. "One thing I'm sure of. Danny Weaver didn't do it and he isn't hiding anything."

Carla looked at him. "How can you be so sure?"

"His eyes, Carla, the way he looked at me when he answered my questions. You'll learn how to do it. When we question Chub Choate and Hunter, watch their eyes. If either one of 'em knows something it'll be right there in their eyes. All you gotta do is learn how to look for it."

# NINETEEN

Hunter ranch headquarters was a monument to old money and the heyday of skyrocketing crude oil prices. A sprawling ranch house built of native stone and caliche mortar sat in a grove of cottonwood trees marking a rare southwestern Texas spring. The sight of a swimming pool and a tennis court in the middle of an empty desert was in stark contrast to a view of the surrounding dry scrub brush that touched the horizon in every direction. Even more out of place was a windmill, blades driven by gusts of hot wind from the south, a sucker rod rising and falling gently only a few yards away from the kidney-shaped pool encircled by a bamboo grove and imported palm trees. A man-made waterfall cascaded into the pool from a concrete and rock fountain, all of it the creation of some well-paid landscaper who built the Hunter family an artificial oasis outside their glass patio doors. Blue heelers barked at them from a fenced dog pen.

"This must have cost a fortune," Carla said as they got out of the Ford in front of a four-car garage. A Rolls-Royce sat in the shade of a row of palms that lined the circular driveway. A bright yellow Mercedes convertible was parked in front of the Rolls.

"The oil boom was generous to some folks," Claude replied as dust from Danny Weaver's pickup drifted across the driveway in a chalky white cloud. Hunter's rambling stone mansion was almost two miles off the main road into the ranch.

Danny parked behind the Mercedes and climbed out, all legs and cowboy hat and Adam's apple. "I'll tell Mr. Hunter you're here," he said, ambling up a red brick sidewalk toward a pair of hand-carved wooden front doors.

Carla spoke quietly. "Why would a rancher with this much money sell part of his land for a nuclear waste dump?"

"Some of these oilmen are virtually broke now," Claude said while Danny rang the doorbell. "They spent money like it was never gonna end. When crude prices dropped it caught a lot of oilmen heavily in debt. It might be a good idea to make a few financial inquiries about Hunter. This could be a cardboard plantation ready to fall."

"I'll bet we saw fifty oil well pumping jacks on the way to this house and not one of them was pumping."

"Crude prices are too low. Twelve bucks a barrel isn't enough to justify the cost of running a pump on deep wells. If memory serves me, all this oil is real deep. I can ask Alfred tonight. He'll know."

Carla turned to him abruptly. "I wish you wouldn't do that, Captain. I'd like to leave Dad out of this until we come up with a solid case to present to the district attorney. Anyone we ask in Sanderson will know how deep these oil wells are."

He frowned, mildly irritated. "What the hell's wrong with asking Alfred a few things about territory he knows? I can't see the harm in it."

"Sorry," she muttered, as a man in blue jeans and a denim work shirt with hair the color of milk opened one front door of the house, looking as much like a working cowboy as Danny Weaver.

Claude started up the brick walkway. The older man came out to meet them, Danny walking beside him.

"Cale Hunter," he said, offering a thick-fingered hand. "I got the call from Walter sayin' you was comin' to see where that gent was when Danny found him." His gaze strayed to Carla, then to her badge.

Hunter's face registered nothing, no smile, no concern that Claude could see. "I'm Captain Claude Groves. This is Ranger Carla Jenkins."

Now disapproval clouded Hunter's eyes for a second or two. "I heard we had a woman Ranger. Some good men quit the Rangers on account of it. There's some things only a man's cut out to do, in my opinion. If I'm too blunt about it, it's just my old-fashioned nature. I'd imagine you took offense, ma'am, but I grew up in another generation where a woman's place was at home. I ain't sayin' you can't do the work—"

"She was appointed because Major Elliot believed she could do the job," Claude broke in. "Now if you don't mind, we've got a few questions. Mostly having to do with Post Oak Jim Feathers." He said it before Carla could reply angrily to Hunter's sexist remarks, and to establish who was in control of this conversation—another bit of wisdom he'd learned from Alfred. Part of a ranger's duty was to take charge of things.

Hunter's gaze returned to Claude. "Ol' Jim didn't kill him, whoever he was. Jim went to work for me an' my father back when his pappy went to prison. He's honest as the day is long an' he wouldn't kill another man for no reason on earth. He can't even make himself spur a green colt that needs spurrin'. He's one hell of a good hand with a horse an' workin' cattle. I'd wager this ranch an' every cow I own he didn't do it. Whoever's tryin' to blame him don't know a damn thing about Jim or his disposition or he'd know better. Some rotten son of a bitch put that hunk of hair in Jim's truck an' you can take that to the bank."

"Ranger Jenkins and I feel the same way," Claude said, with an added note of emphasis on Carla's official status. "We talked to Jim early this morning."

Hunter eyed Carla again, thoughtfully. "We had a Ranger up in Midland a while back by the name of Jenkins. Alfred Jenkins. You happen to be any kin?"

Carla looked Hunter straight in the face. "He's my father. He's retired now."

Hunter's entire countenance changed. He grinned, hooking his thumbs in his front pockets. "Alfred Jenkins was prob'ly the best lawman this part of Texas ever had. I'm real sorry for what I said just now, about women. I met your daddy several years ago, an' read about him in the newspapers all the time. Hell of a man. You've got a big apology comin' from me. At times, I get my foot stuck in my mouth."

Carla merely nodded, although her face was pink and Claude was sure she was wishing the subject of her father hadn't come up.

"Did Mr. Feathers tell you how he thinks it happened or who he believes committed the murder?" Claude asked. "I understand you visited him in jail."

Spiderweb lines crinkled around the corners of Hunter's eyes before he spoke. "He wouldn't tell me a damn thing. Said there was things about bein' a Lipan Indian I'd never be able to understand. He told Walter some story 'bout a ghost, this evil spirit who came back from the dead to scalp the guy like Indians did back a long time ago. It's crazy talk, only Jim ain't crazy, and he never did talk crazy like that before. Now, in case nobody told you, his ol' daddy was crazy as hell, an' a drunk. He drew some sort of pension from the army an' drank up every bit of it. He beat Jim's mama to death an' got sent to prison. But Jim ain't like him at all. Never took a drink in his life. Did his work just like he was supposed to an' made one hell of a ranch hand. Jim never once mentioned nothin' to me about evil spirits or nothin' of the kind, an' I've known him damn near forever."

"Did you see the body?" Carla asked, blurting it out like she'd been waiting for a pause in the conversation.

Hunter hesitated. "Danny showed it to me. I told him to take it down to Sheriff Casey's office. To tell the honest truth I didn't look none too close." A scowl deepened age lines across his forehead. "Some folks think it was meant to scare me out of sellin' part of my river pasture to the NRC. I reckon you know about the dump an' all the legal wranglin' I've been through. I can tell you this—ain't no sumbitch gonna tell me what I can do with my own land. They can pile dead bodies higher'n a five-wire fence out there an' I'll still do just as I damn well please with land that's mine." He looked at Carla. "Pardon my bad language, ma'am, but it puts a hump in my back when somebody tries to push me."

Carla ignored his apology. "Had there been any strangers in town or out here at your ranch before the body was found?" she asked.

"Just that goofball from the NRC, an' he's still here. He makes some folks mad every time he opens his mouth, but he was sent down here from Washington to explain how the dump would work an' why it wouldn't hurt nobody's animals or the drinkin' water. If you're askin' me if I ever saw that dead feller before, the answer is no. I don't see how his own mother coulda recognized him anyway, bad as he was whacked up. I'm sure you know there was worse things done to him than just bein' scalped."

"We know," Carla said. "I understand you have a neighbor who is also planning to sell to the NRC."

Hunter nodded, inclining his head to the west. "The McCloud boy. Robert McCloud. There's thirty thousand acres of his land that adjoins my river pasture. Bobby, they call him. He ain't interested in the ranch. His daddy an' me were friends. When Bob died he left everything to his boy.

Bobby'd like to sell the whole damn thing if he could, only with west Texas crude down so low, nobody's interested. If those damn Arabs don't quit dumpin' oil on the market, oil's gonna be worth less than water. If we had a damn president an' a Congress with any backbone they'd put a big tax on foreign oil. Way things are, those Arabs get richer every day while the rest of us can't afford to pump our own damn wells at these prices."

Claude made a mental note to talk to Robert McCloud. But if the murder were a scare tactic to keep Hunter from selling, McCloud was an unlikely suspect. "As far as you're concerned, you know Jim Feathers well enough to say he couldn't have committed murder under any circumstances."

"None," Hunter said emphatically. "If you lined up every man in Terrell County for that possibility, he'd be at the back of everybody's line."

"Had you noticed any strange vehicles near the ranch before the body was found?" Claude asked. "A car or a truck you didn't recognize?"

Hunter hesitated, appearing thoughtful. "None that I can remember. Wasn't really lookin', to tell the truth. Every now an' then we get oil well service trucks out here to keep pipes from waxin' up, just in case this damn oil can be pumped again. I hate them Arab bastards for what they're doin' to us." He paused again, looking Claude in the eye. "Did you ever find out who that dead guy was?"

"We're still trying," Claude replied. "It would appear he wasn't from around here. Sheriff Casey says no one has been reported missing."

"Likely some hitchhiker who wasn't gonna be missed, one of those damn long-haired hippies we see along the highway from time to time."

Claude looked at Carla. "That's all we need for now, Mr. Hunter. We took some plaster casts of footprints near the cave and we may come back for another look."

"Footprints?" Hunter sounded surprised, then he

shrugged and said, "They'll be Danny's, I reckon, when he followed them buzzards to the cave that day."

As Claude was turning for the car he heard Carla ask, "One more thing, Mr. Hunter. Was Mr. Feathers a religious man? Did he ever go to church in Sanderson, or did he mention anything to you about Lipan or Apache religion?"

"Not that I recall," Hunter answered. "Never saw him in a church, an' if he talked about Indian religion I don't remember it. You can ask Danny or Chub if he ever said anything to them about Apache stuff. Nobody ever thought about him bein' an Indian . . . he was just Jim Feathers, a quiet feller who did his work an' minded his own business."

"We were told he came out here fairly often," Carla said. "Even after he retired. Did he ever explain why?"

Hunter's gaze rolled up toward the sky a moment. "He said somethin' about this bein' where his people used to live, along the Rio Grande. I think his grandpa told him about it. Jim was real close to his grandpa until he died. My daddy knew Jim's grandpa pretty well. That old Indian was an honest-to-goodness water witch. He'd take a forked tree limb an' walk all over the place until the stick bent down. That's where you'd find water. Lots of folks don't believe in water witchin', but my daddy did, an' he paid Jim's grandpa to tell him where to dig for a well. Never struck no dry holes, neither. It works."

"We'd like to ask Chub Choate a few questions," Carla went on, passing over the remarks about water witching.

"He's over yonder at the barn," Hunter said, pointing east to a distant row of cattle sheds surrounded by pipe corrals.

"We'll find him," Claude said, opening his car door. "If you think of anything else, we'll be staying at the Flagship for a few days. Give either one of us a call."

Hunter nodded as Claude started the car. Carla

climbed in, a frown creasing the smooth tan skin of her forehead.

Chub Choate was a stocky young cowboy with an over-sized belly hanging over his belt, wearing a sweat-stained hat similar to Danny Weaver's. Claude and Carla found him shoveling cattle feed into a wheelbarrow in one of the sheds, and he seemed unusually nervous when he saw them coming. He appeared to shove his hands into the pockets of his jeans to keep them from shaking after they introduced themselves.

"I never saw nobody strange drivin' around," he answered, when Claude asked. "I'd remember if I did." His dark eyes flickered back and forth from Claude to Carla. Beads of sweat rolled down his cheeks, although Claude chalked them up to his labors in the heat.

Carla was looking at his boots. "Have you been to the cave where the body was found, Mr. Choate?" she asked.

He wagged his head quickly. "No, ma'am. I know where it is, but I sure didn't have no reason to want to see it or nobody who was cut up like they said he was. I ain't curious about stuff like that."

"Are these questions making you nervous?" Claude asked.

Now there was a slight tremor in both of Chub's arms. "I have to work this ranch. Knowin' there could be a killer on it kinda worries me. I hope y'all catch him real quick so we can all quit worryin'. Some folks in town are sayin' it's because Mr. Hunter's gonna sell land for that nuclear thing. Mr. Hunter aims to sell, so that killer's sure liable to come back."

Claude looked at Carla before he spoke. "I think that's all for now. We may have more questions later."

Chub nodded to both of them and wheeled around to go back to his shoveling. As Claude turned for the car he saw Carla opening the trunk, taking out the bottle of mold plaster. She knelt over one of Chub's boot prints and began pouring a cast.

"He said he hadn't been to the cave or seen the body since Danny found it," Claude said, glancing over his shoulder to see if Chub was watching.

"I heard what he *said*, Captain," she replied.

◇ ◇ ◇

They were driving back to the highway before either one of them spoke.

"We need to question Robert McCloud," Carla suggested, looking over her shoulder westward.

"He's not a likely suspect. He's selling too," Claude said. "We can talk to him in a day or two. Right now, we need to talk to Bill Thompson to find out who's dead set against the dump site and who's made the most noise about it. Our killer didn't want a nuclear dump here. He's somebody who stands to lose if the dump becomes a reality."

Carla stared blankly through the windshield. "I'm sure I picked up something while we were talking to Choate. It wasn't just nervousness. He was too uneasy—I got the feeling he's hiding something. It was just an impression. Nothing specific he said or did."

"Instinct," Claude told her, smiling. "You get it from your dad. You're right. Choate was too nervous."

She let his remark pass. "The key to everything may lie in what Mr. Feathers told Sheriff Casey and his lawyer about ghosts and evil spirits. I still think he's trying to tell everyone something." Carla glanced down at the microphone on the two-way radio. Despite regulations against it, Claude kept it turned off unless he needed it, annoyed by the noise. "I could radio in and run a make on Choate to see if he's got a record, or I can do it tonight on my computer."

Claude navigated around a deep chuckhole. "As far as

I'm concerned you can toss your computer and that damn radio out the window. Choate may be nervous for the reasons he gave us, or he might know something he's afraid to tell us. We'll catch our killer by asking the right people the right questions. In the meantime we'll go over Jim Feathers's house with a fine-tooth comb and we'll talk to Thompson. Could be we'll find something at the old Indian's house that'll tell us who we need to buttonhole." He squinted when glare from the Ford's hood got in his eyes. "You could be right about Feathers. He may be trying to tell us who the killer is without naming names."

"One more thing seems odd. Sheriff Casey apparently didn't question either of Hunter's ranch hands. He didn't even ask Chub Choate to look at the body to see if he recognized him. I wonder why?"

"Pure politics, again, Carla. Casey is afraid of losing his job. You don't win local elections making rich folks mad. Judging by the way Casey acts, he wishes this whole thing would just go away."

Carla didn't appear to be listening, as if her mind were on something else as they headed back toward Sanderson.

"Jim Feathers knows something," she said quietly a moment later. "All we've got to do is get him to tell us what it is."

# TWENTY

THE LITTLE CABIN sat on cinder blocks at the end of a dusty lane, clapboard siding with peeling paint, a rusted tin roof of a type common to cattle barns, a tiny porch in front and back, each with a chair strategically placed to face both the sunrise and sunset. A barren caliche yard around the house had no grass, nor was there any evidence grass had ever grown there. A blue roan dog sat on its haunches on the front porch growling as Claude and Carla drove up in a cloud of dust.

"What a dump," Claude muttered, turning off the engine while Carla returned a search warrant issued by County Judge Roy Green to the glove compartment. Sheriff Casey told them he'd already searched Jim Feathers's shack for a murder weapon and any other incriminating evidence. Claude felt sure Casey wouldn't have the slightest idea what to look for unless he stumbled on a machete or a woodcutter's ax drenched in blood.

"Since we agree at this point Mr. Feathers isn't our killer it seems like we should talk to Thompson first," Carla remarked, smiling unconsciously when she noticed the dog limping down a set of sagging wood steps to challenge their arrival, blue-gray hair prickling down its spine, its growl becoming a series of deep, wolflike barks.

Claude got out of the car. "We only agree he couldn't have done it alone, if he had any part in it at all. I'm playing a hunch we'll find something here that'll tell us more about Post Oak Jim Feathers, or something that shows he might know who committed the murder."

Carla was distracted by the dog's approach. She knelt down with a can of dog food and the opener they'd bought at Joe's Drive-in, along with another six-pack of beer Claude had put in the trunk. "Easy, boy," she said, as Sata's barking became more fierce, more protective of his territory. "I brought you something to eat until your owner gets out of jail." Sata's short, hobbling steps brought a change to her voice, softer, sympathetic. "Mr. Feathers should be out on bond today or tomorrow. We won't hurt you."

Claude thought how similar she and Alfred were, conversing with dogs as if they understood every word, but then he had also carried on one-sided discussions with Spot after his chicken-killing rampage. He took the house key Sheriff Casey had given him and swung wide of Sata's bared teeth to climb the porch steps, one eye on the blue heeler—a breed known for its ferocity even though this dog looked too old and decrepit to be a serious threat.

He unlocked the door, looking in on a tragic collection of battered, worn furniture: a three-legged sofa, an iron bed with yellowed sheets in one corner, an old television set resting on an empty wooden crate marked Oilfield Supply Company of Midland, and an old recliner that could have come from a trash dump with numerous tears in its upholstery. "I've never seen a house that was furnished for less than a hundred dollars," he said over his shoulder, as the dog quieted and began eating from the dish Carla placed on the step. He noticed a dented footlocker underneath the bed—the most likely place to find out about Post Oak Jim Feathers's past.

Before heading for the footlocker, he took in the rest of the place: a stainless-steel sink and Formica cabinet sat at the back with a small window above them. A jar of government-surplus peanut butter sat on the drainboard. The refrigerator was only slightly larger than an Igloo ice chest, badly rusted, another item from someone's junk pile illuminated by the two bare lightbulbs that dangled from pull-string fixtures. The place smelled musty, of old things and neglect. Claude wondered about his own lonely existence. Would his living quarters evoke the same feelings of sympathy when someone saw his house near Austin? He hoped not. He made an effort to clean the place once a month, hauling off old newspapers and empty beer bottles.

Carla walked in and stood beside him. "Christ. It looks like he found everything in a trash heap somewhere."

Claude pointed to the trunk. "We might find something in that footlocker. I'll open it while you look for anything that could be a murder weapon. I suppose we oughtta send every sharp object we find to the lab to test for minute traces of blood, just to cover our asses."

"I'll get some plastic gloves and bags out of the car," she said, "although we both know it's probably a waste of time."

Claude went over to the bed and pulled out the metal box, an old army issue, probably from as far back as World War II. It was unlocked and when he opened its rusty hasp dust rose from the lid. For a moment he squatted beside it, frowning while examining its bizzare contents; a pair of badly worn moccasins, a rotting deerskin shirt with ornamental fringe and remnants of beadwork, a curious necklace of large animal claws—a bear or a cougar, he supposed. A rusted iron bit and pieces of a leather bridle. The frame of an antique revolver missing its cylinder, a cap-and-ball type that had to be at least a hundred years old, both wooden handgrips rotted away. One rusted spur without a rowel.

In a corner of the trunk he found a stack of envelopes

with a rubber band around them, one from the Social Security Administration bearing a postmark of July '88. Another letter from the Texas Department of Corrections, Darrington Prison Unit, dated October 1964, yellowed with age, informing survivors of Big Jim Feathers of his recent demise in the prison hospital. More old letters, addressed to Post Oak Jim Feathers in care of the Hunter ranch, Sanderson, Texas, from a Brazoria County coroner, and a funeral home.

Beneath the meager pile of correspondence were photographs, and one in particular caught Claude's eye as Carla came back into the house. A very old Indian with waist-length hair stared at the camera wearing a fierce expression, dressed in what appeared to be the same deerskin shirt as the one in the footlocker. A backdrop advertising Pawnee Bill's Wild West Show hung behind him. And then Claude noticed the necklace around the man's neck: the same one lay at the bottom of the trunk.

When he turned the weathered photograph over he read a badly faded inscription. "Four Feathers." No date or other notation of any kind.

The next photo was of a man and a woman, both with prominent Indian features, a more modern photograph. He read what was on the back. "Big Jim and White Dove Feathers."

Wordlessly, Claude offered the pictures to Carla, along with a yellowed obituary for White Dove Feathers with no date on it.

"I wonder if the old guy is his grandfather," Carla said, flipping through the photographs.

Claude fingered a few more items of old clothing at the bottom of the trunk before he stood up. "Whoever he is, he sure as hell looks like a real old-time Indian. We'll show it to Post Oak Jim and ask him who he was."

Carla's attention was on the necklace. "He's wearing the same necklace, Captain. I'm more convinced than ever Mr. Feathers is trying to tell us what happened in some

symbolic way. Those Tigua Indians at the reservation outside El Paso were modernized, the ones I saw as a police
officer. Getting drunk, sniffing spray paint, but with no
links to their Indian past I ever could tell. Mr. Feathers isn't
a modern Indian in the true sense. He keeps these artifacts
to remind him of his Apache heritage, and I think if we pry
a little deeper we'll find out he still sees himself as a survi-
vor from another time. If people knew that Feathers went
out to the Hunter ranch because it was the homeland of his
ancestors and he wanted to revisit his Indian past, the killer
could have made the murder look like the work of Apaches
from long ago, drawing attention to Feathers as the only
Indian in Terrell County, then sealed it by placing the scalp
in the back of his truck. I know it sounds far-fetched, but
there's no other obvious explanation for the way the victim
was scalped and disfigured."

Claude gave the cabin another sweeping glance.
"Even if all that's true, Carla, anyone can see that the old
man isn't strong enough to hack up a man half his age. And
nobody in his right mind would just sit there while some
old man tied his wrists, even if he had a bellyful of peyote."

"If the victim was that high and he didn't truly understand what was going on, he might."

Claude gave her a puzzled frown. "Then you're sayin'
the old man could have done it, if the guy was out of his
skull on peyote?"

"I don't think so, but Mr. Feathers would know
enough about how peyote works to pull it off. And I believe he knows who else would have that kind of information—someone who might be our killer."

Claude took a deep breath. "Maybe he doesn't know
for sure. Right now he isn't talking." He opened a drawer.
"If somebody wanted to frame Feathers badly enough to
plant the scalp in his truck, it stands to reason they could
have hidden the murder weapon around here too. Put every one of the kitchen knives in an evidence bag so we can

send 'em to the lab. And see if you can find the pocketknife Danny told us he carried."

Carla put on a glove, placing three plastic-handled carving knives in separate evidence bags. "These wouldn't cut warm butter," she observed. "The murder weapon was razor sharp. It had to be, to make those clean cuts."

"I'll look in the bathroom for a razor," Claude said as he walked into a closet-sized room off the kitchen that held a shower stall and a chipped porcelain sink. But he found only a rusted pair of tweezers, a bar of soap, and three thin towels smelling of mildew. He tucked the towels into plastic bags for a shipment to the lab, even though they showed no traces of bloodstains.

Outside, as they placed items in the trunk of the car, Carla turned southwest a moment, squinting in sunlight reflected off the hardpan caliche encircling the shack. "We need another look around the cave, Captain. I have the feeling we're missing something important out there."

"Could be," he told her, thinking how many times he'd heard virtually the same words come from her father's lips during an investigation. When Alfred got a feeling it was never wise to ignore it, even when it seemed too outlandish to make sense at the time. "Let's go talk to Thompson. Bring those photographs and lock the place up. We can both try talking to Jim Feathers again, after we hear what Thompson has to say. Maybe Feathers will tell us a little more, after he sees that picture of his grandfather."

Unexpectedly, Carla bent to reach into the trunk of the car, examining one plaster cast of boot prints. She picked it up and turned it over, reading a small piece of tape on the bag it was in, then she placed it beside one of the others carefully, for in spite of the heat some of the casts were not yet fully hardened. "Look at this!" she exclaimed. "Here's our first break!"

"What the hell are you talking about?" Claude let his gaze rest on the six-pack of beer momentarily, thinking how good a Coors would taste right about now.

"We've been lied to. These two prints are the same. See the identical hole in the bottom of both soles?"

They *were* made by the same boot, one impression slightly deeper than the other, he thought, although he couldn't grasp the significance of it just then. He looked at Carla for an explanation.

"Chub Choate told us he hadn't been to the cave. I took the impression on the right at the cave entrance. The one that isn't quite dry yet is Choate's, the one I got at the barn. He was there."

# TWENTY-ONE

"This is Harlan. Post Oak's free on bond. Him an' old man Bell just walked out of here. The judge down in Del Rio set the bond at twenty-five thousand, and Cale Hunter had a bondin' company make it. Bell just brought Sheriff Casey the forms. Walter's outside talkin' to Bell right now."

"Interesting. I wonder why Cale didn't post bond himself. He had to pay fifteen percent of the face amount. That's almost four thousand dollars he can't recover. If he's so sure Feathers is innocent he would have used his own money . . . unless he doesn't have it in cash."

"I wouldn't know," Harlan said, glancing through the front window where Sheriff Casey, Feathers, and Bell stood on the sidewalk.

"Where are the Texas Rangers?"

"Out at the Hunter ranch. They wanted Danny to show 'em where he found the body."

"Have they talked to Thompson yet?"

"Don't know 'bout that either. The big guy Groves is bein' real tight-lipped about what they're doin'."

"I'm sure they questioned Cale and Danny and Chub. It may be interesting to see who they question next."

"Walter said this Cap'n Groves has a real bad-assed reputation when it comes to catchin' crooks. Accordin' to Walter he don't give up easy."

"Thompson will fill his head with wild ideas. He'll start pointing fingers—"

"I gotta go. Walter's comin' back inside."

"Let me know if anything develops, but make sure no one else is around when you call."

# TWENTY-TWO

BILL THOMPSON SAT on the edge of the bed while Claude and Carla ate hamburgers from the Dairy Freeze. They met in Claude's motel room for the sake of privacy. He didn't want anyone else listening in on Thompson's theories. Thompson was not the typical bureaucrat Claude expected. He wore ill-fitting clothing, a rumpled short-sleeve shirt, baggy khakis, and tennis shoes, looking more like a scientist than a paper shuffler. He was somewhere in his mid-thirties with thinning blond hair. His wire-rimmed glasses seemed too small for his face. But his handshake was firm and when he took Carla's hand he pumped it no differently than Claude's. He spoke with a crisp, northeastern accent.

"There are two factions at odds over the dump. You have the big landowners and a few property holders with more expensive local residences who oppose it," he began, "while the other side wants the influx of government money generated by the jobs, especially now in a sagging oil field economy. Of course, Cale Hunter and Robert McCloud are in favor of it because they will both profit from the sale of land, significant portions of land, I might add, with state and federal regulations requiring large buffer zones around any dump site, regardless of category. A rancher by the name of Hammond adjoins the Hunter property to the east. Ray Hammond is the largest land-owner in the county, and probably the wealthiest. He has been the most vocal in his attempts to stop us, along with another wealthy rancher named Billings, a crusty old codger whose land adjoins Hammond's to the west. Their attorneys have filed a number of legal actions to halt the dump, seeking a permanent injunction, citing all manner of older studies wherein damage was done to land used as storage facilities for nuclear material and earlier biological and neurological offensive weapons, test sites for nuclear weaponry, and so forth. A great deal of damage was done to soils and underground water supplies during periods before science understood nuclear-material safety and containment requirements. In recent times we've learned what went wrong and how to contain it, however these attorneys play on a generalized public fear of things the average individual does not understand. Billings, I think, is just along for the ride. He and Hunter never really got along. Billings wants this county left in its natural state. He seems harmless enough."

Claude swallowed a mouthful of hamburger. "So you think Mr. Hammond may have either directly or indirectly played a role in the murder, or at least in leaving the body on Hunter's land?"

Thompson frowned. "I have no real proof, although Hammond's efforts to present the court with a petition signed by a majority of residents in Terrell County have fallen significantly short. Men who formerly worked in the oil fields are unemployed now and with the dump offering jobs, most aren't willing to sign his petition. I see this murder as a scare tactic, not necessarily aimed at Hunter or McCloud but to frighten citizens so they'll sign his petition."

"So do you know Cale Hunter or Robert McCloud?" Carla asked.

"Yes, well, McCloud is an odd duck, not a typical rancher by any means. He inherited the ranch from his father, and he's more of a city type who enjoyed spending the money generated by his oil wells. Since crude oil prices dropped he does not enjoy the same lavish lifestyle, I understand. And Hunter is heavily in debt to several Midland and Odessa banks for the same reason. He has mortgaged a sizable portion of his land over the past five years. We investigated the titles to both properties and found liens against several sections. Of course, these liens would have to be released and new surveys taken for the land we wish to acquire. Mr. McCloud agreed to let Hunter arrange for the surveys, although Hammond filed a motion to halt them."

"Why does the land need to be surveyed? If these properties have been in the same families for generations—" Carla began.

"That's exactly why the markers will be difficult to locate," Thompson answered, "requiring the services of someone who knows this part of the country fairly well in case some of the stakes are missing. These old deeds read in an obsolete fashion, things like 'the Hunter survey containing ten thousand acres more or less, taken from field notes derived from the Vasquez land grant,' referencing trees and iron stakes driven in the ground more than a hundred years ago, which may not be there now. We can't purchase land on such generalized legal descriptions, even though Texas law often recognizes de facto boundaries after a fence has been in place for a certain number of years, even if it is enclosing part of another individual's property. Regardless, we require a current survey. If a question as to actual ownership arises, the owners must settle it themselves in court while the purchase money is placed in escrow."

"Had Hunter already begun this survey?" Claude asked, taking a sip of watery lemonade, weighing what Thompson was telling them one piece at a time.

"Not that I'm aware of," Thompson replied. "Facing

drawn-out court battles against Hammond's lawyers, I rather doubt it."

"Why would Hunter offer to pay for the survey when McCloud owns some of the property the NRC wants to buy?" Carla asked, leaving half her hamburger uneaten for now. "It looks like they would share the cost."

"Perhaps they intend to, although Hunter owns almost two-thirds of the land we wish to acquire. I think Hunter simply wanted to get the ball rolling. McCloud is a playboy, spends a lot of time in Hollywood looking for small parts in movies. He tells locals he's an actor."

"So Hunter stands to make the most money off this," Claude observed, wondering if this were somehow a key to part of the puzzle even though a killing on Hunter's property seemed to be at cross-purposes with Hunter's objectives.

Thompson shrugged. "It has to do with geological formations rather than Hunter seeking a larger share of the sale. Last year we conducted drilling core samples on both ranches. Hunter has more of what is required for the storage facility as well as the buffer zone. After numerous discussions with Mr. McCloud I am convinced he wishes he could sell his entire ranch. He isn't the cowboy type."

Claude wiped mustard off his mouth with a paper napkin. "I get the feeling you believe Ray Hammond is the man we should be investigating."

Thompson adjusted his glasses on his nose. "It's quite clear to me the old Indian didn't do it. I've seen him, and I saw the body. Mr. Feathers worked for Hunter and according to what I've been told, the two are friends. Why would an old man like Mr. Feathers perform a desecration on a human body when he has no history of violent behavior whatsoever? And stands to gain nothing? In fact, if the killing was meant to scare people away from approving a nuclear dump here, it would only work to defeat Hunter's efforts to sell, and if Mr. Feathers were the killer, he'd be hurting his friend and employer of many years."

"We agree on that," Carla said, toying with the straw in her strawberry milkshake. "Feathers was framed, as we see it, but we can't come up with the motive behind it."

Thompson nodded as though he had it figured out. "It may have been a ploy, a diversionary tactic. I think whoever the killer is, he knew Mr. Feathers would never be taken seriously by a judge or a jury. People would be distracted while the real killer either covers his tracks or buys time to achieve his personal objectives—as in Mr. Hammond's case, when it is perfectly clear what he wants: a permanent injunction against the site so his land values do not suffer. Like so many oilmen and ranchers in this area, he isn't showing a profit and if he plans to sell his property, hundreds of thousands of acres in his case, he doesn't want the dump lowering land prices."

"Has Hammond listed his ranch for sale?" Claude asked, as he found his admiration for Thompson's logic growing.

"Not publicly, but quite often when a ranch of that size is being marketed, it is handled by private treaty through a broker who has contacts with wealthy clients. It isn't usually advertised in local newspapers since purchasing something that big requires a buyer of considerable financial substance. And it is also possible Mr. Hammond is merely thinking of selling in the future if oil and cattle prices remain low. While most of these ranchers wear blue jeans and cowboy hats, they're still businessmen who must make a profit to stay in business."

"Makes sense," Claude agreed, thinking back to the matching boot prints Carla found, making an apparent liar of Chub Choate. "But we could all be barking up the wrong tree. The killing may not be related to this dump at all. The corpse could be a drug dealer, or some poor slob who got crossways with a bunch of cult lunatics over in Mexico, even. The coroner found peyote in the dead man's stomach—"

"Peyote?" Thompson asked, sounding genuinely surprised. "I didn't know. It grows in the wild in certain regions of the Southwest, I believe. American Indian tribes used it in the previous century."

"Some still use it," Carla said, folding her napkin around the rest of her sandwich. "We've been wondering if there's a tie-in somewhere. Jim Feathers is an Indian. The victim may have been at least part Indian. The average John Doe isn't walking around with peyote in his stomach."

Thompson took off his glasses a moment to rub his eyes. "I suppose this only throws more suspicion on Mr. Feathers," he said thoughtfully, "unless the murder victim had peyote forced down his throat before he died."

"Unlikely," Claude said, getting up from his chair to signal an end to what was, for now, nothing but a discussion of possibilities. "We'll keep in touch. And Ranger Jenkins and I will talk to Hammond."

Thompson took his cue and stood up. "I think you'll find Mr. Hammond to be an arrogant man full of self-importance. He may be rather uncooperative."

Claude pulled a dry smile. "We have ways of getting the cooperation we need, Mr. Thompson. I'll call you if we find out anything important."

Carla gave Claude a curious sideways glance as Claude let Thompson out of the room.

"He was released on bond a couple of hours ago," Deputy Huffman said, staring too long at Carla's chest before his gaze returned to Claude's face. "Sheriff Casey drove him home. He's not supposed to leave Terrell County for no reason 'less he gets an okay from the sheriff or Judge Green."

Claude turned to the office door. "We'll drop by Feathers's house on our way back to the Hunter ranch. By the way, how well do you know Chub Choate?"

"Chub?" The question appeared to puzzle Huffman.

"He's a local cowboy. Works for Hunter. Got a Mexican wife an' kids. He was borned here. Everybody called him Chubby while he was in school. He used to be real bad 'bout gettin' drunk sometimes, only he don't do it much no more. Too many kids an' a wife to feed. How come you ask?"

"Just curious," Claude replied quickly, before Carla told Huffman more than he needed to know. "Tell Sheriff Casey we'll be back to talk to him later this evening. We want to ask him some questions about this dump business and a man by the name of Ray Hammond."

"I'll tell him," Huffman said as Claude opened the door for Carla.

They climbed into the Ford in oppressive afternoon heat. Claude drove slowly through Sanderson and swung off the road to reach the Indian's shack after they crossed the railroad tracks. Carla didn't say any more until they came within sight of the old man's cabin.

"He isn't there," she said, eyes slitted to keep out the sun's glare. "His truck isn't beside the house. I wonder where he went? Surely we can't all be wrong, and he is a murderer, making a run for the Mexican border. . . ."

Claude grinned. "You missed one important detail, Carla. The dog's still sitting on the porch. If Feathers was gonna run he'd have taken his dog with him. When he was in jail that old three-legged hound was the only thing he was worried about."

"You're right," Carla whispered, watching the blue heeler as they drove up to the shack. "He'd have taken Sata with him."

He swung the car around, enjoying himself. "Your computer ain't got eyes or ears. It still takes a cop with good instincts to solve a tough case. Right now we're gonna put a little more of a squeeze on Chub Choate to find out why he lied to us about being at that cave. Watch his eyes real close. I'll lay odds he's about to tell us a hell of a lot more'n he intends to.''

At the Hunter ranch Claude drove past the main house and its swimming pool and tennis court to reach the cattle barns. Danny Weaver's four-door pickup truck sat in front of one of the sheds where they'd spoken to Chub. As he and Carla got out Claude was quick to notice Danny was shoveling cow feed into the wheelbarrow now—Chub was nowhere in sight.

He strode over to Danny with Carla close at his heels. "Can you tell us where we can find Chub?" he asked, gazing across rows of pipe corrals.

Danny wiped sweat from his forehead. "He went home early on account of he said he wasn't feelin' good. I reckon it's this heat got him. He's been a touch under the weather lately anyhow. He don't hardly eat nothin'. Claims his belly hurts all the time so he don't hardly get any sleep. I figure he's got the flu or somethin' like that, if it ain't the heat.''

Claude felt Carla's stare before he turned to her. "Where does Chub live?" Claude asked. "We forgot to ask him a couple of questions."

"On Live Oak Street. Third house on the left after you turn past Joe's Drive-in, just before you git to the tracks.''

"Much obliged," Claude said, taking a step toward the car as suspicion became certainty that Chub had gone home early due to heat of a different kind.

# TWENTY-THREE

Post Oak Jim sat on a high bluff above the Rio Grande, his favorite place on the Hunter ranch, a sacred place where dim carvings in the rocks told ancient stories about Lipan history. His knees were bent so that his feet were underneath him, and he stared across the river at the rugged mountains of Mexico. He could feel the spirit presence of the Old Ones all around him, the spirit of Gokaleh and of his grandfather, Four Feathers, as though they were made of bone and flesh while still invisible to the human eye. Fifty feet below the river passed slowly to the southwest, a muddy ribbon of water crawling toward the horizon, bending like a giant serpent where rocky outcrops forced it to change direction. He sought peace in meditation, communication with the spirits, hoping their timeless wisdom might help him understand what was happening to him. It was on this bluff where he most often experienced the inner voice spoken by Four Feathers—reassurances that he would join his people in the afterlife where he would not be the butt of cruel jokes for being Lipan, and more recently, dire warnings that Earth Mother shed rivers of tears over what the white man was doing to her by overgrazing, drilling holes looking for oil, fouling her dry ravines and creek bottoms with her wasted blood, the oil they spilled that killed grasses and trees, making wild animals sick or leaving them to die.

He looked up at the evening sky. *"Nie habbe weichket,"* he whispered in the tongue of his forefathers. "I am seeking death now. There is no place for me on the face of Earth Mother, for the people here believe I am a killer, that I am crazy. No one understands. . . ." A gust of warm wind carried his softspoken words away. "Hear me. I am ready to die. This is no place for a Lipan Apache. I am the last of the People, my people, and I do not belong among the whites. Take my spirit from my body so I may join my ancestors. I am too old to work, to be useful. I am lonely, and now I am afraid of the place where they will send me, to prison or to a house for crazy people. The whites do not understand what has happened, how Gokaleh took the form of a man to punish those who have destroyed Earth Mother. When I tell them this, they say I am crazy. No one believes me."

He heard only the wind passing through chaparral and sage on the bluff, the rustling of dry creosote stems, and silence. Why did the spirits ignore him when his heart was pure and his mind cleansed of all earthly thoughts? It was the Way. He knew the Old Ones were there as surely as the brush and the rocks and the river, yet they remained silent.

He lowered his gaze to the river, remembering the two Texas Rangers, especially the woman who showed so much kindness for his dog. When Sheriff Casey brought him home he found the empty can of dog food near the steps. The woman who wore the star seemed to have compassion, a gentle nature. He wondered if he could tell her about Gokaleh without being ridiculed by her, the way lawyer Bell and Sheriff Casey ridiculed him. Or was she like all the rest of the whites who laughed at the ancient teachings of his people as they had been handed down since the beginning of time among the Lipans.

Slowly, he lifted his palms toward the sky, beginning the death chant to prepare his spirit for the journey to the Land of Shadows. In a soft, melodic voice he repeated the Lipan words he had learned from his grandfather, hands raised toward the heavens as the sun lowered to the west.

When he came to the appropriate passage calling upon the spirits to show him the pathway he must walk, leaving all his earthly possessions behind, he removed a leather thong with a tiny deerskin bundle affixed to it from his neck and placed it gently on the rocks: the medicine pouch given to him by Four Feathers containing a small blue stone, an eagle's claw, and the mummified paw of a gray squirrel, all having meaning in the life of his grandfather. Offering his *maw-wea* to the spirits, the bundle of magic every Lipan wore during his lifetime, was the final act of preparedness called for in the ceremony. From this moment on he would have no more protection from evil, thus death could claim him whenever the Great Spirit, Powva, was ready.

Later, after the moon had risen above the mountains across the river in Mexico, he uttered a few more chants and came slowly to his feet, knowing what he must do. He turned and began walking along the fence, head bowed, thinking of Sata and what he must do to make himself ready. There was only one man among the whites he might tell about his plans and the words would be difficult to say. Perhaps it would be better to say nothing.

Off in the distance he heard the sounds of an engine, and as he looked eastward he saw headlights from a pickup truck crossing the horizon. He wondered briefly if someone had been watching him, perhaps because of this thing called a bail bond containing words commanding him not to leave Terrell County until he went to trial in Del Rio. Someone seemed to think he might try to wade across the Rio Grande to hide from Sheriff Casey and the two Texas Rangers in Mexico.

He shook his head, continuing his silent walk back to

the spot where he parked his truck. "Let the white men think whatever they want of me now," he whispered, his worn boots making no sound across sun-cracked caliche. "Gokaleh will come again to have his revenge and I will not see it with these tired eyes. I will see only what waits for me in the Spirit World."

He wondered if the Spirit Warrior would pass near his house tonight. Sata would hear the horse long before he did, warning him with a growl. How could he explain to a dog there was no reason to be afraid?

# TWENTY-FOUR

CARMEN CHOATE WAS genuinely afraid of something—he could see it in her face as she stood behind the screen door.

"I do not know where he is, *señor*. Sometime he go for long drive in his truck." A child was crying somewhere in the back of the house. "He drink too much beer sometime."

"Where do you think he *might* go?" Claude asked.

"Maybe so to the river to fish. He like catfish. Other time he say he just drive all over, thinking."

"Has anything in particular been bothering him lately, Mrs. Choate?"

She averted her dark chocolate eyes. "Billy don't sleep so good. He don't tell me why."

Claude nodded. "Tell him to call the Flagship Motel and ask for Captain Groves as soon as he gets home. I forgot to ask him a couple of questions."

"*Sí, señor.*"

◇ ◇ ◇

Claude put six bottles of beer in the sink and covered them with ice—another six-pack he bought after they left

Chub's house on Live Oak Street, upon hearing from his slender Mexican wife that Chub wasn't at home. It was past five o'clock, time for a beer or two, and the bottles in the trunk had been too warm to drink as quickly as his thirst demanded. On the drive back to the Flagship Motel he and Carla discussed their growing suspicions of Chub Choate, and whether he was a murderer or simply a witness, or someone who knew something relating to the killing.

"Chub's wife called him Billy," Carla remarked as she began hooking up a modem to her computer and the telephone. "Chub is only a nickname because he's always been fat."

Claude twisted open a cold Coors. "Well, Billy or Chub, he's either running from us now, heading for the Mexican border, or he's hiding someplace while he makes up his mind what to do. Depends on what he did, I reckon. If he's our killer, he's running. Could be in 'most any direction, not necessarily Mexico. If he was merely a witness to something he wasn't supposed to see, he's trying to decide what to tell us. After you check to see if he has a record we'll know what to do. Sheriff Casey said Choate had never been in any trouble that he knew of."

As Carla was making the connection to DPS computer banks in Austin she said, "He may have gotten in trouble with the law someplace Sheriff Casey didn't know about . . . or Casey could be covering for him, although I can't imagine why he would. Choate can't be anybody important in this county."

Claude took a bubbling swallow of beer. "Remember, he works for someone important. Cale Hunter is no small fry here, even if he does borrow money against his land."

Carla looked at him and smiled. "Kind of early for a beer, isn't it, Captain?"

"It's after five. Besides, I was thirsty. Still am. I'm officially taking myself off the clock long enough to wash the dust from my throat." He grinned and drained his first bottle, opening another before he sat on the edge of the bed near Carla's chair.

Carla frowned. "Traffic tickets. Two speeding tickets and a misdemeanor DWI in 1987 in Brewster County. That's it. William Donald Choate has no criminal record."

"Then we have to conclude he either saw something or he knows something. He'll probably try to talk to somebody he trusts, ask him what to do."

"That could be Danny Weaver," Carla suggested.

Claude thought about it a moment. "Probably not. He'll be wanting an opinion from someone with influence, not just another range cowboy. He'll need to trust the information he asks for, like how much to say, or whether to say anything at all. He may ask whoever he saw at or near the murder scene, if that's what he's trying to hide."

Carla ended her connection to Austin with the flip of a switch and turned off her computer. "We should be looking for him now." She glanced at his Coors.

Claude downed more beer. "Everybody takes a coffee break."

"I didn't know Adolf Coors bottled coffee."

He grinned again. "I could write you up for insubordination for that remark, Miss Jenkins." He did his best not to think about how pretty she was, or stare at her too long, until he made up his mind to offer a superficially harmless observation, one that wouldn't offend her or seem out of place coming from a man his age. "You're a beautiful woman, Carla. If I was a younger man, and if it wasn't for the added complication that you're the daughter of my closest friend, I'd be sending you flowers and candy and all that stuff, trying to win your heart. I never met your former husband, but he was an idiot to let you go. Your dad told me you've been bitter since your divorce. Be patient. The right guy will come along sooner or later. You have, in what I suppose I should call barstool terminology, all the right bait to catch a man who'll make you happy one of these days."

"All the right bait?" she asked, a trace of a smile curling her lips. "I suppose you're talking about my chest, if this is barstool terminology."

He could feel a blush creeping up his neck as he wagged his head. "No, not just that. You have a pretty face and a pretty smile. A nice shape overall. C'mon, Carla. I didn't mean to get out of line with you. It was only a remark and you took it wrong. You're a beautiful lady. Nothing wrong with telling you that, is there?" He felt like a mouse caught in a trap when he really wasn't after the cheese.

She closed her laptop and turned to him, and when her deep green eyes riveted on him he wished desperately he'd kept his mouth shut.

"Nothing wrong with it at all, Captain," she said in a quiet voice, expressionless. "You weren't out of line and I did not take it the wrong way." She stared at him a moment longer. "I take it as a compliment, even though I've never been told I have what you called 'the right bait.' You needn't apologize."

Despite what she said he was still extremely uncomfortable. "It's my big mouth. Gets me in trouble all the time. I should have remembered you're Alfred's daughter, that I've known you since you were nearly in diapers. I'm sorry. Damn near all my life I've made a fool of myself in front of a pretty woman. No reason to expect I'll change. We're partners now. What I said was personal, inappropriate for a field training officer to say to a trainee regardless of the circumstances. I promise you it won't happen again." He finished his second beer and got up to open another, feeling foolish, embarrassed.

He tossed the empty bottle away and twisted open a fresh Coors with his back to her, when he heard her say softly, "That won't be necessary. You can tell me I'm pretty any time you feel like it, only I'd like it better if you wouldn't refer to me as bait."

# TWENTY-FIVE

BILLY'S STOMACH WAS cramping, twisting. It was worse now, worse than when he made the telephone call at the phone booth in front of Barker's Texaco more than an hour ago. It had required all the courage he could muster to make that call, and five beers before he dialed the number. It had been the toughest decision he'd ever made, whether to call the person he saw, or thought he saw, at the cave that night. Or simply hunker down and wait with his guts churning, unable to eat or sleep, so jumpy everyone noticed the sudden change in his behavior, his forgetfulness, and that he was drinking too much. But no one else had seen or heard what he'd witnessed that night, so how could he expect anyone to understand? The shrieking of a dying man's agony still echoed in his memory as vividly as the moment it had occurred, the hours of sobbing cries Billy listened to, only a few hundred yards away from the spot where he'd dismounted when he heard something in the dark ravine, unable to identify it as a human voice at first, since it was coming from a place where no one should have been at that hour, an empty pasture above the Rio Grande. Even his bay horse had sensed something was wrong, snorting softly through its muzzle, ears pricked forward, raising its head to sniff blood on the wind. Billy knew all along he shouldn't have been riding out in that pasture at night, but with so many money troubles hovering over him, the doctors' bills on account of the baby, he sometimes rode alone in the dark, thinking about what to do, occasionally hunting night-feeding rattlesnakes with his .22 to take his mind off other things. He couldn't talk to Carmen about it and Danny would never have understood, not being married or faced with children to raise. It was a bitch, he'd thought a thousand times, to be burdened with so many rising debts and having no way out, no way to escape them because the baby *had* to have medical attention and it cost tons of money. The bank wouldn't loan him any more, not even enough to buy a better pickup for the long drives to the hospital in Fort Stockton, and he could never have asked Mr. Hunter for any more money. His pride wouldn't have allowed that and Danny said Mr. Hunter was having money troubles anyway, with oil prices so low, which was the reason he was selling off part of the ranch for this stupid dump, whatever the hell it was.

He opened another beer, gazing blankly through his cracked windshield at the night sky without really seeing it, his mind on the telephone call, the chance he was taking. His stomach convulsed when he drank more beer and he almost threw up, but he gritted his teeth, gagging. He'd been told to wait here, until the two of them could talk about what he thought he saw, how he must have been wrong about who he believed it was leaving the cave that night, how darkness sometimes plays tricks on a man's eyes. But down deep, Billy was sure of what he'd seen, almost sure of the killer's identity, and this was what didn't make any sense.

"One thing's for damn sure," he told himself aloud in a shaky voice, "it wasn't ol' Post Oak. I'd have recognized him from a mile away even if there wasn't no stars or moon." It was in part the deep feelings he had over the injustice being done to the old Indian that pushed him closer to making the call tonight. Billy couldn't let them send Jim Feathers to the gas chamber for something he didn't do, he'd known the old man too long.

He heard a horse moving across the black prairie hills to the west, the rhythmic click of iron horseshoes striking rock, a sound he'd known intimately all his working life. He got out of his truck and leaned against a front fender with his insides quivering, clutching a lukewarm can of beer as the sounds drew nearer. "What the hell am I gonna say except the truth?" he whispered. "Somebody's gotta tell me what I'm supposed to do."

Billy caught a glimpse of a hatless figure astride a dark horse crossing a brushy hilltop, and for a moment he thought he had to be drunk. The rider looked like an Indian, an old-time Indian with what vaguely resembled a pair of feathers hanging down one shoulder. "What the fuck is goin' on?" he asked under his breath. "I ain't all that damn drunk. Who the hell—?" He blinked, and dropped his half-empty beer can to rub both eyes.

It can't be, he thought. It couldn't be Post Oak Jim out to play some dumb trick on him, because he was in jail. Besides, who other than the person he'd called knew he was supposed to be waiting here in the dark? Yet the rider did look like Post Oak—was it the way he was slumped over the horse's withers?

The churning in his belly became a knot of fear as Billy recalled small details from the night of the killing, things he hadn't remembered until now. He stood there, trembling, as the rider approached, fully aware that what he was seeing now was not an apparition or a figment of his imagination. And he was sure of one more thing. Making the phone call had been a terrible, stupid mistake.

# TWENTY-SIX

CLAUDE PUT THE windows down and turned off the head-lights. They could see the river passing below a bluff where the dirt road ended. A few scrub cottonwood trees lined the riverbank. Light from a pale moon made it easy to see that Choate's pickup was not parked among the trees. A clerk at Joe's Drive-in told them this was a favorite fishing spot: off Highway 90 down a two-rut lane running for miles between the Hunter ranch and Ray Hammond's property all the way to the Rio Grande. The makeshift road had once been dedicated to Terrell County by Hammond to keep so many oil well service trucks from wandering all over his ranch, leaving gates open.

"He isn't here," Claude said needlessly. "We don't have any choice but to notify Sheriff Casey that Choate is a suspect, that he lied to us and now he's missing."

"He's not running," Carla said, sounding sure of it. "He's off someplace deciding what to do, or he's talking to someone. I suppose he might even have driven up to Ozona to talk to that lawyer, Dave Bell. And where is Jim Feathers? I keep wondering where he would go without his dog, why he'd leave home so soon after he got out of jail."

"He may be talking to Cale Hunter. We'll drive over to the Hunter ranch if Choate doesn't show up here pretty soon." Claude reached over the backseat to take a bottle of Coors from the rear floorboard. He glanced at Carla as he was twisting off the cap. "I know. It looks like I'm drinking on the job. I'm officially taking myself off the clock again. It's a privilege of rank, you see, being a captain. I'm doing surveillance on my own time, for the record."

She smiled. "I wasn't going to say a word, Captain. You've become much too defensive about your drinking. What you do with your liver is your own affair."

"It's probably the size of a basketball by now."

The dark night sky stretched before them through the windshield, and suddenly Carla said, "You dislike women, don't you? That's not to say you won't sleep with one, but you won't let yourself commit to a relationship because of what happened between you and your wife."

He thought about it. "Martha taught me to hate women. It was easy, learning to hate her. She's a real bitch, the kind any man could learn to hate if he stayed around her long enough."

"And you cheated on her."

"After I found out I hated her guts. Not before."

Carla kept staring straight ahead. "I've had the same problem relating to men after being married to George for five years. I know all men aren't like him. I guess I'm keeping my guard up."

"No regular boyfriend?"

"No. I've tried going out on dates and for some reason it never works out. I don't like guys who come on too strong and I don't like the ones who just sit there. It's a choice between having someone try to tear your clothes off or being bored to death."

Claude drank half of his beer. "I'd be the guy trying to rip your clothes off, I suppose . . . if I was younger, and if you weren't Alfred's daughter." He grinned a little self-consciously. "First thing I'd try to do is get you drunk. Women are easier to seduce when they've been drinking. It's a fact of life. Women don't really like sex. They merely consent to it because they think they have to in order to trap a man."

Carla smiled again. "My, aren't you bitter? And who told you women don't enjoy sex?"

"We shouldn't be talking about it. It's inappropriate, due to our professional relationship and that you're my best friend's daughter. It's my fault. I started talking about the correct way to seduce a woman."

"The correct way?"

"The only way it works, most of the time."

"You've never slept with a sober woman?"

"Probably just Martha, and she was lousy in bed. I'd have to think to see if I can remember any others."

Carla laughed. "Why did you marry her?"

He sighed. "I wish I knew the answer to that. She was pretty. We got along well, until I married her."

"That's the way it was between George and me. We got along fine until we got married and I went to work for El Paso PD. It went to pieces almost immediately."

"You'll find someone else. Give yourself time."

"Time hasn't helped you find anyone," Carla observed.

"I'm not really looking for something permanent. I've resigned myself to bachelorhood. It ain't all that bad, really. Now, if I could find someone like you I might change my mind." He felt her staring at him as soon as he said it and it made him realize what he'd told her sounded brash, inappropriate.

"That's very sweet of you," she said, lowering her voice. "Dad told me you were really a nice guy, only you'd had some bad experiences with women. He said it was because you looked for the trashy kind, the kind you could never fall in love with so you wouldn't end up in another bad marriage."

"Alfred's degree in psychology came from a cereal box. He hasn't done all that well himself in the marriage department."

"Obviously none of us have. I've given up looking. Every guy I meet turns out to be a jerk."

"Getting drunk might help. It would be harder to tell if a guy's a jerk if you were half-loaded."

"But what happens when you sober up?"

"You admit your mistake and go on to the next guy, hoping he won't be as bad as the one before."

"Then I'd be another trashy woman, wouldn't I? The kind you are so attracted to."

Claude reached for another beer, tossing the empty bottle on the backseat, wishing he hadn't started this conversation with Carla because it made him wonder what she'd be like, not only in bed but as someone he cared about in a romantic way. He suspected he'd already gone too far with their discussion, yet for some vague reason he wasn't ready to stop. "I'd be attracted to you drunk or sober," he said, "if it wasn't for the circumstances."

She leaned back against the passenger door, watching him in an odd way. "I'd be attracted to you too, Captain. I know you wouldn't turn out to be a jerk." She hesitated. "I'll tell you something, even if it may seem out of line, as you call it. I am attracted to you, in spite of all the circumstances. I can't change the fact I'm Alfred's daughter any more than you can deny he's your friend. You're a handsome man and you're very sure of yourself, which is very attractive to women."

Her remark surprised him completely, catching him off guard. "I don't . . . I'm not sure what to say. On the one hand I'm flattered. Really flattered. But your Dad trusted me to show you the ropes, and that doesn't include . . . getting personal with you. If things were different I'd probably make a complete fool of myself over you, if you'd let me."

She grinned impishly. "You wouldn't try to get me drunk?"

He noticed his palms were sweating now, and his heartbeat was faster. "No. You're not the kind of woman I'd do that to. You're different. You're a real lady."

"But what would you think of me if I allowed you to take me to bed? Wouldn't that change everything?"

"Jesus, Carla. I hadn't thought about it because it would be all wrong. I never let it cross my mind."

"How's that? Why would it be wrong?"

"Because of Alfred, first of all. He trusts me. And then there's the official misconduct to consider, if I took advantage of you . . . if I tried to seduce you."

Her grin widened and he wondered if she were only flirting with him, teasing him to see what he would say.

"I never said I'd let you take advantage of me. A seduction by most definitions suggests the consent of both parties, doesn't it? Otherwise it would be rape."

"I suppose so. If you weren't drunk." Was she actually offering him the chance to sleep with her?

"I was curious to see how you felt about it."

"I've said too many of the wrong things already, Carla. I hope you won't hold it against me."

"You haven't said anything wrong. I'm the one who asked you what you would think of me if I allowed you to take me to bed, if it would change things. Remember?"

His thoughts became a blur of all the possible consequences if Alfred or Major Elliot found out he'd slept with his partner. Alfred would probably try to kill him with a large-bore gun before the major could act to have him terminated on grounds of sexual harassment. But when he looked at the soft lines of Carla's face in the half dark, her cheeks and hair bathed in moonlight, an urge stronger than fear stirred inside him. "You're only testing me, aren't you?" he asked. "To see if I'll make an official blunder, or if I'd sink so low as to double-cross Alfred."

"Is that what you think?" She asked in a way that made him wonder.

"The thought did occur to me just now."

"You're wrong," she said, almost a whisper, leaning across the car seat. She kissed him gently on the lips and pulled away before he could respond, returning to her place on the passenger side. "We can think about it, if you want. I'm not willing to jump into bed with you yet. I've got some of my own thinking to do. We've barely become reacquainted. I'm not willing to be just another one of your conquests. I'd want more than that."

"Right. You'd want more than that," he said, his voice turning hoarse as he reached for the ignition key, worried, and at the same time filled with pleasant anticipation over what had just taken place between them when he should have shown more restraint. "Like you say, there's plenty of time to decide."

Claude was still tasting the sweetness of her lips as he started the car and wheeled it around for the drive back to Sanderson. For the time being he'd forgotten all about Billy Choate and their murder investigation, pondering the wisdom, or lack of it, of letting himself become romantically involved with Carla Sue Jenkins.

# PART 2

# TWENTY-SEVEN

BILLY CHOATE'S BODY was so badly hacked to pieces he was all but unrecognizable. Ants were feeding all over the corpse while swarms of green-backed blowflies hovered in filmy black clouds a few feet above him, buzzing incessantly, swirling in a curious series of aerobatic formations like tiny fighter planes until they landed where blood and exposed tissue offered the quickest access to a meal.

"Almost the same as our John Doe," Claude said, examining a deep gash in Choate's stomach. His intestines lay around him in looping curls, almost as if by arrangement, a crude design of some sort. "Get the camera out of the trunk," he told Carla, as Deputy Huffman continued seemingly endless dry heaves behind his patrol car, gagging, gasping for breath. Claude noted the victim's missing scalp, sliced off to bare bone, and it appeared the remaining skin across his forehead had been pulled down to cover his eyes. Choate's penis and scrotum were stuffed into his mouth, resembling a swollen, misshapen purple growth protruding from his lips.

"Goddamnedest thing I ever saw," Sheriff Casey said, "worse than the time that Sante Fe Limited hit Buddy

Johnson's car back in '87. There was pieces of Buddy layin' all over them tracks. I found one of his shoes in the Lopez's backyard an' his foot was still in it. This is worse, because we all knew Chub so good."

Huffman, despite his tough appearance, began vomiting again when he heard the remark about Buddy Johnson, just as Carla walked up with the camera. Claude straightened up. "Get shots of the way his intestines are laid out." His gaze wandered over soft caliche beyond the pipe fence of a corral where the body lay. "Those are a horse's hoofprints, and it looks like a set of real faint footprints leading over to the fence and back to where the horse stood while the body was dumped here. Let's get plaster casts. Whoever killed Choate brought him here on the back of a horse."

"Cattle rustlers from over in Mexico," Casey pronounced, as if he were sure. "They used to cross over on horses all the time to steal a few cows. Maybe Chub saw 'em and they killed him to keep him from notifyin' me."

Claude almost ignored Casey's wild guess. "That still won't explain why they cut him up. Whoever did this was no common cow thief. Why bother to scalp him and cut his genitals off, or toss his guts all over the place?"

Carla took a picture of the corpse.

Cale Hunter, who'd been silent until now, leaning against the hood of his pickup, said, "Jim got out of jail yesterday. If this happened last night it's gonna look bad for him. But Jim wouldn't kill Chub. Hell, they were friends an' worked together on this ranch for years. I don't care what anybody else thinks."

Claude was bothered by something and didn't hear all of what Hunter said. "There isn't enough blood. Choate was killed someplace else. He was brought here on the back of a horse after he was already dead." Then he turned to Hunter and Sheriff Casey. "We went by Post Oak Jim's house yesterday afternoon and again last night, around nine or ten o'clock. He wasn't there. His truck was gone both times. Has anybody seen him since he got out of jail?"

Danny Weaver spoke up from his place next to Hunter. "I saw his truck headin' down to the river just before dark. He was drivin' that old wagon road that crosses the river pasture, only he was west of here by a couple of miles. He goes down there all the time. Just sits on a rock lookin' across the river for hours, like he's thinkin' real hard about somethin'."

Claude rubbed his chin thoughtfully. "After Ranger Jenkins gets pictures and plaster casts, I want you to show us where Jim Feathers goes, that place you told us about on the river."

Carla was squatting down to take a close-up of the body when she asked, "Who found the body this morning?"

"I did," Hunter replied. "I was checkin' floats on those automatic waterers we use in the steer pens, makin' sure none of 'em was stuck. It was right after sunrise . . . maybe seven-thirty or so. Danny hadn't gotten here yet. I seen this lump lyin' in one of the empty pens, so I climbed over the fence an' this is what I found. I called Walter right away. I never heard a damn thing last night, not a sound. Dogs didn't even bark. Danny told me Chub went home early yesterday because he wasn't feelin' good." Hunter pushed away from the truck hood. He aimed an accusing finger at Sheriff Casey. "I've been tellin' you all along this is meant to scare me outta sellin' my land to the NRC," he snapped. "You can forget all that bullshit about Mexican cow thieves an' wild Indians who done this. It's high time you started lookin' right under your nose, Walter, at sumbitches like Ray Hammond who're tryin' to keep me from sellin'."

Casey hooked his thumbs in his polished black pistol belt and shrugged his shoulders. "There's nothin' to prove Ray had anything to do with this or the other killin', Cale. Besides, we've both known Ray damn near all our lives. He wouldn't do nothin' like this. He's payin' lawyers to try to stop you. I know the two of you got crossways over this dump business, but Ray ain't the kind of feller who'd chop up a kid like Chub Choate or whoever that other guy was. Ray Hammond wouldn't kill nobody."

"He paid some asshole to do it. He figures this is gonna scare me, only he's goddamn sure wrong. I'll show the old bastard who's callin' the shots when it comes to sellin' my own goddamn land. He don't run this whole fuckin' county." Hunter gave Carla a quick look. "Sorry for the language, ma'am, but this hadn't started out as no ordinary day. Chub was a good kid with children to raise. One of 'em, his baby daughter, was born blind an' it's been real expensive for him to take her to the doctors up in Fort Stockton so often. I helped him with a little extra money now an' then. Now his wife is gonna have to raise them kids all by herself. She'll have to go on welfare, most likely. Chub's been workin' for me since right after his daddy got killed in an oil-field explosion. I was real fond of him an' he damn sure didn't do nothin' to deserve this."

Claude knew he and Carla were headed for Ray Hammond's place as soon as possible, when everything around the crime scene had been examined and photographed. He noticed Carla had ignored Hunter's apology and gone to climb over the corral fence, bending over one of the prints. The buzzing of so many blowflies became annoying and he went over the fence to see what she was looking at so closely.

"This isn't a boot print, Captain," she said, pointing to one of the footprints he'd seen earlier. "And it isn't a tennis shoe or a dress shoe. There's no heel. The bottom was completely flat, with no markings. He wasn't barefoot because there are no toe impressions. I can't figure out what he was wearing."

Claude suddenly remembered something he found at the bottom of Jim Feathers's old trunk. "Moccasins," he said, keeping his voice down, "like the ones in Post Oak Jim's footlocker."

Carla stared at him, furrowing her brow. "You don't

really think Feathers got out of jail yesterday, put on his moccasins and borrowed a horse someplace to come over here and kill Billy Choate? Why would he do it? Where's his motive? Neither one of us can make ourselves believe he's a killer."

Claude looked past her to the horse tracks. "Maybe that's what it was made to look like. I imagine everyone in Sanderson knew Feathers was out of jail. The killer could have used that to try to frame the old man again. You heard Danny Weaver say he saw Feathers driving down to the river yesterday evening, and we know he wasn't at home last night. I'll be damned if it isn't starting to look like Feathers could be involved in both slayings some way or another. There sure as hell are a lot of coincidences stacking up against him."

"Or one hell of a clever frame job," Carla suggested, just as Sheriff Casey climbed over the pipes to join them.

"It don't appear I have any choice," Casey began, sounding like a man under heavy pressure. "I'm gonna have to bring Jim Feathers in on suspicion of committin' a second murder. He was on this property yesterday evenin' and you said he wasn't home last night. Makes him the only suspect we've got, unless you've got other ideas."

Claude stood up, looking south, toward the river. "One bit of important evidence we haven't found yet is the murder scene. Choate wasn't killed here. And Choate was driving some kind of foreign pickup truck, a Toyota I think it was. We need to find it, too. It's my guess Choate was killed somewhere on the Hunter ranch. A horse carrying a rider and a body couldn't jump any fences. If your deputy can stop throwing up long enough to ride a horse, ask Mr. Hunter if he can borrow one to look for Choate's truck and any traces of blood on the ground. If he can follow these hoofprints, they should lead him to the murder scene. Tell him to be sure not to touch anything. As soon as Ranger Jenkins and I are finished here we'll go looking for

Jim Feathers. We'll question him, and if he can't give us solid answers we'll bring him down to your jail."

"Harlan's got a weak stomach," Casey explained. "He'll be okay in a few minutes. Do you want me to radio our volunteer fire department to send out the ambulance so's they can take Chub down to the funeral parlor?"

Claude glanced through the fence at the body. "We're almost done. May as well call 'em. Hardly any need to ship him off for an autopsy, it's real easy to see how he died. But just in case tell your undertaker not to do anything yet. We may need one more look at him."

"I'll radio you if Harlan finds anything," Casey said. "Tell me what frequency—"

"I hardly ever turn my car radio on, so don't bother tryin' to reach us. We'll be at Feathers's house or at your office in an hour or two . . . if we can find Feathers."

"He may have lit out for Mexico."

Claude wagged his head. "His dog was still at his house last night. I don't see Feathers as the type to run, anyway."

Carla went back across the fence to get plaster for print molds out of the car. Casey hesitated a moment.

"Once the newspapers get hold of this we'll be crawlin' with reporters again." Casey sighed. "More goddamn stupid questions about wild Injuns runnin' loose in Terrell County. I still say this could be some cult of loonies over in Mexico doin' this shit here."

Claude did not bother to comment on it. "Give me directions to Ray Hammond's house before you leave," he said, taking a last look at the horse tracks as he turned for the fence.

The sheriff lowered his voice. "Don't pay too much attention to Cale when it comes to Ray Hammond, Cap'n. They ain't gotten along since this dump issue came up. Ray's got more money an' land than anybody in the county, an' some folks resent him on account of it, includin' Cale. Ray didn't have nothin' to do with this. He's got the best lawyers in Texas fightin' Cale an' Bob McCloud over the dump. He's a prideful old man who don't want no nuclear shit buried close to his property, but he damn sure wouldn't have nobody killed over it. When you turn west out of Hunter's front gate, it's the next iron gate on the left down Highway 90. You'll see, after you talk to him, that Cale's dead wrong to figure Ray's behind this."

Claude stepped wide of the corpse and strolled through an open corral gate to the car where Carla was mixing plaster. Remembering last night, he thought about what she'd said to him, and wondered if she might be leading him on. He'd spent a wonderful night dreaming about it and he had been looking forward to today, until the grim phone call came from Sheriff Casey early this morning.

Cale Hunter walked up behind him. "Me an' Danny will saddle horses to help Harlan look for Chub's truck and the murder scene. I'm wantin' to get to the bottom of this quick, an' I'm bettin' the tracks will lead us straight to Ray Hammond, one way or another. He went too far killin' a boy who worked for me, tryin' to make it look like Post Oak Jim was to blame, an' I'm gonna help you prove Ray done it."

Claude overheard Casey radio for the ambulance. In small towns like Sanderson, firemen were local volunteers and someone monitored a two-way radio day and night to handle emergencies. He finished the call and as Hunter left to saddle a horse Sheriff Casey came over to see what Carla was doing.

"I'll drive to town an' tell Chub's wife what happened to him," he said to Claude. "She called Harlan real early this mornin' when Chub hadn't come home. I'm sure dreadin' givin' her the news. For her sake I think I'll skip some of the details. I sure hope she don't ask to see the body. Christ, what a damn mess. A man who'd do that to another human bein' has got cowshit where he oughtta have brains." He glanced at Carla. "Pardon the language, ma'am."

# TWENTY-EIGHT

"THIS ISN'T GOING to look good at headquarters," Carla said as Claude sped toward the highway. "Another bizarre murder right under our noses. Like Sheriff Casey said, once the news media gets hold of this it'll be everywhere, including Major Elliot's desk. They'll be calling this the work of a serial killer before you know it. Then the major will be asked a hundred times a day why the first woman Ranger, a rookie, was assigned to track down the Midnight Mauler. He'll have a coronary."

Claude dodged a chuckhole in Hunter's gravel road. "It's because we *are* nosing around that Choate was killed, I suspect. The killer either figured we were getting too close, or he found out Choate knew something he might tell us. Choate may even have been a witness to the first killing. Don't worry about the major right now. I'll be the one facing heat from the reporters."

"I think we need to notify Major Elliot now, before he finds out about it from the press. I can radio Austin through highway patrol relay towers if you want."

He scowled at the microphone clipped to the dashboard. "Go ahead, only turn the damn thing off as soon as you're done, so I don't have to listen to all that other crap. First thing we're gonna do is find Jim Feathers. If he isn't at home we've got a problem." As Carla lifted the microphone he continued to think out loud. "Here's a possible scenario. Feathers is a participant in both murders. We can't figure a motive, but both times he's had opportunity. He isn't strong enough to kill two men on his own, so he's got an accomplice who does most of the physical part of each killing. Feathers may be nothing more than an advisor, so to speak, telling his accomplice how to make the murders look like the work of Indian savages."

Carla flipped a switch on the radio. "But Jim Feathers is several generations removed from the days when Indians were scalping people. How would he know how to do it?"

"Maybe his grandfather told him how. I know it's pretty far-fetched, but Feathers is the only one who was seen in the vicinity of both murders."

Carla turned a radio knob. "You're forgetting about Danny Weaver," she said.

It was a possibility Claude hadn't seriously considered up to this point. "I figured he was too dumb, too simple, but he's strong enough to be our killer. Trouble is, we're still missing the most important element—a motive. Feathers and Weaver know each other from working together, but neither one has any motive to commit murder and Choate was their mutual friend. Too many holes in that bucket. There has to be another answer."

"If Hunter sells off a big part of his ranch, maybe Weaver wouldn't have a job. It still doesn't explain why Jim Feathers would help him commit murder, and a ranch hand's job would hardly pay enough for Weaver to risk going to prison or face a lethal injection."

"We've got two very important people to talk to. Possibly three," Claude suggested. "We both believe Feathers knows something, only he isn't saying what it is, at least not directly. Ray Hammond is the power behind trying to halt the dump, so he has the strongest apparent motive, if

Hunter is right about the killings being meant to scare him out of selling. And we haven't talked to McCloud, the other seller. But it won't hurt to do a little digging into Danny Weaver's past, to see if he's ever shown a tendency toward violence."

Carla requested a dispatcher from the Midland highway patrol office. Claude tried to ignore the bothersome crackle of radio static as the car flew across Hunter's cattle guard and then onto the highway.

◇ ◇ ◇

The old Dodge truck was parked in its usual spot. Sata lay on the front porch near his master's feet as they drove up. Jim Feathers didn't seem surprised when Claude and Carla got out. He remained in his mended wooden chair, watching them with no hint of concern on his face or in his eyes, late morning sunlight turning his skin a deep golden color. Sata growled, until a word from Feathers silenced him.

"Mornin', Mr. Feathers," Claude said.

Feathers merely nodded to them.

"We've gotta ask you a few questions, like where you were yesterday evening and last night. We know you were seen out at the Hunter place late in the day. Tell us what you were doin' there."

"Praying," the old man replied. "Seeking the guidance of my spirit ancestors. I know white men do not believe in these things."

"Where exactly did you go?"

"To the sacred place, where the Old Ones left their carvings on the rocks. It is where I always go to speak to the spirits."

"Then what did you do?"

"I waited for the moon to rise and then I spoke with her."

"Who? You mean the moon?"

Feathers gave what might pass for a smile. "You believe I am crazy. No white man can understand. The moon is a sister to the Great Spirit, like our Earth Mother. It is not so strange. White men believe their God has three parts, the Holy Ghost and Jesus, who is also the son of God. To an Indian this seems strange, how the son of God can also be a part of your God. I do not understand how this can be, or how a ghost can also be God."

"You've got a point, I suppose," Claude said, more certain than ever Jim Feathers was not a killer. His gentle voice and mannerisms simply couldn't be part of a brutal murderer's makeup, for if there was one thing Claude prided himself on it was his judgment of human nature. "Did you see anybody on the way back, anyone you knew?"

"No. There were cars on the highway. They honk at me when I drive too slowly, but I do not know the owners of these cars. They go too fast for me to see who is inside, and it was dark."

Claude shifted his weight off his bad knee. "Do you know about Chub?" he asked carefully, ready to gauge the old man's reaction, any suggestion he evidenced no surprise.

"What do you mean?" Feathers asked. "What is there to know about Chub?"

"Somebody killed him last night. Scalped him and cut his belly open just like the other guy they found."

Feathers blinked, staring into Claude's eyes. "No," he said in a dry whisper. Then his hands, resting on the worn knees of his blue jeans, began to tremble. "No," he said again, glancing up at the sky beyond the roof of his tiny porch. A tear formed in the corners of his eyelids. "It is not possible. Chub has done nothing to anger the Old Ones."

"What do you mean by that?" Carla asked softly, watching Feathers.

Feathers wouldn't look at them, his gaze fixed on the morning sky while a tear trickled down his cheeks. "Chub is only a cowboy, like me. He did nothing wrong."

"Are these Old Ones you mentioned some sort of spirits you believe in?"

He finally turned tear-filled eyes on Carla. "You would not understand. Everyone thinks I am crazy. I will say no more. If people believe I am only a crazy old Indian, let them think whatever they want. I am ready to die. My time has come."

"We don't think you're crazy, Mr. Feathers," Carla told him gently. "But you must explain what you're trying to tell us about these Old Ones. We don't believe you would kill Chub Choate, because he was your friend. We don't believe you killed the other man. We do think you know, or have some idea, who killed both of them."

Feathers looked down at Sata, rubbing his neck with the palm of his hand. "When I told Sheriff Casey and the lawyer named Bell who I believe killed the stranger, they said I am crazy and a judge will send me to a place for crazy people."

"I don't think a judge will send you anywhere," Claude said to reassure him. "I don't believe they can impanel a jury in the state of Texas who'll believe you're a murderer. What we're askin' you to do is help us find out who did it."

Now Feathers stared blankly at the horizon. "The Old Ones would not kill Chub, for he is not Earth Mother's enemy. This is all I will say until I have listened to the spirit voices."

"Can you show us this place where you go to pray? Where your ancestors carved things in the rocks?" Carla asked.

He fingered drying tears from his cheeks. "I will take you there," he replied, struggling up from his chair as he looked at Carla. "You showed kindness to Sata by bringing him food while I was in Sheriff Casey's jail. For this, I will show you where my ancestors wrote our history in the stones."

Claude started to turn for the car, until a thought

made him pause. "Have you still got those old moccasins, Mr. Feathers? We had a search warrant and when we looked around, I found them at the bottom of your footlocker. We'd like to look at them again, if you don't mind. Our search warrant is still valid."

"I know nothing of these things, search warrants and bail bonds, but I will get the moccasins for you. They belonged to my grandfather." He opened his screen door and hobbled into the house.

"He didn't know about Chub," Carla said quietly. "He didn't have anything to do with the killing."

"That was obvious," Claude agreed. "Whatever he knows, or what he thinks he knows about the first killing, may be nothing more than superstition or his Indian religion. I have a feelin' we're barking up another empty tree."

"I'm not so sure," Carla said, frowning. "I wish he'd tell us the whole thing, the version he told Casey and Bell."

Noises came from the house, something heavy being pulled across the floor.

"Let's drop that film off at the drugstore before we go back to Hunter's place. One thing keeps bothering me. . . . It's the way Choate's intestines were spread out, forming almost the same type of loops on both sides of his body, like a sick design of some sort that may have meant something to the killer. I know how weird it sounds, but I've got this feeling they were arranged that way for a reason. We've got a killer who follows some sort of ritual, maybe an Indian ritual from a long time ago. I want to show those pictures to Feathers, to see if he can give us any possible explanation."

"It'll be hard on him to look at them," Carla said. "They were friends and they worked together for years."

"It won't hurt to ask—" Claude fell silent when Feathers came out on his porch. His hands were empty.

"They are gone," he said, sounding mystified.

"Someone took them, and the old photograph of my grandfather when he was with a Wild West show."

"I took the picture," Claude said, his mind racing. "It's in the glove compartment of the car. I wanted to ask you who he was, the Indian in the photograph. But we left everything else except some towels and a few kitchen knives, which we took to check for bloodstains. Are you sure the moccasins aren't there?"

"I am sure," Feathers said, and now he seemed frightened, a tremor in his fingers when he reached for a place below his neck as if he were seeking something that was no longer there.

Was it possible that someone would go to such elaborate lengths to frame Jim Feathers? Claude was certain now the footprints near Choate's body would turn out to be made by the same moccasins, if they ever turned up, so a match could be made, but who knew the old man well enough to know they existed in the first place?

Almost everything seemed to be pointing to Post Oak Jim as the killer. Too many things. The odor of phony bullshit was growing stronger in Claude's investigative nose.

# TWENTY-NINE

Jim Feathers sat in the backseat saying nothing, until he gave directions to turn down a narrow lane running south across miles of brushy flats. A rusting barbed-wire fence lay on both sides of the two-rut road, a road showing little sign of use in many years, partially overgrown with broomweed and agave plants, and an occasional scrub mesquite tree.

"The road is very bumpy," Feathers said. "Many rocks are hidden in the weeds. The road ends before we come to the river. We will walk half a mile and there are many rattlesnakes."

Carla turned around in the seat so she could look at Feathers. Claude could tell she'd been thinking hard ever since they left Sanderson Pharmacy where they'd had the film sent off to be developed overnight in Midland. "I want to ask you a general question, Mr. Feathers, about Indian rituals from a long time ago. Was there a ceremony, or ceremonial killing, in which the man—let's say he's an enemy—was cut open and his intestines were spread out on the ground in some special way?"

Feathers watched her silently for a moment. "My grandfather told me stories. There was a band of Lipan

Apaches who followed a war chief named Gokaleh. This was before the white man came. Gokaleh was a mighty warrior. When he captured enemies of the People, my people, he cut them open so death would be painful, and slow. When other tribes, or Mexican scalp hunters, found them they would know it was Gokaleh who killed them. My grandfather said Gokaleh learned this from the Comanches. A Comanche shaman named Isa Tai taught his people how to kill this way. I do not remember if my grandfather told me about doing special things with intestines. He died when I was very young and I am old now, so I do not remember some things."

The left front tire struck a rock, jarring everyone inside the car as Claude muttered, "Shit. I couldn't see it."

"Did you tell Sheriff Casey you think the first killing had something to do with the way your ancestors killed their enemies?" Carla continued.

Feathers looked away, out a side window. "I was wrong to think a white man could understand."

"Captain Groves and I are trying our best to understand what you meant."

Feathers said no more, watching the land pass by, his face empty.

"That's Cale Hunter and Danny Weaver," Claude said, pointing to a pair of horsemen riding along the fence under a noonday sun, coming up from the Rio Grande. They had been walking only a few minutes, having parked the car where the road ended. Claude was sweating profusely in the heat, careful where he placed each foot to avoid a rattler's hiding place.

Feathers, leading them down a faint path that wound around tall creosote and thorny brush, stopped when he saw Hunter and Weaver coming toward them.

Both riders urged their horses to a steady trot. Hunter

was the first to arrive, halting his horse in front of them. He took a leather string with a tiny bag attached to it from the horn of his saddle. He looked at Feathers.

"This is yours, ain't it, Jim?" he asked.

Feathers shook his head, then he looked at the ground. "It was my grandfather's medicine bundle."

"We found it on that ledge above the river, an' that ain't all we found. Sorry, Jim. It breaks my heart to have to show these rangers what's down there, 'cause I know how it's gonna look. Don't think for one damn minute that I believe you went an' killed Chub. You ain't got it in you, an' I know you better than anybody else."

"What else is there?" Claude asked, taking the pouch and leather thong from Hunter.

Hunter let out a deep sigh. "A bloody knife an' a pair of old moccasins. They've got blood on 'em too. Maybe they ain't Jim's. They look like they're older'n hell, nearly worn out. Me an' Danny didn't touch nothin', 'cept that bundle. I knew it was Jim's because he's worn it every day since he come to work for me at the ranch. I recognized it right off. Can't say as I know whose knife it is. It ain't a regular pocketknife."

Claude's thoughts were a tangle of possibilities and for a moment he didn't say anything. "Did you find Choate's pickup?" he asked.

"Not yet. Harlan went east an' we was supposed to ride the river towards each other. I yelled for Danny when I found this an' the other things."

Carla's voice interrupted Claude's next question about the bloody knife.

"Are you all right, Mr. Feathers?"

When Claude turned around he found the old man shaking from head to toe. Tears streamed down his face, forming little damp circles in the caliche between his boots.

Carla reached for his arm. "I'll take him back to the car, Captain, while you take a look at what they found. You can see he isn't feeling well."

"I'll need to go back to get a couple of evidence bags, just in case there are fingerprints." He turned back to Hunter and Weaver. "Are you sure neither one of you touched anything?"

Hunter indicated the pouch. "Just that, 'cause I knew it was Jim's." He looked at Feathers while Carla was helping him back toward the car. "To tell the truth, Cap'n, it crossed my mind to toss that necklace in the river a while ago. It's gonna make it look like Jim had somethin' to do with killin' Chub." He leaned forward in the saddle. "You know he didn't do it an' so do I. Somebody's tryin' to frame him, only they picked the most unlikely man in Sanderson to pin it on. I don't give a damn what it looks like to you or Sheriff Casey or anybody else, Jim Feathers didn't kill nobody. I signed for his bail because I know damn good an' well he's innocent, an' I'll mortgage this whole ranch if that's what it takes to get him out again." Hunter looked across the fence. "If you'll go right over yonder across them hills, you'll find the son of a bitch who's behind all of this. Ray Hammond's spendin' thousands on lawyers to try to stop me an' McCloud from sellin' our land to the NRC. Now he's tryin' to scare hell out of everybody with all these killin's, makin' it look like Post Oak is the one doin' it."

"But why would he try to frame Jim Feathers?" Claude asked.

Hunter frowned, pulling off his cowboy hat. "I ain't got that quite figured out yet. Hell, for all I know he may be tryin' to make it look like I done it myself, usin' Jim as a scapegoat because he used to work for me. If he can make it look like I'm involved some way or another, he winds up with more folks on his side, I reckon, so they'll sign his petition to call for an injunction."

There were too many holes in Hunter's assumption for Claude to buy it, for now. "I'll question Hammond later today. Right now I'll grab a couple of plastic bags and then you can show me where you found the knife and the other things."

Following Carla and the old Indian, he returned to the Ford to remove evidence bags from the trunk. As he walked back toward Hunter and Weaver he thought about another key piece of evidence that was still missing. Where was Chub Choate's pickup truck?

◇ ◇ ◇

On a shelf of flat rock overlooking the Rio Grande Claude found a bloody bone-handled skinning knife. It would be Choate's blood on the blade, he was sure of it. And he recognized the old deerskin moccasins from Feathers's footlocker, their beads and quill decorations just as he remembered them. There were traces of blood on the soles.

He placed each item carefully into clear plastic bags for shipment to the crime lab in Austin, although he already knew what the result would be. The only question he had was: would the Indian's prints be on the knife?

Hunter and Weaver had dismounted to watch Claude bag the knife and moccasins.

"Jim never done it," Weaver said, his first comment since he rode up. "Him an' Chub was real good friends. Chub was madder'n hell when Sheriff Casey arrested Post Oak the first time, 'cause he said Casey knew Jim didn't have no mean streak in him. Jim was always a loner. Stayed off to himself most of the time. He felt sorry for Chub, havin' that blind girl to raise along with them other kids. There ain't nobody in Terrell County who knows Post Oak Jim who'll believe he'd kill his friend Chub."

Claude gave the ledge one more examination. "To tell the truth I can't make myself believe it either. But what's missing is a reason why anyone would go to all the trouble trying to frame an old man who isn't capable of murder, especially not the murder of a friend." He swung away from the river. "We'll send this stuff off to the lab for fingerprints and blood typing. But until we get the report, there doesn't seem to be much choice but to put Mr. Feathers back in jail."

"You'll have the wrong man locked up if you do," Hunter said while Claude's back was turned.

"I feel the same way," he replied, trudging back up the game trail, trying to sort things out in his head. For the life of him he couldn't imagine why the old Indian was being targeted. It didn't make any sense.

"We'll keep lookin' for Chub's pickup," Hunter said as he and Danny mounted their horses.

For the time being Claude was too preoccupied to respond. He was certain Feathers hadn't known his grandfather's moccasins were missing from the trunk. But who else knew they were there? And had the opportunity to take them while Feathers wasn't home?

When he got back to the car he showed Feathers the knife and moccasins. The old man's gaze lingered on the knife in the plastic bag. "I have never seen the knife before," he said as he looked out the car window. "The moccasins belonged to my grandfather. They were not there when I went to the sacred place to pray. I would have seen them."

Claude looked across the roof of the Ford at Carla, and he knew without hearing her say it that she still believed Feathers was innocent as strongly as he did.

"Mr. Feathers told me he left his grandfather's medicine bag by the river," Carla said. "It's his good-luck charm, and he put it there because he believes he will die soon. This is what he was praying for yesterday. It's something a Lipan Apache does to prepare himself for death."

"We've got no choice," Claude told her as he opened the car door. "With all this circumstantial evidence, we have to take him back to jail and book him on suspicion of committing another murder. Casey will insist on it, anyway."

# THIRTY

JIM FEATHERS WALKED quietly into Sanderson's only jail cell and sat down on the same metal cot where Claude and Carla first saw him the day they came to town. Sheriff Casey locked the door while Feathers hung his head, staring at the floor. Casey noted the look on Claude's face.

"You're convinced we've got the wrong man in here, ain't you, Cap'n?"

"I'm almost certain of it." Claude could hear Carla's voice in the front office telephoning DPS headquarters, checking for a record of criminal convictions or arrests for Daniel Lee Weaver.

"You can't believe Danny's the one who done it."

"We're just checking his record," Claude replied, following Casey to the front.

"He's been in a few fistfights while he was drunk over in Dryden. Last time was a few years ago, I think. He was Chub's closest friend. It's plumb crazy to think Danny would do that to Chub. I'm gonna call the border patrol, to see if they've had any reports of weirdos over in Coahuila. Some of that country below the river is still wild as hell and empty as a gourd. There could be a bunch of them shaved heads or some goofball militia group hidin' out in those mountains an' nobody'd ever know it."

To placate Casey, Claude agreed. "That's a good idea. Ask the border patrol if they've ever heard of something like this."

Carla was making notes before she hung up the phone. Claude motioned her toward the front door as he spoke to Casey. "Let us know if they find Choate's truck. We'll leave our car radio on just in case. And if you want you can telephone Ray Hammond to tell him we're coming out to talk to him." Claude was sure Casey had already done so.

Outside, before Carla could tell him what she'd written on her notepad, Claude almost bumped into Bill Thompson, who was looking like he'd slept in his clothes.

"Word is all over town," Thompson said, out of breath. "There's been another scalping, just like the first one. It was a local man this time, wasn't it?"

"A cowboy who worked for Hunter. We're on our way out to Ray Hammond's place. We'll fill you in later."

"Someone said you've arrested the old Indian again."

Claude was impatient to get under way, pulling out his car keys. "He was seen on Hunter's property just before dark, and we've found some other evidence. That's all I've got time to tell you now. I'll call your room tonight."

They left Thompson standing on the sidewalk mopping his brow with a rumpled handkerchief.

Ray Hammond's mansion dwarfed Cale Hunter's home by a great many rooms, and a second floor. Again they found a swimming pool and tennis court surrounded by a man-made oasis, tall palm trees and all manner of shrubbery, enclosed by a six-foot wrought-iron fence in the middle of a brush-choked desert. Hammond's house was older, Victorian, with a steeply slanted roof.

"Now, here's some serious money," Claude said, stopping the car at a tile walkway leading to the front door.

Carla put away her notes concerning Danny Weaver's arrest record, three charges of assault and battery over a span of seven years, which were all dropped. Carla insisted it showed a strong tendency toward violent behavior. Claude dismissed the notion entirely. Carla didn't know enough about cowboys and whiskey on a Saturday night.

"One thing about Cale Hunter," Carla said as she got out, "I never heard him mention a wife, or children, and we've never seen anyone else around the house while we were there. Why build a big house with a swimming pool or a tennis court if you live alone? I guess he could be divorced, like almost everyone else I know. What if a relative who stands to inherit all or part of Hunter's ranch is trying to keep him from selling it?"

"A relative who'd resort to murder?"

"Stranger things happen. That ranch could be worth a lot, enough to kill for. Someone might believe Hunter would sell it and spend all the money, leaving them with nothing."

Claude stopped, intrigued by Carla's logic, something he'd overlooked entirely. "Damn good thinking, Miss Jenkins," he said as the possibilities ran through his mind. "A disenfranchised son. Or a brother who thinks he'll inherit the land if Cale dies first. We should have asked somebody."

"Why not a daughter or an estranged wife?"

"A woman wouldn't be strong enough to subdue a man or carve him up like that."

"Bullshit. I subdued men who resisted arrest all the time at El Paso PD. A woman who knows how can do it easily."

"Your language, Miss Jenkins."

"My language was entirely appropriate for a sexist remark like that. Typically male chauvinist. I expected more from you."

"Pardon me, Miss Jenkins. For a moment there I almost let myself think of you as a woman. I suppose I should be surprised you didn't add the word 'pig' to the label you've given me."

"If the shoe fits, walk in it. Our killer could be a woman who knows physical restraint techniques. Maybe she was in the military. I've taken down men who were bigger and stronger than you, and they didn't have old rodeo knee injuries. Don't tell me it isn't possible. I've done it."

He chuckled over the rising anger in her voice, and a deeper green color in her eyes. "There's too much of Alfred flowing in your veins, Miss Jenkins."

"It's Ranger Jenkins, Captain Groves, and there is nothing funny about looking for a woman as our suspect."

He nodded, still grinning, stepping onto the expensive tiles that led to the house. "First, we have to find either a man or a woman with a motive, Ranger Jenkins. So far, nobody seems to have one, and that's the reason we're here, to see if Hammond has enough at stake to be willing to commit two murders."

Carla was following him when she stopped abruptly. "The yellow convertible!" she exclaimed.

"What?" Claude halted a few steps from Hammond's door. "Are you talking about the one we saw at Hunter's?"

"Of course. What man, especially a tough-talking cowboy type, would drive a yellow convertible? There's a woman inside that house, and we need to find out who she is."

"You're hell-bent on turning this into an equal-opportunity investigation, aren't you?"

"I'm completely serious."

He started up the walkway again. "Maybe Martha did it. She's capable of murder. She threatened to castrate me while I was asleep some night, to keep me from cheating on her. Contact the Santa Fe police on your computer tonight to see if Martha Groves was at home the night of both killings."

"You're impossible, and you *are* a male chauvinist," Carla muttered behind his back. "A cattleman like Cale Hunter wouldn't ride around in a yellow Mercedes convertible any more than he'd be caught wearing pink tights and a tutu."

◇ ◇ ◇

Ray Hammond sat in a leather-bound swivel chair behind a massive mahogany desk in his study. Bookshelves lined three walls. A dark-skinned housemaid with peculiar wavy red hair who spoke broken English had taken them down a hallway to the rear of the house. Every room they passed was full of expensive furniture and fixtures, gilt-framed oil paintings, china vases, elaborate ceramic lamps. Proof of Hammond's wealth lay everywhere.

Hammond rose from his desk to shake hands. Claude could see that he was still muscular and fit, with a flat stomach and thick shoulders, and guessed that he was close to sixty. Only his hand, the one Claude shook, betrayed him as having been a working man earlier in life. His fingers and palm were roughened by old scars and thick calluses. His hair was gray, thinning on top, and his skin bore the lines of age and sun. He wore a tailored silk shirt and casual tan slacks.

He offered Carla his hand. "I've read a great deal about the turmoil your appointment created, Ranger Jenkins. Congratulations for breaking down an important barrier. There must have been a great many difficult times." His voice was deep, resonant yet soft. He smiled when he spoke to Carla, showing off perfect white teeth that could have belonged to a much younger man.

Carla acknowledged his remarks with a nod and a firm handshake. "Pleased to meet you, Mr. Hammond."

"Please sit down," Hammond said, indicating two

chairs set near his desk. "I've been expecting you. As you must know by now, I'm an interested party to the litigation. I initiated it, in fact. Frankly, these murders are . . . puzzling. They seem, on the surface, contradictory. The first victim, I understand, was a stranger. Sheriff Casey tells me you've been unable to identify him. Billy Choate, on the other hand, had worked for Cale for years. One must conclude Mr. Choate was silenced by whoever is responsible for the first murder, fearing Billy somehow knew his identity. What is lacking is a motive for the first murder. I am certain Cale has told you he believes I'm in some way responsible in order to frighten him away from his proposition with the Nuclear Regulatory Commission. However, despite being preposterous, it does nothing to discourage Robert McCloud, a second party to the NRC's offer, although smaller. The manner in which both victims were killed is also impossible to view logically. Why were they scalped and made to look like they were disemboweled by an Indian war party which no longer exists? Anyone who can make himself believe Post Oak Jim Feathers performed these acts knows nothing about him whatsoever. Mr. Feathers is a meek, timid soul who remains lost in his Indian past. There isn't an aggressive bone in his body, yet by all appearances someone is hoping to convince Sheriff Casey, and perhaps even the two of you, that Feathers is guilty. How am I doing so far?"

"Right on target," Claude replied, surprised to find Ray Hammond was an articulate, well-educated man who had come to almost all of the same conclusions he and Carla had. "Up to this point nothing about this makes much sense. Ranger Jenkins and I felt all along the key would be findin' out who the first victim was, and that should lead us to the reason why he was killed, and then why he was killed on Hunter's property. But due to the advanced state of decomposition, we can't ID the corpse, and no one in this area has been reported missing. A dead end, unless our lab can come up with something else to go on. Besides the strange way he was killed, they found peyote pulp in his stomach. I understand it grows wild in this part of the state, but we can't come up with anything to go with it to make it meaningful."

Hammond smiled, tenting his fingers on his desktop. "You may not know Cale is deeply in debt to several Midland and Odessa banks. He borrowed heavily after crude prices dropped, believing they would rise again when the Arab oil cartel became more unified. We've all grown accustomed to a strong crude oil market, and few oilmen were prepared when it collapsed. Cale was misled by investment bankers and stockbrokers, and he enjoys gambling in Las Vegas. He made expensive mistakes too often, and now he needs to sell some of his land to pay the fiddler, so to speak."

"Does he have a family?" Carla broke in.

"Why, yes. I'm surprised you haven't met his daughter by now."

"We haven't," Claude said, aware of a quick sideways glance Carla gave him. "What can you tell us about her? Sheriff Casey hasn't mentioned her."

"She has . . . she has had a drug problem, so I'm told. Cale is long divorced from her mother, twenty-five years or so. Asa was a beautiful woman and Cale was justifiably proud to have her for a wife, however she apparently couldn't adapt to the isolation of a ranch. It can be terribly lonely without close neighbors. Asa filed for divorce at a time when Cale was riding high in the oil business. She had a good El Paso attorney. As I recall she got almost all his cash and investment portfolio, in order to allow him to keep his ranch intact. Asa moved to Lake Tahoe with their daughter, Rose, where I'm told they lived the good life off the millions Cale provided in their divorce settlement. I heard this from other sources, you understand. Cale never talked about Asa or Rose after the divorce. He was heartbroken. He flew out to Nevada to see Rose a few times. Less often the last few years, until she showed up in Sanderson not long ago. A banker I do business with in Midland told me Rose had gotten into some difficulties with the law involving drugs. Cocaine, I believe it was. She spent some time in prison in California. It must have been very hard on Cale. To complicate matters, Asa died of cancer while Rose was in prison. Asa had spent all the money she got from Cale and died virtually broke, leaving Rose with nothing and no place to live. A bank in Nevada foreclosed on her house in Lake Tahoe. Apparently it was mortgaged to the hilt. Rose doesn't socialize in Sanderson. She's rarely seen in town, except when she's buying gasoline for her car. She leaves for several weeks at a time and then returns. No one seems to know where she goes during these absences. Perhaps this is the reason you haven't been introduced to her. She may be away on one of her . . . trips."

"She drives a yellow Mercedes convertible," Carla said, a statement, not a question.

"She does indeed. If you've seen her car then she must be at home now. Odd that you haven't met her."

Claude leaned forward in his chair to ease a nagging pain in his lower back. "Hunter believes you would go to any lengths to halt this dump from coming to Terrell County. He thinks you're behind these murders, directly or otherwise. There's no argument you're opposed to the dump."

Hammond was clearly amused. "I'm spending a huge amount of money to prevent it. As to the allegation that I'd commit murder to keep it out, there is a great deal of hollow logic behind his charge. Cale needs money desperately. Placing a nameless body on his property would never stop him from selling to the NRC at a time when they are the only interested buyers. Murdering young Mr. Choate is equally mindless, unless the unfortunate man saw me performing the first senseless killing, which, as I said, serves no purpose since it does nothing to alleviate Cale's bank debts or his need to sell. I've known Cale since the day he was born. His father and my father were friends and neighbors.

Our property lines join. He's bullheaded. Finding a dozen dead men on his ranch wouldn't stop him from selling if he could. I intend to stop him in court. I want this region to be safe for my grandchildren. The science behind safe nuclear waste storage is unproven over time, no matter what the NRC's experts say. We don't need the potential risk here and I'll fight them all the way to the Supreme Court if I have to, for the right to say no to a proposition that could poison our water supply, kill our livestock, and quite possibly kill citizens of this county in the future."

Claude found it hard to argue against Hammond's position, as little as he knew about the underground storage of nuclear waste. "I suppose you have a point there."

"Do you have a family, Mr. Hammond?" Carla asked.

Hammond appeared to be expecting the question. "My wife lives on San Pedro Island in the Caribbean. I provide generously for her support, by mutual agreement. We have two sons and a daughter, all married and living in other states. If you are asking whether anyone else lives here, the answer is no, other than Cuza, my housekeeper, and Tomo her brother, who attends to my gardens and routine ranch chores. Feel free to question them if you wish, however they speak very little English. They were born in Central America."

"I don't think that'll be necessary," Claude said, getting up stiffly. "We may have more questions later. Thanks for your time, Mr. Hammond."

◇ ◇ ◇

Claude was pulling away from the house when Carla said, "I think we may have found our missing link. Rose Hunter, a convicted drug addict, who disappears frequently for weeks at a time. She hasn't returned to Sanderson for twenty-five years, and when she does, dead bodies start turning up. Maybe it isn't her . . . a boyfriend who's helping her stop her father from selling off her inheritance.

I've got a feeling we're on the right track now." Carla frowned. "I've never heard that name before for a woman."

"You've never heard of Rose?" Claude asked, pushing the car to fifty miles an hour on the gravel road. "Half the barrooms in Texas have got at least one girl named Rose occupying a stool in 'em."

"I'm talking about Asa. It's the first time I ever heard of a woman by that name. Unusual, to say the least."

# THIRTY-ONE

"HERE'S ANOTHER POSSIBLE CONNECTION," Carla said as Claude sped down Highway 90 toward the Hunter ranch, grimacing every time his car radio crackled with a communication between highway patrol units in neighboring Pecos County where an interstate ran between San Antonio and El Paso, a bonanza for speeding tickets written by DPS officers. "The first victim had peyote in his stomach. Rose Hunter is, or was, a drug addict. Maybe she knew the guy. They chewed peyote together. Cale Hunter may even know who he was and he's trying to protect his daughter."

"You're still stuck on the notion Rose killed the guy, and then she had to kill Chub Choate because he knew she did it. It doesn't explain why she would scalp them and stuff their peckers in their mouths. I read something about penis envy once, where a woman wishes she had one, or something like that. Maybe Rose cut them off because she didn't want *anybody* to have one, since she was born with the wrong plumbing."

"I'm being serious. Hammond told us Rose was in prison in California. California is full of offbeat cults and fruits who call almost anything a religion. Rose could have gotten involved with a drug cult of some sort where they practice human sacrifice and mutilation. It's possible."

"Then you're saying the first killing isn't related to the dump at all, and Chub was killed because he saw something that night."

"I'm not sure. But questioning Rose Hunter will be revealing. You can count on it."

"We can't just come out and ask her if she whacked off some guy's hair and his weenie. She'll clam up and then we'll have to dig for everything ourselves. Be careful what kind of questions you ask. We don't want her to think we suspect her of anything."

"She'll know. If she's been a cocaine user and been to jail for it, she'll be wise to the routine. Felons learn a lot from other inmates while they're in prison, as I'm sure you already know."

"I'm still not ready to buy your theory yet, about it being a woman. When I see her, if she looks strong enough physically, maybe I'll change my mind."

"Some of the best martial arts people are small, Captain. Don't let her size fool you if she doesn't look like Godzilla."

"Women don't need martial arts to cripple a man. Men become totally helpless when they're up against a really short skirt and a few open blouse buttons."

"You're speaking from experience, of course."

He shrugged, applying the brakes as they neared the gate at the entrance to Hunter's property, tires squealing. "Superman turned into a kitten around kryptonite. We all have our weaknesses."

"You truly are a degenerate person. Dad was right about you."

"Then I take it you've decided against allowing me to seduce you some night."

"I didn't say that. I merely made the observation you're an opportunist who preys on inebriated women who show their legs."

"Trashy inebriated women. Don't leave out the trashy part."

◇ ◇ ◇

The yellow Mercedes was parked in the shade of a palm tree. "She's here," Carla said. "I've been wondering if she'd run on us after we came out to look at the body this morning."

Cale Hunter's truck was parked beside Weaver's out at the cow barns. "I'd guess Hunter an' Weaver are still lookin' for Chub's pickup. Maybe the girl's home alone. It'll be better that way, less interference from her father if he's tryin' to protect her." Claude stopped behind the convertible and got out.

A knock at the twin front doors produced nothing, even after he tried several times.

"Let's check the swimming pool," Carla suggested, starting around to the back.

They passed through a heavy metal gate in a stone fence around the pool and gardens. He saw her immediately, a bronze-skinned beauty reclining in a chaise longue, wearing a string bikini that covered only the bare essentials. She had long black hair tied back in a braid. She saw them come in and took off earphones connected to a small tape player.

"Afternoon, ma'am," Claude said. "You must be Rose Hunter."

She looked at the badges on Claude and Carla, and at Carla's gunbelt, before she replied, "I am."

He walked up to her, admiring her sleek oiled body and the longest legs he'd ever seen, muscular calves, firm tanned breasts covered with tiny triangles of light blue cloth. "I'm Texas Ranger Captain Claude Groves, an' this is Ranger Carla Jenkins. We'd like to ask you a few questions."

Rose reached for a drink in an insulated plastic glass

on a small table beside her. "What would you like to know?" she asked in a cool, even voice, her angular face frozen in an unreadable mask.

Claude noticed her nose was slightly elongated, the only feature she had that might detract from her stunning beauty. "I guess we'll begin with what you know about the two murders that took place here."

"I only know what my father told me. They sound terribly gory. I didn't care to look at either one of the bodies."

Claude saw tiny needle marks on the inside of her left forearm, and a dark purple bruise the size of a plum. "Did you know Chub Choate?"

"Not really. I've seen him around the ranch a few times."

"If you didn't look at the first body, then I don't suppose you know who he was."

"Sorry, but I can't help you. I never saw him."

"Someone in town told us you lived in Nevada for a while, and that you spent some time in California recently, until you came to live with your father."

Rose swung her magnificent legs off the chaise to sit up and look at him with eyes the color of a raven's wing. "I assume you are talking about my prison sentence. I served twenty-two months for possession of crack cocaine. It was all a mistake, but my lawyer couldn't prove it. I was keeping it for someone else and I didn't actually know what it was."

"Then you wouldn't know what those needle tracks are doin' on your left arm either," he said, deciding to cut through the bullshit when it was clear she was giving them nothing else.

"Do I need a lawyer before I answer any more questions?" she asked, more proof that she was hardened to police procedure.

"Only if you have reason to believe you need one."

She stood up with her drink in her hand. "Then I

think I'll wait until my father comes back so he can call his attorney. I know my rights, Captain Groves."

He took a second look at her because of her height, standing five feet ten or eleven inches. It was easier to believe now that she might be athletic enough to over-power an unsuspecting man close to her size, or even larger. "Call the lawyer," he said, meeting her somewhat defiant gaze with a steely look of his own. "Arrange a time when we can talk at Sheriff Casey's office, or at the office of Judge Green. We have several more questions. In the meantime, we'll request your criminal record from Califor-nia, and check for anything in Nevada, so be prepared to answer questions concerning your drug use and all of your known acquaintances. We'll want names so we can check their records and current residences. I hope you'll be coop-erative, Miss Hunter. Otherwise we can detain you for ad-ditional questioning, and who knows how long that could take. And it could happen again and again, until we're satisfied with your answers. It might get real inconvenient to have to keep callin' that attorney every day or two. There's a possible trip to Austin in this for you too, to see if you can identify the first body. I understand you enjoy taking long trips fairly often. It's a nice drive between here and Austin. Pretty scenery."

Her eyelids narrowed, poorly disguised anger, and then her knuckles turned white around her plastic cup. "I'll have my father arrange everything," she said, turning away to walk to a glass patio door at the rear of the house.

"Have Mr. Hunter call me as soon as possible," Claude said to her back.

She walked inside without saying a word.

◆ ◆ ◆

"Bingo!" Carla said as he started the car, a look of satisfac-tion on her face. "We hit pay dirt with Rose. We may have just come face to face with our killer."

"Don't be so quick to celebrate," he warned. "All we have so far is a woman with a dope conviction who won't talk to us without having an attorney present. She's been through a trial and a prison system, so she's wary. It doesn't make her guilty of murder. If she is, we'll have to prove it. She's the kind of ice-cold bitch who ain't gonna confess to a parking ticket."

"You didn't seem to have any trouble running your eyes all over her ice-cold bitchy body, Captain. I was afraid you'd step on your tongue. And you were drooling."

"She's pretty. Sexy, I guess you'd call it, half-naked like she was. Men can't help starin' at pretty women who don't cover themselves. But I wasn't drooling."

Carla stopped teasing him to gaze out the windshield. "She almost looks part Asian. Dark skin and black hair, with black eyes. Maybe her mother was Asian and that's where the unusual name comes from. She also had a very prominent nose, but then I don't suppose you noticed that, since you were so busy looking at her other parts."

"We'll push her for answers as hard as we can. A lot will depend on how good her lawyer is, and I'm bettin' he'll be good if he represents Hunter." He glanced out his car window. "It would help if somebody could find Choate's truck. I've got a hunch it'll tell us more'n the killer intended. I'm hungry as hell. Let's grab a bite to eat in Sanderson. It's after four, so we'll call it supper. I'll buy some beer and I can fill Bill Thompson in on the latest developments while you're requesting Rose Hunter's record from California. Be sure to have headquarters check in Nevada too. I'm bettin' this bitch has got a string of convictions. She's got enough needle marks on her arm to make a sieve."

"Did you notice her bruise?"

"I notice everything, Miss Jenkins. She could have been in a struggle with Choate when she got it, or she could have slammed the refrigerator door on her arm. It doesn't mean much by itself."

"You're right about noticing everything, Captain. I never saw a woman who underwent any closer scrutiny. Was there something about her chest that you thought might give us a break in our case?"

"You can't prove I wasn't looking for fingerprints," he grumbled.

She smiled. "If gawking leaves prints, she's covered with them today."

Claude's hand tightened around the steering wheel and he stabbed the accelerator, determined not to say any more. Carla was much like Alfred in another regard, always trying for the last word. What he needed more than anything else right now was a beer. Several of them.

# THIRTY-TWO

WALTER CASEY KNEW the voice on the other end of the line and the minute he heard it, he reached for the plastic container of Rolaids in his top desk drawer. Nelda Brooks from the *Weekly Terrell County Times* had already called wanting details of Chub Choate's death for the Monday edition. He hadn't told her much, other than that it appeared Chub was killed the same way the other victim died, and he promised to keep her informed as to the activities of the two Texas Rangers. By tomorrow half the newspapers in west Texas would be calling, and a television crew was on its way to interview him for tonight's ten o'clock news in Midland. What had been a simmering kettle was now at full boil.

"Groves and the woman Ranger came. They didn't know about Rose. I'm sure they tried to question her," Hammond said.

"Cale's gonna be hoppin' mad if you told them about her prison time." He pushed four tablets into his mouth and chewed as rapidly as he could. His belly was already on fire.

"They would have found out anyway. Captain Groves

is an anomaly of sorts. He doesn't say much or ask probing questions the way I expected."

Walter wasn't sure what an anomaly was. "He's sure Feathers didn't do it, but we had to lock him up because of the moccasins. He admitted they were his, and there's blood on 'em."

"Someone is going to great lengths to make it appear he's a murderer, when all logic is against it. The net result, however, is working in our favor. Because of the way both men were killed it draws a great deal of attention to our pending litigation and the dump issue. It will not harm our cause if people believe the killings are someone's effort to stop the site from coming here. You'll be asked by reporters if the two are related, in your opinion. You don't have to stick your neck out, but some of us will be grateful if you continue to suggest such a possibility."

"I can do that. Even Cale believes it, and he'll say it if they interview him."

"I'm quite sure they will. He'll be helping us without realizing it if he connects the murders to the proposed dump. People are like sheep. They frighten easily. More of them should sign our petition now. It helps, in a tragic way, that Chub was a local man everyone knew. It brings the reality of murder much closer to home."

"Cap'n Groves thinks Chub was killed because he knew who killed the first guy."

"It requires no superior intellect to come to that conclusion sign, and the killer left his signature so everyone would know both acts were committed by the same individual."

"Tomorrow's gonna be a long day. This town will be full of reporters an' this goddamn phone's gonna ring off the hook. An' Cale will come stormin' in the minute he finds out those Rangers questioned his daughter, wantin' to know who told 'em about her."

"It promises to be interesting. Let me know if Rose was questioned, and what Captain Groves has to say about her. I've been told he's very thorough. He'll check her record in California, and if that could somehow be leaked to the press, Cale will suffer tremendous embarrassment. Fewer citizens of this county will be inclined to side with him if they learn he has a daughter with drug problems. Voters have little sympathy for a man in any way associated with narcotics. This is a very conservative area. People here will condemn him because of his daughter."

"I ain't so sure of that. Cale's got a lot of friends an' plenty of folks want those jobs Thompson promised."

"Time will tell, Walter. Please keep me informed."

"I was just wonderin'. Who do you think actually done the killin'?"

"I have no idea, but whoever he is, he's doing some of us a service. I can't imagine anything that would draw more attention to our efforts to halt the government from poisoning Terrell County land."

# THIRTY-THREE

CLAUDE STEPPED OUT of the narrow shower stall wrapped in a towel, feeling better after another chicken-fried steak and a slice of apple pie, a shower, and three icy bottles of beer. Carla was in the adjoining room requesting a criminal record report from the state of California for Rose Dawn Hunter, her full name obtained from county courthouse records on their way through town to the City Café. There had been an interesting notation on her birth certificate. In a space where the form called for the race of her mother, a term no longer used on birth certificates to identify nationality, "unknown" had been hand-written in the blank. Asa Hunter's maiden name was listed as "Lone." Carla kept talking about how odd both names were all the way through dinner. "What kind of name is Asa Lone?" she asked over and over again. "Have you ever known anybody with a last name Lone?"

He'd said he hadn't. A number of times.

He walked to the window and peered out at dusky skies over Sanderson before getting dressed. All day he'd been thinking about calling Alfred to tell him about the second murder, to get his thoughts as well as to reassure him Carla was handling the case like a seasoned veteran. Knowing Alfred, he was probably wringing his hands, worrying about her. But the call to Alfred would have to wait until Carla went to bed, knowing how she would feel about it.

He had opened another beer and was sitting down to drink it, when a knock on the connecting door to Carla's room halted him. "I'm not dressed yet," he said. "Give me a minute."

"Neither am I. Cover up and open the door. I've found something very important in Sacramento."

He adjusted the towel around his waist so nothing showed and opened the door. His gaze immediately fell to a towel wrapped around her damp body and another around her hair, twisted in the manner of a turban.

"This looks like a Turkish bath," he said as she walked in carrying a yellow notepad filled with scribbling.

Carla perched on the end of his bed, showing more leg than he wished she had, though her full attention was on her notes.

"Rose served twenty-two months just like she said, in a minimum security facility at Glendale. But it was her *second* conviction. When she was nineteen she was remanded to the Nevada State Youth Commission for her escape from a halfway house in Carson City, where she'd been sentenced to a drug rehabilitation program. She was legally an adult when California authorities picked her up in Los Angeles on charges of intent to distribute a controlled substance. They sent her back to Nevada. No report yet from Nevada on what else she may have been charged with there."

"Nothing in any of that makes her a killer," he said, his gaze wandering from Carla's bare legs to her face. "We've got nothing but suspicion and old drug charges. No history of violent behavior."

Carla dropped the pad on her lap, obviously frustrated. "You refuse to believe she's capable of murder because she's a woman."

"I'm not refusing to believe anything, except that you'd better cover yourself or I might be inclined to think wicked thoughts."

Her expression softened, then she smiled. "Are you staring at me the way you stared at Rose?"

"I'm trying not to, although it's difficult when a half-naked woman comes into my room while I'm hidin' behind a skimpy bath towel."

She stood up, holding the top of her towel tucked between her breasts. "Are you thinking wicked thoughts now?" she asked and her voice was changed somewhat, husky.

He took a quick swallow of beer. "I'm afraid I am, Carla, and I know I shouldn't."

She came closer to him. "So am I, only there's a difference. I'm not feeling guilty." She stood on her tiptoes and kissed his lips gently, staring into his face. "I shouldn't have done that, but I'm not sorry. No regrets."

Claude wasn't sure what to do. He wanted to take her in his arms and kiss her, yet something held him back. "I'm not sorry either," he told her. "I've got no luck, you see. I find a woman I desire and I can't do anything about it. I'm stuck like a fat pig under a gate. We'd be putting ourselves in serious jeopardy if anyone found out. It's not only improper professional conduct between law enforcement officers, I'd be betraying the trust of my best friend. It's my bad luck you're Alfred's daughter, and that I'm your field training officer."

"But you do find me . . . desirable?"

"Very. Too damn desirable. It's all I can do to keep from kissing you back."

"Then you *can* be a gentleman. When you really put forth the effort."

"Not very often. Standin' here without taking you in my arms is harder than I thought. Let's not talk about this now. Maybe it's the beer, but I'm in a weak frame of mind."

She dropped her notes on the floor and slowly put her arms around his neck. "So am I. I've decided there isn't anything wrong with a kiss or two. I haven't thought about taking it any farther. It's reassuring to know you can be a gentleman. You've got a very bad reputation."

"Yeah. I probably earned it. This is different because you are different."

"I'm not trashy enough? No miniskirt?"

"You know what I mean, Carla." He put his beer bottle down on a cheap Formica-topped dresser behind him and placed his hands behind her back. "I'm gonna take a big chance here," he said, little more than a whisper. He bent down and kissed her, tightening his embrace, allowing his lips to linger on hers. He felt a small shiver run down her spine and pulled back, wondering if he'd shown too much passion, although she kept her body pressed against his in a way that suggested she took no offense.

"That was nice," she said, smiling. "You can be very gentle too." She continued to keep her arms around his neck while she added, "I suppose we should stop before this goes too far. We agreed we're both in a weak frame of mind."

He let go of her waist reluctantly, dropping his hands to his sides. "No matter what you may think of me or what I just did, I want you to know how I feel. You're a real lady, Carla, not the kind of woman I've had to settle for since my divorce. I'm not sure I know how to act around a lady. Haven't had much experience. I know it's wrong for me to think of you in some sort of old-fashioned romantic way. I'm almost old enough to be your father. I've got nothing to offer a woman like you, but that doesn't stop me from wishin' I was younger, and that I wasn't a close friend of Alfred's."

"Maybe you're being too hard on yourself, and I think you worry too much about what Dad would say."

She took her arms from his neck, grasping the front of her towel again. "I might come to regret allowing you to seduce me, although I don't think so. Since George and I divorced I haven't found a man I was interested in. I hardly ever think about it now, devoting myself to my career, keeping busy with other things. But there is something about you that fascinates me. I'm still not ready to hop in bed with you. Perhaps I never will be. If we both decide it's what we want, no one would ever have to know. I'll keep thinking about it."

"So will I," he whispered, torn between a feeling of deep loyalty to Alfred and desire for his daughter.

# THIRTY-FOUR

AS HE WAS bolstering himself with yet another beer before calling Bill Thompson, his telephone rang. Carla was next door dressing and he'd been thinking about their kiss, their discussion of the possibility they might become lovers, weighing the good against the bad, knowing himself too well to believe he could pass up the chance if she agreed, despite the risks.

"Shit," he muttered. He answered the phone by simply saying "Groves."

"Cap'n, this is Walter Casey. I've got a problem on my hands. Cale Hunter just called me boilin' mad. He said you questioned his daughter, an' that you upset her by askin' all about some trouble she had in California a while back. He said he don't see no reason why you had to dig up all that crap. It don't have nothin' to do with Chub or that other guy who was killed. He said you wanted to ask her a bunch more questions, an' he's madder'n hell about it. He's done called his lawyer over in Midland."

"I don't care if he calls the president. Rose Hunter lives on the property where two bodies were found. We wanted to know if she saw anything, or knew either of the dead men. She told us she had only seen Choate a few times, and never saw the first body. She became uncooperative after that. We've run a criminal records check on her in California, and we're still checking in Nevada. We're going to question her again, whether she is willing to cooperate or not. If I have to, I'll get a search warrant for Hunter's house and detain Rose in your very own jail until she's given us satisfactory answers. If Miss Hunter and her father want to play hardball, I'm ready to play."

"It don't have to come to that, does it? Cale's a good man an' it ain't his fault the girl got in trouble. Her mother was the one who raised her wrong. His ex-wife hardly ever let him see his daughter. He'd just as soon not have everybody in Sanderson knowin' about that trouble Rose got in, now she's back livin' with him. He's been tryin' real hard to straighten her out. It'll look bad if you bring her in for questionin'. Folks will be askin' why."

"It's my job, Sheriff. She said she wouldn't talk to us without a lawyer being present, after we asked her a few questions this afternoon. If that's the way she wants it, we'll do it her way. You can call Hunter back and tell him exactly what I said. She cooperates fully, or we bring her in and hold her for questioning behind bars. We can hold her on suspicion of aiding and abetting, suspicion of drug possession or any number of things. If Hunter wants to keep his daughter's past a secret from the citizens of Sanderson, he's goin' about it the wrong way. If she's done nothing wrong she's got nothing to fear from answering our questions."

"I'd sorta hoped you'd understand, Cap'n. This is a small town where a reputation can get ruined real easy."

"We're not out to ruin her reputation. We intend to find out who killed two men on Hunter's property. For all we know our John Doe could have been a friend of hers from out of state."

"You don't think she's . . . involved, do you?"

"We won't know until she talks to us."

"Hell, she's just a girl who made a mistake. I wish you'd go easy on Rose. I'll call Cale an' tell him what you said, only he ain't gonna like it."

"You can tell him I don't care if he likes it or not. He's got forty-eight hours to arrange for a meeting, with or without a lawyer. If we haven't heard from him by then, we'll bring her in." Claude hung up before Casey could reply.

"Hunter blew his lid because we questioned Rose," he told Carla later.

Carla sat in a chair next to the bed wearing a pair of tight blue jean cutoffs and a T-shirt, brushing her damp hair while she listened to Claude's story of the phone call. "We hit a nerve. Hunter is worried we'll uncover a connection between Rose and our John Doe."

"He could have been an old boyfriend, or a previous associate in the drug business in California. It might explain why nobody's been reported missing around here."

"It's all beginning to fall together, a believable scenario with Rose in the middle. I knew it the minute Hammond told us about her."

"You're jumping to conclusions too soon. Prior drug convictions don't make Rose a murderer."

"A prime suspect, then."

"Maybe. Two things are still dangling. No one has found Choate's truck, and we still haven't talked to McCloud, the would-be movie star. Don't forget he has a stake in this."

"Left field, as Dad used to say." She looked down at her tennis shoes. "I wish I hadn't said that. No clear motive is what I mean. McCloud is desperate to sell to the NRC. Why would he do anything that might throw a monkey wrench into the deal?"

"He probably wouldn't. But we don't *know* he

wouldn't. He's next on our list tomorrow morning—" The phone rang again. He made a face and picked it up, expecting to hear Bill Thompson's thin voice. "Groves," he said into the mouthpiece.

"Claude? This is Tom Elliot."

"Yes, Major." Carla stiffened in her chair.

"I got the report on a second murder. Scalped and cut all to hell just like the first one. What the fuck is goin' on out there?"

"We don't know yet. We believe the second victim was most likely a witness to the first killing. Our murderer silenced him before he could talk. It's only a guess so far."

"Got a suspect?"

"Nothing solid. A few leads."

"Jesus fuckin' Christ! The DPS public information officer has been gettin' calls all afternoon from every goddamn television station an' newspaper in the state, wantin' to know if this is a new serial killer runnin' loose across Texas. Some shithead at the crime lab, one of Wally Baker's assistants, gave a copy of one of the morgue shots of the first victim to the *Austin Statesman*. I had the son of a bitch fired. It'll be on the fuckin' front page of tomorrow's edition. Is Carla Jenkins sittin' right there?"

"No," he lied, crossing his fingers, "she's in her room down the hall." He glanced at Carla, watching her complexion pale.

"Find some way to get her out of there, before the media finds out she's on this case. They'll have a field day when they learn we've got our token woman handling something like this, not to mention the number of Ranger veterans in Company E who'll damn sure complain they didn't get a case in their jurisdiction. I let you pick the one you wanted, Claude, hoping you'd choose some routine investigation so the goddamn newshounds would forget about her for a while. I'm tired of readin' about her every time I pick up a newspaper."

"She's doing an excellent job, Major. Very professional, and she found an important lead I'd overlooked. I'd like to keep her on the case. She knows what she's doing."

A pause. "I've got a feelin' you're saying that because Alfred was your partner. You'd protect her if you could."

"That isn't true. I'm askin' you to give her a chance. You won't be disappointed, and if we find this killer like I'm sure we will, it'll look good, like you made the right choice when you selected her in the first place."

Another pause, longer. "All right, Claude. I can't think of another man I've got who I'd let talk me into this. It's the goddamn reporters. I hate reporters. I want you to keep me posted on a regular basis. Find this crazy son of a bitch an' do it as quickly as you can. Too goddamn many people will be watchin' every move both of you make."

"Thanks, Major. I'll keep you informed."

When he put down the phone he saw tears in Carla's eyes.

"He wanted me taken off the case. Did he give you a reason?" she asked.

"He's worried about the press, what they'll say about having a woman investigating something like this. He's letting you stay on with me, so stop crying."

"I'm NOT *crying!*" she snapped, jumping out of her chair with her face turned away, slamming the door of her room behind her as she left. He heard the dead bolt slide into place.

"Two more calls to make," he mumbled, reaching for his beer and then the telephone. It wouldn't take long to bring Thompson up to date, but calling Alfred, if Claude told him the whole story including the call from Major Elliot, would take time and a delicate hand. Alfred would be wounded by the major's request. He wondered if he should mention it at all.

◇ ◇ ◇

Claude turned off his bedside lamp at ten-thirty, after he told Bill Thompson about the latest developments. He'd tried to call Alfred several times, but kept getting a busy signal and gave up shortly after ten.

"It's probably Miz' Wilkerson calling to complain about Spot killin' more chickens," he said to himself sleepily, yawning, balling his pillow underneath his head before drifting off to sleep, beginning a dream about Rita and her huge breasts because it was safer to dream about his new neighbor than to allow himself to imagine what Carla would be like in bed. He shouldn't have returned her kiss this evening. No matter how they both might justify it, becoming involved with each other would be like tap-dancing across a minefield.

# THIRTY-FIVE

THE PHONE JOLTED him awake when it seemed he'd barely closed his eyes. He reached for it in the dark, fumbling, putting the wrong end to his ear on the first try. "Groves."

"It's me, Claudie. Carla Sue called. She told me what you did when Tom phoned you. Just wanted to say thanks for stickin' by her."

"I tried to call you but your line was busy forever."

"We had a good talk. She actually told me about the case, the second victim, the rancher's daughter with a record, how the old Indian is bein' set up to take the fall. I couldn't believe my ears when she discussed it with me. She sounded upset right at first, but then she told me what you said to Tom. You're a good friend to both of us, Claudie. I owe you."

Claude winced, wondering what Alfred would feel he owed him if he knew what had happened earlier this evening with Carla. A .45-caliber armor-piercing slug through Claude's black heart? "I did the best I could, Alfred. Carla's doin' a helluva fine job. She has a lot of your instincts for reading people and she's real careful not to overlook little things. She matched a couple of boot prints that turned one of our possible suspects into a liar. He's the guy who got killed. He was probably a witness to the first murder and the killer silenced him. It's a mess. The local sheriff is a hick with too many political ties on both sides of the nuclear dump issue, caught in the middle, tryin' to appease everybody. There's no clear suspect with a motive yet, and everything hinges on findin' out who the first victim was, which we haven't been able to do."

"I asked Carla if I could come down there to help. She said no, even after I promised to stay out of the way entirely. But I was glad she called. We really talked. It's been a long time since we did."

"I'm glad too. She feels she has something to prove and she wants to do it by herself. Be patient with her and don't take it personally."

"If she helps you break this case it'll really help her with Tom an' the others, the old-timers who didn't resign when she was appointed. I'd like to see her rub it in their faces, includin' Tom's. Tell me one thing—who stands to gain the most if the dump comes to Sanderson?"

"A rancher by the name of Cale Hunter, the father of the girl with the drug record in California. He's sellin' the most land to the NRC, and he's in debt to several banks. He needs to make this land deal."

"Always remember to follow the money, Claudie, when it looks like you're lost. Look for a paper trail. Go over every official record in the county with his name on it. Look real close to see if anybody else wins if Hunter loses."

"Loses what?"

"The money. Haven't you been listenin'? See if a neighbor stands to win if for some reason or other the NRC decides to move the dump in another direction."

"One of his neighbors is the power behind the effort to stop it from comin' to Terrell County at all. A rich bastard. We haven't had a chance to talk to the other neighbor yet, a rich man's son who wants to be a movie star. But the guy from the NRC has already told me there's some kind of rock under Hunter's land that doesn't reach far enough across this guy McCloud's. As it stands now, Hunter is the only one who's willin' to sell who has the right kind of rock. I don't understand most of the scientific bullshit."

"Keep followin' the money. Carla thinks the girl is involved, that she could be the killer."

"It's possible, I suppose. We don't have enough on her yet to start tightening any screws. Tom's nervous. He wants this put to bed in a hurry."

"Tom's a good commander. He's been under a lot of pressure from the governor lately. There've been some fuck-ups, as you know, makin' the Rangers look bad. I figure Tom's gonna retire pretty soon. He told me his ulcers are killin' him."

"We're working as fast as we can. Seems there are too many angles, and the weird way both victims were killed makes this even harder to figure. When's the last time you looked for a murderer who scalps his victims, in addition to all the other meat carving he does?"

"He, or she, is putting their name on it. Follow that angle as far as you can. That's what I told Carla Sue. Find out if that old Indian can explain it. He isn't your killer, but he may suspect who the killer is or why someone wants it to look like he did it. Get some sleep. I'll call you in a day or so. I've got an old friend in Midland from when I commanded Company E. He may know a thing or two about Hunter an' what's goin' on down there."

"G'night, Alfred. I'll call you."

◇ ◇ ◇

"I called Dad last night," Carla said as he was pinning his badge on a clean white shirt. She hadn't mentioned crying or her door-slamming episode since coming into his room this morning.

"I know. He called to tell me. You made him real happy by discussing the case with him."

"He gave me an idea, so I made another call this morning. I called Ray Hammond, apologizing for the early hour. It's been bothering me ever since we saw Rose's birth certificate, the name of her mother. Hammond has been a source for some of our dirt, so I asked him if he had known Asa, or where she came from, and her nationality because the name Lone is so unusual. He said Hunter met her in Oklahoma years ago while he was there making a deal to sell his crude to Sun Oil Company. Hammond said hardly anyone in Sanderson knew her, and he didn't know much about her, either. She stayed at the ranch and rarely went to town. Hammond said she was beautiful, with a dark complexion and black hair just like her daughter, but their marriage only lasted three years. Hammond's wife went over to meet her one time and Asa wouldn't invite her in. When I told Hammond her maiden name was Lone, and spelled it for him, he sounded very surprised. He hadn't ever heard it before. It's an unusual name."

"You're hung up on the wrong name, Carla. Rose is the one we should be checking on thoroughly, her friends in California, anyone who might have been arrested with her. One of them could be our John Doe. Then we'd have enough to make an arrest, something to take to a grand jury."

"Headquarters still doesn't have a report back from Nevada on Rose. They could radio us when they did, only the guy I talked to said you never turned on your radio, even after several reprimands, so he'll leave a message at the hotel desk."

"I did *not* get several reprimands. Just two. I hate the damn thing, all the noise it makes. I'd rather listen to an old Hank Williams tune if I have to listen to something."

"Hank can't help us solve two murders."

"Neither can a damn two-way car radio. You solve murders by questioning people and looking for evidence.

Which reminds me, I've got to check with Casey to see if they found Choate's pickup. It can't just vanish into thin air."

"If they haven't found it, it's because the killer hid it, or got rid of it someplace."

"Findin' the actual murder scene could be just as important. Footprints, or hoofprints like the ones at Hunter's cattle pens."

"Hunter isn't going to cooperate now, because of Rose."

"Screw him. We'll look anyway."

Claude walked to the door, placing his straw Stetson on his head at just the right angle, the brim low in front.

"I'm sorry about last night," Carla said. "I lost my temper when I heard what Major Elliot wanted you to do."

"Forget it. It was the end of a really long day."

◇  ◇  ◇

Sheriff Casey stood before several reporters on the front steps of his office, using his hands now and then to punctuate some remark. A video camera was aimed at him while a woman in navy slacks and sport coat held a microphone. A van parked at the curb bore a sign saying KXEL El Paso News.

"The shit's really in the fan now," Claude muttered, cutting down and across Main Street to the City Café in hopes of avoiding reporters. "Major Elliot said a morgue photo of our John Doe will be in today's Austin paper. Some guy working at the crime lab tryin' to make a few bucks. Elliot had him fired." He parked at the curb and took a deep breath. "Now all the quack theories by journalists will come out, that this is another Son of Sam or Jack the Ripper hysteria. This is what Ray Hammond wants, like Thompson said, to keep Terrell County voters scared if this is linked to the dump. Maybe we need to look a little closer at Hammond."

"You still don't think much of my theory about Rose, do you? And your theory about Hammond falls apart because he'd have used hired killers, and nobody we've talked to has seen any strangers, not Hunter or Danny or anybody else—other than our John Doe, that is, and I hardly think Hammond would hire both a killer and a victim. More pertinent is the undeniable fact that our killer had to know Jim Feathers, his habits, about the moccasins, times when Feathers was at the Hunter ranch. And he had to know the lay of the land at the ranch to find that cave. We could ask Feathers if any strangers have come to his house recently, asking about his Indian heritage, perhaps getting a look at his grandfather's memorabilia. I still say that's way out in left field. Rose Hunter is a much stronger suspect in my book."

"Let's eat some breakfast and talk to McCloud, the last of the principals involved in the money trail. Then we'll talk to Feathers again. And we've got to find out where Chub's Toyota is."

◇  ◇  ◇

The McCloud ranch was similar to Hunter's, a house built of native stone, a swimming pool but no tennis court, all nestled inside a circle of towering palm trees shading the house and lawns. There was another difference. The place showed signs of neglect: wilting hedgerows drooping in blast-furnace heat without regular watering, a red tile roof with a few clay tiles broken or missing. A silver Lincoln Town Car sat in front of a more modest three-car garage. An older model Chevrolet pickup was parked several hundred yards northeast of the house where cattle feed yards stood empty, next to a few saddle horses in one corral beside a low-roofed hay barn. A pair of dogs barked at their car from a fenced enclosure behind the house, and Claude noticed several rows of cages, like chicken coops, close to the dog pen.

"McCloud raises falcons," he said as they drove up in a cloud of yellow dust after following a mile-long gravel road leading from the highway.

"None of his oil wells were pumping," Carla observed. "Not a single one we passed on the way in. It looks like McCloud needs money more desperately than Hunter, if you can judge by the outward appearance of things here."

Claude looked at his watch. "It's almost nine. Let's wake him up if he ain't up already."

Several rings of a doorbell were required to bring someone to the front door. A bleached-blond woman wearing hoop earrings, a tank top, and shorts took a careful peek outside before she spoke. "You're the law. I've been real careful about opening this door since that Indian went crazy again. Bob told me he's back in jail, but I'm still being careful. Some folks don't think it was him."

"Is Mr. McCloud available?" Claude asked, smelling liquor on the young woman's breath.

"He drove over to Alpine last night. He told me to keep the doors locked and not let anybody in. It's just me and the maid, Consuelo."

Claude glanced at her left hand. "Are you his wife?"

She chuckled. "A friend. Bob isn't the marrying kind. I'm an actress. I'm from New York originally. I've been giving Bob acting lessons this summer."

Claude could easily imagine what type of acting she did, in videos where bare bodies, a generous bosom, and groaning were at the top of the talent requirements. "We were told Mr. McCloud has aspirations to become a movie star. When will he be back?"

"He didn't say. Probably tonight. It was some sort of meeting."

"Did he say what kind of meeting it was?" Carla asked.

She shook her head. "I didn't ask. Didn't give a shit, if you'll pardon the way I put it. He hasn't been paying hardly any attention to me lately and I'm sick of our . . . arrangement, if you know what I mean. I know he's seeing another woman. I hate this part of Texas, too. This has got to be the ugliest, hottest place on earth. He broke a bunch of promises he made, to buy me new clothes and some nice jewelry in exchange for acting lessons. He lied to me. He didn't tell me he was almost broke. He can't sell any of his stinking oil. He says the price is too low."

"Just tell him when he gets back that the Texas Rangers would like to talk to him," Claude said. "We're staying at the Flagship Motel. Just a few questions."

"About those murders? He doesn't know anything. He said the crazy Indian probably didn't do them because he's too old. He's been worried it'll screw up a chance he's got to sell part of this ugly ranch. I don't understand all of it and truthfully I just want out of here, as soon as he gives me some traveling money. There's nothing to do around here besides drink."

"Do you mind if we look around for a minute?" Carla asked, puzzling Claude with her intent gaze.

"Help yourself. Look all you want. I'm sick of looking at this place."

◇ ◇ ◇

"Those are peregrine falcons," Claude said, pointing to a dozen or more birds in the rows of cages. "You can tell by the spots on their chests."

"His taste in birds is considerably better than his taste in women," Carla remarked, leading him past the cages to the barn and corrals. "Now, that's what I would call a trashy woman."

"Just my type," Claude told her. "I'll say it before you do. Why are we going to the barn?"

"McCloud has three horses but no cows. I wanted to

see if they are wearing horseshoes. Whoever delivered Choate's body to the Hunter ranch was riding a shod horse. It'll seem odd if he keeps shod horses when he doesn't appear to need them."

"I don't think a hoofprint with a shoe proves anything. I'd bet every cow horse in the county wears iron."

"A computer can often make a match out of tiny scratches or the slightest differences in a print."

"You took castings of the horse tracks at Hunter's?"

"Of course I did. They could turn out to be critical bits of evidence."

They came to a pipe corral where the horses stood, a bay and a sorrel and a gray. A tin hay barn sat beside the fence, with a combination lock holding its sagging doors closed.

"Two of them are shod, Captain. I'll go get the car and drive down so I can make molds of both horses' hooves, front and rear."

"Very thorough," he admitted, "but probably a big waste of time."

She ignored him, striding off toward the Ford. He wondered what sort of meeting Bob McCloud attended last night. Claude couldn't remember a case where there were so many loose ends.

# THIRTY-SIX

SHERIFF CASEY WAS in a foul mood. Deputy Huffman was on the phone at a smaller desk explaining to a reporter that the Terrell County Sheriff's Department would issue a written statement before noon. An ancient manual typewriter sat before Huffman with a piece of blank paper in it—the unfinished statement, Claude supposed.

Casey glowered at them, a half-empty plastic container of Rolaids near his elbow. "I knew it was gonna be like this," he said, "only it's worse than the last time. Some guy from the Dallas Morning News keeps callin' back every fifteen minutes. He wanted to know how come we don't have a fax machine. There's a picture of the first guy we found on the front page of the Austin paper. Two television stations from Austin are sendin' film crews out here. They want permission to take film of Chub's body. I can't let 'em do that to Carmen. She keeps askin' me what she's gonna do, how she's gonna feed them kids or pay the doctor bills. What the hell am I supposed to tell her?"

"She'll be eligible for Medicaid and other programs," Carla said. "I'll call a regional caseworker with the Welfare

Department. In the meantime, we'd like to talk to Mr. Feathers again."

Casey tossed a key on his desktop. "Help yourself." Now he looked at Claude. "By the way, Cap'n, Cale's calmed down a bit, only he still wants his lawyer there when you question Rose. He ain't as mad as he was, but he's still agitated. He did ask me if you'd try an' keep things quiet. He'll call you to arrange a meetin' out at the ranch when his lawyer can be there."

Claude took the key, glancing at Huffman. "Has anybody found Choate's truck?"

Casey wagged his head. "Nope. No tracks either. It just ain't there. Cale said to search Hammond's place. He's bettin' that's where it'll be."

"And what do you think, Sheriff?"

"Ray didn't do it. I called the border patrol office in El Paso. They say they never heard of nothin' like this. The area commander laughed when I told him we'd had two men scalped. He didn't believe me right off. But he did say there could be all sorts of crazies over in them mountains south of us. He said he'd talk to the *comandante* of a Mexican army post over in Ciudad Acuna to see if they've heard anything."

Carla took the key from Claude as if she'd heard enough of Casey's Mexican cult theories, entering the hallway leading to Feathers's cell.

"We'll talk to Feathers and then drive out to Hammond's," Claude told him. "We tried to question McCloud this morning. A young woman with booze on her breath told us McCloud drove over to Alpine for a meeting last night. Got any idea what kind of meeting that would be?"

Casey reached for his Rolaids. "Bob ain't nothin' like his ol' daddy. Robert was a good feller, an honest rancher. Made a lot of money durin' the oil boom. But that boy ain't much. He's a playboy. Thinks he's gonna be a movie star, only he ain't been one yet as far as I know. It don't surprise me none the girl was drunk so early. Her name's Sherry somethin' or other, an' the only time anybody in Sanderson sees her is when she's at the liquor store next to Joe's Drive-in. Usually drunk, of course. She ran over Miz' Darnell's best sow a while back. Claimed she couldn't see it, somethin' as big as a pig. Tore hell outta that front bumper on Bob's Lincoln, only there wasn't much I could do. The pig got out an' wasn't supposed to be on the highway. Bob paid her a fair price for the sow. . . ."

Claude walked away from the desk before Casey was finished with his pig story, since he clearly had nothing to add to their knowledge of Bob McCloud.

Carla was sitting in the cell with Feathers, saying, "We'll feed Sata again today. I want to ask you one very important question, Mr. Feathers. Think back carefully. Has anyone come to your house to talk about Indian lore recently, anyone you might have shown your grandfather's moccasins to? It might not have been someone you knew very well, or it could even have been a total stranger."

Feathers kept his eyes glued to the floor as though he was in some sort of trance. A moment later he spoke softly without looking up. "There was the girl. She asked me what it was like to be the only Indian in Sanderson, and what tribe I came from."

"What girl?" Carla asked too quickly, revealing too much sudden interest, in Claude's opinion.

"Mr. Hunter's daughter. Her name is Rose. She asked me many questions. She told me her mother was part Indian. We talked for a very long time and I showed her my grandfather's war shirt and moccasins, the eagle claw neck-lace, and the medicine bundle he gave me. She was very nice, and very pretty. She told me she would visit me again. She has lived in another place for a very long time. I do not remember where."

Carla turned a satisfied look toward Claude before she spoke to Feathers again. "What kind of questions did she ask?"

The old man appeared to be thinking. "We talked about the Four Spirits. Other things I do not remember."

"Her mother's maiden name was Asa Lone. That's an Indian name, isn't it?"

For the first time, Feathers looked at Carla. "Asa is the Comanche word for 'star.'"

"So her mother was at least part Comanche."

"She did not tell me. My grandfather spoke some Comanche. I do not remember but a few words he taught me. That was many *taums* in the past, when I was a boy."

"Please try to remember anything else she asked you, or what she talked about," Carla persisted, eager now, knowing she was onto something important.

The Indian's eyelids fluttered briefly. Claude was sure it was a sign Feathers recalled something he wasn't sure he should say because of his loyalty to Cale Hunter.

Finally the old man spoke again. "She asked if my people practiced the peyote ceremony in the old days."

"And what did you tell her?"

"That I do not know these things. My grandfather never talked to me about them. I was too small to understand the power of visions given by the sacred plant."

"Did she ask you if you could find some for her? This may be very important, Mr. Feathers."

There was suspicion on his weathered face now. "Why is this important?"

"Because the man you found in the cave had peyote in his stomach."

Feathers looked up at his cell window. "I do not remember if she asked this question," he said. "I am an old man. Many times, my memory is not good. I will say no more about the girl or what we talked about. Mr. Hunter is my friend. Send me to this place for crazy people, or to prison. Very soon I will begin my walk to the Land of Shadows and nothing in a white man's world will matter to me."

❖ ❖ ❖

As Carla returned the cell key, Sheriff Casey stood near a
front window watching another television crew arrive with
KTRC Big 4 News lettered on its side. "Just what I need,"
he muttered, wearing a sour look, "another goddamn
bunch of reporters wantin' to know if we've got Indians on
the warpath in Terrell County. When I showed 'em Post
Oak last night, they acted real disappointed. They don't
believe me when I tell 'em he's the only Indian we got."
He noticed Claude and Carla. "Did he tell you anything he
ain't told you before?"

Claude answered quickly, "Not much, really. He
doesn't want to discuss it, says he's ready to die and nobody'll believe him anyway."

Casey nodded like he understood. "Who the hell's
gonna believe all that Apache ghost crap? He's already told
his lawyer enough to get him sent to the loony bin. Told
me the same damn thing when I found that scalp. He's
headed for the fruit farm, unless you can find us an Indian
ghost wanderin' around someplace."

"We'll check back with you later, Sheriff," Claude
said as he ushered Carla to the door, hoping to avoid two
newsmen getting out of the van. "Tell Mr. Hunter we'll be
in touch with him."

❖ ❖ ❖

"Get me to a telephone," Carla said as they drove away
from the sheriff's office. "Let's go to the motel so I can
hook up my computer modem. At last we've got what
we've been looking for, a tie between Rose Hunter and
Indian ceremonies involving peyote."

"It's startin' to look like you could be right about
Rose," Claude said. "Too much smoke for there not to be
any fire. She may not have killed either one of the victims,
but it's beginning to look like she knows a helluva lot more

than I thought she did. Nice work, Ranger Jenkins. You bought the information we needed with cans of dog food. Why do you need to hook that toy to a telephone? We've got enough to confront Hunter and his daughter the way things are."

"My 'toy,' as you call it, will give me access to our main computer banks to find out about Asa's background, to verify her Comanche bloodlines. Then I'll contact a good anthropologist who can tell us if they used peyote in any sort of ceremony or ritual killing like the one Post Oak Jim mentioned. We might get enough on Rose to get an indictment from the district attorney."

"All circumstantial, but take a shot at it. While you're punching buttons I'll drive out to Hammond's, just in case we're following a false trail, and see if Hunter's right about Choate's truck bein' on Hammond's land. I'll bring back some burgers from the Dairy Freeze."

"Leave me a shipping container so I can send the hoofprint molds to the lab. I'll walk them down to the bus station if you don't get back in time."

"If you're so damn sure Rose Hunter did it, why bother with the hoofprints from McCloud's horses?"

"It's so obvious I can't believe a man with your background missed it. McCloud is clearly attracted to sleazy women, something the two of you have in common. He and Rose may have been in on this together. Rose Hunter is as sleazy as they come. I'm merely checking every angle."

He turned into the Flagship parking lot. "I should resent that remark about my background."

"Your record speaks for itself, Captain Groves. As Romeo of the rodeo set, you're an expert on women with low morals. I have it on good authority."

# THIRTY-SEVEN

Ray Hammond didn't sound pleased when his maid summoned him to the front door. "Can't you understand searching my property is a waste of time, Captain Groves? If I killed Mr. Choate, I most certainly would not leave his truck parked anywhere on my ranch."

"It hasn't turned up and I intend to cover every inch of this country until I find it, or convince myself it isn't here. It could contain some important clues to the killer's identity and possibly some fingerprints. I'm askin' your permission to drive around or I'll have to get a search warrant."

"By all means look, then. You won't find anything. I own more than three hundred thousand acres. It could take considerable time."

"I have binoculars. I'll be looking near the river, mostly, and close to Hunter's property. If Choate drove down there, or if his truck was driven by someone else, he probably used one of the oil well service truck roads."

"You'll need a master key to a few gates. I'll get it for you."

◇ ◇ ◇

Spiny ocotillo stalks bearing tiny golden leaves and bristling thorns grew in clusters across a flat leading to the Rio Grande. Thicker stands of creosote were bunched in other spots, intermingled with cactus beds, cholla plants, and occasional yucca. Claude stood in front of the car, passing his binoculars along the riverbank, pausing near a rare cottonwood tree or a drooping willow at the water's edge. Across a barbed-wire fence to his left was Hunter land, not far from the place where Jim Feathers had led them to his medicine bundle and the bloody moccasins. They'd found Choate naked just like the first victim. "The killer probably tossed his clothes in the river," Claude muttered, the sound of his voice a pleasant diversion from the constant cries of the desert cicadas, a locust that somehow survived in this region no matter how dry summers were. Their eerie noises could grate on a man's nerves, a never-ending chorus of insect screams from dawn until dusk.

He'd driven bumpy ranch roads for more than two hours and found nothing other than grazing herds of Mohair goats between windmills and water troughs often a mile apart.

*How can a pickup truck just disappear?* he thought. Unless someone drove it away from the murder scene. Hammond had been right, of course, to assure Claude that if he had killed Choate he wouldn't have left the truck anywhere on his property to incriminate himself. But the killer, especially if it turned out to be Rose Hunter, could have put Choate's truck on Hammond's ranch to remove it from the actual murder scene and throw suspicion on Hammond. Despite everything Carla was finding out about Rose, he couldn't quite make himself believe she was the murderer, at least not acting alone. It wasn't enough that her mother may have been part Indian, or that Rose had questioned Jim Feathers about peyote and knew about the moccasins, although it did tend to point to her involve-

ment. An important piece was missing, he felt, but he had
no idea what it was at the moment.

Claude lowered his field glasses. "It just ain't here,"
he said, as though he spoke to the shrieking locusts around
him. Before giving up he would search the abandoned road
between Hunter and Hammond, even though they'd
driven it before with Feathers when they were shown his
moccasins and the knife.

Alfred would know where to look, he told himself,
getting back in the car. Alfred had a feel for this sort of
thing.

◇ ◇ ◇

He stood on the bloodstained ledge where they'd found
the murder weapon and moccasins, noticing crude etchings
in the rocks below, drawings of men on horses, a rising
sun, symbols Claude didn't recognize, a pictorial history of
Post Oak Jim's people. He imagined what the old man
must have looked like sitting on this bluff, praying to his
spirit gods, a rather sad image of a lonely man lost in another time, living a solitary existence in his tumbledown
shack with a dog as his only companion.

*Not all that different from the way Alfred lives now,* he
thought, *and a likely fate for Claude Groves unless something
changes drastically.* "I don't even have a dog," he said, again
talking to himself, experiencing a rush of loneliness, wishing he could have a few days to visit with his son, a chance
to get to know him.

He turned away from the river feeling empty inside.
The hours spent searching Hammond's property had been
a waste.

On his trek back to the car he avoided the deadly
rattle of a diamondback hidden in some brush near the
footpath. He hoped Carla and her computer were doing
more to solve these murders than he had this morning.
He'd have been just as well off going fishing, although like

Alfred he hated the taste of fish and found trying to catch them too boring.

Another bleak thought crossed his mind as he was driving back toward the highway. This investigation was moving slowly and Major Elliot wanted results. Claude envisioned a stopwatch ticking on the major's desk, or was it a time bomb under Claude's law enforcement career? A remark Alfred made when he called awakened in Claude's memory, something about following a paper trail when all else failed. Courthouse records, he'd said, but what could he hope to find there? He drove past a locked gate into Hammond's property and an oil well pump jack, idle like all the others. Beside this well was a small rusted tin building with a faded sign, Sun Oil Company, above a padlocked door. Probably a tool shed, he thought with his mind on other things.

When he arrived at the house to return Hammond's key he saw a cowboy, his face hidden by the brim of a straw hat, riding a horse into the hallway of a barn. "Probably the maid's brother Hammond told us about," he muttered, unable to recall his name.

◇ ◇ ◇

Her name was Mildred Anderson, and her official title was Terrell County Clerk. She had to be close to seventy, past the usual retirement age, her silver hair worn in a bun. She had asked all the expected questions first, if the Texas Rangers had a suspect in the murders, did Claude believe Post Oak Jim was guilty, were the killings designed to frighten Cale Hunter away from selling to the NRC. She seemed puzzled by his request to see deed records for land belonging to Ray Hammond, Cale Hunter, and Robert McCloud. In a giant bound ledger she dutifully looked up each recording on yellowed, timeworn pages.

"They've been in the same family for years," she said, "and the only recent notations were made when an heir inherited each parcel of land. Very little real estate changes hands in this county. We're a settled community here, mostly stable people who don't move away unless they can't find work. The drop in crude prices has forced some families to move. As county clerk there isn't much to do besides handle automobile registrations and a handful of filings the bank requires when someone borrows money against collateral, a few birth and death certificates, things like that."

"Mr. Thompson with the NRC told me the deeds are vague in some of their descriptions of property lines. If one of these landowners wanted a new survey, who would do it?"

"That's hard to say, Captain Groves. Mr. McKinney was the only licensed surveyor we had, and he died of a heart attack almost two years ago. Mr. Ingram in Ozona retired. When a house is sold, Mr. Cunningham at the bank uses a registered surveyor in Fort Stockton to provide the title company with a deed. His name is Mark Herring, although I'm told he is very busy most of the time. There is a younger man in Alpine, a strange-looking boy. He came here to buy official copies of county plat maps. He filed a copy of his registration in Terrell County, however it was several years ago. He isn't the type of individual decent folks would trust, in my opinion. I remember he looked filthy. He hasn't done any survey work here that I'm aware of, and it's no wonder. Bathing more often might help his business. Cleanliness is next to godliness. I'm sure you know your Scripture, Captain."

"Who would Cale Hunter be most likely to use to satisfy the NRC?"

"I assume that would be Mr. Herring, if he wasn't too busy."

Claude jotted down a note to call Mark Herring, to see if Hunter had contacted him about doing a survey. "I guess that's it, Miz' Anderson. Thanks for your time." His search for a paper trail was looking as though it had also been a dead end.

"I hope you catch the man who did those awful things," she said as he started for the door. "Mr. Feathers is not capable of such brutality. Now, his father, on the other hand, was a holy terror until he got what he deserved by going to prison. He killed his poor wife with a sledge-hammer while under the influence of distilled spirits. I am against the sale of alcohol in Sanderson, Captain Groves. It is scriptural, straight from the Bible. I close my eyes every time I drive past Joe's Drive-in and that dreadful liquor store he owns next door. If it had not been for the sale of alcohol in our town, Post Oak Jim might have had a proper family. The evils in alcohol turned his father into a demon, an instrument of the devil, until he got his just reward. 'Vengeance is mine, saith the Lord.' "

Claude tipped his hat and left the clerk's office, vowing to watch out for Mildred Anderson if she happened to be driving past Joe's Drive-in while he was buying beer, forewarned that her eyes would be shut, apparently believing the Lord would guide her car past the devil's depot where Joe Gomez acted as Satan's disciple by supplying bottled evil.

Across Main Street, Sheriff Casey was again planted near the sidewalk in front of his office being filmed by a television news crew, reading from a piece of paper while curious citizens were gathered nearby. Claude walked quickly to his car to avoid being seen.

# THIRTY-EIGHT

WALLACE BAKER CAME back to the telephone with a report from Ron Cherbak, his top lab chemist. Ranger Carla Jenkins was on the line calling from Sanderson, and after the huge embarrassment accompanied by a blistering dressing-down he'd gotten from Major Elliot when the morgue shot was sold to the *Statesman*—stolen by the now-unemployed lab assistant—Wally desperately wanted to cooperate with any Ranger request. "It was peyote," he began. "Mescaline, the most active alkaloid present in the buttons of the Lophorphora cactus. It produces psychotomimetic effects similar to those found in LSD like alterations in mood, changes in perception, reveries, visual hallucinations, delusions, depersonalization, mydriasis, and very strong psychic dependence. May as well call it LSD. It's almost identical chemically."

"Visual hallucinations?" she asked. "Is there any known pattern to them? Paranoia, or something consistent among frequent users?"

"I'd have to do some checking. It's addictive as hell and we've seen lots of cases where mescaline or LSD causes the overproduction of adrenaline. Some subjects develop almost superhuman strength while they're on it. Ask any police officer who's ever tried to arrest someone really buzzing on LSD. Some guys can lift a car by its front bumper. Your John Doe from Sanderson had needle marks everywhere. It took Dr. Grossman a while to find them, between his toes, all over his thighs. Whoever he was he'd been on drugs a long time. We don't expect to be able to ID him for you. But he'd swallowed a bunch of peyote, if that helps. Ingestion is one way to get it in the bloodstream and it lasts longer that way, a continuous high if he kept eating it. By the way, we're real sorry about the photograph."

She seemed to ignore his apology. "I'm sending some plaster casts of horse tracks, front and rear hooves. They're labeled. See if any of the A series is a match for the B series. I need to know as soon as possible. Also the blood on the knife should be a match for the sample I took from the second corpse. I'm sure you're loaded up with other things, but try for that match too, as quickly as you can."

Horse tracks? He recalled the grisly autopsy he witnessed with the first victim. Was some clown riding a horse all over west Texas scalping people? "We can probably do the horses' feet with a computer enhancement using the Townes method for normalizing size. Then we'll use the image analyzer to look for differences or similarities. I can't remember ever being asked to compare horses' feet before."

"Please do it as soon as you can. Major Elliot wants this wrapped up in a hurry."

"That could be the understatement of the decade," Wally replied. Major Elliot had bellowed into the phone so loudly he couldn't keep it near his ear when Elliot learned about the missing picture. "By the way, we've got three matches on those boot prints you sent us the other day. Three in the A series are the same as three in B."

"Three?"

"I don't have the sequence numbers in front of me. I'll have to call you back."

"Do that. It means one more possible suspect may have lied to us about being at the first murder scene."

"I'll get that to you as soon as I can. One more thing Grossman didn't notice at first. John Doe's intestines had dirt all over them, so he surmises they had been out of the body lying on the ground until someone, probably the mortician in Sanderson, put them back in the body cavity through the midline incision."

"Just like the second corpse," Jenkins remarked. "It almost looked like they'd been arranged in some sort of pattern."

"How weird," Wally said. "Sounds like you've got a schizoid killer on your hands."

"*That* may be the understatement of the decade," Jenkins told him. "Hardly any of this is fitting together. As soon as you call me with those series matches for the boot prints, we may be able to identify at least one more individual involved in this mess who's having trouble with the truth. Thanks."

Wally hung up, thinking that Ranger Jenkins wasn't the meter maid everyone predicted she would turn out to be.

# THIRTY-NINE

JIM FEATHERS LAY on his back dreaming, remembering Rose and how beautiful she was, how sincere when she asked about the Way, his grandfather, the history of his people. They had talked for hours that afternoon and evening. If only he could have found a woman like Rose to share his life with he would have been happy, content, less lonely in the world of white men. She reminded him of his mother, what he remembered of her when she wasn't crying, or when her face was not covered with bruises and blood from the beatings his father gave her.

The questions about Rose, asked by the Texas Ranger woman, could only mean one thing: they suspected her of being involved in Chub's murder and the death of the stranger. Their asking about the sacred plant, if Rose wanted him to find some for her, was more proof they suspected her. It had been a mistake to tell Ranger Jenkins about their discussion of the peyote ceremony, and he'd been careful not to mention how he'd given Rose several bulbs he kept hidden underneath his house, or told her how to bake them to make the pulp tender, easier to chew. These were things known only to an Indian. Rose already

knew most of them, handed down by her Comanche
mother in the way all secrets and stories from the past are
given to the next generation of a people who lived upon
the face of Earth Mother before the white man came.

*I should not have told Ranger Jenkins anything*, he
thought. He had told her what Asa meant in the Comanche tongue, and when he realized his mistake by saying
this, he'd lied about being unable to remember what else
he and Rose talked about, hoping to protect her. This
white Ranger woman was clever, pretending to care for
him by feeding Sata and telling him she did not believe he
killed anyone, when all she really wanted was information.
He had given her too much. Ranger Jenkins tricked him
into saying things he should not have said about Mr.
Hunter's daughter.

When Sheriff Casey or the Texas Rangers asked any
more questions, he would give them nothing but silence.
Rose could not have killed the white man he found in the
cave, or Chub, although he did wonder about the man she
said she visited in Alpine who gave her the peyote, someone who knew the ceremony. Whoever he was, he had to
be an Indian to know these things.

He wished for a few buttons of cooked peyote now so
he could enter the world of strange visions, even though
some of them were so terrifying, dark and mysterious, full
of visitations by Spirit Warriors from the past. Gokaleh had
come to him during a peyote vision many times, warning
him of what was to come, leaving him fearful, trembling,
more afraid than he had ever been in his life. And as Jim
knew they would, Gokaleh's predictions had come to pass
even though Chub had done nothing to deserve the anger
of the Old Ones.

# FORTY

CARLA WAS BEAMING when he came into her room with a sack of hamburgers and french fries, and an envelope with seven pictures of Chub's mangled corpse in his shirt pocket.

"Wait till you hear this," she said, sitting by her computer wired to the telephone. "I talked to the crime lab. John Doe was covered with needle marks. Somehow the medical examiner missed them the first time, possibly mistaking them for ant bites. Now we've got a strong link between John Doe and Rose." She watched him put the hamburgers on her nightstand. "There's more, a hell of a lot more. Nevada sent Rose's record to Austin. Three juvenile arrests for drug possession, the first when she was fourteen. She was sentenced to sixteen months in a Nevada Youth Commission drug rehabilitation facility in Carson City. I called them and spoke to a counselor who pulled her file. She was in numerous fights with other girls and adult supervisors. A staff psychologist made several notations concerning her violent behavior. She escaped, as we already know, was picked up in California during a drug bust, and sent back to Carson City. As soon as she was released she went back to L.A., where she was arrested again, this time as an adult, sentenced to twenty-two months at Glendale. That's when her mother died, and she showed up here about a year ago. Her mysterious disappearances begin, according to Hammond, and they last for weeks at a time. Then she just happens to drop by Mr. Feathers's house to ask about peyote and look at his Indian memorabilia, including the moccasins found on the Hunter ranch with blood on them. Feathers says they were stolen from his footlocker."

"You and your electronic toy have been busy," Claude said, tossing the envelope full of photographs on Carla's bed. "Don't look at those before you eat." He took a burger and fries from the bag and handed them to her.

She continued, ignoring her lunch for the moment. "I was directed to the Joint Tribal Council at Lawton, Oklahoma, where records are kept on Comanche Indian families who live or have lived at the Fort Sill Indian Reservation. Everything is computerized, but it still took a while to find any record of Asa Lone. Her full name was Asa Lonetree, and she was three-quarters Kwahadie Comanche. She worked in a bar in Lawton, where she must have met Cale Hunter and later married him. They had no further information on her or where she went and they weren't aware of her death."

Claude settled on the bed to eat his sandwich. "I'll agree it's strong stuff. When we question Rose we'll push her on it, especially the part about visiting Feathers, seein' his old moccasins, proving she knew where they were."

"Precisely, giving her the opportunity to take them while Feathers was in jail the first time."

"You're guessing on that one, but it's probably a good guess after all you've found out. Good work, but no hard evidence. When the lab tells us what kind of knife was used to kill Choate, what brand and so forth, we may be able to trace it. I searched Hammond's property and couldn't find the truck. Then I went to the courthouse to look at deeds to all three ranches, Hunter's, Hammond's, and McCloud's. I asked Miz' Anderson, the county clerk, who would do a survey on land the NRC wants. She said either a guy named Herring in Fort Stockton or some other guy in Alpine whose name she couldn't recall. I'll check out Herring, but it's interesting that Alpine is where the sleazy woman, as you branded her, said McCloud went for his meeting. Maybe it's a coincidence. Or maybe he's askin' the weird guy to do a survey now. Miz' Anderson told me Herring was always busy. She also gave me a sermon on the evils of alcohol. She closes her eyes every time she drives by Joe's, so she won't see the devil's brew bein' sold in Sanderson. It's a wonder she hasn't run over half of Joe's regular customers."

"I was also told to do some checking over in Alpine," Carla said, thoughtful now. "I requested the names of anthropologists who were considered experts in western Indian practices, and I found the name of a professor at Sul Ross State University in Alpine who's an authority on Plains tribe culture, a Dr. Roger Evans. He's written several books on the subject."

Claude chewed a moment. "Looks like everybody is tryin' to send us to Alpine. You can see if this Indian expert knows or has a guess as to why Choate's guts were arranged like they are in those pictures, if it's an Indian thing to whack off a guy's most useful parts and stuff 'em in his mouth."

"Most useful parts? Don't you think your brain is your most useful part? Or would you rather be without a brain than without your penis?"

"Depends on what I'm doin'," he replied, grinning despite a mouthful of greasy fries.

"According to my source, the type of woman you typically use your penis on, or in, doesn't require a great deal of intellectual stimulation in order to peel off her underwear."

"Booze works better. Quicker, too. I've never talked

my way into a woman's panties, not that I remember. Just get 'em drunk and roll 'em over on their backs. It works almost every time."

"It won't work on me, I'll promise you."

"Don't be so sure. I haven't tried yet. It's an age-old method with proven results. Ask any guy sittin' on a bar-stool."

"Do you really intend to try?" she asked, playful by the lilt in her voice, a mock frown lightly creasing her forehead.

He stopped eating to look at her. "No," he replied softly, thinking about the call from Alfred. He was still serious when he added, "There's such a thing as forbidden fruit, Carla. In spite of all the swipes you take at me for my bad track record, I do have a conscience. Not much of one maybe, but it's there. You want to know the truth? I'm scared, scared of what I'd do, the chances I'd take if I became . . . involved with you romantically. But you know what scares me the most?"

"What?" she asked, her frown deepening.

"I'd still do it if you gave me the chance, and that scares the hell out of me."

She didn't say anything, reading his face, and once again he found himself wishing he'd kept his mouth shut.

◇ ◇ ◇

"Mr. Herring, this is Texas Ranger Captain Claude Groves. I need to ask you a question regarding an investigation in Terrell County."

"Those awful murders in Sanderson?"

"It's related. Did Cale Hunter or Robert McCloud ever ask you to survey land being offered for sale to the Nuclear Regulatory Commission for a low-level dump site?"

"Cale did, only I told him I couldn't get to it for months. I told him to ask that boy over in Alpine. The kid ain't got a phone, but he's registered an' I hear he's pretty good with old boundary markers. Somebody in Alpine takes phones messages for him. I met him a couple of times. Can't say if Cale ever talked to him. McCloud did call once, but my secretary told him I was down in Presidio County an' wasn't schedulin' any work till after Christmas. He never called back."

"What's the young man's name in Alpine?"

"Gary Smith. They tell me he lives in some cabin up in the Glass Mountains without no electricity or runnin' water. Now, I wouldn't want to be quoted on this, but I've heard tell he does smoke a little dope. He's one of them hippie-lookin' kids who grows his hair near' long as a woman's. Don't get me wrong. He has his registration on file here at the courthouse, an' folks have told me he's good, knows the business. There ain't many of us in this neck o' the woods. It gets hotter'n blazes in summer an' colder'n a polar bear's ass in winter. Damn near everythin' out here is big, an' it takes lots of time to run a survey. If you don't already know, not much land changes hands here either, so it's hard to make a livin' at this."

"Thanks for your time, Mr. Herring. I won't mention dope smoking when I talk to Smith."

Claude hung up and dialed Hunter's phone number. He should have asked him about a survey a long time ago. No one answered the telephone at the Hunter ranch.

While Claude was thinking about Alpine, Carla stuck her head through the connecting door.

"I finally reached Dr. Rogers at home. Summer school at Sul Ross is over and fall classes haven't started. He agreed to look at the pictures and tell us what he thinks. I described what was done to the bodies and he said it sounded like a very old wartime practice by tribes who spoke variations of the Shoshoni language, which includes Comanches. They cut up their enemies in a number of cruel ways so they would suffer for an extended period. He'd heard about the scalpings here, although he didn't know about the other forms of mutilation. He sounds like the expert we've been looking for."

"The surveyor in Fort Stockton couldn't get a survey done at Hunter's in time, so Herring referred Hunter to the guy in Alpine by the name of Smith. No phone, lives up in the mountains. Somebody takes messages for him. A hippie with long hair who smokes marijuana, accordin' to Herring. Nearly everyone from my generation believes guys with long hair smoke pot. Maybe surveying is just a sideline with him. He could be in the marijuana business."

"We need to go to Alpine," Carla said, chewing her bottom lip.

"I agree. We'll go first thing in the morning. It's late, and the trip is a couple of hours. We may need all day to find where Smith lives, if it turns out we need to talk to him. The Glass Mountains are rugged as hell and it'll be dark soon."

Carla didn't appear to be listening. "What if Smith turns out to be our John Doe? He smokes pot, and what if he uses, or used, other drugs? He hasn't been reported missing because he lives alone, without a phone, and whoever takes messages for him believes he's off somewhere doing a survey. Think about it, Captain. What if he came to the Hunter ranch to do a survey and someone murdered him, for reasons possibly related to drugs. Maybe he and Rose did drugs together. He gets high on peyote and she kills him. . . . Somehow, Choate sees what she did or knows she did it and she has to keep him quiet. It all fits together."

Claude ran it through his mind quickly, wondering if Carla could have sniffed out an important clue. "She would have tossed his body in the river, only she wasn't strong enough to carry him or she was too high on drugs, maybe the same peyote they found in John Doe's stomach. It may even have occurred to her in a drug-induced hallucination to scalp him the way her ancestors did. But there are problems. A surveyor would have a truck of some kind. If Doe is Smith, then where the hell is Smith's truck? That leaves two trucks missing and one truck would be a damn hard thing to hide."

"I think I've got a plausible answer. Instead of tossing bodies in the river, those trucks could be at the bottom of the Rio Grande. And McCloud could be Rose's accomplice. Remember when his so-called acting instructor and girlfriend said he was seeing another woman? It could have been Rose."

A slow feeling of certainty crept into Claude's thoughts as he weighed everything Carla said. "McCloud went to Alpine for a meeting. Maybe he panicked and drove over there to destroy any evidence at Smith's, anything that could connect him to the dead surveyor when he was told we were here to investigate the murder. But we're still missing a motive: Why kill a surveyor?"

# FORTY-ONE

AFTER INSTRUCTING CARLA to begin calling cities like Abilene and San Angelo looking for an experienced scuba diver, what would sound like a moronic request coming from a place like Sanderson in the middle of a desert, Claude dialed Bob McCloud's phone number. If McCloud was at home he would only ask benign questions, carefully avoiding any mention of Gary Smith or a survey until he and Carla went to Alpine to check out her theory, a theory that was making more and more sense the longer Claude thought about it.

"Hello." A woman's voice, slurred, syrupy.

"Captain Groves, ma'am. We met yesterday. Is Mr. McCloud there?"

"No. The bastard hasn't even called me."

"Sorry to bother you. I guess he's still over in Alpine."

"Wherever the hell he is, he's with another woman."

"What makes you so certain of that? He could be there on business."

"I *know* him. He's been seeing someone else all summer."

"Has he admitted it?"

"Hell, no. He goes off at night, making up some excuse, but a woman knows these things. You can tell. In plain English, he hasn't punched my ticket but a couple of times since June."

"Not gettin' your ticket punched, as you put it, is enough to prove he's been with someone else?" Her remark about McCloud going places at night was what really caught his attention.

"Right. He used to want it all the time. I'm getting the hell out of here. This whole state sucks."

"Thanks for your time, ma'am. Make sure he calls me at the Flagship motel if he does show up. By the way, did he ever say where he was going or what he was doing when he left at night?"

"He'd take one of those stupid birds with him. He said they hunted rabbits and snakes at night. It's a crock of shit."

"Thanks again," he said, having serious doubts that falcons were night hunters.

As soon as he hung up something dawned on him—what should have been obvious the moment the woman told him McCloud had not returned. No one was answering the phone at Hunter's house. It could be coincidence, or it might mean something when neither McCloud, Rose, nor Cale answered. Had Cale grown suspicious enough of the questioning of his daughter to help her leave the area? Or even the country? He'd already shown his protective side. McCloud could be running too, if Rose had warned him about the questions she was asked. What didn't make sense was why McCloud would run when he owned tens of thousands of acres of land here, and was on the brink of selling part of it . . . unless he was running from a murder charge.

Claude dialed Hunter's number again. After a dozen rings he hung up. It was time for a fast trip to the Hunter ranch to make sure of his suspicions—before he called the

highway patrol with license numbers for a yellow Mercedes, a Rolls Royce, and Hunter's four-door pickup truck.

He stuck his head into Carla's room. "McCloud still
isn't home and nobody answers at Hunter's. I'm goin' out
there to see if Rose took off on us. Before you look for any
more divers to search the river, call the Brewster County
sheriff's office and ask them what they know about the
surveyor Gary Smith. Find out where he lives and how to
get there. Ask if anybody's seen him lately and who takes
the phone calls for his surveying business. Call that number
to see if they've heard from him. I smell shit and the stink is
gettin' stronger."

"Why not ask the Brewster County sheriff to check
Smith's cabin?"

"Do you want some idiot like Walter Casey disturbing
any evidence we might find?"

"You're right," she replied, jotting down notes as
quickly as she could. "I should have thought of that."

◇  ◇  ◇

He came into his room carrying two six-packs of beer.
When Carla heard him she appeared in the connecting
doorway with a question on her face.

Claude opened a beer and put the others in his bathroom. "I talked to Danny Weaver. He said Hunter told him
to tell us, if we asked, that he and Rose had gone to Midland to talk to his attorney. I'm not sure I'm buyin' it yet,
but don't call DPS with their license numbers now. We'll
give them the benefit of the doubt until tomorrow morning."

"That could be too late. She could be on a plane for
Brazil by then. I checked with the county clerk and the
convertible isn't licensed in her name or Hunter's in Texas.
I've got calls in to California and Nevada."

He slumped into a chair, sucking thirstily on a Coors.

"I am well aware tomorrow could be too late. Tell me what Brewster County said about Smith."

"Virtually nothing. They know he's a registered surveyor who bought a deer-hunting cabin somewhere east of Alpine in the mountains. He's only been there three years. You were right about the sheriff there, another stumblebum like Casey. Maybe worse, if that's possible. A young woman who works at a café in Alpine takes calls for Smith, and when I dialed her number I got an answering machine. She could be at work. I found a diver in Odessa, a high school biology teacher who gives classes at the YMCA. School hasn't started yet, so he'll dive the river for a flat fee of a hundred bucks and an additional twenty per hour, for as long as it takes. I told him to be here day after tomorrow because we'll be in Alpine tomorrow. He sounded surprised when I told him we were looking for pickup trucks."

"You've got a good logical mind, Carla. I won't say it's just like your dad's because you don't want to hear it, but you'll turn out to be as good an investigator as he was, as good as he still is, maybe better." He got up to open another beer. "Who's the girl who takes phone calls for Smith?"

"Ramona Silva. I left my number on her machine, asking her to call me here collect. I didn't say anything about being a Texas Ranger. If Smith smokes pot, it might scare her. I said I wanted to talk about a survey, which is partly true. I've been wondering what to make of it if she doesn't call back. She may be scared if Smith is missing and she doesn't know where he is."

Claude opened a fresh beer and sat on the bed. "I think we've covered about all the bases we can for one evening. I'll call Hunter's house again tonight. If there's no answer we can be pretty sure he's helping Rose leave the country. Same could be true of McCloud if he was involved in either of the murders. His boozy acting teacher told me again she's sure he's been seeing another woman nearly all summer because he doesn't punch her ticket the way he used to."

"Punch her ticket?"

"Slang for gettin' laid."

"So you could punch my ticket?" She laughed.

He couldn't allow himself to think about it and drank more beer without looking up at her. "I drove past a little Mexican food place on the way in. Never noticed it before. We'll try it for supper tonight. How does Mexican food sound?"

Carla smiled her impish smile and went back into her room, leaving the door open between them. A moment later he heard the shower running, another temptation he denied himself, not thinking about what she would look like naked, dripping wet, soap suds clinging to certain parts of her perfect body.

Instead he thought about recent developments in their case, wondering if they could be sitting here like bumps on a log while two killers escaped.

# FORTY-TWO

IT WAS ALMOST ten o'clock when they returned from supper at La Fiesta Café, a feast of enchiladas, rice, refried beans, and hot sauce. As a form of insurance against almost certain indigestion he bought more beer at Joe's, knowing what the green *salsa verde* usually did to his stomach. He went to the telephone with beer in hand to dial Cale Hunter's number while Carla went next door to change. They'd had pleasant dinner conversation without any further mention of involvement or seduction, and for that he was grateful. The only scar on an otherwise enjoyable evening with Carla had been the stares from other café patrons and a question from their Mexican waitress as to whether or not the killer had been caught. He had given some thought to a stop at the county jail to show the photographs of Choate's body to Jim Feathers, deciding against it when the hour grew late. Finding out if Danny Weaver had told him the truth about Cale and Rose's whereabouts seemed more pressing now.

Claude waited through a dozen rings before he gave up. They could have spent the night in Midland, he thought, not altogether sure he believed it. And there were no messages for either of them at the front desk. So McCloud had not come home, and Ramona Silva wasn't returning calls for Gary Smith. But would he be acting prematurely if he called in an APB for Cale and Rose Hunter? He would look like an utter fool if the DPS picked them up on their way back from the attorney's office.

"It'll keep," he mumbled, pulling off his boots. A cold shower sounded inviting after a long day in the heat.

A soft tapping on the inner door distracted Claude from a television news report dealing with the murders in Terrell County, an interview with Walter Casey in which Casey read, in stumbling, awkward fashion, from a written statement prepared by Huffman—a real-life instance of the halt leading the blind.

Dressed only in underwear, he slipped into a pair of pants and let Carla in. She was wearing her cutoffs and T-shirt.

"I was listenin' to Casey. He can't read worth a damn and it was Sanderson's boy-genius Huffman who wrote what Casey is reading. I saw Huffman working on it between phone calls from reporters."

Carla stood in front of the television set until the report ended and a weather forecast began. "He's too dumb to be embarrassed by the way he sounds. I never noticed before, but his eyebrows jump up and down while he talks. He could have been doing a standup comic routine in a nightclub somewhere."

When it came to noticing things it was impossible not to notice she wasn't wearing a bra when her chest was outlined by the TV screen. "Major Elliot won't think it's funny if this is on Austin television. I suppose I should have called him today to tell him we've got some stronger suspects."

Carla turned to him as he drank the last of a beer. "We'll have some solid information by tomorrow evening, if we're right about any of this."

Claude went for another beer. "What worries me is what we say to him if we're wrong. Our commander don't want bad news."

"It's because of me he's pushing so hard. I'm your biggest liability right now."

"That isn't true, Carla. You've put pieces together I failed to connect. Relax. We're doing about all we can."

"I can't relax. There's too much at stake. I don't think I'll be able to sleep a wink tonight, wondering what we'll find in Alpine."

"Have a few beers. It'll help you sleep."

"Are you attempting a barstool seduction without the beer signs? Or is this good medical advice?"

"I'm not trying to get you drunk or seduce you. It probably wouldn't work without a jukebox playing a slow Hank Williams tune anyway." He pulled a Coors from his ice-filled sink and offered it to her, after opening one for himself.

She took it, surprising him. "A jukebox wouldn't make any difference." She twisted off the cap and took a swallow. "I'd know what you were up to, and this stuff tastes awful. You'd never get me drunk with this."

He sat on the bed, leaning back on pillows piled against the headboard while a television weatherman droned on about more hot and dry weather. Claude wanted to avoid the topic. "I called Hunter again and no answer. If he put Rose on a plane in Midland, she's already headed for parts unknown. I didn't see her convertible at the ranch, although I suppose it could have been in the garage. Hunter's truck was gone too. If they went to Midland, why would they take two cars?"

Carla sat on the edge of the bed next to him, sipping on her beer. "As you said, her car could be in the garage. For some strange reason, I don't think she's running. She was too cold when we questioned her, too sure of herself. If she's doing anything, it's trying to cover her tracks. She wasn't afraid of us the other day. In fact, your questions made her mad."

"I noticed. She tried to stare holes through me. We'll wait until we see what's in Alpine, or what isn't. But you're forgettin' about Rose's history of running. She took off for California that time."

Carla noticed the long scar on his bare chest, just below the left side of his rib cage. "Is that the old knife wound you told me about?"

"This guy got me before I could get the cuffs on. I wasn't expecting a knife. It was my mistake. Gettin' careless can get you killed in this line of work, but I'm sure you know that from being a cop in El Paso."

"A scar like that can have its advantages for a man like you. It probably gets you sympathy from women who aren't too drunk to see it when you take your clothes off."

"You're gettin' more like Alfred every day, never letting me forget what kind of man you think I am."

"I'm teasing. I already know what kind of man you are and it isn't what you think. You're a very kind person underneath your hard exterior. You can be very gentle and understanding, when you choose to be."

"Don't credit me with too many good traits. It'll ruin my image, if word gets out. Someone might mistake me for a human being instead of a lecherous seducer of boozed-up trashy women. Your dad has done everything in his power to promote that image of me among the general public and my co-workers, and it keeps all the decent women away."

She watched his face for a time, then she got up and turned off the television set, leaving the room almost dark, the only light spilling from the partially closed bathroom door. "Not all the decent women," she said, returning to the bed, sitting closer to him now. "I consider myself a decent woman and nothing I've heard about you keeps me from finding you attractive. Like all of us, you have a good side and a dark side."

"*You* have a dark side?"

"Of course."

His heart beat faster because she was near, and because of what she said. He wanted to take her in his arms and kiss her the way he had before. "Don't say things like that to me or you'll give me false hope. I've already admitted I'm afraid of what I'd do if you gave me the chance."

"Can there be that much wrong with a few nice words and a couple of kisses between us?"

"It's what it might lead to that worries me."

"It can't lead to anything unless we both agree on it." Her voice was noticeably quieter when she said it.

"I'm not man enough to draw the line where I should. It has to be up to you. If I try to go too far you have to stop me."

She smiled, took a swallow of beer, and put her bottle on the nightstand. "I will. If I want you to stop. I still can't make up my mind. My only concern is how it might change us the next day and thereafter, if we'd behave differently toward each other, if it would change the way we worked together. We'd both regret it if becoming involved ruined things between us. Right now I think you respect me. I wonder if you would if we became lovers."

"Respect wouldn't be the issue," he told her, fighting back powerful urges, "and working together could be the same. It's where we'd take it from there. We couldn't let anyone know, at least not now. We'd have to hide it from . . . everyone."

She leaned forward, putting her palms on his chest before she kissed him, her lips merely brushing against his. When he took a deep breath she smelled faintly of shampoo, toothpaste, and beer. He left his hands at his sides on the bed without wrapping them around her the way he wanted.

"Was that so scary?" she whispered. "You said you

were afraid of what you'd do, yet you're behaving like a perfect gentleman again."

"I'm tryin' real hard to behave myself. It ain't easy."

"It was only a kiss. Does it worry you that I'm too aggressive? Or do you prefer timid women? George felt threatened by what he called my aggressive tendencies. He wanted to be the aggressor. With some men it's a macho thing."

"I'm not macho, but I am used to doing most of the hustling myself."

"By 'hustling' you mean ordering another round of drinks?"

He grinned. "More or less. It's a little more compli-cated than that. You gotta develop a few lines that work, ways to get women to my place without coming right out and saying you'd like to take 'em to bed. I shouldn't be admitting this to you. It makes me sound bad. Devious."

"I suspect you *are* devious with other women. I'm glad you aren't playing that game with me." She kissed him again, longer this time, and he put one palm behind her back to draw her closer while he returned her kiss.

She pulled back a moment, staring into his eyes, trac-ing a fingertip gently down a laugh line in his cheek. "It would be so easy to give in," she said.

Her nipples rested on his chest, separated only by the thin cloth of her T-shirt, worsening his aroused state of mind to a point where he knew he was on the verge of losing control. "It has to be your decision, Carla. You know I'd be lying if I said I didn't want to make love to you. I'm not blind or senile. I have no choice but to wait until you've made up your mind either way, but it's damn sure hard, this waitin', kissing you like this without tryin' to push you. Old habits, I guess, going after something I want."

"It helps to know you want me." She sighed, and came even closer, resting her head against his cheek, her breasts pressed to his chest. She whispered in his ear, "You won't think I'm cheap or trashy if we go any farther?"

"No," he answered, hoarse with desire for her, feeling the beginnings of an erection rise inside his pants, hoping for some odd reason she wouldn't notice.

"I wish I could be sure you'd say the same thing tomorrow morning. That's my big gamble."

"You're worrying about the wrong thing," he told her gently as he moved his hand higher on her back, applying more pressure. "It's what could happen if anyone else finds out. . . ."

# FORTY-THREE

SHE SLIPPED OUT of her T-shirt in a way other men might not find seductive, a quick pull to bring it over her shoulders and head before she dropped it on the floor, her breasts swaying with each slight movement of her body. His gaze fell, lingering perhaps too long on the sheer perfection of her, her slender waist, in the faint light coming from the bathroom.

"You're staring at me," she said. "It makes me uncomfortable. Sorry. I'm not very experienced with this sort of thing. I haven't been naked in front of a man since my divorce." She closed her arms across her breasts. "All of a sudden I'm nervous and I can't explain it. I thought I could go through with this, but now I don't think I can. You'll think I'm a tease. Please don't be mad at me." The strain in her voice was unmistakable. She couldn't look at him, closing her eyes with her head bowed.

"I'm not mad," he told her, pulling her closer to him very slowly, gently, so her chin rested on his shoulder. "I really do understand, Carla. I shouldn't have stared at you. Like I told you before, I'm not sure how to act around a lady. The women I'm around like bein' stared at, I suppose.

It's okay to be nervous and it's okay to change your mind. There's a helluva lot more to this than the physical side. There could be serious consequences. I've probably been leading you on, to a degree. We've had some frank discussions about sex and seductions and all that. It started out as a joke, more or less, because of all the things Alfred told you about me. To make it worse, we're both a little lonely. It's tempting as hell to think we'll find a solution by making love in this motel room. But I don't think you're ready yet, and I'm most likely not the man you're lookin' for."

Her slow breathing whispered across the side of his neck. He felt her relax somewhat.

"I think you are the right man, Claude. I don't know what's wrong with me. I wanted this . . . at least I thought I did, and now I'm freezing up. I don't know why."

"It doesn't matter why. Something about it doesn't seem right to you. It's okay. If you want to know the truth, I expected it. You're too much like me, one of the walking wounded, afraid to let yourself go because it hurts if things don't work out. In my case it's safer for me to find an easy woman I could never fall in love with so I don't run any risks of getting hurt again. I imagine the same thing's going through your mind."

Carla wrapped her arms around his shoulders. "I am afraid I'll fall in love with you. I wasn't scared of it until now."

"I understand. No need to explain. Down deep, I'm sure I'm afraid of the same thing."

She shivered in his arms, but only once, and it could have been due to the air conditioning.

"Will you just hold me like this for a while?" she asked in a small voice, "or would that make me a tease? I'll put my shirt back on."

"You don't need the shirt. You're safe the way you are, in spite of all the bad things you've heard about me."

She snuggled against him. "I do feel safe when I'm in

your arms. That's what doesn't make any sense. I want intimacy with you, and at the same time I'm afraid of it. I'm confused."

He rubbed the small of her back with his fingertips, trying to think of a way to explain the way she was feeling. Claude was sure it had something to do with his closeness to her father even if she denied it. "We've known each other in different settings, under different conditions. I knew you as a child, and you knew me as your dad's friend. I taught you how to ride a Shetland pony when you weren't big enough to climb in the saddle by yourself. Now we meet again and you're all grown up, a woman, one of the most beautiful women I've ever seen. It changes everything. . . . I stare at you because you're beautiful, not the knobby-kneed little kid I used to know, and I can't put the two images together."

She giggled. "I know. I remember you as this great big guy wearing a cowboy hat who was always smiling. You were so patient with me when my dad wasn't, and I was never afraid of making a mistake around you. I suppose I really did think of you as a member of my family back then."

"Maybe you still do, unconsciously."

Carla kissed the nape of his neck. "I don't think so. I'm physically attracted to you and it was weird at first, wondering how I could feel that way about a man I'd known most of my life. I didn't want it to happen. I kept telling myself it was just a passing fancy because you are handsome, and so damn sure of every move you make. I see women staring at you and you don't seem to notice."

"I only pay attention to stuff like that when a woman's on a stool under a neon sign advertisin' beer. There has to be the right atmosphere."

She let out a sigh, then she raised her feet off the floor so she was lying beside him, wriggling until she was comfortable in his arms, still resting her upper body across his bare chest. "But you noticed me tonight. I feel so foolish. I wanted you to notice me and when you did, I turned into an ice cube."

"You go into your shell, Carla. Like I do, only I do it in a different way."

She kissed his lips. "Would you mind holding me like this a little longer? Or does it make things worse?"

"Don't mind at all. In fact, I'm enjoyin' it." He couldn't tell her of his own confusion, a bewildering mixture of frustration and relief. Stroking her hair again, he pushed out of his head what might have been. He could be a gentleman, he told himself, only it damn sure wasn't easy.

# FORTY-FOUR

CLAUDE DIALED HUNTER'S number at seven o'clock the next morning, as they were leaving for Alpine. He got an answer on the third ring.

"Mr. Hunter, this is Captain Groves."

"Danny told me you were lookin' for me. We went to Midland to talk to my attorney. Mr. Wheeler wants to be there when you question Rose. He said you'll either have to charge her with somethin', or let her go."

"That's more or less the way it works. We can hold her for a spell. He can get a writ of habeas corpus, but it'll take some time. There's no need to go that far with it if she'll answer my questions truthfully."

"She ain't done a damn thing wrong."

"Perhaps not recently. Is she there now?"

"Where else would she be? She's asleep. You ain't gonna question her without Wheeler bein' present. That's the law."

"I know the law pretty well, Mr. Hunter. Have your lawyer there tomorrow afternoon. We can ask our questions out at your house if you think it'll save you any embarrassment. Leave word here at the Flagship what time

Mr. Wheeler can be here. And be sure to tell him that if her answers don't stack up, we'll hold her in Casey's jail as long as we can. We've found out a few things that could be enough to convince the district attorney to ask for an indictment." Claude wondered if Hunter would know he was bluffing. He wanted to see how Hunter reacted under pressure, if Hunter already knew or guessed his daughter might have knowledge of the killer's identity. It was worth a shot.

"What the hell are you talkin' about? What are you gonna charge her with? How the hell can you believe she's got anything to do with Chub or that other guy gettin' killed? That's plumb stupid. You've been listenin' to that bastard Ray Hammond too long."

"We've questioned Hammond too. One more thing. I talked to a surveyor named Herring who said you asked him to do the survey for the NRC. He told you he couldn't get to it, and he referred you to a surveyor over in Alpine. Did you ever ask Gary Smith to conduct your survey? I understand he's new around here, but Herring said he was a good surveyor."

A slight hesitation. "He told me about some other guy, only I never called him. Smith sounds like the right name. I've got it written down somewhere. I wouldn't trust anybody besides Mark Herring to do somethin' like that. I'm waiting till he gets done in Presidio."

Hunter's answers seemed to ring true enough, with a possible exception being his assertion Rose was at home asleep. Was he merely buying her more time to hide from the law? "We'll question Rose tomorrow afternoon. We're looking into a few other things first." He made no mention of the scuba diver or their drive to Alpine, hanging up before Hunter could launch into another tirade about Ray Hammond.

"What did he say about Rose?" Carla asked, standing near the door holding her computer case.

"He says she's asleep. We can't question her without the attorney present."

"It's bullshit," Carla said. "He's covering for her while she covers her tracks. She may have already destroyed important evidence."

On a hunch he dialed McCloud's number again and waited while the phone rang. "Maybe so. We can't do much until we've got something solid for the DA. . . ." A voice on the end of the line ended what he was saying.

"Hello."

"This is Captain Groves again. Has Mr. McCloud showed up?"

"Hell, no. I hope his pecker rots off. I'm out of vodka and the liquor store won't let me charge any more to his account. I hate his lousy guts."

"Sorry to bother you, ma'am. Tell him to call me at the motel when he gets back." He hung up quickly to avoid further discussions of McCloud's suspected philandering.

"McCloud isn't there and Rose may not be asleep at home like her father says," Carla said as they left his room. "It's looking more and more like they may be in it together. I should have run a background check to see if *he* has a record."

Claude started the engine. "You can radio headquarters on the way to Alpine."

As he was backing away from the curb, Carla's tone changed. "I'm sorry about last night. I feel like a first-class bitch for leading you on. Thanks for being so understanding."

"I do understand, Carla. No need to apologize. Besides, it had benefits. I got the chance to hold a real lady in my arms for a while. I enjoyed it."

She didn't look at him, switching on the radio and asking for a DPS relay from Midland to Austin. It may have only been morning sunlight on her cheeks, yet it did appear she was blushing.

An hour later, as they were speeding west on Highway 90, a static-muted voice reported no wants or warrants for Robert A. McCloud, Jr., and no criminal record in Texas.

◇ ◇ ◇

Brewster County Sheriff Cletus Boyd was in his thirties, with close-set eyes in a narrow face mottled with freckles. A mop of carrot-colored hair hung down from the front of his straw cowboy hat. His office was in the basement of an old brick courthouse, a single room with a battered desk cluttered with papers that fluttered in the breeze from a ceiling fan. The guy couldn't keep his gaze off Carla's chest while Claude asked him about Gary Smith and Ramona Silva. Snuff made a bulge in his lower lip. Between questions he spat noisily into a Styrofoam cup.

"Ramona works at the Cactus Café. I asked her 'bout Gary right after yer female partner called. She acted kinda funny. Said he was likely off somewhere doin' a survey, only he hadn't called her to see if he had any other messages. Unusual, she said, that he hadn't called in. The Cactus is over near the college. Keep goin' down Highway Ninety. It'll be on the right. She can tell you how to git to his cabin. I haven't been up in that part of the Glass range since I was a kid. No reason to go. That Smith's a real sissy type. Wears an earring. He don't hardly talk to nobody when he comes to town for groceries. He ain't from around here. *Nobody* from round here wears an earring, not even them college kids. Most of them's cowboys. Sul Ross has always got one hell of a college rodeo team. A sissy would get his butt kicked all the time if he went to school at Sul Ross."

"What kind of truck does Smith drive?"

Boyd looked at the ceiling. "Seems like it's an old International, a rusted-out white International. Got a camper shell on the bed. Has he broke the law? Kinda unusual fer Texas Rangers to be lookin' fer a man who ain't." He said this while staring at Carla's badge. Or her bosom . . . Claude couldn't be sure.

"Not that we know of."

Boyd finally looked at Claude again. "His cabin's off of Highway Sixty-seven someplace. You turn east. Them roads'll be rough as hell. Watch you don't tear yer muffler off. There's big rocks in places up in them peaks. They'll rip a car muffler off afore you know it. Don't nobody go up there 'cept durin' deer season, hardly. No electricity. It's county roads, mostly, only we don't blade 'em till deer hunters git here. No reason. The Silva girl can tell you which road to take when you turn off the highway." Boyd frowned. "I wish the city council would pass a law where a man can't wear no earrings while he's in Alpine. It just don't look right on a man. Same goes fer long scraggly hair, if you ask me. Has this got somethin' to do with them chopped-up bodies over in Sanderson? I seen one of the pictures. The killer's gotta be somebody who got loose from a mental hospital someplace. Nobody whose head works right would do somethin' like that. Sheriff Casey called the other day to ask if we had anybody reported missin'. I told him we ain't."

"We aren't sure yet. Thanks, Sheriff," Claude said, heading through the office door to a set of stairs that led from the basement.

Outside, walking to their car, Claude said, "Now you see why we didn't ask Sheriff Boyd to help us before. If I ever decide to take up bank robbing, this is where I'd start. He'd loan you a wheelbarrow to carry the money in before he realized what you were up to."

"He's even dumber than he sounds over the phone," Carla added without the slightest suggestion of humor in her voice. "This would be the perfect place to rob a bank, but you'd better not be wearing an earring while you're pulling the job."

◇ ◇ ◇

Ramona Silva was clearly nervous. A slender Mexican girl with bobbed hair, she hid her hands underneath her apron as soon as Claude asked for her at the Cactus Café, then started with his first question.

"He is somewhere close to Sanderson doing a survey, I think. I have not heard from him in more than three weeks. He always calls me to ask about messages. I worry if a rattlesnake might have bitten him or something."

"Are you his steady girlfriend?"

"No, sir. We are friends. He pays me twenty-five dollars a month to take telephone messages."

"If you're worried about him, how come you haven't asked the sheriff to have someone look for him?" Claude asked, noting that Carla had also been alerted by the mention of Sanderson, leaning across the table of their tiny booth, reading Ramona's words and mannerisms, the inflection in her voice.

Ramona turned her face to a café window. "I am afraid. He told me never to talk to the police about him, or tell anyone where he lives. I do as he asks because I need the money he pays me every month. I do not ever ask him why he said these things."

"We know he's a registered surveyor, but to your knowledge is he involved in anything illegal?"

"No, sir," she replied quickly, giving a brief, fluttery nod. "If he is, I would not know anything about it. I don't see him very often, only when he comes to town for his messages."

Claude knew he'd found a soft spot. "How about drugs? Does he use 'em once in a while? Marijuana, maybe? Anything else?"

"No, sir. I really don't know him that well."

"I want you to give us directions to his cabin, Miss Silva."

With her fingers knotted in her apron she said, "I have only been there a couple of times."

"You can draw us a map. Just show us where to turn the best you can recall. We'll find it." He took a paper napkin from a metal dispenser that sat between salt and pepper shakers on the tabletop, offering the white square to her with his ballpoint pen.

Then Carla asked a question he'd entirely forgotten to ask.

"Do you remember the name of the man who asked Mr. Smith to conduct a survey in Sanderson?"

Ramona began drawing lines on the napkin representing roads and main highways. Her writing hand trembled slightly. "I don't remember his name," she said. "I have it at home in my notebook, along with his telephone number, unless Gary tore off the page."

"Could it have been Cale Hunter?" Carla asked.

"I think that was his name," she replied without looking up.

Claude glanced at Carla while Ramona finished her map. It wasn't necessary to say it aloud. Cale Hunter had lied about who he called to survey his land.

# FORTY-FIVE

"GARY SMITH IS John Doe," Carla stated flatly as they drove north on Highway 67 following Ramona's map.

"We may have uncovered a love triangle. If McCloud were involved with Rose as his screen queen seems to indicate, then he could have killed Smith in a fit of jealous rage when he found Rose with the surveyor one night. Or Rose and McCloud might have killed Smith for the drugs he was carrying. Either way they decide to cover it up by framing Mr. Feathers, and later they repeat the process when they find out Choate knew something."

Claude swerved around a curve with the Glass Mountains off to their right, virtually barren rocky peaks the color of rusted iron jutting into a clear morning sky. "All within believable limits," he agreed. "Keep watching for a silver-painted corner post in this fence. We've come almost seven miles, so it shouldn't be far till we make the turn. We'll probably have most of our answers when we search Smith's cabin."

"Maybe," Carla said. "But I wonder who else besides Cale Hunter is lying?"

"I've got a feeling Cale knows everything. He's faced

with a choice. Lying to save his daughter's ass while he lets Feathers take the blame, knowing a jury will never convict him—or telling the truth and watching his only daughter get sent away. But why would Hunter ask Smith to do a survey if he knew Rose was involved with him, either through drugs or a romantic interest? And if Smith is Doe, and if he went to Sanderson, how come nobody reported seeing him? Boyd said Smith wore an earring, but our autopsy report doesn't mention one."

"I think we'll find that earring where we find Choate's truck, which is where I think we'll find Smith's International. At the bottom of the Rio Grande."

"There's a silver fence post," Carla said suddenly. "And a road, if anyone can call *that* a road—" She was interrupted by a woman's crackling voice coming from the two-way radio, a call to Claude's unit number. She'd forgotten to turn it off, turning the squelch button instead. She took the microphone. "Ranger Unit Forty-three, go ahead."

"Midland DPS dispatcher with a microwave relay to Ranger Captain Groves from Terrell County Sheriff Casey. He says his deputy found peyote buried under the old man's house in a sack, and another human scalp. A dog was digging it up. He says to tell you it solves everything. A Mr. Jim Feathers has signed a written confession to both crimes. Shall I relay a reply or patch you in to Sheriff Casey's telephone?"

Carla kept her finger off the transmit button, staring at Claude while he braked for the silver fence post. "Feathers confessed?" she asked. "There's no way in hell—"

"Tell her we'll call Casey in a couple of hours, and have her tell him I said not to release anything official on it yet."

Claude swung into a lane bedded with red volcanic rock, two ruts cutting through a washboard surface overgrown with weeds and bunchgrass, while Carla repeated his message to the DPS dispatcher. He waited until Carla signed off, carefully navigating a jolting roadway leading into the heart of the mountains.

"He was probably coerced into making a confession by Casey when Huffman found the peyote and Choate's scalp. You can see it in the old Indian's eyes, Carla. He's given up. He may even be trying to protect Rose, believing he's doing Cale a favor. Let's hope we can clear all this up when we find what's inside Smith's cabin."

"Let's hope," Carla replied, bouncing in the car seat when they hit a bump. After a moment she added, "I wonder what caused Huffman to go to Feathers's house today?"

◇ ◇ ◇

Driving at a snail's pace over a particularly rocky ridge between two mountains where the road made a sharp bend, Claude suddenly put on the brakes. In a mesquite-forested valley below he saw a one-room plank cabin beside a windmill, and deeper into the trees, a clear plastic dome supported by metal ribs.

"A temporary greenhouse," he said, "the cheap kind you can put up or take down in a hurry. Looks like Mr. Smith was into marijuana farming. It's hidden under those trees so DEA aerial surveillance planes can't spot it. The windmill gives him water for his plants and he's probably got propane heaters to keep 'em warm in winter. This is what I'd call pay dirt."

"There's a Jeep of some kind parked behind the cabin," Carla said. "I can see its rear bumper and the back of a canvas top."

Claude put the Ford in reverse and backed off the ridge to keep out of sight. He turned off the motor and got out, walking to the trunk of the car as quickly as his bad knee would carry him. "I'm goin' down there," he said, taking a pump twelve-gauge shotgun from the trunk, jacking a shell containing a solid lead slug into the firing chamber. "Take the other shotgun and find some cover along this ridge." He put a few extra shells into his pants pocket. "Mr. Smith may have a partner, or a caretaker. I want you to stay put, no matter what happens. If I run into a bunch of heavy gunfire, radio DPS and the Sheriff's Department with our location. Don't try any heroics on your own."

"I can shoot, Captain," she said, taking his spare shotgun off the floor of the trunk, a hurt look on her face.

He looked at her while strapping on his pistol belt. "I'm quite sure you can, Carla. That isn't the point. We call for backup like we're supposed to if there's more'n two or three men shootin' at us. That's an order. If anybody's down there, we ain't lettin' 'em get away."

Claude turned west, staying off the crest of the ridge with his shotgun balanced in his left hand, pulling the snap off his holster for quicker access to his .45 automatic.

◇ ◇ ◇

It had taken a half hour to creep up on the cabin through a tangle of mesquite. Sweating profusely, his shirt clung to his back like a second skin. He stopped behind the greenhouse a moment to peer inside. A forty-foot Quonset with lightweight aluminum ribs and a clear plastic skin allowed sunlight to fall on rows of six- or seven-foot marijuana plants growing in long, narrow water-filled pans. Beyond the greenhouse a late-model red Jeep with a black canvas top was parked next to the cabin. The cabin had small windows on three sides and a door facing south; with the windows and doors closed the heat inside would be stifling.

*Can't be anybody in there,* he thought, *or they'd suffocate.* Not a sound came from the building, although soft noises would be obscured by the chorus of chirping locusts feeding on mesquite beans in the trees around him.

Shotgun at the ready, he crossed open ground to the cabin door, prepared for the moment when someone shouted an alarm, or started shooting at him.

Slowly, Claude twisted the tarnished brass doorknob

with his left hand, aiming his Remington shotgun into the opening. The door swung inward easily, hinges creaking, causing every muscle in his body to tense, his trigger finger poised.

He was greeted by a sight more bizarre than anything he'd seen during his entire law enforcement career. A man lay on a warped plank floor in a pool of crimson, his entire body covered with some sort of white paint. He was naked. A long gash from his sternum to his pelvic bone lay open like an unzipped purse. Twin coils of purple intestine were arranged on either side of him, almost in the shape of a bird's wings.

"Shit," Claude whispered, taking note of the fact that some of the blood had not completely dried in spite of furnacelike heat in the cabin. He made sure no one else was in the room before he stepped inside for a closer look, breathing through his mouth.

The dead man's genitals were hanging from his lips, and like the corpse of Chub Choate, this victim had been scalped. He had thick, corded neck muscles, muscular shoulders and arms, and his face bore strange markings, black lines under his eyes and across both cheeks that looked like fingerpaint used for a Halloween costume. His eyelids, tightly closed, were also painted black, contrasting with the white body paint covering the rest of him from head to toe.

"What kind of fuckin' fruitcake would paint himself up like this?" he asked aloud. The dead man's identity loomed as the primary question. If this was Gary Smith, then their theory about John Doe was out the window. He bent closer. No, this man had no earring or holes in his earlobes. The full body paint was a new wrinkle. And the dead man was powerfully built. Rose Hunter would never have been able to butcher a man this size, not without help.

Only then did Claude notice a collection of decorations on the cabin walls, a bleached goat skull with curved horns painted with colorful designs, a pair of crossed spears with flint tips, a round shield made from dried animal skins, adorned with clusters of feathers. Twin bunk beds sat against each side wall. At the back, a stove fueled by propane tilted on one broken cast-iron leg. A wooden box in one corner held several rolled maps collecting dust and cobwebs, more evidence that surveying had only been a sideline for Gary Smith. His income came from the greenhouse, a rather imposing harvest of marijuana plants.

Claude's gaze wandered to a blackened tin cooking pot on the floor near the corpse. He peered down at its contents. Something resembling a boiled green onion, pulled open to reveal its center, lay in the bottom of the pan.

"Peyote," he said, almost choking on the coppery stench filling the room. He'd seen enough. Whoever the dead man was, his identity would answer questions about Rose Hunter, Gary Smith, and Robert McCloud. And this time, the only known Indian resident of Terrell County was back in jail. Scalp or no scalp buried underneath his old house, Feathers would soon be a free man. Whoever was trying to frame him had made a serious mistake.

Claude walked outside, cupping his hands around his mouth as he yelled up to Carla, "Bring the camera and evidence bags down!"

◇ ◇ ◇

Carla took nine pictures of the body, the interior of the cabin and the items hanging on the walls, her complexion a little bit chalky as she stepped around the corpse to shoot another angle.

"This has to be ceremonial paint of some kind, a form of dress called for by some Indian peyote ritual," she said, taking more shots of the cabin walls while Claude took blood samples.

"The poor bastard hasn't been dead all that long," he told her, placing the onion-shaped bulb in a plastic bag.

"As soon as we know who he is, I'm convinced we'll have our killer pinpointed."

Carla stepped outside for a breath of fresh air. "I think I already know who he is, Captain," she said as he followed her out carrying evidence bags.

"It isn't Smith, if that's what you're thinkin'. Neither one of his ears is pierced."

"Smith is John Doe. The guy in there is Robert McCloud. He hadn't come back from Alpine this morning. He's been missing for several days. And all we've got is her father's word that Rose Hunter is at home sleeping. She's our murderer. She killed McCloud while he was high on peyote, dressed up like some Indian mystic as if he were playing a role in a crummy movie. Remember, he wants to be an actor. Rose convinced him to paint his body and face like some old-time tribal medicine man so they could hold a peyote ceremony and get really high, see things, hallucinate. Maybe she promised him what she's got between her thighs if he indulged her fantasy."

"It won't wash," Claude replied, "even if that is McCloud in there, which isn't likely if the two of them were lovers doing drugs together. Did you see the size of him? All those muscles? A woman couldn't subdue that guy. He's too big and strong. If she did it, she had to have some help."

"Unless his mind had been turned to mush by mescaline, or a combination of drugs. And in case you've forgotten, I have taken down men his size. You're still hung up on all that weaker-sex bullshit. And there's a way to be almost certain this guy is McCloud right now." She disappeared around the back of the cabin before he could apologize for being a chauvinist—again.

◇ ◇ ◇

A radio call to Motor Vehicle Registration with the license number confirmed Carla's belief as they waited for the

Brewster County coroner to arrive with Sheriff Boyd. The red 1990 model Jeep parked behind the cabin was registered to Robert Alvin McCloud, Jr.

Carla placed five evidence bags in the trunk of the Ford containing personal effects, blood samples, the peyote bulb, and a set of fingerprints Claude had taken from the body after wiping off a coating of oily white paint. Claude didn't want to think about what Major Elliot would say when a third body turned up. Although Carla made no mention of it now, he was sure she was thinking the same thing.

# FORTY-SIX

◆

SHERIFF BOYD GAZED down at the body, forgetting to spit when he first saw what had been done to the corpse, a trickle of brown tobacco juice dribbling from a corner of his mouth. "What the hell was goin' on in here?" he stammered, uneasy, shifting his weight to the other foot, resting his hands on his hips, blinking several times before he finally spat on the floor. "Looks like somebody was tryin' to field dress a deer carcass. Wonder how come he's all painted up like that? It didn't look like that guy in the newspapers was painted white with black marks on his face. Enough to make a man sick to his stomach."

"There's a greenhouse out back full of marijuana plants in hydroponic pans," Claude told him. "We also found what looks like a peyote bulb in that pan on the floor. We think we know who this guy is, but get a good look at his face to see if he could be Gary Smith."

"That ain't Smith," Boyd replied. "Smith was a freaky type, but that ain't him. Smith was smaller. Shorter, an' you can see he ain't wearin' no earring. Never saw this feller before in my life, only it's a little hard to tell with his pecker an' nuts in his mouth, painted up like a damn ghost, his hair pulled off. This was done by the same loony bird who done them killin's in Sanderson, don't you reckon?"

"We're pretty sure it's the work of the same killer," Claude said.

"The meat wagon is outside. I'll tell the boys to come in an git him, if'n yer done here. I'll telephone the DEA in El Paso to tell 'em about the dope. Likely they'll burn it. Never had no idea Smith was raisin' pot out here. He had this paper sayin' he was a legal surveyor. You reckon his girlfriend Ramona was in cahoots with him on them marijuana plants?"

"She told us she'd been out here a few times, so she had to know about it. I'm sure the DEA boys will question her."

"This here's gonna be big news in Alpine, Cap'n Groves. We don't have much crime round here to speak of. Mr. Turner at the *Alpine Herald*'s gonna want pictures fer his newspaper. It's sure gonna make a lot of folks sick when they see 'em." He glanced over his shoulder, making sure Carla was outside. "What's the new woman Ranger like? I read about all the stink in the papers when Joaquin Jackson an' them others resigned. She sure has got nice tits."

Claude bit down before he replied. "She's one of the best investigators I've ever worked with. Top-notch. As to your remark about her anatomy, I wouldn't say any more about it if I were you. Women voters in Brewster County might not want a sheriff who talks about nice tits on a law enforcement officer in the middle of a murder investigation, come the next election."

"Sorry," Boyd mumbled, spitting again, "but a normal man can't help but notice 'em." He turned his back on the body. "We can count on havin' Alpine swarmin' with reporters an' such, just like they done to Casey. What the hell am I supposed to say? We got us a serial killer runnin' around who whacks off three guys' dicks and hair, stringin' their guts all over the place? I can tell you this much . . . every sumbitch in Brewster County who ain't got a gun will be buyin' one today. I'd better call the college an' tell 'em to be on the lookout for any strangers. They've got ol' man Martin fer a security cop, only he couldn't stop a stray dog from pissin' on a flagpole. I've got two part-time deputies, so I'd better ask the city council to make 'em full-time fer a spell, till we catch whoever done this. You got any good suspects yet?

"No one we're certain of. The old Indian in Sheriff Casey's jail couldn't have done it. The blood is still damp in places so I figure it happened late last night or early this morning. I'd keep one of your deputies on guard at the greenhouse until the DEA gets here. We'll talk to the Silva girl on our way out of town. If we think she knows anything at all about this we'll bring her over to your jail to hold her for further questioning. We can probably charge her with complicity in an attempt to distribute a controlled substance anyway. She was real nervous when we asked her for the directions out here, although she claimed she barely knew Smith."

"Where do you figure Smith is?" Boyd asked, walking out of the cabin behind Claude where an old panel truck with Wollard Funeral Home painted on its sides was parked.

"He may have been the first victim in Sanderson," Claude replied. "To tell the truth, we aren't all that sure of anything yet except the identity of the second victim, a local cowboy who worked for Cale Hunter."

Sheriff Boyd spat into a patch of dry buffalo grass. "Cale is a good feller, only he's made a lot of enemies lately with all that ruckus over sellin' land fer a nuclear bomb plant."

Claude motioned Carla toward the car without bothering to correct Sheriff Boyd's understanding of the proposed dump site. "We'll question Ramona Silva and if she doesn't come off squeaky clean, we'll bring her to your office."

"You've got my full cooperation, Cap'n Groves. Just

say the word. When all them reporters start showin' up I'll
tell 'em to talk to the Texas Rangers fer an official statement, 'cause I ain't rightly sure what to say 'bout this
mess."

◇ ◇ ◇

Dr. Roger Evans unlocked his office door on the second
floor of a brick building on the Sul Ross University cam-
pus. The room smelled musty. Bookcases lined every wall
of a cramped office space with a single dusty window overlooking a parking lot. He was well past sixty, round shoul-
dered, with a gleaming bald spot on top of his head.

"Please sit down," he said. "You'll have to move some
of those files in that chair. Just put them anywhere. I'm not
at all sure I can help you. The mutilations in Sanderson
sound like the behavior of a psychotic madman. The fact
that they were scalped may be incidental, or someone trying to make the deaths appear similar to wartime practices
of early Plains tribes. A kook who read something about
Apache or Comanche torture. All six of the Kiowa tribes
adhered to brutal forms of slaughter, however I doubt
you'll find any of this was done by an Indian. There are
very few purebloods left in Comanche or Kiowa tribes due
to intermarriage, a modern society that lures them from
the poverty of reservation life."

Carla placed the envelope of photographs on Evans's
desk before she sat down. "There is a third murder now,
Dr. Evans. This one occurred close to Alpine in the Glass
Mountains. In this particular case the corpse we found was
somewhat different. His entire body was painted white
with what appears to be grease paint. Black lines were
drawn under his eyes and across his cheeks. But he was
butchered in precisely the same fashion as the first two. I
want you to take a look at these photographs of the second
victim, and if you will, pay particular attention to the arrangement of the intestines on both sides of the body."

Evans frowned as he opened the envelope, taking a pair of reading glasses from his shirt pocket. "I hadn't heard about the one found here." He paused. "Good grief! This fellow was disemboweled. I presume those are his genitalia in his mouth . . . it's hard to tell from this angle."

"All three had their penis and testicles pushed into their mouths," Claude said.

Evans looked closely at another picture. "I see what you mean about the intestines. The way they are placed around him is clearly not a random act." He glanced at the other photographs and put them down to remove his glasses, his brow furrowed in thought. "You must remember I'm an anthropologist and I know absolutely nothing about criminal behavior. One thing you've told me arouses my curiosity. You said the victim found here was covered in white paint with black markings. It jars something in my memory. I'd need to make a phone call to an old friend at New Mexico State University. His specialty is obscure religions from all over the world, occult beliefs and that sort of thing. He has written a number of professional journal articles over the years."

Carla came to the edge of her chair. "You sound as if you don't believe this is an imitation of an early Comanche form of murder or torture. Can you tell me why?"

"Several reasons. First, the scalpings are quite different in that the entire scalp was removed. Plains tribes only cut off a token lock at the front of the scalp as a trophy, proof of the death of an enemy which they kept on lances or on special stakes in front of their lodges. Also, there is no record whatsoever of any practice by Plains tribes of placing the intestines around the body, nor were male genitals usually removed. Comanches made pouches of womens' breasts, but in general they did not sever male organs. What you've shown me and told me about actually bears almost no similarity to Native American torture methods, except in a very vague way."

"Then what is it?" Carla asked, visibly deflated when

her theory pointing to Rose Hunter seemed to be unraveling.

"I'm not certain. I'll call Philip Carter for you. He may be away for the summer conducting a graduate field study in South America or Africa. But I will try to reach him, if you wish."

"Can you take a guess?" Claude asked, feeling as though they were wasting time now.

Evans took another glance at one photograph. "Have you ever heard of Santeria, Captain Groves?"

"Can't say as I have. What is it?"

"It is a very old form of sacrificial religion originating in Africa. It came to the Caribbean islands hundreds of years ago by way of slave ships. I don't know much about it, however Phil Carter will. I read an article he wrote about it, along with a few other rare forms of human sacrifice practices still being followed in Jamaica and parts of Latin America. The description you gave me of white paint and black markings on the victim's body is mentioned in Phil's article, I'm quite sure, and I'm almost certain there was one group who did something with the internal organs, something with significance to followers. I can give Dr. Carter a call if you feel it's important."

"It could be *very* important," Carla insisted.

Dr. Evans opened a desk drawer to retrieve an address book.

# FORTY-SEVEN

◆

'I SEE," EVANS said into the phone, scowling when he looked at a photograph of Choate's body. Evans made several notations on his desk calendar during the conversation. 'Can you estimate how widespread this group may be, or why it would show up suddenly here in west Texas?"

A deeper frown and more notes, leaving Claude wondering what appeared to confound Dr. Evans.

"Yes, the Texas Rangers say they have photographs of the one who was painted for sacrifice. I'll give them your address and ask them to send some to you, although you sound fairly positive of what you've told me."

More silence and note-taking. Carla seemed nervous, trying to read what Evans wrote without being too obvious about it. She took out her ballpoint and notepad, turning to a blank page.

"Good-bye, Phil. And thanks again. You've been a great deal of help."

Evans hung up and glanced across his desk. "Phil is fairly certain what this is, based on what you told me. Quite frankly I've never heard of it until now. The symbolic placement of the intestines, a full calvarium scalping, removal of male genitalia and painting the body white with specific markings is an indicator of a very old form of human sacrificial religion from Africa known as Palo Mayombe. It has been found in Haiti and Belize in recent years, also parts of Honduras and Guatemala and Venezuela, even among some Mexican Indian tribes in lower states such as Michoacán. How it showed up in Texas in anyone's guess, according to Dr. Carter. It is a drug-based belief system, often seen as satanic, and Phil says in more modern times, cocaine or a similar hallucinogenic is consumed before the ceremony is begun. The number of believers is thought to be quite small, although as you might imagine, it can only be a guess. No cases of this form of human sacrifice have ever been reported in the United States, as far as Phil knows. He's considered a world authority on the subject. He is very curious to see your photographs."

"Palo Mayombe?" Carla asked, jotting it down as she spelled it out.

"Correct," Evans replied.

"And you, as well as Dr. Carter, are certain this can't be a form of American Indian practice, in particular a Comanche type of symbolic disfiguration?"

"I'm quite sure of it. Phil recognized it almost immediately when I described it to him. Two or three Comanche bands were particularly cruel to their enemies, staking them out in the sun with their eyelids cut off so the fluid within the eye caused the eyeball membrane, the conjunctiva, to burst. There were several other brutal forms of torture, however they were all rather crude compared to what was done to the man in these pictures."

Claude shifted his bad knee. "You say it's come as far as southern Mexico, according to Dr. Carter. Then I suppose we could have a Mexican illegal who came north to work in the States who was a believer. What you've told us won't fit with some of the evidence we've found with the other victims . . . one in particular, the ranch cowboy. He wasn't involved with drugs as far as we know, and neither one of the first two were painted. This stuff about Palo Mayombe or whatever you call it don't wash with the connections we believe we've uncovered between our victims and a possible suspect. We were sure we had a relationship established between at least two of the victims, and we believe the cowboy was killed because he saw the first murder bein' committed, or he knew who was responsible."

Dr. Evans shrugged. "I told you I'm not a criminologist, Captain Groves. I can't tell you *why* this happened. Phil was of the opinion that what I described to him was a Palo Mayombe human sacrifice. He told me he'd seen it twice before, once in a tiny village near Tegucigalpa, Honduras, and again a few years ago in the Orange Walk District of Belize. He said the intestines are meant to represent a means of travel to the heavens, a pair of wings allowing the deceased to reach their god. By preparing the human to be sacrificed with hallucinatory drugs, it is believed they experience no pain. Phil did say something about the man's genitals. He said some scholars theorize those who were sacrificed were being punished for infidelity or some sort of sexual misbehavior. By cutting the genitals off and placing them in the mouth, it supposedly offers proof the man will be unable to commit this act again in the afterlife. Crude, obviously without logic, but none the less a part of Palo Mayombe beliefs."

"Incredible," Carla said quietly, "that it can still exist in these times."

"It's highly localized, Phil said, and quite rare, usually found among very primitive people in remote locales. He was stunned to hear of it occurring in Texas."

Claude pushed himself up from the chair. "We appreciate your time, Dr. Evans. You've sort of thrown us a curve with the Palo Mayombe stuff. It leaves us with a bunch of apparently useless information. We've got one common factor left with two of the victims—they both used peyote. I suppose we take it from there."

◆ ◆ ◆

"Shit," Carla muttered, slamming the car door, her features pinched in a deep frown. When she realized Claude heard her she said, "Sorry. I can't make myself believe I was wrong about Rose and her Comanche mother. I was so sure it was where she learned about scalping and peyote ceremonies and some of the rest of it. She's still in this up to her neck as far as I'm concerned, but where would she learn anything about Palo Mayombe? That needs to be the first question we ask her tomorrow—if she's ever heard of it. I'll know if she's lying."

Claude started the engine. "I hate like hell to admit it, but that idiot Casey may have been right all along. We could have a group of Palo Mayombe weirdos across the border, comin' over at night. That still doesn't account for the connection between the victims—all three were, in various ways, involved with the dump site. And why would the same crazies follow McCloud all the way to Alpine to kill him? It don't add up. Right now we're gonna arrest Ramona Silva and pump the hell out of her for information about Smith and the drugs, everything she knows. When I tell Major Elliot what we found out today, along with another body, he'll blow his stack. I may be the one who gets a transfer to Siberia." He drove away from the parking lot wishing Alfred could be here. Alfred would know what to do with the new information they had, where to begin. "Radio Sheriff Casey and ask him to come to Alpine to identify McCloud. The girl at the ranch is probably too drunk by now to make the drive without killing somebody or runnin' over another farmer's pig."

◆ ◆ ◆

At an apartment complex on the west side of Alpine Claude asked the manager to unlock number 107 when no one answered his knock. Ramona had gone home from work early, complaining of a virus, they were told. Claude was sure the girl was running.

"She ain't here," the manager said. She told them Ramona drove a white Nissan with a dent in one door, which wasn't in the parking lot. She let them in. "I saw her loadin' some things in her car about an hour ago."

Carla went straight to the closet in the bedroom. "All her clothes are gone, Captain. I'll radio for a license number so we can notify DPS to have her picked up. Maybe I can find some old letters, anything from her family or a friend that might tell us where she's going."

Claude walked out of the stuffy little apartment while Carla gathered up various personal effects belonging to Ramona. One of their prime sources of information was making her escape and if she knew the back roads in Brewster County, she might get away clean as a whistle, either to old Mexico or elsewhere. Another dose of bad luck had just reared its ugly head.

# FORTY-EIGHT

DEPUTY HUFFMAN WAS clearly annoyed when Claude told him to release Jim Feathers.

"We got proof he done it," Huffman said, aiming his thumb at a green plastic garbage bag in a corner of the office. "That's Chub's scalp an' six peyote buttons in that bag yonder. Found it right there under Post Oak's shack buried in the ground. If you ain't heard yet, he signed a full confession to both murders. I typed it out for him an' he signed it right here at this desk."

"Release him," Claude said again, growing irritated, tired after the long return trip from Alpine. "He didn't do it and we have nothing we can hold him on. There was another murder while Feathers was in jail. Somebody put the scalp under his house to throw suspicion on him. We'll take him home."

Huffman got up from his chair with the key. "Walter said the one in Alpine was different. He ain't gonna be happy when I tell him I let Post Oak out."

Claude's jaw turned to granite. "I don't give a damn if he likes it or not, Mr. Huffman. In case nobody taught you the law, a prisoner has to be charged with something and any charges against him are about to be dropped. His confession is worthless. Open the fuckin' cell and let him out."

Huffman went quietly to unlock the cell door. Carla smiled and turned to an office window. Her dislike for Huffman helped her enjoy watching the deputy back down in the face of Claude's sudden outburst.

"Thank you, Captain," she said, and he knew the way she meant it, a show of gratitude for putting Huffman in his place.

The old Indian came slowly into the outer office. He gave Claude a momentary stare, questioning him with his eyes.

"You're free to go, Mr. Feathers. We'll drive you. As of now, any charges against you will be dropped. You may be asked to testify at a subsequent trial, if we ever find out who's doing this, but you'll only be asked to tell a judge and jury what you know about certain events, if you know anything at all. Get in the car and we'll take you home."

"I signed the paper," Feathers said, his voice so soft it was hard to hear.

"We think we know why you signed it," Claude replied after a brief glance in Huffman's direction. "Make a paper airplane out of your confession, Deputy, and see how far it'll fly across Main Street, because that's all you'll ever be able to do with it."

ata was sitting on the front porch when they drove up and when the old man saw his dog, he smiled. Claude had been careful not to ask Feathers any questions until now.

"Your dog's glad to see you," Carla said. "He's wagging his tail so hard it may drop off."

Claude put the Ford in park. "We want to ask you a couple of things, Mr. Feathers. My partner and I are tryin' real hard to find out who's doing this and put a stop to it.

Someone, for reasons we don't understand, wants people to think you did it. A third victim was found this morning in Alpine. All this time we've been thinkin' it was made to look like an Indian scalping so suspicion would fall on you. But an expert on that sort of thing told us what it really was—a cult practice that began over in Africa called Palo Mayombe, and it's come across the ocean as far as Mexico. We think we know who the first victim was now, a surveyor from Alpine by the name of Gary Smith. Maybe you saw him out at Hunter's ranch one day—he drove an old white International pickup. We believe the third victim is Robert McCloud. Can you tell us anything about any of this?"

Feathers sat quietly in the back seat for a long time with his face to a side window. He replied in his typically soft voice, "I saw the stranger in the white truck two times. He was looking through a looking glass on three poles and then he wrote something down. I watched him for a while. He did not see me."

When Feathers said no more, Claude asked, "What else can you tell us? We really need your help."

Another lengthy silence passed before the old man spoke. "I sometimes gave peyote to Mr. Hunter's daughter and I showed her how to cook it so the middle is tender enough to swallow. She did not know these things. She is a nice woman. Her heart has been troubled. She is also an Indian. Her mother was from the Sata Teichas tribe. In the white man's tongue, she was Comanche."

"Do you believe she is capable of killing someone?" Claude continued, doubting he would get a truthful answer if Feathers thought Rose might be a killer.

Feathers shrugged. "I only know her heart is troubled. I gave her peyote and told her how to seek a spirit vision to put her heart at peace. She wanted to know. A warrior seeks his spirit vision before he goes to fight the enemy. Mr. Hunter's daughter is not a warrior." He watched his dog limp over to the car door wagging his tail

"I must feed Sata now. I am very tired, for I cannot sleep in Sheriff Casey's jail."

Carla turned around to face the rear seat. "We have to find out who the killer is and we need your help, even if what you tell us is something white people don't understand. Compared to what we heard in Alpine today about Palo Mayombe, nothing you say will sound too strange or unbelievable. Someone killed your friend Chub Choate, and whoever it is, he or she wants everyone to think *you* did it. Please help us, Mr. Feathers."

Feathers looked at Carla, making a study of her face. "If you come back tomorrow . . . I will tell you the story of Gokaleh and the Spirit Warriors, how they can take the shape of a man to come from the Land of Shadows." His eyes flickered to Claude, then back to Carla. "Come alone, Woman Who Wears the Star. I will repay the debt I owe you for feeding Sata while I was in jail."

" 'Woman Who Wears the Star,' " Claude said in a mocking way as they drove back to the motel. "It's a very catchy name. I like it." His expression turned serious. "You've broken down his barrier at last. I think he'll tell you more than he wants to if you ask the right questions."

"I still believe Feathers is protecting Rose out of loyalty to her father. We'll see. Digging that out of him will be hard and any direct questions will put him right back in his shell."

"You're sniffing the wrong scent, Carla. Where does Rose learn a Palo Mayombe ceremony or how to kill a man in a sacrificial way?"

"Prison, perhaps. As soon as we get to our rooms I'll get all I can on Palo Mayombe from a computer search. There's our favorite sheriff just back from Alpine. . . ."

Claude slowed the car to park in front of Casey's office. Sheriff Casey saw them as he was about to open the office door. He turned around and came to the curb as Carla was lowering her car window.

Casey came right to the point, ignoring Carla to speak to Claude. "It's Bob McCloud, all right. What a mess they made of him. Any idea why he was dipped in paint to look like a Halloween spook?"

Deputy Huffman came out on the front steps as Claude was giving his answer. "It's something from over in Africa called Palo Mayombe. We talked to an expert on it."

"Africa?" Casey exclaimed, bushy eyebrows curling. "We ain't got no goddamn Africans round here. Hasn't ever been one lived in Terrell County that I remember. I reckon you could say we don't encourage that sort of thing."

Carla's cheeks went tight. She fiddled with the strap on her computer case.

"We'll fill you in with more details later, Sheriff," Claude said, putting the Ford in reverse. "By the way, I told Huffman to release Feathers. We took him home. I'll call the DA down in Del Rio to have all the charges against him dropped. Call that attorney and tell him Mr. Feathers's bond will be lifted."

"But what about that second scalp an' all the dope Harlan found under his house?"

"Somebody put it there, obviously. When we find out who did it, we'll have our killer. You might ask any of the old man's neighbors farther up that road if they saw a car drivin' down to his house. It probably happened last night, or the night before."

Casey was angry now. "We ain't got no blacks here. Hell, they would stick out like a sore thumb so's everybody in town would notice if one came through killin' folks. Maybe the expert you talked to don't know shit about Terrell County."

Claude backed away from the curb without a reply, heading up Main Street toward the Flagship.

"God, I hate that man," Carla mumbled, gripping the

strap on her computer case with a white-knuckled hand. "Between him, his dim-witted deputy, and Sheriff Boyd there aren't enough brain cells to fill a thimble. I didn't know idiots like them really existed, and these guys are licensed to carry guns."

Claude's mind was elsewhere, on a phone call he wanted to make while Carla was busy with her computer. By running all the new information they had under Alfred's nose, he was sure Alfred would pick up something they'd missed.

At the Flagship Claude was informed there were eleven phone messages from newspapers and television stations waiting for him to call back with an official statement regarding the deaths. He took them down hurriedly, eager to make a far more important call first.

"It's simple, Claudie. Can't believe you didn't figure it out yourself. You've gotten lazy since you quit workin' with me and it's showin', the way you're handlin' this. I already told you where to look."

"The paper trail doesn't go anywhere, Alfred. The courthouse records are full of old field notes having to do with the surveys from a long time ago. The first victim was probably a surveyor named Gary Smith, the guy who was raising the dope, and we know Hunter lied to us about not calling him. But why would Hunter have his own surveyor killed? That don't make any sense."

"He didn't like somethin' the surveyor found out. Maybe a property line ain't where Hunter thought it was, so he killed the surveyor to keep his mouth shut. He could have found out he doesn't actually own the land he's tryin' to sell, a fence that's been in the wrong place for fifty years, somethin' like that."

"I suppose that's possible—"

"Possible, my ass! It's your missin' piece. If I was

down there I'd have that case wrapped up before sundown. You're after some trashy woman you found there and you're thinkin' with your dick."

Claude flinched. If Alfred even suspected he had so much as considered intimacy with Carla there would be one more dead body found in this part of west Texas. "Where does a rancher like Cale Hunter learn about Palo Mayombe?" he asked, to head their conversation in virtually any other direction.

"That's what the state of Texas is payin' you to find out. Put Carla on it. She knows how to dig deep. By the way, how's she doin'?"

More guilt feelings tweaked him. "Great. She's convinced the old Indian to talk. She's just fine. A damn good investigator. Don't worry about her. I'm gonna have to call the major and tell him about the third body. Keep your fingers crossed that he won't go through the roof."

"If you an' Carla would let me come down I'd have the whole thing solved in no time. Tom would never know."

"Carla wouldn't like it. I've told you why."

"Alice poisoned her against me. Let's not talk about it. Put Carla on that Mayombe thing. Find out if another surveyor, or the guy who was too busy, is a friend of Hunter's. Everything else will fall into place if you stay on the trail of money. I bet I've told you that at least a thousand times, Claudie. . . ."

# FORTY-NINE

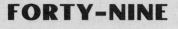

"THIS IS HARLAN. There's been another killin'. It was Bob McCloud, killed nearly like them others. Walter drove over to Alpine to identify the body. He said McCloud was painted white with black marks on him. Those Rangers found a bunch of marijuana where they found McCloud, at some surveyor's cabin way up in the mountains. But get this. The Rangers told Walter some expert says this ain't the way an Indian kills people. It's something else with a long name an' it come over from Africa. Walter's so mad he could eat nails. He told 'em we ain't got no Africans here in Sanderson. That Cap'n Groves made us let Post Oak go 'cause he was in jail when McCloud was killed. They're gonna drop all charges against him."

"What did the Rangers say about the surveyor?"

"Walter didn't tell me. He called Sheriff Boyd over in Brewster County right after he heard what Cap'n Groves said. Walter was cussin' so bad I didn't pay much attention, only I think Walter said the guy's name was Smith. I never heard of him. After he hung up Walter drove out to talk to Cale, mainly to get away from all the reporters comin' by the office. Cletus Boyd told him they was all over Alpine too, stickin' microphones in his face, takin' all sorts of pictures. I know Walter asked Cletus if they had any black folks in Alpine, an' Cletus said they only had two, an' he didn't believe either of 'em had enough sense to come in outta the rain. But he's gonna bring 'em in anyways to question 'em, maybe keep 'em in jail overnight. Cletus told Walter the Rangers never said a word to him 'bout this bein' somethin' from Africa."

Silence for several seconds.

"I called soon as Walter left 'cause I figured you wanted to know right away."

"Yes. Thank you. I wonder if the Rangers believe there were any witnesses to McCloud's murder."

"They're lookin' for a girl who knew the surveyor, she took off right after Cap'n Groves questioned her about the dope. The highway patrol has her license number, Cletus said. The Rangers didn't know McCloud was up there dead till after they talked to her. We got a call from Midland DPS to look for her white Nissan—name's Ramona Silva. Walter said to forget about it, that she wouldn't come this way. I've never seen him so mad. He's blamin' it all on the woman Ranger."

"I see. I wonder why Walter drove out to talk to Cale in person?"

"The Rangers wanna question Rose tomorrow out at the ranch. All Walter said was, he needed to talk to Cale in private. He stormed outta the office an' damn near slammed the door off the hinges. He was boilin' over just as bad when I told him I had to let Post Oak go, like me findin' Chub's scalp under his house didn't mean a damn thing. When that Mexican woman called to tell me I oughtta look under there, it was real hard to understand her. Wish I knew who the hell she was . . . how she knew Post Oak put it there."

More silence. "Thank you for calling, Harlan. Let me know the minute anything changes. Your cooperation won't be forgotten. We need a good candidate for sheriff in

Terrell County. Walter is trying to straddle the fence, hoping to keep everyone happy, which could eventually make him a number of enemies if he takes it too far. He hasn't been keeping me informed the way I'd hoped he would. I'm counting on you to keep me aware of new developments."

"I'll sure do it. You got my word on it."

## FIFTY

IT WAS TOO hot to sleep in this part of the afternoon even though he had told the two Rangers he needed rest. He wanted to be alone more than anything else, to think about what he should do, the words he could say to the Star Woman without bringing harm to Mr. Hunter and his daughter. And how could he explain a thing he did not understand himself? How Chub's scalp came to his house, buried with the peyote? In his heart Jim was sure it was the work of Gokaleh, but how could he explain this to a white woman who knew nothing about the Land of Shadows, the Way, or Spirit Warriors? He had seen Gokaleh many times at night after the man was found in the cave, the spirit rode a horse across the empty flats behind his house, land belonging to Mr. Billings. They would say he was eating peyote and this was only a vision, not a warrior made of flesh and bone. Perhaps it was true, that it was a vision. When his mind traveled the pathways revealed by peyote he was never quite sure what the eyes of his spirit could see and what actually existed in this life in a physical form. Gokaleh had powerful medicine. If it was the wish of Powva that Gokaleh come back to Earth Mother with the body of a man to punish those who harmed her, it would be the fulfillment of a promise made by the Old Ones long ago, a story told to each generation of the People until the People were no more. Jim had known for many years he was the last of the Lipans. His would be the last Lipan eyes to see Gokaleh's revenge upon the white man, but he could never tell these things to the Star Woman.

He struggled out of his chair as the sun lowered and the slanting rays of light outlined tracks leading up to the back of his house. When he first saw them he wondered if his mind had wandered into a dream. But as he moved stiffly away from his porch to take a closer look he felt a strange chill in spite of the heat. The tracks were real, tracks made by a horse.

He knelt beside them, tracing a fingertip over the edges to learn how old they were, how long they had been in his caliche yard. The prints were recent, made only a day or two before, crisp edges still there in powdery soil.

He followed the tracks with his eyes, back into the yucca and cholla thorns. A rider had come to his house, then turned back in the direction from which he had come.

He was suddenly afraid. "He came looking for me, bringing me the scalp as more proof of his return from the Land of Shadows."

He stood up slowly, looking south across empty pasture land owned by Tyson Billings. The tracks made by Gokaleh were real, not part of a peyote vision. The bare-chested warrior with two feathers tied in his hair he had seen on those other nights was as real as these hoofprints. He had not imagined it.

*I will show these tracks to the Star Woman tomorrow,* he thought. *Now she will know I am not crazy. Gokaleh has taken the shape of a man to kill his enemies and he rides a horse the way he did when he fought the Mexicans and white men. I have proof Star Woman can see when she comes.*

Sata whimpered behind him. "Be quiet, foolish dog, for I am thinking of the words I will say tomorrow."

One thought still puzzled him as he walked back to his porch to watch the sunset, a question he could not answer. Why had the Spirit Warrior killed Chub? How could it be possible that a Spirit Warrior with the wisdom of Gokaleh made a mistake?

# FIFTY-ONE

◈

"PALO MAYOMBE IS an ancient form of ancestor worship,"
Carla began, reading from pages of notes. "It came to Cuba
from Africa on slave ships. It has spread throughout the
Caribbean and parts of Central America. A *palero*, the high
priest of Palo Mayombe, is a representative of their god,
Sambianpungo, and believers are required to perform
whatever acts the *palero* ordains. They have been known to
conduct both animal and human sacrifice. They are particularly hard on homosexual men. Homosexuality is forbidden in Palo Mayombe. According to several informants
who contributed to what I found at Washington State University, if a man is promiscuous, the *palero* may order his
sacrifice to appease Sambianpungo. His hair is removed,
then his genitals are pushed down his throat and as Dr.
Carter told Roger Evans, the intestines are spread out to
form symbolic wings. Painting the body white with black
facial lines is found in a highly secret form of Palo
Mayombe known as Orisha, in which the human to be
sacrificed is painted to resemble a spirit, a *nganga*." She
looked across the room at Claude while he was finishing a

beer. "No mistake about it, Captain. What's happening here is Palo Mayombe."

"Tom Elliot is never gonna believe it. I'm not sure I can believe it. How the hell does some mumbo-jumbo African religion wind up in this part of Texas? Who would know anything about it in the first place, even if it were just a copycat? And what does it have to do with a nuclear dump or Cale Hunter and Robert McCloud sellin' land for it?"

He walked to the sink and opened another Coors. "I've got no idea what to do next or where to take it from here. I suppose we question Rose Hunter tomorrow and you talk to the old Indian. That's about our only hope, if we can find out who's tryin' to frame him." He drank deeply, frustrated by today's strange revelations. "See what you can find in those letters and stuff we bagged at Ramona Silva's and Smith's cabin. I've got to have something solid to tell Major Elliot when I call him, even if I cross my fingers and tell little white lies. If we don't zero in on a suspect real damn quick, both of us will be on our way back to Austin while Tom replaces us with Rangers who can get the job done." He looked closely at Carla now. "There's one man who could help us break this wide open, only you're so sensitive about accepting his help you won't hear of it. Alfred offered to come down here to help us unofficially. Right now I sure as hell wish he was here."

She turned to the window in Claude's room. "That would be like admitting I can't do it without him," she said. "I won't do that." She opened one of the evidence bags taken from Ramona Silva's apartment and took out a small spiral notebook.

"Hell, I'm admitting it," Claude said, walking to stand by Carla in front of a blazing sunset that lit the western skies while she flipped through pages of scribbling. "Nothing wrong with admitting we got stumped on the case. He gave me his word he wouldn't get in the way—

"Look at this!" Carla exclaimed, interrupting his thoughts.

He saw her pointing to a notation. "I'm drinkin' beer. Tell me what it says."

She hesitated a moment, following the tip of her finger across a line. "We've been wrong all along about Gary Smith and the survey," she said, barely able to conceal her excitement. "Cale Hunter didn't call Smith to request a survey of his property. Here's what Ramona wrote down. 'Survey. Eastern boundary lines. Bosque Redondo grant, Terrell County. Call Mr. Raymond Hammond at 915-326-3188. Must be done immediately.' "

Claude turned away from the window. He and Carla shared a look. "Hammond? I thought she said it was Hunter?"

"We asked her if Hunter was the right name. She said she thought so but she would have to check. The name written here is Ray Hammond, and his phone number."

"Shit," Claude whispered, forgetting his thirst for now. "We've been on the wrong trail."

# FIFTY-TWO

◈

THE PHONE IN Carla's room rang while Claude puzzled over Ray Hammond's request for a survey of his property. Why would Hammond need to know where *his* property lines lay? His land was miles from the proposed dump site. Was he simply fulfilling a requirement in order to sell his ranch to someone else, a large investor, perhaps? Thompson had said this sort of thing usually was handled by private agreement with a ranch as big as Hammond's. But then why was Gary Smith killed? Why was his body found on Hunter's land?

"Shit," he muttered, downing more beer. It was no ordinary killing, this Palo Mayombe stuff. Where the hell would Ray Hammond learn anything about African cult practices? If Hammond wanted to keep the dump from coming to Sanderson badly enough to kill in order to accomplish it, then why not execute Cale Hunter along with McCloud? And why not just shoot them and dump their bodies in the Rio Grande?

Trying to explain all this to Major Elliot would be virtually impossible. The first order of business would be to confront Hammond with what they knew about Gary

Smith and the survey, to gauge his reactions. Hammond would have an answer, but would it be the truth? Could Cale Hunter have been right all along, that Ray Hammond was behind what was now three murders? Hammond seemed too analytical and intelligent to continue with the executions while Texas Rangers were in Sanderson looking for the killer or killers.

Carla hurried through the connecting door. "Listen to what the lab just told me," she said, reading from her notes. "They have matches on three sets of footprints. Choate, Weaver, and Jim Feathers were at the cave, which we already knew. There were three more sets of prints. One is a size six, which makes it a woman's print—I remember one of them being small. A fifth and sixth print don't match any of the others. One could be McCloud's. The woman's footprint has to be Rose. The other is probably our killer. None of the hoofprints are a match for the tracks at Cale Hunter's corrals, so we haven't found the right horse yet. The knife has no markings so it'll be hard to trace. Who else among our suspects owns horses?"

"Can't think of anybody," Claude replied. "Besides that, I can't buy the notion that Rose knows all this Palo Mayombe crap. If she's involved at all, somebody had to help her, somebody who knows Palo Mayombe. It damn sure isn't the old Indian. Which leaves us right back where we started."

"Rose is the key, Captain. I'm sure of it."

"She was in Midland with her father talking to a lawyer at the time McCloud was killed."

"Hunter *said* she was with him. He could be covering for her if he suspects she's involved with either the deaths or drugs."

"Another woman who may know the answer is Ramona Silva," Claude said. "Let's hope DPS picks her up before she vanishes." He gave the window a passing glance as dusk came to Sanderson. "I can just hear Tom Elliot calling me back to Austin, putting me on a ninety-day leave of absence without pay while I undergo psychiatric evaluation."

Carla sank to the edge of the bed. "It means I'll go down in flames with you, I suppose." She dropped her notepad beside her.

Claude headed for the bathroom for a fresh beer. As he was twisting the cap off his Coors he heard a soft knock at the door. "Probably a goddamn reporter," he said as he put the beer back in his sink.

Carla opened the door. Claude could tell by the look on her face she was surprised.

"Come in, Mr. Feathers," she said, opening the door a little wider so Claude could see the old Indian standing there.

"I have something to show you, Star Woman," Feathers said in a quiet, almost inaudible voice. "I had planned to wait until tomorrow. My grandfather spoke to me in a vision, that I must show you now. I drove over here. I do not have a telephone. I want to show you the tracks of Gokaleh, the Spirit Warrior of my ancestors, so you will know I am not a crazy old Indian. Many times he has ridden near my house in the night. I have seen his shadow moving among the ocotillo. He came again while I was in Sheriff Casey's jail."

Carla gave Claude a quick look. "We'll be right there, Mr. Feathers. And thank you so much for coming. This may be the break we need."

Feathers bowed his head politely. "When I show you the tracks, you will know it is Gokaleh. The white man has caused Earth Mother to shed black tears, to die slowly, and for this Gokaleh has returned in the body of a man to make white men pay for what they have done to her."

"It's just like I said from the beginning," Carla told him as they drove up to Feathers's dark shack. "In a symbolic way he's telling us who's behind all of this. He knows who the killer is. He believes one of his ancestors has inhabited the physical body of someone here in Terrell County, this Spirit Warrior he calls Gokaleh. It's his way of pointing us at our murderer."

Claude killed the engine and turned off his headlights. "I have to be convinced. Horse tracks close to the old man's house won't, by themselves, prove a damn thing."

"You're wrong, Captain," Carla said as she opened the car door. "Someone on a horse brought Choate's body to Hunter's cow pens. I suspect the same person rode a horse here to put that scalp under Feathers's house. I'm going to follow these tracks if it takes all night. I'll get a couple of flashlights out of the trunk, and some mold plaster. I think our killer just made his, or her, first big mistake."

Claude got out of the Ford. Carla Sue Jenkins was once more showing just how much like her father she truly was. He had the strange sensation that having Carla with him on this investigation was a helluva lot like having his old sidekick along.

# FIFTY-THREE

"HORSE TRACKS AND boot prints," Carla said, kneeling at the rear of Feathers's shack to pour plaster across faint impressions while Claude held a flashlight above her. Jim Feathers stood a few feet away, watching.

"The tracks were made by Gokaleh, the Spirit Warrior," the old man said in the softest of voices.

Claude wanted to keep Feathers talking, in the hope that he would add something solid they could use. "What does he look like? Have you seen him up close?"

"I have only seen him in darkness. I hear the sounds made by his horse. He is only a shadow, moving through the brush."

Claude glanced over his shoulder. "Where do you figure the tracks lead, Mr. Feathers? Who owns the land south of here?"

"The land belongs to Mr. Tyson Billings." He offered no opinion as to the destination of the hoofprints.

"How come there's no fence around it?" Claude continued, when Feathers said no more.

"An old fence fell down many years ago, when the

land became too poor to graze cattle. Mr. Billings is in the oil business. He has no need for fences now."

"What sort of man is Billings? We haven't talked to him yet."

"He is very old, more than eighty. He has a sickness. I do not remember what it is called."

"You never did say where you believe those horse tracks are going. Just tell us where you think they'll take us if we follow 'em tonight."

Feathers seemed uneasy. He looked down at the ground for a moment. "I do not know," he said later, too quietly.

Carla stood up while the plaster was drying. She walked over to Feathers, standing directly in front of him. "Surely you understand Captain Groves and I *must* follow these prints. Someone has killed three people. Perhaps you believe Gokaleh has entered the mind and body of someone who lives in Terrell County who acts out Gokaleh's revenge. Think of your friend Chub, his wife and small children. I think he would want you to help us."

Feathers couldn't look at her. "This is one thing I do not understand, how Gokaleh could make such a terrible mistake. Chub was like me, a cowboy. He did nothing to harm Earth Mother." A glistening tear slid down one side of the old Indian's face. Without a word Feathers looked to the south. He stared at the dark horizon.

"Will they take us to Mr. Hunter's house?" Claude asked. "Is that what you're afraid to say?"

"No," Feathers whispered, then he fell silent again for several seconds. "I followed them until it became dark after my grandfather spoke to me." He waited again. "I will show you where the tracks come to a fence. This is all I will do. Do not ask me to betray the spirits of my ancestors."

Claude was satisfied, but Carla wanted more.

"Your grandfather spoke to you in a vision, asking

you to show us these hoofprints. He wants us to find out who killed Chub.''

More tears filled Feathers's eyes. He took a deep breath, still watching the dark skyline. "I am afraid," he told them in a strangled voice.

"Afraid of who? Or what?" Claude asked impatiently, wondering how the old man could be afraid of something he believed was a ghost.

Carla touched Feathers's shoulder. "Are you afraid that what you could tell us might harm Mr. Hunter's daughter?"

He turned and stared into Carla's eyes. "I will not betray the spirits of my ancestors or the daughter of my friend. Do not ask such a thing of me."

Carla nodded slowly. "I have one more question. Why would Mr. Hammond call a surveyor to mark his property lines? He isn't selling to the NRC, and his fences should tell him where his land begins and ends."

For a moment Feathers appeared puzzled. "Some of the fences washed away in the big Rio Grande flood when I was a boy. This was the flood that killed Mr. Hunter's father. He drowned on a horse trying to save some of his cattle. The fences were put back after the flood by Mr. Hammond and his father. I remember my grandfather saying some of the fences were in the wrong place."

Claude let out his breath explosively. "There's our motive for the murder of Gary Smith. Hammond ordered a survey because he knew Hunter would be required to conduct one to satisfy the NRC. If Hammond knew he had some of Hunter's land behind the fences they put up after this flood a long time ago, he had to figure he'd be discovered. So Hammond called Smith. If he paid Smith to keep his mouth shut about the fences being wrong, he'd have his boundary lines recorded. Only Smith wouldn't play ball for some reason, and Ray Hammond had no choice but to kill him. There's dozens of oil wells along that fence between Hammond and Hunter. Hammond would owe Hunter all that back oil revenue from years of pumping wells on land that was actually Hunter's. It could be millions of dollars."

Carla was watching him. "And Chub happened to see the murder, probably by accident, so Hammond had to silence him. It still leaves us without a motive for McCloud's murder, but I think we're getting close. I can't see an old man like Hammond actually committing the killings, and none of this explains how Rose was involved or where the Palo Mayombe came from."

"I suspect most of our answers are at Ray Hammond's place," Claude said, turning off his flashlight. "Let's drive out there unannounced."

Carla hurried over to lift her plaster molds into evidence bags while Claude's thoughts whirled through all the possibilities. A soft voice interrupted them both.

"Be careful of the one called Tomo," Jim Feathers warned, his face turned southward again.

"Who the hell is Tomo?" Claude asked.

The old man folded his arms across his chest. He merely wagged his head from side to side, refusing to say any more.

# FIFTY-FOUR

THE FORD CAREENED wildly at over a hundred miles per hour on the dark, empty highway. Claude watched the roadway for deer while Carla gave him her thoughts about what they'd just learned. It crossed his mind again how much it was like listening to Alfred putting the facts in a case together.

"Always follow the money," Carla said. "We thought all this had to do with the sale of land to the NRC. It's peanuts, compared to fifty or sixty years of oil production from land above big oil pools." She paused. "This guy named Tomo might know about Palo Mayombe. But how is he connected to Hammond, and where does McCloud fit into all this—unless he stumbled onto the truth somehow and had to be silenced, like Chub Choate? One thing I'm sure of now—Jim Feathers knew who was doing the killing all along. He kept silent because he thinks Hunter's daughter is involved." Carla stared into the beams of light from the headlamps brightening the highway in front of them. "Maybe it was through Rose that McCloud found out what was going on. McCloud may have been in on the drug angle. We know he was using peyote. The pan we found at Smith's cabin was proof of that."

Claude hit the brakes suddenly, squealing tires sliding on asphalt when Hammond's ranch came in sight. "Locked," he muttered. "No problem. I've got some armor-piercing slugs in the trunk."

The car skidded to a halt in front of two heavy iron gates blocking the road into Hammond's property. Claude threw the Ford into park and jumped out to open the trunk.

He filled an empty clip with black mambas while Carla looked on, then slipped the clip into the butt of his .45 automatic. In the glare of the headlights he aimed for the plated lock holding the gates together.

"They'll hear the shot," Carla said. "Hammond will know something is wrong."

"I doubt if he's gonna like a damn thing he hears tonight," Claude said as he gently squeezed the Colt's trigger.

The concussion of a gunshot echoed up and down Highway 90 as metal ruptured, causing one of the gates to sway on impact as a titanium-tipped bullet tore through the plate steel encasing the lock mechanism.

"Get in the car," Claude snapped, when Carla stood there too long. "We're about to break a few rules. If this case goes to court you're gonna forget what you just saw. This goddamn gate was open when we got here. Remember that." He kicked the gates apart and strode hurriedly back to the Ford, placing his .45 on the seat beside him, feeling a rush of adrenalin course through his veins. There was no feeling in the world like coming down on a crook when you knew you had the goods on him.

◇ ◇ ◇

The mansion was dark, no lights behind any of the windows on either floor. He turned off the car and switched off the headlights. A dog barked somewhere near one of the barns.

Carla pointed to a small white house off to one side, in back of the swimming pool. "There's someone there. I saw something move at the window."

"Get a shotgun out of the trunk," Claude said as he climbed from the car. "Just in case. I ain't in the mood for a real close haircut or a belly operation, if we're right about any of this."

"We're right," Carla assured him quietly while Claude eyed the front door of the mansion.

"I'll talk to Hammond first. You stand behind the car and keep me covered, just in case this Tomo shows up."

"Aren't you going to take your gun?" Carla asked, pumping a shell into the shotgun's firing chamber.

"No reason to believe I'll need it," he replied, heading for the dark front porch.

He knocked several times, and rang a doorbell. It was just past eight o'clock, too early for Hammond to be in bed. He rang the bell again. No sound came from behind the door.

After several more attempts he walked back to the car and switched on the radio. "I'll have Midland DPS give us a phone patch. Give me that number from Ramona's notebook. Maybe Mr. Hammond will answer his telephone, since he don't appear to be inclined to come to the door."

Carla read him the number in the car's interior lights. After several minutes of static-filled conversation with a DPS dispatcher, they heard a ring coming through the radio speaker. All the while Carla kept an eye on the house, and the quarters behind the swimming pool, resting the butt of the shotgun on her hip.

"Hello?" a deep voice inquired.

"This is Texas Ranger Captain Claude Groves, Mr. Hammond. I want you to open your door. My partner and I are outside and we have some questions."

"Isn't it a bit late?" Hammond asked, sounding irriated. "I am quite sure it can wait until morning. Unless you have a search warrant, Captain, you are on my property illegally. The front gate was locked."

"Somebody must have forgotten to close it. We drove right on in. And the questions won't wait, Hammond. We want answers now."

"What are these questions that won't wait?"

Claude was becoming irritated now. "Let's just say they have to do with some fences that got moved a long time ago, back when the Rio Grande flooded."

A long, heavy silence. "I won't let you in until I've called Judge Green to see if he gave you a lawful search warrant, Captain. I know my rights. Call me tomorrow and I will arrange to have my attorney present. I have no idea what you are talking about regarding moving fences after a flood. You must have been given bad information."

"You're not as well versed in legal matters as you think, Hammond. My partner and I will say we had reasonable cause to conduct a search for controlled substances, or stolen property, or any number of other things. I'll take my chances with the district attorney. Now open the goddamn door!"

A soft click ended their phone conversation. Claude clamped his teeth together and tossed the radio microphone onto the floor of the car. He turned to Carla. "Let's see who's in the servants' quarters. I'm tired of this bullshit."

Claude slammed the car door, stalking off toward the swimming pool with his mouth set in a grim line. Carla hurried to keep up.

"You know Hammond's right, Captain. If we find any evidence, we'll have taken it illegally."

"You worry too much, Carla," he said. "Leave the worryin' part to me."

The dog's bark grew louder as Claude came to the door of a one-room adobe cottage with small darkened windows. He spoke to Carla over his shoulder as he raised a fist to knock. "Back up a bit an' keep me covered, just in case these folks don't want to cooperate." He banged on the door several times. "Open up!" he shouted, then remembering Hammond said his housekeeper spoke very little English, *"Esta policía!"*

All was quiet inside. He knocked again, harder this time.

A sound behind him made him turn, the soft scuff of a foot in grass. From behind a palmetto a dark figure lunged toward Carla. "Look out!" he cried, too far away to reach Carla before the attacker did.

Carla whirled, just in time to miss the swish of a machete blade aimed for her throat. Claude made a dive for the man's wrists, every ounce of strength he had driving his legs like coiled springs.

Something struck Claude's left temple, sending him spinning to the ground seeing stars, winking lights across his field of vision that almost blinded him. A searing pain exploded in his skull, and his arms and legs refused to move.

He shook his head violently, dimly aware that Carla's life might depend on him, and yet he still could not force his limbs to respond. He lay on his belly in the grass between the cottage and the pool, fighting to remain conscious.

He caught a glimpse of two dark figures struggling one broad and muscular, the other much smaller. A single thought went through his addled brain: *why doesn't she shoot him?*

One figure went to the ground, and Claude knew that this man would kill Carla before Claude could gather his senses and come to her aid. Furious with himself for being so careless, he managed to climb to his hands and knees, blinking furiously to clear his vision.

A thudding sound abruptly ended a series of grunts from the site of the struggle. One figure lay still. In a flash of clear thinking Claude wondered how he could ever ex-

lain to Alfred why he had allowed Carla to be in a posi-
ion where she lost her life to a deranged madman.

Then: "I got him, Captain," Carla gasped, out of
reath, coming slowly to her feet above the motionless
ody on the ground. "I had to hit him pretty hard with my
ervice revolver. He's out cold. I'll roll him over and cuff
im. Are you okay?"

Relief washed through Claude's brain. He felt blood
rickling down his left cheek. "Yeah. I'm okay."

◇ ◇ ◇

thick-muscled man, perhaps thirty years of age with the
uggestion of Indian features in his face sat handcuffed in
e backseat of the Ford, illuminated by the interior dome
ght. Claude held a handkerchief to a bleeding gash in his
ft cheek while he waited for Midland DPS to dial Ray
Iammond's telephone number again. A series of knocks
d shouts at front and rear doors produced no response
om Hammond shortly after Tomo, the housekeeper's
rother, had been secured in the car.

"Hello, Captain Groves," a soft voice said when a
onnection was made. "I've heard you outside. I won't let
ou in without a warrant. I'm warning you, I have a gun. I
lled Sheriff Casey to inform him of your illegal entry on
y property. He's calling your superiors in Austin as we
eak."

"Don't figure we need a warrant now, Hammond,"
laude said. "We've got Tomo, and he damn sure tried to
ll me and my partner—just like you had him kill the
her people who got in your way. As to that gun you say
ou have, we've got some of our own. I'm placing you
der arrest, Hammond, for suspicion of complicity in
ree murders. You've been pumpin' Cale Hunter's oil for
helluva long time and a new survey is gonna prove it.
ou'll probably owe Hunter millions. And you'll be writing
e check from prison."

Hammond cleared his throat. "I was warned you were a very thorough man, Captain Groves."

"My partner figured most of it out. Now unlock the door or we'll have to shoot it open. Don't make this any harder than it has to be."

"I congratulate you and your female associate. Some unfortunate circumstances necessitated the loss of two more lives. Had it not been for the others, Mr. Smith's death would have remained unsolved. Good-bye, Captain Groves."

A click signaled an end to the connection. Moments later, as Claude put the microphone in its clip, a muffled gunshot came from inside the mansion.

◇ ◇ ◇

He was seated behind his desk in his leather swivel chair, blood pumping from a temporal artery, when they found him. His silk shirt was drenched in blood. A .45-caliber automatic lay in Hammond's lap, still clenched in his right fist.

"Call an ambulance," Claude said as Carla felt Hammond's neck for a pulse. He was already dead, but Carla knew they'd need the ambulance to take the body away. She made the call.

# FIFTY-FIVE

◈

THE LANDING OF a Department of Public Safety helicopter
in a vacant field at the outskirts of Sanderson created quite
a stir. Major Tom Elliot, looking fit at sixty-three despite a
paunch his belt emphasized, ignored the crowds and reporters outside Sheriff Casey's office, listening to Carla
while he perched on a corner of the sheriff's desk. Deputy
Huffman stood guard at the door, keeping everyone else
outside.

"Continue, Ranger Jenkins," Elliot said while Claude
looked on from a chair behind Huffman's desk.

"We have our murder suspect in custody, Major. It
has been difficult to question him because he speaks a combination of Spanish and Nahuatl, a Central American Indian language, and very little English. We found the scalp
of the third victim in some sort of ornamental box inside
his house, the one he shared with his sister at the Hammond ranch. At this point, we don't believe the sister was
involved. The suspect's name is Tomo Otero, according to
the immigration papers we found among his personal possessions. He has not confessed to the murders, however he
did acknowledge his familiarity with an obscure form of

religion known as Palo Mayombe, and he admits to being a *palero*, a type of religious leader in this cult. According to an expert on Palo Mayombe we contacted, they are known to practice human sacrifice in some instances. Otero came to the United States from Belize, where Palo Mayombe groups are known to exist. He and his sister were sent to the Hammond ranch by Hammond's estranged wife, who lives on an island there. The ritual form of killing we found in all three instances is consistent with Palo Mayombe, according to our expert; the complete removal of the scalp, severed genitals placed in the victims' mouths, and slicing open the stomach cavity to pull out the intestines and arrange them in a ceremonial way. We discovered numerous other objects at Mr. Otero's residence which will be enough for a conviction in all three murders."

"Why did he kill them?" the major asked, watching Carla closely.

"We believe he was ordered to do so by Raymond Hammond, in order to protect a deception committed by Hammond and his father more than fifty years ago. After a flooding of the Rio Grande washed away a number of fences, the fences were replaced covering a part of the Hunter ranch which held rich reserves of oil. No one knew, since Cale Hunter was a child and his father died in the flood. Hammond then sold oil off what was actually Hunter's property for the next fifty years, oil that was probably worth millions of dollars. But when Hunter decided to sell part of his land to the NRC for a nuclear waste site, a current survey was needed. We believe Hammond contacted the first victim, a surveyor from Alpine by the name of Gary Smith, a heavy drug user whom Hammond thought he could bribe into recording false property line as being correct. Hammond learned about Smith from Hunter's daughter, Rose, who is a convicted drug user She visited Smith in Alpine to use marijuana and peyote She met Smith by accident, she claims, one night at a bar in Marfa. Rose had been sleeping with Otero and taking pey

ote with him for several months. Smith was on the adjoining property, Hammond's, conducting a survey when he
saw their fire one night. The three of them did drugs together. The following day Smith informed Hammond that
his fences enclosed over a thousand acres of Cale Hunter's
property. He apparently refused to file a false surveyor's
report and this gave Hammond no choice. He ordered
Otero to kill the surveyor, and to make it look like an old
Indian by the name of Post Oak Jim Feathers was to blame
by placing Smith's scalp in the back of Mr. Feathers's truck.
Hammond must have concluded that a brutal killing of this
type would help him fill a petition to have an injunction
handed down, halting the dump from coming to Terrell
County. This would discourage Hunter from having his
own survey done. The second victim, Mr. Choate, had the
misfortune to witness the killing of Smith while he was out
on the Hunter ranch. Choate must have recognized Otero
and notified Hammond of what he'd seen. Hammond had
no choice but to order another execution, to silence the
only witness to Otero's crime."

"This gets complicated as hell," Elliot said. "I think
I'm still with you. Keep going."

Carla flipped to another page of her notes. "A rancher
by the name of Robert McCloud, who also intended to sell
property to the NRC, became involved with Rose Hunter
early this summer. He slept with her on a number of occa-
sions, according to her, and he was a regular drug user.
He'd been buying marijuana from Gary Smith, but after
several phone calls to Alpine, he became suspicious when
Smith failed to meet him at a rendezvous point with the
drugs. Or he simply got curious as to Smith's whereabouts.
We haven't found Smith's girlfriend, Ramona Silva, yet to
get her side of the story. In any case, Robert McCloud
drove to Alpine to look for Smith, to find out what was
wrong with his marijuana and peyote connection. Hammond had become worried that there might be a copy of
some record of the true boundary lines among Smith's ef-

fects from when he conducted the survey in his personal
effects, so he sent Tomo Otero to Alpine to destroy any
evidence of the survey. We found Smith's field notes in
Otero's living quarters at the Hammond ranch, so we have
to assume McCloud was there when Otero carried out his
orders, and he was forced to kill McCloud, too. That part
is speculation, until someone who speaks Nahuatl can in-
terrogate Otero thoroughly. But it's fairly clear Otero took
Smith's field notes back to the Hammond ranch, after he
killed McCloud. Why he did not destroy them is anyone's
guess. It is entirely possible that Ray Hammond was with
him on the night McCloud was killed, since Otero does
not read or speak English. Hammond's suicide prevents us
from getting that information, until, and if, Otero is willing
to give us a statement. But Otero wouldn't have known
what the surveyor's report said. Someone had to be there
with him to locate the right documents."

"Could that be Rose Hunter?" the major asked, a
question Claude had been asking himself ever since they
arrested Rose.

"She isn't saying any more, on the advice of her attorney," Carla replied. "We've got enough to indict her on
several charges as it is—conspiracy to commit murder, drug
possession. A search of the Hunter ranch yielded several
pairs of peregrine falcon feathers in Rose's room. The old
Indian who found the first body saw falcon feathers at the
death scene. McCloud has peregrine falcons. Mr. Otero
had similar falcon feathers at his living quarters. They may
have been part of some drug ceremony which all three of
them participated in. We also found both trucks, the one
belonging to Smith, and Billy Choate's, at the bottom of
the Rio Grande where it fronts Hammond's property. If it
weren't for our scuba diver from Midland, no one would
have found them unless the river ran dry."

Tom Elliot smiled for the first time since his arrival in
Sanderson. "Nice work, Ranger Jenkins. Very thorough.
We can give the press a statement now. You've got all th

facts, so I'll ask you to do it. Step outside and tell them what you've told me. This is making news all over the country. You'll be hounded to death with questions. Just be careful what you give the bastards, so we don't contaminate our case. Until formal charges are filed, use the hell out of the word 'alleged.' Best word in the English language, in my opinion. In law enforcement, it keeps a peace officer's ass out of a crack, so to speak."

"I understand, Major."

Elliot swung off the desk, looking down at Carla. "You've done us proud, Ranger. Captain Groves tells me you broke this whole thing open, tracing down all this Palo Mumbo crap, backing it up with solid detective work. Congratulations."

Carla stood up and took the handshake Major Elliot offered her. "Thank you, sir. It was all fairly routine."

Elliot gave her a wink. "Don't bullshit me, Miss Jenkins. I spent my share of time out in the field. This was a complicated case. There was a time when I counted on your father to handle some of the tough ones. You're a helluva lot like him. I'll call him when I get back to the office. Now get out there and feed those damn news hounds what we have. When you get back to Austin we'll call a press conference. Get your speech ready. You'll be doing it, along with our public information director. Hell, he uses the word 'alleged' more than I do. That's why I gave him the damn job."

# FIFTY-SIX

CLAUDE SWUNG OFF the highway as DPS patrol cars continued toward Del Rio with Tomo Otero and Rose Hunter manacled in the rear seats. Carla's request to stop at Jim Feathers's house was somewhat puzzling. He drove up in front of the house and parked while Carla got out. The old man was sitting on his front porch with Sata curled near his feet.

"We brought these back to you, Mr. Feathers," Carla said, taking his deerskin medicine bundle, his grandfather's moccasins, and the photograph of Four Feathers from an evidence bag. She stopped at the foot of the steps leading to the porch.

Feathers stood up and accepted the items without a word. He looked down at Carla. Sata was wagging his tail.

"Thank you, Mr. Feathers, for helping us with this case," she continued. "Without you, we might still be looking in the wrong places."

Feathers spoke softly. "My heart is heavy for my friend, Mr. Hunter. He loves his daughter. What I told you will send her to jail."

"You must understand, that's where she belongs, Mr.

Feathers. She broke the law, several laws, and she told Tomo about your moccasins in order to help Ray Hammond frame you for the murders. When you think about this from now on, remember your friend Chub and his family. He didn't deserve to die. You did the right thing. As an honest man, you really didn't have any choice."

"It was my grandfather's spirit voice. He told me what to do. What I must do."

Carla smiled. "I'm sure Four Feathers is proud of you, and I wanted you to know how grateful Captain Groves and I are for helping us."

Feathers fingered the medicine bundle a moment, reading Carla's expression. "Your heart is good, Star Woman. A Lipan knows these things. . . ."

They were driving back toward Austin, after sending the evidence bags to the district attorney in Del Rio by way of a highway patrolman. Major Elliot wanted Carla to be ready to give the press a statement regarding the case tomorrow morning.

"I called Alfred," Claude confessed, watching the sun drop below ridges of the distant Davis Mountains. "Don't tell him I told you this, but he broke down. He could hardly talk. He's so damn proud of you he's about to bust wide open. He's taking the bus tonight to Austin, so he can be there for your press conference tomorrow morning. I just had to call him, Carla. He's been my friend all these years. I figured you'd be mad about it, but you've got to understand. I owe your father too much."

"You gave me too much credit for breaking this case," she said. "We did it together and you know it."

He thought about it a moment as the Ford went around a curve in the empty west Texas highway. "Not really, Carla. You kept peeling away the bullshit everyone was giving us until you got to the truth. I couldn't have figured the damn thing out by myself. You won the confidence of old Jim Feathers. You read him right, whereas I didn't. He trusted you, and finally told us what we needed to know. That's the way Alfred used to do it. He could read people like a book. I know you're tired of the comparison, but even Major Elliot noticed it."

"As the Ranger in charge of this investigation, you should have been the one to talk to the press."

Claude grinned. "Tom did that to take some of the heat off you, and himself. But you deserved every bit of the recognition for solving a complicated case. I wish you'd stop questioning everybody's motives. Typical of a woman, in my experience, to look for a double meaning behind everything a man does. I guess it's true some of the time, but not always."

She looked across the car seat at the scar on his face, the stitches required to close the gash made by Tomo's machete. "Is that your way of saying there was a double meaning behind the things you told me the other night at the motel? Or should I have questioned your motives a little more? Maybe you said all those things because you couldn't get me drunk enough to weaken my resolve. You only pretended not to care whether I slept with you or not. It made you angry when I couldn't, only you wouldn't say so."

"That isn't true," he said, remembering that night. "You said you weren't ready, that you hadn't made up your mind. I was being honest with you."

"Dad told me you've never been honest with women." She was teasing him now.

"I reckon that's partly true. But for the record, I was honest with you."

"You aren't mad at me for chickening out at the last minute?"

"Never was. It's different with you, Carla. You're a lady, not a tramp. The decision was always yours to make.

We'd both be risking our careers if we'd gone through with it.''

She stared at the highway a moment. "What would you say if I told you I'm still considering it?"

He felt his palms grow damp on the steering wheel. "I'd say I'm flattered, first off, but I'd still say the same thing if you decided against it. I suppose I'm too weak to say I wouldn't go through with it. You're a beautiful woman, even if you are my best friend's daughter. I know myself too well to say I'd refuse if you gave me the opportunity. That would be an outright lie."

Carla giggled. "We'll be passing dozens of motels on the way back to Austin. Would you believe me if I tell you I'll be thinking about it every time we drive by one?"

He gripped the wheel a little harder. "I wish you hadn't told me that," he said. "I'll slow down every time I see a motel sign, just in case. I'll just be making sure you have plenty of time to let me know if you've made up your mind. . . ."

# ABOUT THE AUTHOR

FREDERIC BEAN is a native Texan who used to raise and train quarter horses. He was formerly editor of a national livestock magazine and he has written more than thirty historical novels, including *Pancho and Black Jack, Lorena, The Pecos River, Hell's Half Acre*, and *Black Gold*. He lives in Austin, Texas.

If you enjoyed MURDER AT THE SPIRIT
CAVE, don't miss the next exciting
installment in Frederic Bean's Texas Ranger
mystery series,

# THE HANGMAN'S TREE

When wealthy West Texas rancher Walter Lacy finds his
son hanging from a blood-red madrone tree, he wants
revenge. Calling on the Texas Rangers he demands they
send their best investigators to handle the case: Captain
Claude Groves and Ranger Carla Jenkins. As the body
count rises and time runs out, Claude and Carla find
themselves tracking a desperate killer who strikes too
close to home—and who will do anything to protect the
most deeply buried secret of all.

Coming from Bantam Books in Fall 2000